INSIDER

OWEN MULLEN

Boldwood

First published in Great Britain in 2021 by Boldwood Books Ltd.

Copyright © Owen Mullen, 2021

Cover Photography: Shutterstock and Jared Murray

/ Unsplash

The moral right of Owen Mullen to be identified as the author of this work has been asserted in accordance with the Copyright, Designs and Patents Act 1988.

A CIP catalogue record for this book is available from the British Library.

Paperback ISBN 978-1-80048-426-9

Large Print ISBN 978-1-80048-425-2

Hardback ISBN 978-1-80162-974-4

Ebook ISBN 978-1-80048-427-6

Kindle ISBN 978-1-80048-428-3

Audio CD ISBN 978-1-80048-420-7

MP3 CD ISBN 978-1-80048-421-4

Digital audio download ISBN 978-1-80048-422-1

Boldwood Books Ltd
23 Bowerdean Street
London SW6 3TN
www.boldwoodbooks.com

To Christine

PROLOGUE

James Stevens – Jazzer to his friends – ducked into the hotel door-way, ran a wet hand over his face and shook water from his hair; 'a drowned rat' was the cliché in his head. That didn't matter; he wasn't here for his good looks. On the phone, the woman with the New York accent had told him he'd been recommended – she didn't say who by – outlined the job and asked if he was interested. Yes or no? Jazzer sensed if he hesitated, the conversation would be over, the opportunity gone. He'd said yes and was glad, because, as the details emerged, what she wanted was a nice little earner: nothing he hadn't done before. Too bloody right he was interested.

They'd arranged to meet in the hotel on Lime Street. Before the call ended, he'd asked, 'How will I recognise you?'

The reply was strange, maybe a joke. 'I wouldn't worry about that.'

'What should I call you?'

'Why do you need to call me anything?'

'I like to know who I'm working for.'

'You're not working for anybody yet.'

'Tell me your name.'

'It's Charley.'

Jazzer clocked her immediately at a table near the back of the bar, and understood why she'd been confident about being recognised. The bar wasn't busy but if it had been he would've still been able to pick her out: mid-thirties, long red hair, red lips and a full figure only a real man would take on; a 1950s movie-star type, striking and challenging, even from a distance. They didn't shake hands. No small talk or would-you-like-a-drink malarkey. And Jazzer quickly realised two things: his wasn't the only name on her list – maybe not even her first choice – and the lady languidly crossing her legs was no ordinary female.

The money she was offering was impressive, generous even. It soon became clear why. It wasn't just one job. She gave him an envelope, soiled at the edges as if it had been carried in a pocket until she found the right person to give it to.

'Any questions?'

'No, no questions.'

'You're straight about what's required?'

'Absolutely.'

'Who you use and how many will be your decision. Don't be greedy; to make it work will need a minimum of three. Any less increases the risk.'

Jazzer knew a dozen guys who'd fit the bill. 'We won't fuck it up.'

Her reply confirmed his assessment. 'If I believed there was the slightest chance of that, I wouldn't be sitting here. A word of warning: these aren't boys you'll be going against. The plan's simple. Stick to it and it'll be all right. We won't talk again until London. I'll meet you at the flat the next morning with the rest of the money. Are we clear?'

Jazzer weighed the envelope in his hand. Foolishly, he made a joke. 'Tempted to get a taxi out to John Lennon Airport and disappear. Somewhere sunny would be nice.'

She smiled, a lipstick smear like blood on her teeth. 'I'd find you. No matter where you went, I'd find you.'

Jazzer believed her.

PART I

1

Friday 8.57 p.m.

Ethel brushed a strand of stray hair from her eyes, wedged the little that was left of the cigarette in the corner of her mouth, and kept the oranges in the air with the deftness of a piano virtuoso. Her voice was an emotionless monotone her ex-husband would have no trouble recognising. Ethel was thirty-three years old, brunette, hard-faced and divorced with two kids. A lot of people would struggle with the job she did – the controller at River Cars – especially on Friday nights when everybody in Lambeth and their granny wanted a taxi. She chain-smoked Benson & Hedges, sipped a cold coffee that hadn't been over-warm to begin with, and matched the requests for taxis to the nearest available cars.

It was still early. She was in a dull-yellow monstrosity of a porta-cabin on an unlit piece of spare ground behind a Spar food store. Ten vehicles, left by guys out on the road, were parked on the uneven earth. When the shifts changed at six in the morning, they'd disappear; others would take their place; she would go home and fall into bed.

The taxi game was a twenty-four-seven operation – drivers coming and going until the clubs and late-night pubs finally closed. Ethel wasn't alone. Winston, her boyfriend, an unemployed painter and decorator from Jamaica who occasionally drove part-time for the firm, was with her, stretched out on a busted sofa, flicking through an old newspaper somebody had left behind.

Ethel put a fresh cigarette in her mouth and lit it off the one between her fingers.

'Car for Victoria Mansions, South Lambeth Road. Going up West. Who's nearest?'

A tinny voice replied through the static. 'I'll get it. Be there in six minutes.'

Winston looked up from his paper. 'Sort us an E, will you, love?'

Ethel ignored him. He tried again. 'C'mon, sort us.'

She turned emotionless eyes on him. 'Got any money? 'Cause if you haven't, forget it.'

'But...'

'Yeah... that's what I thought.'

Ethel swore under her breath and brought her attention back to the phones. Winston was a freeloader, a loser she should never have got involved with. The reason he was here instead of with his pals in the pub was in the two black bin bags at her feet. While she worked her arse off, his plan was to get out of his head for fuck all, but she'd had it with him; he was on his way out. Winston had been a drunken error made one night when she'd still believed every black man was a stud – a mistake she'd kept repeating even after he'd proved it was a myth. What did she need him for, anyway? This job paid well – great, actually – Ethel could afford the life she wanted. All she needed from a bloke was sex, and Winston was no Idris Elba in that department.

Her voice bounced off the portacabin walls. 'Car for Black Prince Road. Any takers?'

* * *

Ronnie hurried along the pavement, one hand in his pocket, the other carrying a sports bag with Nike on the side. When he reached his destination, he left the street, ducked into the shadow of the cars parked on the waste ground and hunkered down in the darkness. Jazzer had reckoned a couple, maybe three at the most, but a Scouser, especially one with a shooter, could handle three London lads any day of the week, no problem.

Ronnie rubbed his fingers together, feeling the sweat on them, unzipped the sports bag, drew a balaclava over his head and ran to the portacabin door. A flat female voice drifted outside. For a minute he paused, listening, hearing nothing but her nasal drawl and male south London accents through the static. He threw the door back and charged in, levelling the gun at the people inside. The surprised man and woman raised their hands on a reflex; Ethel's cigarette fell from her fingers and smouldered on the carpet that hadn't been cleaned since the day it had been tacked to the floor.

'Give us what you've got and you won't get hurt.'

Ronnie pronounced it 'heert'.

She answered defiantly. 'There's no money until the shifts finish.'

Ronnie said, 'Why don't I just blow you and your shite chat away? I admire your bottle, Mrs, but save it. This is the wrong time to be a smart-arse. It isn't appreciated. I'll take whatever cash you've got but I'm not after money. So, don't fuck me about!'

Winston said, 'Give him what he wants – the money, the dope – give him all of it. It isn't ours.'

Ethel pushed a bin bag along the floor with her foot.

Ronnie said, 'Now the other one.'

Her lip curled in a sneer. 'I feel sorry for you.'

'Really, why's that?'

'You're making the biggest mistake of your life and don't even know it. If I were you, I'd drop those bags and start running.'

At the door, he stopped. 'And if I were you, I'd think before I called the police. "They stole our drugs" won't play well.'

He dipped his hand into one of the bags, brought out two blue pills and tossed them on the filthy carpet. 'Enjoy the rest of your night.'

*Eamon Durham, Independent Bookmakers, Lewisham, South London
Friday 9.00 p.m.*

They moved swiftly, confidently, shotguns raised, their faces hidden by balaclavas. Tosh stayed by the door. Jazzer walked to the middle of the floor littered with discarded pink betting slips. On a television mounted above their heads, the runners and riders were under starter's orders for the last race of the day at Newmarket. Die-hards gathered to watch their four-legged addiction play out. Hungry for fresh failure, the rest studied the racing pages tacked to the walls, convinced the evening meet at Uttoxeter would change their luck.

Behind the screen, the manager and a woman counted cash. Neither noticed the stranger until he fired into the ceiling, bringing down tiles in an explosion of noise and a cloud of dust. His second shot silenced the TV, the shell casing fell to the ground and he had their attention. He stood with his feet apart, surveying their fear through the eye-holes of his bally, the gun comfortably resting against his shoulder, fingers on the stock behind the trigger guard. His mate rotated his weapon in the general direction of everyone. Without the masks they would've been alarming, with them, the robbers were terrifying.

The voice wasn't London. 'Hands in the air. It's a lovely night. Don't spoil it by being stupid, eh?'

He lobbed a canvas holdall over the Perspex and trained the shotgun on the nearest cashier, a blonde, overweight woman in her forties with a film of sweat on her top lip.

'Fill it up before Eamon gets here.'

Behind the bally, he chuckled at his joke.

The manager took half a step forward, his face tight with anger. 'Do you idiots know what you're doing? Who you're ripping off? There is no Eamon. Never was.'

'Fill the fucking thing and shut it!'

Not London: Liverpool.

'Listen, lads, this isn't wise.'

'Told you to shut it, didn't I?'

The bullet shattered the screen of the pay-out window and blew a hole in the counter, sending Formica and jagged shards of wood into the air. One barbed fragment, seven inches long, pierced the manager's shoulder, passing through the flesh and out the other side. Instantly, his white shirt turned red. The woman saw it and fainted.

Suddenly, it was going wrong.

The guy at the door loaded a cartridge into the chamber and levelled the gun on the crowd underneath the shattered TV, more nervous than he'd been a minute ago.

'Hurry it up, Jazzer. Let's get out of here.'

They'd seen *Reservoir Dogs* and agreed not to speak their names. 'Jazzer' was a mistake.

Jazzer shouted, 'Give me the bag! Now!'

The manager gripped his arm with his other hand; lifting the holdall was a non-starter. The thief reached over and grabbed it. Inside was filled with fivers and tenners and twenties – more money than he'd ever seen. He smiled. The plan had worked – they were going to get away with it.

'Good doing business with you.'

The injured man was losing a lot of blood; his next stop would be Accident and Emergency. He gritted his teeth and screwed his eyes up against the pain – there was pity in them.

'You bloody fools. Nobody steals from the family.'

Jazzer had the last word. 'Says who? Tell Luke, Charley was asking for him.'

2

The steps to the basement flat in Moscow Road were worn smooth from a century's worth of wear; weeds that would die in the summer heat sprouted between the stones. In his tiny room, George Ritchie picked the final chips off a plate and drained his mug; the tea had gone cold, but it didn't matter, he'd enjoyed it well enough. After almost thirty years in the south, the abiding memory, the thing he missed most about Newcastle, was a decent fish supper on a Friday night.

In many respects he wasn't so different from the young George who'd stepped off the train at King's Cross station with the clothes on his back, twenty pounds in his pocket, and a deserved reputation as a hard man. He remembered that morning well: scraps of paper blown along the platform by a cold wind at the beginning of another grey day in the north; his mother clutching her heavy skirt beside Hannah, both pretending to be happy as they saw him away on his great adventure. Ritchie could still picture them, the old lady, especially, waving a frail arm in the air, until they were out of sight.

He would never see her alive again.

In close on three decades, apart from for her funeral, he'd been back less than half a dozen times. When Hannah's much-loved idiot son, Jonjo, had insisted on following his uncle south and got himself killed, Ritchie's sister had cut him out of her life, severing the only remaining connection with what had been. George had warned him; Jonjo wouldn't listen. Telling her that wouldn't bring her boy back to her or change her opinion of George.

Newcastle was the past. London was home.

Money and what it could buy had lost its power to impress George Ritchie long ago – if, indeed, it ever had that power. Seeing people relentlessly wage war against each other when they already had more of everything than they needed made not joining in an easy decision. One he hadn't regretted.

He could easily have afforded some flash gaff. But what was the point? He'd better things to do with his cash, like funnelling it into rehabilitation programmes that used money raised from charities and social investment groups to help ex-cons rebuild their lives, giving young fools the chance he'd never had. Ritchie was a career criminal: the irony didn't escape him. His life of crime had been inevitable. That didn't mean it was all he was capable of. Unlike almost everyone in the game, he wasn't in it for the money, the power or the women. He was here because he was great at this; the mistake he'd made was not realising it sooner, and taking crap from ignorant lowlifes.

Thanks to Luke Glass, that was behind him.

But Luke had a vision, a vision George didn't share. Laundering money through real estate, construction and LBC, the private members' club in Central London, no doubt, made business sense. George Ritchie wanted no part of it: the old dog had no use for new tricks. He'd swapped the streets of Newcastle for the streets of London – streets were what he knew. Luke realised he wouldn't back down and let him have it his way. Now, Ritchie ran everything south of the river, leaving him free to build his new empire.

Of course, with the idiots who crossed Ritchie's path, violence was a necessary part of business. But, in the grand scheme, it was a minor part.

If the offer to join the firm had come from Luke's older brother Danny Glass, he would've turned it down on the spot. Danny was exactly the type of boss he'd needed to shuck off – a thug who thought fear was the key to loyalty, and breaking bones the answer to every situation; a psycho, thick as shit, who, in the end, lived a violent life and probably died a violent death.

Depending on the day of the week, urban myth had Danny on a beach in Spain, South Africa or Brazil, drinking Cuba libre or twelve-year-old Glenfiddich over ice, with a blonde, a brunette, or a couple of teenage black chicks: fairy tales to help others like him sleep at night.

Ritchie believed he was a lot closer to home – under the abandoned warehouse in Fulton Street where he'd tortured so many unfortunates, or at the bottom of the river. Put there by his brother.

On the surface, Luke Glass was respectable: a modern villain trading in crimes that left his conscience clear and hands clean, happy to leave the street businesses for Ritchie to manage his own way without interference. Luke was smart and climbing to heights his brother could only have dreamed about. But that meant doing business with the likes of Jonas Small, and it was a shrewd move despite the fact Small could be added to the list of crazies Ritchie had spent too many years shielding from the consequences of their misjudgements. Luke could handle the bastard, though if getting involved with the unpredictable East End gang boss blew up in their faces... well, that was what George was for.

He looked at his watch and dragged his shoes towards him across the carpet where they'd landed when he'd kicked them off. The pub would be jumping; he'd be fortunate to get a chair, probably forced to drink his customary two pints standing up. Once maybe, not now: he was too long in the tooth for that malarkey – if there were no seats, he'd go somewhere else.

A mobile vibrated on the table; he lifted it and listened, his expression suddenly serious. Once or twice he nodded but didn't stop putting on his shoes.

His tone softened. 'You aren't hurt, are you, Ethel?'

'No.'

'Then take a deep breath and tell me exactly what happened. Was he on his own?'

'Yes, and he had a gun.'

Ritchie spoke slowly. 'A bastard pulls a shooter out. Takes a bit of getting over. What did he say?'

'He wasn't after money.'

'The exact words.'

Ethel dredged her memory. '"I admire your bottle, Mrs, but save it. This is the wrong time to be a smart-arse. It isn't appreciated. I'll take whatever cash you've got but I'm not after money. So don't fuck me about!"'

'Then, what?'

'Made me give him the stuff.'

'How much?'

'Two bags.'

'Had you seen him before?'

'I don't think so.'

'And you haven't called the police?'

'I called you, like you told me to.'

Ritchie sighed; he was getting too old for this. 'Good girl, good girl. Now, here's what I want you to do. Lock the cabin up and write down everything you can remember. Picture the details in your mind – height, accent, tattoos. Sit quietly and it'll come to you. Sounds like an amateur chancing his luck. He'll have made a mistake. They all do.'

In the background he heard Winston speaking. 'I was meeting my mates in the pub.'

Ritchie hid his irritation. Ethel was more valuable than she realised – finding people who'd stick the job without dipping their mitts in the till wasn't easy. Pity she was involved with a moron.

'Tell Winston the pub will still be there when you're finished. Bring what you've got to my office tomorrow. It's above the King of Mesopotamia.'

'I know where it is, Mr Ritchie.'

'First thing, Ethel, 9 a.m.' He added a reminder. 'We keep this in-house. We sort it ourselves.'

The mobile hadn't left his hand when it rang again. Ritchie cursed. The manager in Lewisham launched into a tale that had suddenly become familiar. Ritchie felt outrage build inside him.

Somebody was having them at it.

'I'll be there in twenty minutes.'

Then, he made a call of his own. 'Felix. Contact all our guys. I need them up and on their toes. Meet me at the bookies in Lewisham.'

'What's happened, George?'

'We've been turned over. Two locations at the same time.'

'What? Who? Who'd have the balls? It doesn't make sense.'

'Well, they've stepped in it big time. Tell the boys they're on duty till I say they can stand down.'

Felix tried to take it in. 'Nobody's dared lay a glove on us in years. Where's Luke? Does he know?'

'Keep Luke out of this until we understand what's going on.'

'Is it true we're hooking up with Jonas Small?'

'Ask him yourself when you see him.'

Felix hesitated. 'George... could it be him?'

'No, Small wouldn't play games; he'd come at us head-on, go for the heart. It's somebody else.'

* * *

'"Up and on their toes".' Ritchie repeated his phrase to the empty room. It sounded like a call to arms. In fact, it was nothing of the kind: he was reacting for the benefit of the troops, signalling in case some other chancers decided now was the right time to move on them. Unlikely. But so was what had happened. Whatever was going on didn't feel like the start of a war. George Ritchie had survived a few of those and knew the difference. The rules of engagement never changed: hit your enemy hard and fast, inflict as much damage as possible and wait for the response. Tonight, only three shots had been fired. Nobody was hurt if you didn't count the manager – even that was accidental.

Some bastard wanted to get their attention. Well, they had it.

The next move was theirs. But the insult – for that was what it was – wouldn't go unanswered.

Ritchie wouldn't tell Luke all of it. He'd keep back a piece of information inadvertently let slip by one of the robbers in Lewisham. A name: Jazzer. Jazzer from Liverpool.

He dialled a number and waited for his contact to answer. Ritchie said, 'Eddie, long time. Got something for you if you're interested. Right up your street, I'm thinking. Nothing complicated. Already have a name. Need a face to pin it on.'

Saturday 1.30 a.m.

The VIP party swept from the limo through the paparazzi on the pavement outside the club. Shouts for the star to smile were ignored: Alondra Constanza Melosa Vasquez, better known as Vicky Messina, was in a particularly prickly mood. The third of five sell-out concerts at the O2 Arena hadn't gone well. Problems with the sound in the middle of one of her many show-stopping numbers had embarrassed her and she was fuming. And when the boss wasn't happy, everybody heard about it; tomorrow an engineer would be looking for a new job. The diva was a perfectionist, at least where other people were concerned. She'd fought her way up from humble beginnings in her native Puerto Rico and had sworn she wouldn't take shit from anybody – a promise she was in no danger of breaking.

A freelancer jumped in front to take a picture. Mark Douglas, Messina's muscular Scottish minder, snatched the camera out of his hand, crushed it under his heel and shepherded his client inside.

'Hey, that's a Nikon!'

Douglas called over his shoulder. 'Sue me.'

Nina Glass was sipping her Southern Comfort and Coke at the bar when the entourage arrived. Heads turned. Star fuckers, the lot of them.

The reservation had been made and cancelled twice already. Not unusual. Since her brother, Luke, opened the club, Nina had got used to rubbing shoulders with famous people. Some were a pleasure. Others – like the millionaire upstart being shown to a booth by the manager – were in a club that had been named after them and they didn't even know it.

LBC – the Lucky Bastards Club – was the hottest spot in London. Pictures of Vicky Messina on the front pages of the tabloids stumbling into the street in the early hours of the morning were gold, more valuable than any amount of advertising. Nina was the face of the club. Meeting and greeting the punters, fake smile plastered on, hating every bloody minute of it. Luke had asked her to do it and said it would "only be for a few weeks".

That was six months ago.

Over in her own corner of the family empire, the successful real-estate business she'd built, Nina came up against well-heeled tossers with more money than sense every day of the week. She didn't need another dose of the same at night.

Yes, sir, no, sir, three bags full wasn't her style.

If Luke didn't get somebody else and soon, no matter what he said, she was walking. He'd be left to do the arse-licking himself, instead of waltzing in like the lord of the manor when it suited him. Finding a replacement for her would be anything but easy: it took confidence in who you were to pander to fragile egos and make them believe they were the top priority; the only priority. For all their success and ridiculous good looks, A-listers were delicate flowers, constantly in need of reassurance they were still number one.

The singer would pout and complain and be a royal pain in the arse. But she'd spend.

Plenty.

Nina's job was to make sure she got that chance.

* * *

The briefcase contained two hundred thousand pounds in neat bundles, strapped together and tied with currency bands. Jonas Small took a last look at the banknotes, closed the lid and kissed the case lovingly. Behind him, he knew Luke Glass's minders would be laughing. That was okay: Jonas liked a good laugh.

'For luck. I'm sending my babies on their journey. It's a rough old world.'

The smirking minder took the case off him. 'Whatever you say, Mr Small. Want me to sign anything?'

Jonas Small's expression hardened. 'If I did, a scallywag like you wouldn't be getting near it.'

'I was only—'

'Being a smart-arse is what you were only. Money isn't a laughing matter. People worked their socks off for what's in there and don't forget it. My wife's right, these days young guys think five thou isn't a lot of cash. Well, try saving it up.' Small walked them to the door, back to his cheery self.

'You boys do what your mothers told you and don't be talking to strangers, eh?' He winked. 'Drive carefully, lads.'

The men got into the van, shaking their heads. Freddy, the driver, made a U-turn and headed back to the city. Over his shoulder he asked, 'What's the crazy bastard like tonight?'

'Mean as a rattlesnake and daft as a fucking brush.'

'So, the usual, then.'

'Yeah, but don't underestimate him or he'll have your arm off.'

* * *

Vicky Messina's bodyguards set up a perimeter around her booth, their unsmiling faces encouraging admirers to keep their distance. The lights in the seating areas were designed to flatter, though it would take a lot more than clever backlighting to make some of these princesses look good falling out of the door at 4 a.m. on their Botoxed faces.

Messina's own security had every hotel and venue on the tour covered – eighty-three shows in twenty-one countries. A tall order. On the London leg, Mark Douglas and two guys from Celebrity Security were responsible for her safety beyond the bubble they'd created. Of course, there were exceptions: yesterday, against his advice, the singer insisted on jogging in Hyde Park, her slim figure in white shorts and T-shirt boxed between burly minders pushing people aside to clear a path, breaking a sixty-eight-year-old man's arm in the process.

Not how Douglas would've handled it. Predictably, the newspapers had had a field day with the pictures and the pensioner had been advised to sue.

The rest of the time, the star kept to her bedroom in the Dorchester and there was little for Douglas and his men to do other than drink coffee and talk football. Late in the afternoon, she'd left by a side entrance in a blacked-out car for a sound check, returning to the hotel a couple of hours later for a light dinner and her ritual massage to loosen up before the show.

At that point, everything was under control; everything was cool.

After the concert the plan started to unravel. Word didn't reach them until the last minute about Messina's demands: the previous night, a Michelin-starred restaurant in Mayfair had been persuaded to open late for one over-indulged guest. Tonight, it was LBC's turn to be blessed by her divine presence.

Across the club the diva was making the most of her grand entrance. Nina smiled a cynical smile. The woman could sing. Big fucking deal! She hadn't discovered a cure for cancer.

Christ alone knew how much work she'd had done – boob jobs, eye jobs, rhinoplasty. Every damned thing under the sun. If life gave you lemons, a simple operation could give you melons. And for what? Thirty years down the line, she'd go to bed beautiful and wake up looking like a dummy rescued from a fire at Madame Tussauds. Nina studied her own face in the mirror behind the bar. Not the teenage rebel who'd been expelled twice from school, but not bad. Her skin was her best feature, smooth and unlined, though that wouldn't last if she was here every bloody night. Too many drinks and not enough sleep would see to that. Luke's promise about how long she'd be doing this came back. Resentment washed through her. She emptied her Southern Comfort, and snapped her fingers for a refill at the Latin guy juggling a cocktail shaker who thought he was Tom Cruise.

Nina saw Mark Douglas coming towards her and felt her nipples stiffen against her silk blouse – whatever he wanted the answer was yes. Douglas flashed his ID and introduced himself. 'Celebrity Security. I need to check the exits but the manager seems to have disappeared. Any idea where I can find him?'

Nina sipped her drink and made him wait. 'No.'

'Can you okay it?'

She tilted her head. 'What's in it for me?'

Douglas played the game. 'The satisfaction of helping a guy do his job. Did you have something else in mind... Nina?'

Nina – he knew her name. And, no doubt, who she was.

The rolling accent was a bonus – she hadn't had a Scotsman. Nina crossed her legs slowly, giving him time to check them out. He was asking for permission; she'd give him a lot more than that.

'Do you need someone to show you where everything is?'

Her eyes met his, daring him to look away. He glanced over his shoulder through the dance-floor crowd to the prima donna sipping obscenely overpriced champagne in the booth. Nina savoured the tiny victory. One nil to her. Nice. Though not as nice as being totally dominated by a handsome man who knew his way around a woman's body.

Douglas said, 'Thanks, I usually find what I'm after.'

Nina peered at him over the rim of her drink. 'I bet you do.'

* * *

Freddy Bennet – Freddy The Mouth – was the low man on the totem pole; as an orphan shunted from one foster home to another, something he was well used to. He'd gone from an introverted kid to one that couldn't shut up. Almost inevitably, he crossed the line and for eighteen months laid his confused young head on a bunk in Cookham Wood young offenders' institution in Kent. From there, his criminal baptism travelled a predictable route leading to more of the same, this time in Feltham in Hounslow where he learned to drive, followed by two years for burglary and three for credit-card fraud. Freddy would be twenty-six on his next birthday and already his life was over. He was the best wheel man in London but, because he rabbited nineteen-to-the-dozen, nobody was keen to work with him. His constant diatribe rattled nerves that needed to be steady.

The van passed the infamous Blind Beggar on Whitechapel Road; the pub was closed but a light was on inside. Its dark history was well known. Freddy shared it anyway, he couldn't help himself; his talkaholism, the compulsive condition he lived with, wouldn't let him.

He said, 'That's where Ronnie Kray murdered George Cornell in 1966. Did him in front of witnesses, cool as you like.'

'You should be a tour guide, Freddy.'

'You reckon?'

'Absolutely. You're a natural.'

Freddy was off and running. 'Course, nobody would testify against him, would they? Against Ronnie Kray? No chance. Bullet went right through Cornell's skull, so they say.'

'Do they?'

The sardonic response went over his head and he finished his thought. 'Have to give it to him, old Ronnie had bottle.'

The continuous prattle unnerved the men in the back. A ghost story to remind them the city was full of crazy bastards and always had been wasn't needed; they reached for the cold reassurance in their pockets. This was the fourth time they'd ferried money across the city. A low-key operation few were aware of. So far, there hadn't been a problem, though the risk was obvious.

A rough voice contradicted Freddy's version of the myth. 'Ronnie Kray was a psycho. Bottle never came into it.'

'Just sayin' it was ballsy.'

'Yeah, well, do us a favour. Don't.'

Freddy couldn't leave it alone; seconds later, he was at it again. 'They done him for it. Done him good and proper. Took three years but they got him. He died—'

'Shut it. Or I'll shut it for you.'

This time, the message got through. 'Sorry, lads. Can't help it. Always worse when I'm nervous.'

'Understood, Freddy. No problem. Now put a fucking sock in it.'

The van turned right into a deserted Great Eastern Street and on until traffic lights on City Road stopped its progress. The engine idled, the acrid smell of diesel drifted on the air. Freddy tapped the wheel with his finger. 'He was a homo, old Ronnie, did I mention that? Queer as a bottle of chips. And Reggie was bisexual. Had sex with each other to keep it a secret. God's honest. Ronnie admitted as much to some geezer writing a book about them. Not many—'

The bullet exploded the side window, ending the monologue, entered his heart, killing him instantly. The rear doors flew open. A rapid burst of fire from a semi-automatic carbine sprayed the inside, thudding into the minders, making them dance like drunken puppets; they were dead before they could draw their guns. One of the assassins manhandled Freddy's lifeless body into the passenger seat, while the other two got into the back beside the slain guards. When the lights turned green, the van pulled away. Nobody saw. It wouldn't have mattered if they had. In this part of town people were smart enough to keep their noses out of what didn't concern them – no different from the night Ronnie Kray had walked into the Blind Beggar and shot George Cornell.

It had taken all of thirty seconds to kill three men and steal two hundred thousand pounds.

Freddy would've been impressed. What a story that would've been.

* * *

Nina watched Mark Douglas leave, imagining her thighs circling his hard body, feeling a quiver between her legs. On the other side of the room, Vicky Messina pulled out what looked like a diamond-studded Shisha Sticks Sofia, and if it was possible Nina despised her even more – giving wealth to an idiot: what a waste.

Nina was a demanding and aggressive sexual partner, an unapologetic predator who usually got what she wanted. Too much for most of the lovers lucky enough to get the chance to take her on. Men were there to be used and discarded when some new entertainment came along; she wouldn't change, even if she could. Rules were for other people, people prepared to abide by them. That wasn't her. Nina was a Glass.

Her mobile rang. She picked it up and cupped a hand to her ear, smiling, already on her way to the door. 'Mr Drake. What a surprise. I was just thinking about you.'

4

It was 1.55 a.m. Further along, Islington had more than its share of raucous party bars and clubs, jumping with late-night drinkers. Where they were on the main drag was like an abandoned film set.

They kept to the speed limit. With three dead men in the van, attracting unwanted attention wasn't wise. In twenty minutes, they'd seen two black cabs, a Renault with no lights on travelling in the other direction, and an old woman, probably homeless and hungry, rummaging in a bin. Others would rouse themselves from the shadows and join her, the underworld of pimps and prostitutes, sellers and pushers, addicts and alcoholics who hid in the day and lived by night while the rest of London slept.

The late Freddy The Mouth was propped in the passenger seat, blood pooling under him from the fatal wound in his chest. It had taken death to silence Freddy – for once, he had nothing to say. Neither did anybody else. The men crouched in the back, focused on where they were going and what they would do when they got there.

At Lloyd's Bank on Gray's Inn Road, a police car with two uniforms was parked on the opposite side of the street. As they passed, the van driver watched for the telltale puff of exhaust smoke in his mirror that would mean they had a problem. The plan depended on nothing unexpected getting in the way – there was no legislating for being tugged at two o'clock in the morning by a couple of bored constables. It would end badly for the coppers, no doubts about that. But dead policemen were an unnecessary complication, a complication with repercussions. The force looked after its own: the case would never be closed and, if need be, they'd be hounded for the rest of their lives.

When the neo-Gothic architecture of St Pancras was behind them, the driver put his foot to the accelerator and raced along Euston Road. At the end, he turned left into Great Portland Street and relaxed for the first time since they'd spotted the police car. 'Nearly there,' he said, as much to himself as anyone else – a sentiment his colleagues understood – turning his head so his face wouldn't be caught on the CCTV camera trained on the street. His accomplices pulled on their masks and crouched, tensed and ready, gripping the heavy handles of machetes.

Down the lane behind the club, a shaft of amber from the basement cut the darkness. In it, two security guards waited for the van to roll to a stop, eyes on the main road in case uninvited guests decided to join the party. None did. They banged twice on the side of the van and stepped back. A nod passed between them – the cash was here; everything was okay.

And in that reassuring moment, their concentration slipped. Just for a second. Three at most. But the difference – as they were about to discover – between living or dying.

The back doors flew open. Machete blades, thick and sharp, designed to cause maximum hurt, glinted in the light: the first blow landed on a neck releasing a red gusher that arced in the air and landed on the dull plaster wall in a crimson spray; the second effortlessly separated fingers from a hand; the third hacked a leg that would never walk again.

The minders hardly had time to register the pain. No time to draw their guns.

A second. Three at most. The difference between living or dying.

* * *

The club's security guard's teeth were even and white, his arrogant eyes heavy with marijuana. He probably imagined he could handle himself because of the endless hours he spent at the gym. It took a lot more than that. Weights didn't fight back. But it was a nice idea if you were him. His hair was short and dark and slicked with gel. Over a black T-shirt, the jacket bulged slightly on his left-hand side. Hiring this one had been a poor decision. Douglas suspected the sister he'd just spoken to was responsible: looking good in a T-shirt could've swung it. The bouncer hadn't let his pock-marked skin give him an inferiority complex; confidence and indifference oozed from him in equal measure. Mark Douglas recognised the type – he'd met scores like him – ace at standing around playing the tough guy. No damned use when it mattered.

Douglas flashed his ID and breezed through, his footsteps echoing in the dusty stairwell, the pulsing R & B groove of Khalid fading behind him. Halfway down, he heard a cry and saw a security guard rush towards it. Douglas didn't hesitate. He ran back the way he'd come, talking low and urgently into his mic.

'Trouble at the back door. Secure the client.'

The guy with the marked face stared but didn't react. Douglas reached inside his pocket and relieved him of his weapon. 'We've got a situation. Get your men. Now!'

Douglas edged down the stairs, holding the unfamiliar gun in both hands. It didn't take a trained eye to realise the guard on the concrete floor was beyond help. Out in the lane, a second guard lay still. Voices drifted from an inner door. Douglas couldn't make out what was said over the relentless pounding from the club upstairs. Difficult to believe people were dancing, drinking, playing footsie under tables, totally unaware of what was happening yards away.

A female screamed, a man laughed, and Douglas looked round the frame. In the middle of the room, a guy in a mask held the blade of a machete to a terrified woman's neck; a thin red line trickled down the pale skin of her throat and disappeared into her blouse. Ending her life would be easy, a flick of the wrist, no more. His mate kneeled in front of the safe.

Mark Douglas's famous client wasn't in danger.

Through sheer bad luck for the thieves, he'd stumbled on a robbery. He pressed his shoulders against the wall, counted to three, and stepped into the room. Until he said, 'Hands up. Hands up or I shoot,' nobody had known he was there.

The guy on his knees stopped what he was doing and looked round. His friend was unfazed, understanding the advantage he had, and stayed where he was.

Douglas spoke again. 'Get your hands in the air!'

The machete tightened against the woman's flesh; the blood flow quickened and she shuddered. Her captor pulled her closer to him. 'Don't know who the fuck you are, friend, but if you've got even half a brain, this is the time to use it. You've no idea who you're messing with. Put the gun down and walk over to the corner.'

'Not happening.'

'Then this is down to you.'

The blade bit deeper; the helpless woman started to cry. 'Please, please. I don't want to die. I only work here.'

'Listening to that? She doesn't want to die.'

Douglas trained the gun on him. 'The question I'm asking

myself is how you feel about it, given that a second after you kill her, I'll kill you?'

Footsteps would mean the club's security was arriving. There was only silence.

Machete Man said, 'All right, you've made your point. Good for you. Now get away from the door or I'll slit her throat. What comes after...'

He shrugged and Mark Douglas believed him. 'Okay. Take it easy.'

The robbers backed towards the exit, still using the woman as a shield. When they reached the street, Machete Man tilted her head back and drew the blade across her flesh in one continuous stroke. Her eyes rolled and she collapsed. The callousness of it caught Douglas by surprise. Before he could react, the robbers were racing up the lane towards a third man behind the wheel of a car. The rear door was open. Douglas steadied himself and took aim. The first shot hit the one with the sack of money, killing him, the second struck the assassin in the shoulder spinning him round. He stumbled and fell, got up, grabbed the bag and dived into the back seat. The car roared away, leaving carnage behind.

Douglas got on his knees and tenderly cradled the woman's head. Her eyes were closed, already unconscious, unaware of him: dying without knowing why. Stemming the bleeding was impossible; blood gurgled in her severed windpipe like percolating coffee; there was no hope. He held her hand, gently rubbing the cold fingers, whispering it was going to be all right, hating himself for the lie.

When the last breath left her body, he took off his jacket and covered her. Inadequate, but the least he could do. The killing had been unnecessary. She'd served her purpose; the man could've let her go. It hadn't been about escape or protecting themselves from capture: it was murder, cruel and deliberate; the act of a sadist.

you've no idea who you're messing with

Yes, he did. What he'd come up against was pure evil.

* * *

The men in the van had died quickly: a sudden flash, a nanosecond of pain and gone from the world. The guards at the back door hadn't been so fortunate; their injuries had been excruciating, crippling and ugly. Douglas didn't let himself dwell on the woman.

Security had taken their time. When they finally arrived, it was all over. His assessment of them had been sadly accurate: clowns in designer suits who wouldn't last two minutes if the shit really hit the fan. A celeb with too much champagne down their neck was as much as they could handle.

Vicky Messina was on her way back to the Dorchester, her svelte frame wedged uncomfortably between his men; her night had been cut short. She'd take her displeasure out on whoever was handy. Telling her it was for her own good would be a waste of time. The singer was the client. Douglas should've been with her. With his shirt soaked in innocent blood, the temper tantrums of an overpaid brat were unimportant – he couldn't have cared less.

He spoke to an Armani suit. 'Who are you?'

'Luigi. Front of House Manager. I heard a noise and came down.'

'Who's in charge?'

The terrified guy pointed to a corpse on the floor with its throat cut. 'He is. Paul Fallon.'

'Okay, call Mr Glass. Now.'

Douglas sensed the T-shirt who'd surrendered his gun too easily behind him. 'Where've you been hiding? Start doing your job. Seal the lane. Those bodies, get them out of sight. Put them in the van, lock it and give me the keys. Move, for Christ's sake! There's a pack of paparazzi around the corner who'd sell their granny for a photograph of this. That can't happen.'

'What about the police? Shouldn't—'

'No police until we understand what's going on. Where's Nina?'

'Haven't seen her.'

'Fuck! Find her and make sure she calls Luke.'

5

Kelly's blonde head was resting on my chest, one lean leg draped over me in post-coital togetherness, when my mobile vibrated on the bedside cabinet. She rolled away and covered her beautiful breasts to punish me, sighing an exaggerated sigh. She wasn't happy. And she wasn't the kind of girl to keep something as important as that to herself.

I'd promised a night without interruptions – no phone calls, no meetings, no I-have-to-stop-off-for-a-minute diversions: a romantic evening, just the two of us. Until now, I'd been as good as my word. The restaurant in Mayfair had cost an arm and a leg. If there was a difference between what it served and the lasagne we could've had in Clapham at a quarter of the price, it escaped me. But Kelly liked the idea of going up West and it was only money.

These days, not something I was short of.

She mouthed 'tell them go to hell'. I would've obliged, except the manager of LBC, Luigi Giordano, was blowing like he'd run to Marble Arch and back again; his broken accent didn't help me understand.

'We've got a problem, boss. Need you here.'

'What kind of problem?'

'Better don't talk on the phone.'

I was out of bed and on my feet. Cryptic conversations in pidgin English irritated me.

'Damn it, Luigi, what's wrong?'

If it was hard to say, it was even harder to listen to. He struggled to get the words out.

'We've... we've been attacked.'

'How bad?'

Most of what he told me didn't register – our men were down; bodies and bullets and blood; lots of blood; guns and knives and something about a woman who worked in the office whose name I'd forgotten. Luigi Giordano was from Sicily. Mafia country. As a boy, he'd witnessed violence. But not like this. He was in shock and couldn't tell a story if his life depended on it. Maybe it did. His track record at some of the top hotels in London was impressive. I'd hired him for his front-of-house skills; this wasn't his territory. Paul Fallon was Head of Security. Why was I talking to a freaked-out Sicilian?

I forced myself to calm down – Luigi was hysterical enough for both of us.

'Put Paul on.'

'Paul's dead, boss.'

Icy tendrils snaked round my heart and squeezed.

'The briefcase. Did they take the briefcase?'

His answer crystallised any details I'd missed.

'What briefcase? No briefcase.'

'Then, give me Nina.'

'We can't find her. Mark said—'

'Mark! Who the hell is Mark?'

'I don't know. He's here with some celebrity. He stopped them.'

Five minutes away from the place and the roof had caved in.

Kelly could be as pissed-off with me as she liked. This was more important. I said, 'I'm on my way,' and headed for the door.

* * *

George Ritchie was old-school. Twenty-first-century crime, spread-sheets and wire transfers and not getting his hands dirty sat badly with him. His wheelhouse, what he did better than anybody, was run the street scams I'd been distancing myself from since taking over Danny's operation. Nice earners, for sure. But drugs and girls, knocked-off cigarettes and booze weren't where I saw myself ten years down the line. Glass Houses, Nina's estate agency, the construction company I'd started, and LBC in Central London, were the future.

Businesses with potential. Real potential. The kind of money you could spend without worrying about getting caught.

From what I'd heard, tonight we were in George country.

He answered right away – at this time of the night it should've made me suspicious. I missed it. 'Meet me at the club. Now.'

He didn't ask why. He didn't ask anything. He said, 'I'm on my way,' and hung up.

* * *

George Ritchie sat at his desk in the office above the pub; he hadn't gone home. Ritchie knew Luke wouldn't contact him in the middle of the night unless he had a good reason. A very good reason. He hadn't been unduly worried by the hits on River Cars and Eamon Durham in Lewisham. It smacked of small-time: young Turks trying their luck in the big league. Nuisance value. Letting slip a name – Jazzer – was an amateur error. One they'd pay for, late or soon. This was different. This was the club. Earlier, he'd put the troops on alert for show more than anything. Suddenly, the threat had become real.

He lifted his car keys off the desk and headed downstairs. On the bar, the beer pumps were like soldiers on parade in the dull glow of a nightlight. Ritchie locked the door of the King Pot behind him and looked warily up and down the street, seeing nobody – hardly a surprise at twenty minutes to three in the morning. He had a well-deserved reputation for caution – few survived as long as he had without it – though at times it was obvious, even to him, he was being paranoid.

That wasn't the case tonight. Something weird was going on.

* * *

When I got there, Ritchie was talking to a well-built guy with blood on his shirt who looked like he could handle himself. In the light from the back door, every year of his life and a few more for luck were etched on George's face. He'd been in this game a long time; tonight, it showed. I searched for the word to describe him and found it; it wasn't difficult. Old. George was old. The young bruiser from Newcastle who'd come to the capital to shake the trees and make a name for himself had done a runner. But I'd still think twice about taking him on.

I said, 'Where's Luigi?'

'Sent him back upstairs. Anything he knows, this guy told him.'

The stranger made eye contact and held it.

George said, 'Mark Douglas. Luke Glass.'

'What happened? The short version.'

'Short's the only version I've got. I was checking the exits and ran right into them.'

'How many?'

'Three.'

'Recognise them?'

'They wore masks. But you might. One of them's in the van. Dropped him, winged his mate, the third got away.' He pointed up the lane. 'A car was waiting on the main drag. Be interesting to get a look at the CCTV.'

'He would've been more useful to us alive. Why kill him?'

'Didn't give me a choice.'

Luigi had described carnage. I didn't see it. 'Where're the bodies?'

He hooked a bloodied thumb in the direction of the van. 'Dumped them in there in case some paparazzi bastard got an anonymous tip-off and wandered into the scoop of his miserable life.'

This guy had been thinking on his feet. Impressive.

'Before you open it, it's not pretty. There was a lot of blood. I had it hosed away.'

'Good work.'

'They used machetes. Unusual, to say the least. Especially since they'd killed what I'm guessing was the original crew.'

'And you know that, how?'

'There were no gunshots, which means they were already dead when they got here. Which also means machetes weren't some random pick. They had guns and didn't use them. What does that say?'

'You're doing fine on your own.'

'Okay. Two things jump out: the attackers intended to do damage. The guy who killed the woman did it to prove he could – not the MO of ordinary villains – and I believe the safe was secondary. That makes the van the key. I don't know your routine, but I'm guessing armed security guards sitting at the back door in a vehicle isn't part of it. So why the van?'

Mark Douglas was sharp. I wouldn't be telling him about the briefcase full of Jonas Small's money.

I opened the van doors; he hadn't exaggerated. I'd seen worse but couldn't recall when. Death hadn't distinguished between the good and the bad: arms and legs, heads and bodies, piled on one another like shop-window mannequins the day after the place closed down. On a couple of them, the skin was already beginning to pale as gravity drew blood away from the surface into the tissues; mottling would be next, though by then they'd be in the ground. Paul Fallon was near the bottom, his fancy title – Head of Security – no defence against the blade that had almost decapitated him. The woman from the office lay close by.

Ritchie was beside me. He said, 'I've called Felix. We'll take care of this.' His eyes settled on the female, his mouth turned down and I guessed what was in his mind. Females were off limits in George world.

'The woman was a civilian. Did she have family?'

From nowhere, it came to me. 'Rose. Her name was Rose.'

He repeated his question. 'Did she have anybody?'

'No idea. If she had, square them up.'

Mark Douglas pointed. 'That's him. That's the guy.'

The assassin was a stranger. Ritchie closed the van – we'd seen all there was to see.

'What about Nina?'

George reassured me. 'On it. Somebody will know where she is.'

Mark Douglas overheard. 'We were talking a couple of minutes before it kicked off. I'm pretty sure Nina wasn't involved.'

'Talking, where?'

'In the bar.'

'You said there was a car waiting. Is it possible they took her?'

Douglas thought about his reply. 'With the press at the front door it would be difficult.'

Ritchie had the keys of the van in his hand, anxious to get moving. He edged away from Mark Douglas: there was more. 'Didn't call you earlier because there was nothing to say.'

'Nothing to say about what?'

'This isn't the first attack. We were hit earlier tonight. Twice.'

'Twice! Christ's sake, George. What the fuck's going on?'

His hand was on my shoulder, his voice almost a whisper. 'Nothing like this. Completely different. For a start, nobody was hurt.'

'Where?'

'Lambeth and Lewisham. River Cars and Eamon Durham.'

'Any other surprises, or is that it?'

'It's under control.'

I checked my watch. 'The club's closing in an hour.'

'Until then?'

'Until then it's business as usual.'

* * *

'Business as usual'? Who was I kidding?

Kelly's notion of uninterrupted time together was in the bin. Agreeing to it had been a mistake I wouldn't be making again. LBC was the single most significant investment I'd ever made or probably ever would make; more money than I wanted to think about, and if it was as successful as I imagined, we'd be clearing most of the bent earners in London: a great game when you were winning. At the moment, we were being hammered. And failure wasn't an option.

We'd been open six months and the cash was flooding in. Already there was a waiting list for membership and maybe I'd taken it for granted. Not any more. The van with its gruesome cargo was on its way to a quarry somewhere in Surrey or Kent. I wouldn't ask, George Ritchie wouldn't tell me. We'd been lucky a guy hired to stop some drunk-as-a-skunk pop star falling on her well-known face in front of a gaggle of photographers had been here.

Mark Douglas was crouched on one knee, his shoulders sagging like his head was too heavy for his body, the adrenaline rush that had synchronised his mind and body ebbing. Soon, he'd be so exhausted he'd happily lie down on the pavement and sleep.

I owed him. More than I could repay. Half a dozen shirts from Turnbull & Asser would be a start. He was low-key – possibly not appreciating exactly what he'd done. But I did. The club could've been on the front page of every newspaper in the country, police crawling all over the place, and me fielding calls from irate villains with money on the line – the kind of villains it was better not to upset.

That was for tomorrow.

Right now, Nina was missing. We'd been on the receiving end three times in one night, and couldn't be sure there wasn't more on the way. Then there was the little matter of two hundred thousand pounds belonging to Jonas Small, a man not known for his forgiving nature. If he found out – make that when he found out – he'd go mental. He already had a head start, for Christ's sake.

* * *

I walked Douglas to the end of the lane and waited until his taxi arrived. He was a man of few words. After his performance tonight, I didn't intend to lose him. In a mediocre world, he was top-drawer. I gave him my card and asked him to call me tomorrow, or was that today?

Ritchie had assured me the attacks in Lambeth and Lewisham didn't match the carnage at the club. I wanted to believe him and arranged to meet at the King Pot to get a handle on what the hell was happening. Before that, there was another call to make.

Stanford took his time answering. When he finally did, I heard sleep in his voice and a female complaining in the background about being woken up – his wife, the fragrant Elise, a natural-born lily of the field, who neither toiled nor spun, yet lived a life far in excess of her husband's salary and never thought to ask him how he managed it.

Stanford was a rising star in the Met, tipped to go all the way. Nobody deserved it less. He was a smug bastard, permanently amused at some secret joke, and as bent as they made them. Bad guys came in all shapes and sizes: Oliver Stanford was copper-sized, and the only side the policeman was on was his own. If you understood that, he'd never surprise or disappoint you. In a very real sense we were partners, though neither of us would appreciate that description. We each held the other's future in our hands – not the most comforting thought I'd ever had. Ollie had been quiet of late, not earning his corn: time he did.

He growled into the phone. 'What the hell do you want at this hour?'

'LBC was attacked tonight. My sister's missing.'

I left the two hundred grand out of the picture. I'd deal with that myself, one way or the other, and settled for imagining him in his blue-and-white-striped pyjamas, smug as ever.

'Attacked? Who?'

'Unknown. Except, they used machetes so they planned on making a mess.'

'Nasty. Could be personal. Who have you been noising-up?'

I ignored him. 'Personal or somebody going after the club's rep. Bad news, either way.'

'And you're looking for me to do... what?'

The wrong response.

I put it aside for the moment and carried on. 'If the club is the target some public-spirited individual who happened to be passing at half-two in the morning, as you do, might tell the police about seeing something suspicious. That wouldn't be helpful. Squash any attempt to follow up on it.'

'Okay. What else?'

'Trace my sister's phone and give me the location. And, I'm sending you a picture of one of the attackers. Get me a name.'

His tone was dry, as if what I was asking was a chore. He sighed. 'Text me her number.'

Stanford couldn't have cared less about Nina. But LBC was important to him. He understood that if it went down, we'd all go down with it and he could say ta-ta to the lifestyle him and his Mrs liked so much. He'd been to the club half a dozen times, playing the big shot with faces who might be useful in his climb up the greasy pole; ordering champagne and fifteen-year-old Armagnac and running up a tab he'd never intended to pay.

Losing a perk was the tip of the iceberg and that concerned him.

'Going back to the club, what might this person have to report?'

'For a start, seven dead bodies, Oliver.'

6

Nina had known he'd call. Late, but not too late – the surprise was how long it had taken Algernon Drake to get his bottle up. Strong females made some men uncomfortable. Smart women didn't advertise their superiority – there was nothing to be gained by making the darlings more insecure than they were already. Mustn't do that. Yet, even the best of them didn't realise how vulnerable, how easy to control, they were.

Females matured faster, lived longer and had more orgasms.

Who'd be a man?

She turned her mobile off. Screw Luke. If he could do a no-show, she could have an early night.

She paid the taxi and walked between the warehouses on Shad Thames that had stored tea, coffee and spices in another age. Nina had been here during the day, when Algernon Drake viewed the flat. Late at night was a different experience, like wandering into a

Charles Dickens novel: the original brickwork, the winches and faded signs on the walls all still there, and, above her head, the walkways used to roll barrels between the stores criss-crossed the street.

The City of London was a mile north-west on the other side of the river, which meant many of the wealthy residents walked to work. Thieves with an office, Danny would've called them.

Paid-up members of the Lucky Bastards Club.

Algernon Drake would fit right in.

He was older than her by thirty years – a detail the barrister didn't intend to let stand in his way. Grey and balding, tanned and brimming with confidence nurtured by a string of high-profile legal victories throughout his career, his phone numbers were on the contact lists of celebrities who considered the front pages of the tabloids their second home and politicians who'd prefer they weren't. Seeing justice served had made Drake famous in the circles he moved in.

At their second meeting, his hand had brushed hers and he'd said, 'I'm aware who your brother is.'

'My brother?'

A smile flickered at the corners of his mouth. 'Thus far, he hasn't needed my talents, but you never know.'

It amused her to let him think he was clever. He knew who her brother was; he didn't know her. Algernon Drake was only the latest entitled chauvinist to cross Nina's path – tossers who believed any woman they wanted was theirs for the taking. A little bit of effort and the result was guaranteed. With some females, flattery and flowers were enough. Others placed a higher value on their dubious virtue. Of course, if the man was young and attractive it was easy to let nature take its course, though there were other things to consider here: Drake was neither young nor attractive and didn't fit the bill. But he was ready to spend – her commission would run to six figures – for that kind of money, she was prepared to overlook his shortcomings and thinking about the Scot who had made her horny.

Drake had teased her. 'Somebody recommended you.'

'Really? Who?'

'I'd rather not say.'

'Who recommended me?'

'Bill Sutherland. You sold him a house, remember?'

The boys had been talking.

Sutherland was an investment manager with Deutsche Bank in Great Winchester Street. Nina had had a short-lived affair with him – exactly ten torrid weeks – ending when she'd caught him in bed with two hookers. But not before he'd shelled-out six million for an eight-bedroom detached house on the edge of Kingston Hill, a minute from Richmond Park.

She'd made a mistake with Sutherland and let her guard down. If he hadn't blown it, they might even have had something. Drake was different: an unsubtle predator, hot for her or anything in a skirt – all she had to do was reel him in.

They'd viewed one property after another. From the beginning it had been clear he was as interested in her as in anything they were seeing. Eventually, he'd settled on a fourth-floor flat in Butlers Wharf: 2,500 sq ft, with the most spectacular uninterrupted view of Tower Bridge, the River Thames and the City of London skyline – a snip at three and a half mil. In five years, it would be worth double. At the end, they'd shaken hands, him holding hers longer than he needed.

And Nina knew she had him where she wanted him.

* * *

He was holding two glasses of champagne, casually dressed in a fawn cashmere sweater, younger-looking without the pin-striped suit. She took a glass, thanked him and stepped inside, surprised to find the flat unfurnished apart from a sheepskin jacket draped over a wooden chair.

Sheepskin in this weather?

Drake closed the door behind her; she felt his warm breath on her neck. He whispered, 'Thank you for coming,' believing he was in charge, certain he was on a sure thing.

Making him wait was part of the pleasure, hearing him beg – and he would beg – part of the fun. She said, 'When is your furniture arriving?'

The question caught him off guard. 'Any day now.'

Out on the balcony, Nina was reminded why a simple warehouse conversion four miles from the West End was priced in the millions – the view was jaw-droppingly spectacular, a floodlit Tower Bridge a cascade of twinkling light across the water.

Algernon Drake drew her to him and kissed her hard on the mouth, smelling the strawberry and vanilla bass notes of her perfume, tasting champagne on her lips.

'I've wanted you from the first time I saw you.'

Nina answered, her voice husky. 'Are you used to getting what you want?'

'Yes.'

'Then, you're a lucky boy, aren't you?'

Their mouths locked again in a long kiss. Drake led her inside, deftly unbuttoning her skirt and the cuffs of her blouse before starting on the front. Her clothes fell away and he gasped: she wasn't wearing underwear.

'Christ. Bill said he couldn't get enough of you.'

'Bill was a fool. He blew it.'

'The poor bastard still thinks about you – he admitted it.'

'He was in love with me only he didn't realise until it was too late.'

Drake threw the sheepskin on the floor, lifted Nina and lowered her onto it.

'Were you in love with him?'

In the light her skin had the luminescent glow of ivory.

'None of your business, Mr Drake.'

'Algie.'

'Algie.'

'Can I take that as a no?'

'Take it any way you like... Algie.'

Friday had been warm and sunny. The forecast for Saturday was more of the same, but as I got out of the car it started to rain. Not heavy, a freak shower, lasting just long enough to clean the air. I raised my head to the starless sky and closed my eyes. The drops were cool, an angel's touch, washing layers of tension I hadn't been aware of from me. Then, as suddenly as it began, it stopped and I was alone on the street wondering if I'd imagined it.

There was a light in the window above the King of Mesopotamia. I let myself in and locked the door behind me. Sitting in the corner of the bar, hidden in the dark, two men I didn't recognise watched me without curiosity, as if somebody creeping into a darkened pub in the middle of the night was the most natural thing in the world. Not long ago, I would've known everybody who worked for us. Not any more. When George Ritchie had taken over, he'd brought his own people, guys who were loyal to him, into the fold.

His call.

He heard my footsteps on the stairs and had the bottle and

glasses ready. George was the most insular individual I'd ever met. He didn't smoke, rarely drank in company, and only spoke when there was something real to say. He could be friendly, funny, too, sometimes, although there was no escaping the suspicion he didn't need you. How he lived – even where he lived – was a secret. I didn't doubt it would be modest. The whisky gave a lie to all that: fifty-year-old Glenfiddich. I'd read whisky stopped maturing when it was bottled. On the desk was a fragment of time from half a century into the past.

He was pouring before I sat down and pushed mine across to me.

'We need clear heads but a couple won't do any harm.'

I thanked him and emptied it in one go. Ritchie didn't comment – good decision.

'Any word on Nina?'

His jaw worked and I knew he was trawling for positives and not finding any. He settled for the truth, or a version of it. 'Nina's—'

'Headstrong? That what you were going to say? Reckless?'

'A free spirit. She goes where she goes. Somebody remembered seeing her on her mobile on her way out the door. On her own. The barman confirmed it.'

'On her own? So, she called somebody or somebody called her. The attackers might've lifted her – they could've, it's possible – except, that's an assumption. There's no proof. She isn't answering her phone. Got Stanford doing a trace.'

I checked the screen for a message from the policeman. Nothing. Which reminded me I hadn't heard from him about the other two hits, either. Oliver Stanford was getting sloppy.

Ritchie said, 'He'll be wasting his time. I've tried her number a dozen times.'

'Which means—'

'It's turned off. Can't reach her until she turns it back on. That's as much as we know, Luke.'

He was giving a masterclass on staying in the moment. Unfortunately, I wasn't in a place where I could hear it. Anger and resentment burned in me. If Nina was fucking us about, I'd kill her myself.

He gave me a refill and turned the bottle round so I could read the label. 'Fifty years old. Do it justice. Sip the bloody stuff.'

Ritchie ditched the let's-all-be-calm act. 'She's not at her flat. Even had her office in Waterloo checked out in case she went there. A long shot, but you never know. Nothing. We'll keep looking. For whoever attacked LBC, Luke Glass' sister is a prize and a half. If they had her we'd have heard from them by now. The fact there's been radio silence tells me they haven't.'

It made sense. There was no more to be said.

He moved on to LBC. 'Let's leave the security guard out of it for the moment and concentrate on what we know.' His eyes hooded; his expression changed. 'The first two hits at Lambeth and Lewisham had the same MO. Masked men with shotguns.'

'How bad?'

'Bad enough. It should never have happened. Threats but no actual violence – the only injury was to the manager, and that was an accident. He's all right, by the way. We lost a day's takings from Eamon's and drugs from the taxis.' He made a face. 'Not serious. We'll survive.'

'What's your thinking, George?'

'Hitting the club complicates it. Before that, their out-of-town accents and the cheeky bastards asking for you told me somebody was sending us a message. I tightened everything up in case there was more on the way and waited for their next move.'

'Asking for me? What do you mean?'

'Said to tell you Charlie was asking for you.'

'Charlie? Who the hell is Charlie?'

Ritchie shrugged. 'LBC is different – doesn't fit the same pattern. It was ugly because they wanted it ugly. Machetes guaranteed they got their wish. The big mystery, the puzzle I'm trying to get my head round, is why. The three of our guys who collected the cash from Jonas Small were dead before the van got to the club. They already had the money.' Ritchie frowned and shook his head. 'I don't get it.'

'Unless they *are* sending a message – showing us it can go down hard or easy.'

He toyed with the amber in the glass. 'Just so you know, I've put a call in to Newcastle. By lunchtime tomorrow, the cavalry will have arrived.'

'How many?'

'Enough for a war, if that's where it's headed.'

He was planning for a battle. After three years in total control south of the river it didn't seem real. Except, it was. We were in the dark, scrambling around trying to understand what the hell was happening.

Ritchie said, 'In case you're wondering about the two down-stairs, until we figure this thing out, they're yours.' He held up a hand before I could object. 'You're Luke Glass not Nina, that makes you the number one target for an enemy. I believe your sister's safe. She'll turn up at the door, bloody raging at me for hunting all over London for her.' He smiled. 'Nobody will be happier when she does, and, whether she likes it or not, we'll have a team on her, too.'

For a while, we didn't speak. Then Ritchie said, 'How much did we lose?'

'Two hundred thou.'

'Of Jonas Small's money.' He pursed his lips. 'Couldn't make this stuff up, could you?'

'Make it up's exactly what we'll have to do. We'd collected the cash, which means it was our responsibility. Small will get his money. But it'll take a lot of talking to persuade the others thinking about putting their business our way.'

Ritchie said, 'Going back to this Mark Douglas character. Him showing up when he did prevented a bloodbath. You're short a head of security. Sounds to me like he'd be perfect – if he's bloody stupid enough to take the job.'

7

We came downstairs into the bar. The men in the corner had their orders and stood, ready to go wherever I was going. It was still early, yet all over the city guys like them would be in position, watching and waiting for an unknown enemy to show face, squeezing information from reluctant mouths. We'd had south London to ourselves for too long. Been kings of the castle. And it hadn't been good for us; we'd gone soft and paid the price. George Ritchie, as seasoned a pro as I'd ever met, had to be spitting nails. Ritchie saw me check out his guys and guessed what I was thinking. His hand touched my arm to stave off resistance. 'Don't fight me on this.'

He'd read it wrong – fighting him was the last thing I'd do. I'd seen the bodies in the van, riddled with bullets, hacked like butcher meat. If he hadn't made moves to keep me safe, he wouldn't be doing his job.

The same couldn't be said for our pet copper, Oliver Stanford. So far, he'd been as useful as a one-legged man in an arse-kicking competition. I hated surprises. He was supposed to make sure I didn't get any. The policeman had forgotten his place and was due a reminder.

I said, 'Let's get a couple of hours' sleep and meet again around lunchtime. Whoever's behind this might have shown their hand and we'll know what we're up against.'

I'd arrived at the King Pot in the middle of the night. Now, a dawn sky, pale and streaked with grey, broke over London. Orange tinged the horizon to the east: it was going to be a sunny day.

Glass Houses had put me in the way of a two-bedroom flat in a new development in Balham, the kind of place a thrusting executive like myself should lay his weary head. I liked it. Not as much as the old place, but well enough. What I found told me there wouldn't be much thrusting for a while: the wardrobe doors were open, clothes hangers were scattered on the bed, and the drawer of one bedside cabinet was on the floor. Kelly had left and taken her stuff with her.

Not entirely unexpected.

On the coffee table in the lounge, she'd gouged her anger into a yellow Post-it.

THIS ISN'T WORKING.
   K

Usually I was the one to call time on relationships though not always. Losing Kelly hardly registered. I didn't feel sorry. I didn't feel anything. In the kitchen I dropped the note in the bin under the sink and made coffee. Before it brewed, I changed my mind and lay back in the chair beside the fire. My eyes closed and I was asleep in seconds.

The mobile ringing brought me back into the land of the living. I grabbed it without checking the ID and got my character handed to me. When it came to anger, Kelly was a novice, a beginner barely scratching the surface.

My sister was the real McCoy.

* * *

From the balcony, Nina followed a dry-bulk cargo barge loaded
with sand as it passed on its way up river, waving to a man in grey
overalls and a flat cap standing in the prow, smiling when he waved
back. Her mood was high and no wonder. Drake's cheque was
clearing at the bank and he'd acquitted himself passably in bed.
She took a last look at Tower Bridge and the Tower of London
behind it. He'd got his money's worth – in more ways than one –
and would need the rest of the weekend to recover. The poor
darling was still sleeping. Let him. Egged on by her, he'd beaten his
personal best and almost killed himself in the process.

The male ego at work once again, imagining he could satisfy a
younger woman without bringing on a heart attack. Still – ten out
of ten for effort.

At one point, he'd made a sound in his throat like dolphins
talking to each other and she'd thought he wasn't going to survive.
But he had. On Monday, Algie would be boasting to his colleagues
about the foxy lady he'd tamed on Friday night. Nina expected to
hear from him again. But that wasn't happening. Before she left, she
laid an LBC platinum membership card on the bedside table. The
girls at the club could satisfy his demands in future; he'd had all he
was getting from her.

Her mobile rang while the guy on the barge still had his hand in
the air. Nina wasn't a fan of George Ritchie and resented the influ-
ence the Geordie had with Luke. Hearing from him was never good
news. She steadied herself. 'George. What can I do for you this
bright, beautiful morning?'

Ritchie didn't rise to it; he had more on his mind. 'Where the
hell are you?'

His tone set her on edge. 'Sorry. Didn't realise I needed your
approval to go out.'

'Where are you, Nina? It's important.'

She thought about not telling him. Something in his voice changed her mind.

'Butler's Wharf, if you must know.'

'What were you doing there?'

'None of your fucking business.'

'Okay. You're right. Stay where you are. A car will pick you up in twenty minutes.'

Nobody did awkward-little-girl better than Nina Glass. She said, 'No, thanks. I'm going into town.'

Ritchie wasn't listening – the fool didn't appreciate the danger she was in. By the time she did, it could be too late. 'Twenty minutes, Nina. If you're not happy, take it up with your brother.'

* * *

She didn't scream. Didn't shout. Her fury was beyond that. Instead, Nina quietly spat into the phone, articulating each word so her message couldn't be missed. 'Who do you think you are?'

'Nina – the club was hit.'

She raved on. 'No man tells me what I can or can't do, do you hear me? No man. George Ritchie has just given me an order. Put your flunky back in his box. Get him off my case. Or else.'

The line died in my hand. Immediately, it rang again and I roared. 'Hang up and I'll break your fucking neck!'

Oliver Stanford didn't hide his amusement. He chuckled. 'Wouldn't dream of it, especially when you put it like that.' He took a few seconds to enjoy the joke. 'Your sister's mobile switched on five minutes ago. She's at Butler's Wharf.'

For the third time in two minutes, my phone rang. Nina was calm. 'The club was hit? When?'

'After you left.'

Suspicion crept into her voice. 'And that's why Ritchie's ordering me around?'

I exploded. 'You stupid bitch. People died. Ritchie's doing his job, which is more than could be said for you.'

'A friend called me.'

The response was weak, self-serving – I'd expect it from a child.

'I don't want to hear about your "friend". There's a car on the way for you. Get in the back and keep your mouth shut. And when you see George Ritchie, you owe him an apology.'

* * *

Sunlight glinted on the abandoned tinfoil containers and stained cardboard lids littering the floor; the smell of curry filled the flat. In the centre of the room on a beat-up coffee table, a half-eaten onion bhaji shared a white plate an inch thick with scraps of cold paratha and the survivors of two unnecessary portions of pakora.

The previous night they'd downed Strongbow – nowhere near as good as the Old Rascal they drank back home – blown triumphant smoke rings in the air and talked about how overrated these London types were. It had been easy. Easier than any of them had dared hope.

Jazzer lay in bed watching dust motes float in the air. His head ached. Cider did that to him. Since the Holiday Inn in Lime Street, not a day had gone by when he hadn't thought about the woman. His obsession concerned him: females were warm-bodied distractions. Not this one. This one was different. This one he wanted.

At the sink he splashed water on his face and filled the battered electric kettle. Whoever was here before them had left a crumpled bag of sugar and a jar of Maxwell House in the cupboard, caked hard and months beyond its sell-by date. Vile, though better than nothing. He made himself a cup, sipped it and screwed up his face – the bloody Mersey tasted better.

Ronnie was at his elbow. 'I wouldn't have minded one.'

Jazzer set him straight. 'You think that but you'd be wrong. Help yourself.'

Tosh surfaced from under the sleeping bag on the floor, rubbing his eyes like a sleepy child.

'What time's this tart coming?'

Jazzer wanted to punch him; he didn't like Tosh calling her a tart. 'Don't worry. She'll be here.' He kicked the holdall of money and drugs. 'Got this to collect, hasn't she?'

In Lewisham, terrorising the punters had been fun. Now, his palms were clammy and he didn't feel well. He blamed the shitty coffee. The truth was, he was nervous. When the doorbell rang, Ronnie pressed the entry buzzer and they waited.

The top buttons of her white dress were undone; beneath, the bra was losing the struggle to contain the pale-cream swell of the breasts. Red hair fell to her shoulders, red lips – the lips Jazzer saw when he closed his eyes – parted when she smiled. Something amused her.

'Been having a party?'

'Just a few drinks to celebrate.'

'Is there a law against opening a window in this country? My Christ, it stinks in here.'

She was older than Jazzer remembered – strangely, that made her even more desirable. Her voice was strong and deep, almost masculine. 'Any problems?'

'No.'

The others hadn't seen her before. Jazzer watched their reaction – they couldn't take their eyes off her; it wasn't just him. When she lifted the bag, her dress tightened across her rear. Behind her back,

Ronnie made a crude gesture. Jazzer hated him for it but understood: she was messing with them because she could.

And Ronnie wasn't wrong: doing her would be a challenge, a battle he'd willingly lose.

She pushed their share of the money across the coffee table, giving them another eyeful of her ample tits, aware of the stir she was causing, playing to the audience.

The lounge of the Holiday Inn hadn't diminished her and Jazzer had imagined he was squiring a movie star from the forties or fifties, a full-bodied seductress he couldn't put a name to.

Every second sentence had a double meaning. Or, that was how it had seemed. In a blunt New York accent, she'd said, 'If it's too much for you, now's the time to tell me.'

Like that. She wanted it. The bitch wanted it.

'It isn't. I've been here before.'

'Yeah, you have, but not like this. Last time you got caught. That isn't an option.'

The reminder of his five years in Leeds, Armley Gaol, for robbing a sub-post office in Moss Lane had taken Jazzer by surprise. She'd done her research, all right.

'You can handle it, yes or no?'

There it was again.

'Yes.'

'Be sure. I don't do disappointed.'

And again.

'What should I call you?'

'Why do you need to call me anything?'

'I like to know who I'm working for.'

'You're not working for anybody yet.'

'Tell me your name.'

'It's Charley.'

In Liverpool, he'd considered moving on her there and then.

His instincts warned against it. There was a coldness that both attracted and repelled him so they'd discussed the plan in detail. At the end, she'd handed him an envelope of ten- and twenty-pound notes to get the ball rolling, and left. He'd stalked her with his eyes through the hotel's front door onto Lime Street, devouring the sensuous sway of her buttocks underneath the leather skirt.

Tosh and Ronnie had been inside, too, and knew prison ate away at your self-belief till you had nothing. Some cons never got it back, especially when they discovered the wife had another man to keep her warm at night – usually a boring bastard with a job. Cash on your hip reclaimed lost ground, helped you believe in who you were. Tosh and Ronnie were getting what they'd been promised. Jazzer was depressed. The money wasn't important.

He followed her downstairs to the pavement hoping to engineer a last chance for himself. It was about his needs not hers, releasing the pressure in his head and the heat in his groin.

His throat was dry. He stammered like a teenage virgin. 'Wh- who are you?'

She stared, as if the question offended her, and he said, 'How... will I contact you?'

The red lips he ached to kiss twisted in a sneer. 'Contact me? Why the hell would you contact me?'

'Because... I want to.'

She looked him up and down, her foreign accent sharp and flat at the same time on the London street.

'Back in your box, Sonny Boy.'

8

This is what I know: when George Ritchie was right, he was right. Arguing with him was a waste of breath because George wouldn't back down. Until we had a clearer understanding of what we were dealing with, it made sense to be cautious. Unfortunately, my sister railed against any attempt to rein her in and always had. Danny had tried, failed and eventually given up. Yeah! The great Danny Glass beaten by a girl with pigtails and freckles. Wise men said watch and learn. I had. Under the surface, Nina was the same difficult teenager she'd always been. Though, if her attitude didn't alter we'd be having a serious chinwag, her doing the listening for a change. An honest mistake was one thing – I'd made plenty of those in my time – being a reckless fool was something else. We were doing okay. Better than okay. Except, this was London, the city was rammed with people who'd love to take what we'd built away from us. Glass Houses was making money – I gave her credit for it. But it was just one revenue stream among many in the family business. LBC – however much she hated having to be there – was the new baby. Babies demanded attention and kept you up at night.

It was time Nina started pulling her weight.

I slipped my gun inside my jacket, drove to a greasy spoon in Balham that did the best fry-up south of the Thames and sat at a table near the window, keeping an eye out for my shadows. I didn't see them, which meant they were good. Nice to know.

The tea was always the same in this place: a hair away from undrinkable served in thick mugs it took both hands to lift. The sheer normality of florid-faced customers casting cholesterol concern to the winds and getting stuck into sausage, egg and chip breakfasts behind the toxic pages of the *Daily Mail* and *The Sun* relaxed me, and by the time I pointed the car in the direction of the King Pot, I felt better.

Ritchie looked like he'd been up all night; his tie was undone – his only concession to tiredness. George Ritchie had been a man when I was still a boy. Sometimes I'd joked about him advising his boss, Albert Anderson, to permanently discourage two lads by the name of Glass from stealing cigarettes from corner shops he was supposed to protect. Fortunately for me and Danny, Albert had ignored his advice, otherwise we would've ended up with sixty tons of cement on our arrogant young heads and spent the next hundred years in the foundations of a mega-storey monstrosity scarring the city skyline.

Ritchie said, 'All quiet on the Western Front,' and qualified it with a whispered, 'so far.'

And while I was stuffing Cumberland sausages and scrambled eggs down my throat, he'd been busy. Sheets of paper covered his desk: bullet points and lists, scribbled and scored out as new ideas occurred. Ritchie was a thinker as well as an enforcer – in my experience, a rare combination. He twirled a pencil between his fingers. 'We're barking up the wrong tree, Luke.'

'How so?'

He lifted the last sheet he'd been working on and read what he'd written.

'Because of how the timing went down, we assumed the attacks were related.'

'You don't think so?'

'Two of them definitely were – Lambeth and Lewisham. There's evidence to justify lumping them together.' He tapped the paper with the pencil. 'The timing, the weapons – shotguns – the accents.' Ritchie paused to gauge my reaction. 'This point is key – they didn't hurt anybody. In fact, they were almost friendly. And they knew you. "Tell Luke, Charlie was asking for him" remember?'

He realised his tie was loose and straightened it. 'Also. What did they steal? Not much. Some cash. A few drugs. Serious criminals would've approached the whole thing differently. For a start, they wouldn't be satisfied with what this crowd got away with.'

I didn't disagree with anything he'd said. He'd marshalled his thoughts and aligned the information. But none of it was new.

'What's your point, George?'

'I'm saying the first ones couldn't be further from the hit on the van and club if they tried. We're looking at separate incidents that, by coincidence, happened on the same night.'

'Which means two enemies.'

'Right.'

I wanted to laugh – could it get any worse?

'Is that better? I'm confused. Two hundred thousand versus spending money. A serious blag or a jolly for the boys.'

Ritchie added, 'Yeah, and a message behind both.'

I remembered Mark Douglas's description of the killer as he'd ended an innocent life. Career criminals – unless they were psychos – would be in and out. Cash would be their only motive. This crew had gone beyond that. London didn't need another gang war and, since I'd taken over from Danny, I'd established ties with every outfit in the city with a vested interest. Until now, those agreements had held.

'Looks very like it. The violence in the second hit was over the top. Hurt for its own sake.'

'You're saying brutality wasn't just a part of it, it *was* it. Killing the guys and driving to the club. Slitting the woman's throat... For what?'

The question remained unanswered because footsteps on the stairs interrupted us. Ritchie held up a hand, suddenly alert, the hours without sleep gone from his face. Instinctively, my fingers closed over the gun inside my jacket as he reached for the revolver in the drawer where he kept the whisky.

The door opened. My grip tightened. The barman stood in the frame.

Ritchie said, 'What do you want, Harry?'

'Somebody... to speak to you.'

'Not a good time. Tell them—'

She swept into the room like the Spanish Armada in a fitted white dress with black polka dots and a scarlet scarf tied like a turban round her hair. The red-painted nails matched her lipstick, and in her ridiculously high stilettos she was taller than both of us; stunningly sensual, like a Hollywood leading lady from before my time. I loosened my hold on the gun, searched my brain for the right word and found it: voluptuous. Five hundred years ago, Rubens would've draped her naked over a chaise, stuck a few winged cherubs in the background and immortalised her in oils.

I'd no idea who she was or what she was doing here, but I was about to find out.

She tossed a Nike holdall on the desk between us.

'No need to count it. It's all there, minus my expenses.'

At least one of the mysteries was resolved – we'd been thinking Charlie when we should've been thinking Charley.

Maybe because she was a woman, or maybe because paying to be robbed rubbed him the wrong way, but George lost it.

'Expenses? We're being charged for you robbing us? Who the fuck do you think you are?'

Charley tilted her head towards him and spoke in an American east-coast drawl out of the side of her mouth. 'Doesn't get it, does he?'

I pointed the gun at her. 'But it's a good question. Answer it before I blow your fucking head off.'

She brushed the threat aside with a manicured talon, parked her ample arse on the edge of the desk and pouted like a little girl who knew how cute she was and how much she could get away with because she'd done it before.

'That's no way to speak to your long-lost sister.'

PART II

9

It was as if the air had been sucked from the room. I searched her doll-face for a crinkle at the eyes, a twitch at the corner of her mouth; some hint she wasn't serious. The tension grew until she broke it, laughing like she'd just been told the best joke in the world. And I realised she wasn't kidding.

The last fourteen hours had been more difficult than any in the three years since I'd taken over. George Ritchie felt it, too. Anger stirred in me. I'd never hit a woman. Right now, I was prepared to make an exception.

She poked the holdall as though it were a dead animal. 'Open it.'

The zip peeled the canvas apart. Inside were plastic bags of pills and smoke and 'H' from River Cars in Lambeth beside wads of money, counted and tied, ready to be deposited in the night safe of Lloyd's on Lewisham High Street.

I lifted a bundle of twenty-pound notes, turned it in my fingers, and let it fall back into the pile. George Ritchie was right about the hit on the club not being connected to the other two. This woman was bold and brash and in your face. She'd gone out of her way to get noticed, but I didn't see her sanctioning the atrocity in the lane behind LBC.

'Where's the rest?'

Her answer was unapologetic. 'Like I said, I had expenses.' She shrugged the deficit away. 'You know how it is.'

Beside me, Ritchie was incandescent, incensed by her casual dismissal. 'You had... you paid the people who robbed us with our own money?'

She smiled. 'Thought you'd appreciate it. Except, you've missed the best bit.'

An alabaster digit pointed to the holdall and the paper, creased and old. I'd never seen a New York birth certificate before; the important part was the last two lines from the bottom.

MOTHER'S NAME: Frances Glass
FATHER'S NAME: Daniel John Glass

My parents.

Ritchie leaned over, took it from me and scrutinised it. Too quickly, he said, 'She's at it. This is a forgery.'

The woman didn't react. Her expression stayed exactly as it had been. 'I'm not and it isn't.'

The pantomime had gone on long enough. I said, 'Supposing this fairy story is true, did you really imagine making fools of us was the best way to introduce yourself?'

'Got your attention, didn't I?'

'Only until we kick you into the street.'

'Really? You should be thanking me.'

'Thanking you? For what?'

'You're vulnerable. I showed just how vulnerable.'

'No, no, you didn't. What you did was reckless. Worse, it was stupid. Nobody in their right mind would do what you did. Now, we'll track your guys down and won't stop until we find them. And when we do, we'll break their legs.'

She didn't respond. Her eyes stayed locked on mine and I saw Danny staring back at me.

'Exactly what did you think these amateur dramatics were going to get you? What the hell are you after?'

The red lips opened. Behind them, the tip of her tongue darted over white teeth.

'I've been on the outside my whole life. Now, I want in.'

Of course, she did. Her and half the villains in London.

'Whether you like it or not, I'm part of this family. I didn't go away. Someone took me away. Now, I'm back – not looking for a handout, not asking for something for nothing. I'm prepared to work. But I want my share.'

Ritchie had heard enough. 'Why're we wasting our time? She's not worth it.'

She took a folded note from inside her bra, laid it on the desk and smoothed it out with the exaggeration that, even in our brief acquaintance, I'd come to expect.

'George can do all the checking he wants. It won't change the facts. Contact me when you're ready to talk seriously, Luke.' She winked. 'But don't leave it too long, eh, brother.'

The call that had convinced Kelly she was always going to come second, or third, or even fourth or fifth, seemed a long time ago. The saddest thing, sadder even than losing her, was that she was right – the business took everything I had and then some. Bringing George Ritchie in had been one of my better ideas and for thirty-eight months we'd run like the proverbial Swiss watch. Danny would've described it as 'money for old rope'. London had become the most peaceful crime-infested city in the world. Overnight, that had stopped being true.

Ritchie and Nina didn't get along and were always locking horns. Knowing how difficult she could be, I'd naturally assumed she was to blame. Now, I realised it was more complicated. Another side to George Ritchie had been revealed, a side I hadn't known existed until now. George was a bad loser.

As we watched the woman leave, he was clearly unhappy. 'I can't believe you're letting her go.'

'What would you like me to do?'

'Make an example of her.'

'And how exactly would I do that?'

He didn't answer and I said, 'She made fools out of us, George. Spotted we were weak and took advantage. If it hadn't been her, it would've been someone else.'

Ritchie disagreed. 'Deal with her the same way we'd deal with any chancer who tried it on. Otherwise, we're putting out the wrong message.'

'No. The wrong message is that you can turn Luke Glass over and get away with it. That isn't what's happening here.'

Ritchie broke eye contact. He wasn't convinced – he was going to have to live with it. Lambeth and Lewisham had been done to make a point and, though George didn't like it, the woman had exposed us and she was right. We were vulnerable.

One mystery solved. If only the club were as easy.

* * *

George Ritchie was against her. That was only to be expected. Nobody appreciated being made to look foolish, least of all one of the most feared gangsters in the city. He'd make a dangerous enemy but she'd tackle that problem when she had to. It was Luke she'd had to impress – he'd need time to process the bombshell she'd dropped on him. Meanwhile, Ritchie could dig as deep as he liked; the birth certificate was genuine. She was Charlene Glass, the child her mother was carrying when she'd left her father. Danny, Luke and Nina were her family. Together at last.

That called for a celebration. Charley lifted her phone and dialled the number.

* * *

Jazzer pushed through the crowd, elbowing people, spilling their drinks. Any who objected got a mouthful and were pushed aside. He was in a foul mood and doing his best to hide it from his friends. The humiliating rejection in Earls Court Road had left him down and he was taking it out on whoever got in his way. At the bar, he raised his hand in the air, snapping his fingers, daring the staff to ignore him. They caught the hard set of his mouth, the meanness in his eyes, and took his order.

'Three lagers.'

'Three lagers coming up.'

Jazzer said, 'How much?'

The barman told him.

'Should be wearing a mask, mate. Fucking daylight robbery.'

'Take it up with the management. I only work here.'

The Liverpool boys had asked a taxi driver to take them some-where good and been dropped outside the Princess Louise on High Holborn, a wood-panelled Victorian homage of tiles, mirrors, mosaic floors and elaborate ceilings, on a sunny Saturday, rammed to the rafters. Tourists and city types overflowed out onto the pave-ment. Ronnie and Tosh were in great form. They loved it, laughing and joking, their spirits lifted by the knowledge they were going home with money in their pockets. When Jazzer came back with the pints, he said little; they didn't notice. His brain was on fire, still thinking about the woman, wanting to slap her face, kiss the red off her lips, make her naked. Anything to regain his lost masculinity.

The buzz from the crowd was so loud and constant, he almost missed the call. She was the last person he expected to hear from. Jazzer turned from his friends and waited for her to speak. Her voice sounded far away. He pressed his ear to the mobile, his heart beating in his chest.

'Where are you?'

'I'm not sure. In some pub. Why?'

'Meet me at the flat.'

Jazzer was too stunned to reply.

'That's what you want, isn't it?'

'When?'

'I'm already here.'

* * *

Decades with Albert Anderson and then his idiot son, Rollie, had been enough insanity to do George Ritchie for ten lifetimes. Luke was smarter than his brother, less reactive, able to look into tomorrow, gauge the consequences of actions taken in the heat of today and choose a wiser course than most. Ritchie liked his boss, respected him even. Nobody else would've talked him out of retiring. But this time, he was wrong.

They should be sending out a message. A serious message. The attacks on his side of the river would be discussed in every bar and street corner from Balham to the Isle of Dogs. No one would be surprised by what happened next and the lesson had to be hard enough to deter any other wide boys with similar ideas, lurking in the shadows, waiting their chance.

Violence as a deterrent – not a way of life. Bones broken in a good cause so lessons could be learned and the status quo maintained.

Despite what his boss thought, this interloper, with her hips and her lips, a Nike bag of money and drugs and a claim so outrageous it just might be true, meant he was sure the lady was trouble. Ritchie would check her claims, though he didn't doubt she was telling the truth. She was a Glass – it screamed out of her. The world already had two – Luke and Nina – more than enough. In Danny's time, there had been three: nobody could forget how that had worked out.

Charley had tossed pebbles into the pond, his pond; he'd deal with the ripples in his own way. That only left what was going on up West. A hit on LBC was always inevitable. Flying high made them a target; somebody had them in their crosshairs.

* * *

Jazzer climbed the stairs to the flat in Earls Court Road, more nervous than he'd ever been in his life. His legs were close to buckling, his heart pounded in his chest, and his palms were damp with sweat. This was his fantasy, the thing he'd dreamed about every day since meeting her in Liverpool, yet he almost wished it weren't happening. Excitement was destroying him. When he'd told his friends about the call, he'd acted as if it were no more than he'd expected and basked in their envy and admiration, draining his pint and casually wiping his mouth on his sleeve.

'So, the lady wants me.'

Ronnie had pressed for details. 'Christ Almighty. Did she actually say that?'

'Her very words.'

Tosh said, 'Then you're a lucky bastard.'

He'd smirked. 'Luck had nothing to do with it, Tosh. But I'm not sure.'

'Not sure about what?'

'This is a pretty nice boozer. I'm happy to kill time until the train with you guys.'

Ronnie said, 'You can't be serious. She's sensational.'

Jazzer drew nicotine-stained fingers through the stubble on his chin, keeping the pretence going. 'It's been a good trip. We did what we came to do. I'm enjoying myself where I am.'

Tosh elbowed him. 'Then, you stay and I'll go. Don't bother sending out a search party if I don't come back. Seriously, Jazzer, pass on this and you're off your head.'

'You think I should go?'

'Absolutely. And give her one for me while you're at it.'

The door was ajar. He pushed it the rest of the way, expecting to see her in the centre of the room, waiting for him. She wasn't. She was on the bed, covered from the waist down by a crumpled sheet, her long hair arranged over her breasts, hiding them. The tinfoil containers and cider bottles were where they'd been. Jazzer didn't notice. She tossed her head back, and slowly drew the bedclothes away.

10

The good weather had brought the crowds out and Regent Street was even busier than usual. I was angry and irritable; the shock of somebody claiming to be a long-lost sister did nothing for my mood. Stop-start traffic was the final straw. An opportunity to take how I was feeling out on a dark-green Vauxhall Astra dawdling in the middle of the road was too good to miss – I blasted the horn, flashed the lights and waved my arms until he got the message and moved over. As I passed, he stuck two fingers in the air. My reaction told me all I needed about my emotional state: I wanted to grab the bastard by his stupid hair, drag him into the street and beat the living shit out of him. Luckily for me, at Swiss Cottage, he faded from my rear-view and the chance to land up on a road-rage charge disappeared.

I put my shades on and forced myself to relax: it was what it was.

Ritchie would confirm if this Charley-woman's birth certificate was genuine. Whether we were related remained to be seen although, even from the few minutes in the office, I'd recognised an unfortunate family resemblance: what she'd done was bold and arrogant, over the top and excessive.

Who did that remind me of?

I had no memory of my mother, and whenever I'd ask Danny about her he'd get mad, give me a slap and tell me to shut it. Eventually, I stopped asking. But the questions hadn't gone away. Had he known she was pregnant when she left? Was Danny angry because she'd chosen her unborn child over us? Had she run from more than a stupefied husband? And, most burning of all, why hadn't she taken the three of us?

North London wasn't my turf – I rarely came here – with the hot sun bleaching the pavements it could've been a pleasure. Except, there was too much to think about to allow it in.

Stanford seemed to have forgotten there were more important matters to be addressed – like talking to people who'd be within their rights to doubt my promise their money would be looked after.

Beginning with Jonas Small.

Then there was Ritchie. He wanted rid of Charley, that was clear. Sending her back to wherever she'd come from would've been easy. Something had stopped me: was it because if she was blood there was a chance she'd have answers to the questions I'd been asking myself since I was old enough to understand my mother had abandoned me? Or could it be I'd immediately recognised she was exactly what we needed to run the less-publicised membership benefits of LBC?

Nina hated the club; anything that meant she didn't have to be there should be good news. Nina discovering her replacement was her sister wouldn't go down well and I didn't have to be clairvoyant to predict Class A dramatics in my future.

* * *

Superintendent Stanford hadn't stuck a pin in the map and ended up pitching his tent in this leafy part of the city by accident. The Oliver Stanfords of the world didn't do anything by chance. Hendon – seven miles from Charing Cross – was London without the hassle. He'd get more for his money or, to be more accurate, more for my money.

In the past he'd been valuable to us, invaluable at times, but a mole had infiltrated his team. Danny had taken care of it the way Danny took care of everything, though the lesson had been clear – no paper trail, no communication except on burner phones. And on the rare occasion I met Stanford it was face to face at the derelict factory in Fulton Street, well away from prying eyes.

My brother's relationship with him had been fractious. The policeman had been made to suffer a deluge of insults and small humiliations calculated to remind him Danny had his foot on his neck. I'd made a decision not to go that road. We didn't have to like each other, in fact I detested the smug bastard, but if the association was to flourish it needed, at least, to be civil. Bludgeoning him with insults was unnecessary and, ultimately, self-defeating. He was on the payroll because he could be useful; the day that was no longer true, he'd be gone. Last night he hadn't been – his jacket was on a shaky nail.

The whitewashed mock-Tudor building set back from the road was impressive. So were the cars parked in the drive – five of them, carefully squeezed together so as not to scratch the expensive body-work. Stanford's blue metallic Audi A6 was one of them.

I'd heard that when the Stanfords gave dinner parties, their guest lists were a who's who of lawyers, senior Met officers and the odd High Court judge. Elise's cooking talents weren't required. Her husband hired an up-market catering company to do the food so she could concentrate on how she looked. By all accounts they were jolly affairs, the wine bill alone a couple of months' honest toil for most people. I'd never been invited to his shindigs and tried not to take offence.

I followed the sound of voices and barking dogs, along a flag-stone path, through a wrought-iron gate in a brick wall to the rear of the property, and stood for a moment in the shadows observing the scene. Oliver Stanford had a reputation for being tough with the men under his command, especially the younger ones. If they'd been standing where I was, they'd see a tall guy in a sky-blue T-shirt and white shorts, turning sausages on a barbeque, a pair of metal tongs in one hand glinting in the light, a glass of white wine in the other. And they'd never feel intimidated again.

His wife left the couples milling on the quarter acre of mani-cured lawn and came over to him. Elise Stanford was wearing a lemon print dress and sunshades, her slim legs still tanned from their holiday in St Kitts, Antigua, or wherever – somewhere beyond anything his salary from the Met ran to.

She touched her husband's shoulder in a small moment of inti-macy, threaded her arm through his and gazed up at him.

It was impossible not to envy them. They had it all, hadn't they? Beautiful people living in a bubble, removed from the trials and tribulations that beset most of the planet. And on top of that, they were obviously in love. I studied my shoes, giving them a little longer before I broke in uninvited and spoiled it. Three of my places had been robbed and, though I didn't expect Stanford to stop it happening, he hadn't bothered to contact me.

Not our deal. Clearly, he needed a reminder.

Elise returned to the guests, doing the rounds with a bottle, topping up drinks that had barely been touched, while two grey-and-black Scottie dogs with tartan collars ran beside her, looking up with their old-man's faces. I liked dogs: they were loyal; you could depend on them. More than could be said for their master.

Stanford wiped sweat from his brow on the top of his sleeve, lost for a second in a haze of charcoal smoke – just an ordinary bloke having friends round on a Saturday for a few beers, the odd over-cooked pork chop and warm potato salad: a modern English tradition.

When I stepped into the light, his expression hardened. His wife called to him; he ignored her and came towards me, smiling as if I were an acquaintance who'd decided to visit at an inconvenient time and had to be shepherded away from the party before I got ideas about staying.

Through clenched teeth he hissed his displeasure. 'What the fuck are you doing here?'

His arm snaked round my shoulder, forcing me to walk through the gate to the front. Resolutions about civility went out the window. My fingers closed round his sun-burned hand and bent it back, watching the corner of his mouth curl as the pain arrived. Behind full lips his teeth were perfectly straight. I said, 'Touch me again and I'll lay you out.'

Stanford stood his ground. 'Don't threaten me, Glass. This is my home.'

The anger was real. For a moment, I thought he was going to punch me, a mistake guaranteed to put our fragile relationship on a different footing. He said, 'I can think of half a dozen reasons why you shouldn't be here.'

I could think of more than that.

'Why are you?'

'If you need to ask, you're not doing your job, Superintendent.'

'What's happened?'

'You really don't know, do you?'

His irritation with me spilled over. 'Fucking tell me and be on your way. I have people waiting.'

Stanford might have added, 'This is a respectable neighbourhood.' Wisely, he didn't.

'You know, Oliver, there was a time you would've known what was going on before I did. I miss those days. Could rely on you then. You've taken your eye off the ball. Too busy dipping your snout in the trough with the rest of the pigs and living it large. It doesn't feel like I'm getting value for money any more and that makes me unhappy.'

'What the hell's happened? Spit it out!'

'Three of my places got hit last night and I have to tell you about it?'

'Three? You said it was the club. I heard about the bookies. What else happened?'

Anger leapt in my chest. I had to stop myself punching his well-fed face. Seconds passed while I fought the urge to choke the fucker. I'd been wrong to treat him like a human being; it didn't work. With scum like him, fear was the key. However deeply he'd resented the barbs and slurs and slights from Danny, he'd taken them because he'd been scared of him.

He wasn't scared of me. But he soon would be.

When I had myself under control I said, 'And two's okay, is it? Two's all right? No need to contact me, see what I might need, if it's only two?'

'That's not what I meant.'

'Really? What did you mean?'

His shoulders fell, exasperated with my reasonable expectations. 'The report I got this morning said we responded to the bookies in Lewisham. Shots were fired. Nobody was hurt. There was no mention of anything else. You're telling me there were three attacks. First I've heard of it.'

'And why would that be? Go on, take a stab in the dark.'

Sweat that had nothing to do with the barbeque filmed his forehead. Behind the blue eyes, he was torn between answering my question and telling me to get the fuck off his property, a dilemma better left unresolved. From the garden, his wife called to him, genteel irritation in her well-modulated voice, impatience disguised for the benefit of the guests.

'Oliver! Oliver! Where are you, darling?'

I guessed the sausages were burning and that would never do.

Stanford heard her and concentrated on me instead. Good decision.

'Where else?'

'River Cars in Lambeth at exactly the same time as Lewisham.'

'Anybody hurt?'

Like he cared.

'We didn't involve the police in case they sent an honest copper by mistake. Three hits and you know sod-all about them.'

Stanford didn't speak, obviously affected by what I'd told him. Eventually, he said, 'There wasn't a word on the streets. Not a word. Otherwise, you would've known it was coming. Which means they're tourists.'

'Yeah, the first ones are. Shotguns with Liverpool accents. A different story at LBC. Entirely different. Did you get anything on the picture I sent?'

'Still waiting. I'll call as soon as I have something.'

I didn't believe him.

Oliver Stanford was a lot of things, stupid wasn't one of them. He'd correctly gauged where he stood with me and was trying to mend his fences. 'What about cameras? Did they give you anything?'

'That's been covered, there was nothing.' I ignored his sudden rush of interest. 'Okay – here's an easy one to get you started. An ex-Glasgow copper called Mark Douglas. I want everything you can dig up on him. Everything.'

'I'll get straight on it as soon as my guests leave.'

I started to walk away; he was beginning to make me sick. Over my shoulder I shouted, 'Too little too late, Ollie!'

* * *

I drove down Hendon Way, past Brent Cross, and on until traffic lights brought me to a halt, furious with myself, gripping the steering wheel so hard my hands hurt. Stanford was an easy target but he wasn't to blame. The arrangement with him was a carry-over from my brother – his 'tame copper', he'd called him. I'd left it in place because it had suited me. But it was beginning to look like it had run its course. Whatever happened from here on in, Superintendent Stanford would have to give more than he'd become used to giving if he wanted to be in the plan. It wasn't just George Ritchie who'd lost his edge, Oliver Stanford had, too. With no one in our way, it had all got too easy. Until last night when it wasn't. The policeman's true feelings had been on show in his attitude. Arrogant. Unapologetic. Unaccountable. Climbing fast and high had warped his perspective. He'd started believing his own publicity. Whether he knew it or not, he'd gone rogue.

Near the North Star pub, I pulled in to the side of the road. The sun was warm, the sky still blue. About now, Elise Stanford would be passing out cutlery for the dessert. Probably strawberries and cream. What could be more English? Perfect with a bottle of bubbles, and a great way to end a wonderful day. I hoped they enjoyed it, because their reign as lord and lady of the manor was coming to an end.

The trip to north London had clarified things that would've been self-evident if I hadn't had so many bloody oranges in the air. Elise's husband was out of order and needed a slap and I had just the man to see he got one.

At the other end of the line George Ritchie was subdued even by his taciturn standards. Like most people who were good at what they did, he was his own biggest critic and I pictured him at his desk above the King Pot, mulling over what could've been done to avoid the attacks, giving himself a hard time in the process.

He greeted me without enthusiasm. 'Luke, how did it go?'

'It didn't. Danny had the right idea about Stanford. Under the cosh is all he understands. He's enjoying himself so much he's forgotten where his nice life comes from. And how easily it can end. Thought it was okay to have the local cops handle last night without contacting me, would you believe? Refresh his memory, will you, George?'

'It would be a pleasure.'

'Leave the wife and kids out of it.'

'If you say so.'

'And the dogs. They haven't done anything.'

Ritchie sounded disappointed; I was cramping his style. 'Not giving me much to play with, are you? How hard a slap does he get?'

'Enough for him to reassess his priorities and remember what a lucky boy he is.'

'A silly boy.'

'He's living the dream, George. Wake him up before it turns into a nightmare for the rest of us.'

* * *

The Princess Louise was less busy than it had been and Ronnie and Tosh had snagged a booth to themselves. As he walked towards them, they applauded, welcoming him like a hero returning from the war. Jazzer held up his hands to quiet them down and went into the act he'd worked on in the taxi from Earls Court. He dropped into the seat, smiling, although he didn't feel like it.

'Thanks, lads, thanks. But first things first, eh? I need a drink.'

He waited until the pint was in front of him before giving them
what they wanted.

Ronnie said, 'C'mon. Spill.'

Jazzer pretended he didn't understand. 'Don't know what you're
on about.'

'Sure, you do. What was she like?'

He held the glass with both hands so Ronnie and Tosh wouldn't
see he was shaking, took a long drink from his lager and licked his
lips. His friends would believe he'd given the woman a good seeing-
to because they wanted it to be true. But it wasn't true.

She'd owned him from the first touch to the last. Mounting and
remounting him, crushing him between the creamy thighs he'd
fantasised about parting, until he'd thought his heart would
explode. When he'd begged her to stop, she'd laughed and kept
going, drowning him in her flesh, using him for her own pleasure.
The headboard had banged against the faded wallpaper like an
untethered shutter in a storm; he couldn't breathe and prayed for it
to end. In the midst of panic the words, spoken with contempt,
came to him.

back in your box, Sonny Boy

11

People were expecting to hear from me; it would be unwise to disappoint them. Tomorrow would be time enough to deal with the others. Today, my priority was Jonas Small.

When I called, he answered right away, his voice like gravel. Of course, he knew already what had happened and agreed to meet me later in Brick Lane at a Bangladeshi restaurant he owned called Chittagong. His parting shot had been, 'Don't worry about it, Lukie boy. We'll have a curry and a powwow. I like a good curry.'

It wasn't difficult for him to be relaxed. It was his cash, but it was my loss. Replacing what had been stolen was down to me. He wasn't going to be out of pocket and we both knew it.

* * *

Jonas Thomas Small had never been young – one look at his wizened face, partly hidden by a beard, proved the adage about the impossibility of putting an old head on young shoulders wasn't true. He had the wrinkled leathery skin of a man whose working life had been spent out in the open. Loose skin sat in folds over the collar of his shirt and when he grinned – which he did a lot – a gold filling glinted in the light. Small's exact age, as with so much about him, was unknown, though his reputation for being loyal to his friends and ruthless with anyone who crossed him wasn't disputed.

He was sitting at a table at the back and didn't get up or shake hands – an indication of how the conversation was going to go. Now we were face to face, 'Don't worry about it...' wasn't where we were. He was wearing a grey three-piece suit with a large yellow check running through it and looked like a music-hall comedian, the kind who told the same bawdy jokes every night and laughed at them himself. The chain of a fob watch disappeared into the waistcoat; he ran his finger along it and spoke out of the side of his mouth, as if he were letting me in on a secret.

'My father gave me this watch. The only fucking thing he gave me.' He coughed into his hand. 'Had a meet one time with your brother. At this very table, as a matter of fact. Wasn't everybody's cup of tea, a right handful, but I liked old Danny.'

'He respected you.'

The first of many untrue statements I expected to make before the night was over.

Small took the compliment in his stride, finding no reason to disbelieve me.

'Always wondered what happened to him.'

Said with wistful curiosity.

For a while after my brother disappeared, I'd been asked the same question every other day. My answer had never altered and didn't now. 'No mystery. He got out while he could, Jonas, same as anybody with any sense.'

Small shrugged like the suspicion had come from me instead of him. 'The business we're in... we make enemies. Worth a thought.'

No, it wasn't. This guy was the undisputed governor of the East End and had been for almost three decades. Long before my brother plundered Albert Anderson's territory like a ninth-century Viking on acid, he'd marked out his manor and given everything west of Aldgate Pump a wide berth. The metal head on the pump symbolised the last wolf shot in the City of London. To my knowledge, Small hadn't shot any animals, but he'd brought the lives of more than a few people to a premature end. Becoming his enemy wasn't what I had in mind.

He sipped the lager he was holding, stabbed a finger at its frosted neighbour on the table in front of me and explained his philosophy. 'Nothing goes with an Indian like lager. Tried beer. And wine. No use. Took the liberty of ordering, hope you don't mind, Lukie boy.'

He sat back in his chair and surveyed the room. 'Been coming here every Saturday night for years. Haven't had a dodgy curry yet. Why I bought the place.'

I nodded as if never having been poisoned was all the recommendation any reasonable person could ask. Now wasn't the moment to tell him Indian wasn't the same as Bangladeshi; he wouldn't have appreciated it. The clue was subtle: Chittagong.

He smoothed the red-and-white-checked tablecloth lovingly. 'Sometimes I just sit after the staff have gone home and breathe in the smells. You're not vegetarian or anything weird, are you? No allergies? Nuts or nothin'? 'Cause what's coming up wouldn't do.'

I assured him I was okay and he pointed to the two men standing inside the door.

'Old George Ritchie's idea, I'm guessing. Look like a couple of his. Want us to feed them, as well?'

'No, they're fine.'

Waiters carrying metal trays piled with plates glided between noisy diners like ballet dancers at Covent Garden, while the scent of green cardamom, toasted cumin seeds and crushed fenugreek painted aromatic pictures of faraway places with strange-sounding names on the flock wallpaper.

Nina had gone crazy when I told her we were getting involved with Small. 'Are you out of your skull? We shouldn't go near that guy. He's as unpredictable as a scorpion.'

He snapped a poppadom between his fingers and returned to my brother. 'Queer though, wasn't it? How he just upped and left like that.'

'Maybe he got bored with the enemies you mentioned and he's sunning himself somewhere, knee-deep in bronzed women with big tits.'

He turned his sharp eyes on me. 'Ever get a postcard?'

'Danny's not a keep-in-touch kind of guy.'

'See, if it was me, I'd want every bugger to know.' Small drew his vision in the air with a crisp shard. 'Copacabana on the front – beach, blue skies, all that. And "Wish you were here" smudged with suntan oil scrawled on the back. Yeah. That would do it.' He paused. 'Did he tell you he was for the off?'

I'd lost two hundred thousand pounds of his money; the advantage was with him. This was the only chance he'd get to quiz me and he was taking it. His questions were anything but innocent.

'I mean, did he actually say to you he'd had it, or even hint about wanting out?'

I measured my reply. 'We weren't as close as we'd been. We weren't communicating much. One day he was there, the next he wasn't.'

Jonas pushed his luck. 'What's your theory? Think something occurred, do you?'

He'd had it his own way long enough. Time to push back. 'Something occurred, all right. He fucked off and left me to deal with the lot of it.'

My phoney anger only half convinced him. 'Big shoes. Couldn't have been easy stepping into them.'

'Didn't have a choice, did I?'

'Mmmm. Still, it's an ill wind, eh? You've done well. Your name keeps coming up. Luke Glass this, Luke Glass that. Said to my wife, "Is he taking over the fucking world, or what?"'. He smiled his crooked smile. 'Lily said, "How can he, Jonas, when you own half of it?"'. He shook his head. 'Thirty-five years and that girl still makes me laugh.'

'The secret to a happy marriage.'

Small was reminding me how powerful he was, warning me not to mess him about. I hadn't a clue if he'd ever met my brother. The Danny chat was him letting me know he didn't trust me. The feeling was mutual and I remembered George Ritchie's assessment after I'd spoken to Jonas for the first time, before we'd got into bed with him.

'He's a slippery bastard. Keep an eye on him.'

'I intend to.'

'I'm serious, Luke. If there's money to be made – fine. Don't let him near anything else. Jonas is a snake.'

'Nobody's perfect, George.'

'Did he mention his wife?'

'How do you know that?'

'Because he always does. It's one of his... quirks.'

'Since when did talking about your wife become a quirk?'

Ritchie smiled and looked away.

* * *

There was enough grub to feed the Russian army. Small loosened his tie and lifted his cutlery, poised to begin. 'Smell that. Great, isn't it? Some men go down the boozer on a Saturday night, other guys have sex with their wife or, if their luck's in, somebody else's wife. Me, I like a curry. My Lily's a great cook, nothing fancy mind, don't get me wrong, but she can't do spices. Never could. They go for her stomach, so I come here.'

He drew the watch from his waistcoat and weighed it in his hand, heavy, tarnished with age, then opened it and held it for me to see. A girl still in her teens smiled at me. The picture wasn't recent, faded and worn at the edges. Jonas Small spoke with pride. 'That's her, that's my Lily.'

'You're a lucky man.'

He was already digging in and didn't comment.

For the next twenty-five minutes, he devoured everything in front of him, eyes darting from one dish to another, forking chicken and lamb, okra and onions and mixing them together. When he was done, he pushed his plate away, opened the bottom two buttons of the waistcoat and mopped his brow with the biggest hanky I'd ever seen.

'Overdone it, as usual, haven't I? Never learn. Pay for it in the morning, but what the hell? There's always a downside. Can you live with it? That's the question.' He leaned towards me. 'Now, speaking of living with things, what's happened to my cash?'

It had taken a while but we were finally there.

Small was sly and straightforward at the same time.

I said, 'Your cash is fine. You lost nothing last night.'

My reply pleased him. 'Appreciated. Saves us getting into a scrap about it. Nobody wants that. But I like to stay ahead of the game and it raises the issue of security, doesn't it?'

'I had three armed men in the van and backup at the club.'

'Except it wasn't enough. Also, the word's out all over the city. Questions will be asked. Unavoidable in the circumstances. Like: is Luke Glass up to it? Can he be depended on to deliver?'

I felt my hackles rise. 'I said your money's safe.'

He focused on something over my shoulder. 'Yeah, this time. What if it goes off again? Cover that as well, will you?'

I laughed a brittle laugh. Small had annoyed me. 'There won't be a next time. Anybody keen to have another pop better be prepared for a fucking war, because I'll come after them.'

'Who's "them"?'

'Don't know yet... but I'm working on finding that out.'

We stared at each other across the table. Small's lip curled and I got a glimpse of his gold filling; it matched his timepiece. He spread his hands, palms up, and tutted. 'Lily will be disappointed when I tell her. The money doesn't bother me. I'm not worried about the money. I know you'll make it good. In fact, if it's tight for you right now, we'll leave it till it's more convenient. Can't say fairer.' He picked a forgotten scrap of onion bhaji off a side plate and put it in his mouth. 'But that kind of cash... will always be a target. I was thinking along the lines of a partnership. Me and you. There isn't a firm in London who'd dare go up against us. It was Lily's idea. Makes sense, doesn't it?'

To him, maybe, not to me.

'Sorry, Jonas. You understand what happens if I open that door. The rest would want in. Kenny and Colin Bishop up in Chalk Farm, Bridie O'Shea out west. Besides, I already have a partner.'

'Your sister.'

'Right. My sister. Nina wants everything kept in the family. She wouldn't go for it in a million years, no matter how much sense it made.'

'And she couldn't be persuaded?'

'She's a woman, Jonas. You know what they're like.'

He nodded as if some great truth had passed between us.

'Indeed, I do, son. Indeed, I do.'

* * *

Off the top of my head I could think of three dozen things I'd rather do than spend Saturday night with Jonas Small, starting with sticking hot needles in my eyes. 'Slippery bastard' was bang on, though he'd been right about the curry. Very tasty. And, as it happened, Small was surprisingly relaxed about his 200 K, generously offering to defer repayment until it was convenient. But his enquiries about Danny's abrupt departure, casually dropped into the conversation, told me he'd been ferreting away in the background since our first meeting to get to the bottom of my brother's disappearing act. Clearly, he'd been unsuccessful. If he had proof, he'd have laid it on the table, flashed his gold-toothed grin, then blackmailed me. Becoming partners in the club wouldn't have stayed a suggestion; he'd have me where he wanted me and my plans for LBC would be in the bin. Also, as I'd explained to him, Kenny and Colin Bishop and Bridie O'Shea would feel understandably slighted.

My life lacked many things, more enemies wasn't one of them.

* * *

George Ritchie was never off duty but noise in the background threatened to make talking impossible. It stopped and I said, 'Where are you?'

'Outside a pub. Can hear bugger-all in there. Everything okay?'

'Not exactly how I'd put it.'

'How did you get on with Small?'

'He's all you said and more.'

I imagined him nodding grimly. 'Oh, yeah? What's he up to now?'

'He's suggested we go into business together.'

George's opposition hissed down the line. 'Bad idea, Luke. I mean, a really, really bad idea. The guy's a fucking nutter.'

'Don't worry. It's a non-starter. He doesn't buy Danny just packed it in. Got close to coming right out and saying it. I had the impression he thinks it was him who hit us.'

'He's reaching. Sniffing around for something to give him an edge.'

'I agree. Yet he was cool about the money.'

Ritchie laughed cynically. 'Because he knows it's as good as in the bank. When the dust settles, that bastard will have lost nothing.'

George was right. I changed the subject. 'Anything at your end?'

I meant on the redhead claiming to be my sister.

'Not yet.'

'For Christ's sake don't mention her to Nina.'

'That's your job. The perks of being a brother.'

'Believe me, there aren't any. I'm expecting to hear from Mark Douglas. How's he checking out?'

'So far, okay. He left the Law School at Strathclyde with a degree and went straight into the force. Sometimes that means an educated dick the regular coppers hate and make jokes about behind their back. Not this guy. Word is, he was going places. Already had a couple of scalps to his name. Ever heard of Tommy Walsh?'

'Should I? Who is he?'

Ritchie corrected me. 'Who was he, you mean. Only the fourth biggest drug dealer in the West of Scotland. Died of a brain haemorrhage in Shotts prison. Douglas put him away.'

'Impressive. So, what happened to his glittering career?'

'It went off the rails when he did.'

'How?'

'Got caught with his hand in the till. Didn't go quietly, either. Smacked a DCI on his way out the door. Not a good look for the boys in blue north of the border, so he wasn't charged – the whole thing was swept under the carpet. Douglas washed up in London nine months ago, started working with a security firm in Barnet and moved on to the celebrity stuff. He's impressed some famous faces; a couple offered to relocate him to Los Angeles and go full-time with them.'

'And?'

'He turned them down.'

'Why?'

'Word is he's happy where he is.'

'What about family?'

'Parents both dead. Killed in a car accident when he was sixteen. Got an older sister in Cape Town he hasn't seen since the funeral. No love interest, far as I can tell.'

Ritchie had unearthed a helluva lot in a short time; if there was more, he'd find it.

'What do your instincts tell you?'

He inhaled deeply. 'By all accounts he's a bright boy. Handled himself great under pressure last night.'

Was it really only last night?

I heard the reservation in his tone. 'I'm sensing a but coming on.'

'You mean, apart from him being an ex-copper? Yeah, there's something. Can't put my finger on it.'

'Once a policeman, always a policeman?'

'Maybe.'

'Could be somebody pushed him down a road he didn't want to go. You have to give me more than that, George.'

He tried. 'Okay – the hit on LBC goes off exactly when he's around to save the day. Does that seem too convenient to you?'

'It's just how it happened.'

Ritchie's legendary caution kicked in. 'Mmmm. I don't know.

The only loyalty bent cops have is to themselves. Witness Stanford. We work with him, but we don't trust him and never will.'

I said, 'Have you considered that if Douglas hadn't been where he was, they were going upstairs to the club?'

His silence told me he wasn't convinced and I felt myself lose patience with him.

'Anything else?'

Ritchie heard my frustration and qualified his opinion. 'He's hard. And he's smart. But let's not forget the only thing keeping him out of prison is that bringing his case to court would embarrass people who don't appreciate being embarrassed. I'm seeing a guy who goes his own way and isn't as clever as he thinks he is.'

'That could be you and me you're describing.'

He laughed. 'Suppose you're right. I'll keep digging. When's the next money due to arrive?'

'Wednesday. Wouldn't be surprised if the Bishops change their minds. I'll meet them tomorrow, try to keep them on board, but I'm not hopeful.'

Ritchie said, 'You'll manage, it makes business sense. They'll want assurances security has been beefed up, of course.'

'That's where Mark Douglas comes in. If he's up for it, I'll need him to start right away.'

'He turned down the celebrity offers. He won't be cheap.'

'We can't afford to let him go, George. There's too much riding on this. On second thoughts, get a number for him, text it to me and I'll call him myself.'

* * *

The air still held heat from the day, there were stars in the sky, and a breeze gently rustled the branches of the trees outside my flat.

Further down the road, the men George Ritchie had on me pulled into the kerb and killed the headlights.

It had been a long day for me. It would be an even longer night for them.

Like it or not, having them there made sense.

Jonas Small was trying to get his head round the idea Danny might be staging a guerrilla assault on his old operation. He was wrong. Well wrong. Whoever had ordered the violence and stolen Small's money was still out there.

I kicked off my shoes and poured three fingers of twelve-year-old Chivas Regal, cradling the glass in both hands; just holding it renewed my strength. The whisky was honeyed apples and butter-scotch. I helped myself to a second glass, lay back on the couch and closed my eyes. A lot had happened. Too much to take in. Less than twenty-four hours earlier I'd tasted wine on Kelly's breath as she matched my thrusts with her own. Though we hadn't known it then, we were making love for the last time.

George Ritchie's text arriving on my phone drew me back from the edge of sleep. I tapped the number he'd sent and listened to it ring. My timing was off. Vicky Messina was still in town. Douglas would be working and wouldn't be doing his job if he allowed anything to come between him and the diva.

I called the club. 'How're we doing, Luigi?'

'Very well, Mr Glass.'

'Are we expecting Vicky Messina's party tonight?'

'No, though it's still early.'

'Okay. Let me talk to Nina.'

'She isn't here.'

I looked at my watch. 'Has she left?'

He thought about how best to reply. 'She hasn't been in tonight. Not that I've seen.'

All I needed was Nina playing silly buggers. I called Ritchie again. 'George, Nina didn't show up at the club.'

He was relaxed. 'She's at home. Been there since this afternoon. She's fine.'

'Well, she won't be when I catch up with her.'

* * *

Sometimes, the best you can hope for is to get through the day. I'd managed that – just. But it had drained me. In the bedroom, I lay down on top of the covers without bothering to undress and fell into a disturbed sleep filled with ugly images. When I woke it was still night and I'd missed a call. I returned it and heard it ring out somewhere in the London darkness.

Mark Douglas wasn't answering.

12

Nina made coffee, black and sweet, and took it back to the bedroom. She pulled her Chinese silk dressing gown round her, lit a Gitanes from a fresh soft pack and drifted over to the window. The street outside was Sunday-morning quiet. Across the road, the two men in the car were still there. She drew hard on the cigarette and let the smoke out in a slow stream as her mouth tightened.

Nina had never trusted George Ritchie and believed Luke had given him too much power. His reputation as the Andersons' enforcer for over two decades impressed her brother. It didn't impress her; they'd had words about his goons following her before. Ritchie was paranoid. Seeing a threat around every corner. His claim that he was only doing what Luke wanted was partly true. But the old woman lifting her skirts and running if there was a mouse in the house was all him. She struggled to imagine anybody being frightened of George Ritchie. Once upon a time maybe, not now. He'd be more at home pruning roses in a garden on the south coast, bemoaning the effect of blackfly with his next-door neighbour, worrying about frost on the marrows he'd entered for the local show.

Nina couldn't remember when she'd last spent a Saturday at home but felt better for it; she'd been running on empty. Luke didn't appreciate how difficult managing Glass Houses during the day and being at LBC at night was. He soon would, because she was done with it. The club was his dream, not hers. She'd tried to get him to settle for what they had. He wouldn't. He'd wanted distance from Danny and all he'd stood for; she didn't blame him for that. At the end of the day that was what she was doing with Glass Houses. The difference was, she was happy with what she had now. Luke wanted more. Much more.

Tomorrow, Peter Conrad, an American working for a New York bank, was viewing two properties. After a succession of cordial emails between them, she'd narrowed the search to a six-bedroom house off Belgrave Square and an apartment at Cambridge Gate, opposite Regent's Park.

Conrad had no interest in living in London; this was an investment, pure and simple. He'd booked a junior suite at Claridge's and would probably be there now.

Thinking about the money she was about to make mellowed Nina. She got onto the circular bed, propped herself against the satin pillows and opened her computer.

The email had been sent some time during the night. It was unsigned and offered no explanation, and read as if it had been written in haste by a stranger.

My plans have changed. I have to cancel.

Nina had just lost commission on a ten-million-pound sale.

* * *

Mark Douglas had thirty-odd hours to get through before the tour flew to Europe and he could wash his hands of Vicky Messina; he wouldn't be sorry. Some stars were spoiled brats, indulged by managers and record companies making a ton of money off them. Most were just people constantly being judged and scrutinised. Occasionally, it got too much and they snapped. That didn't apply to Vicky Messina – she'd been a bitch from day one and she was still a bitch. Tonight was her last show in London. Tomorrow, his counterpart in Berlin could carry the weight.

He was stepping into the shower when his mobile rang. Caller ID told him who was on the line and he steadied himself before answering.

Luke Glass didn't bother with pleasantries. He said, 'We need to talk.'

'Okay.'

'I mean, we need to talk now.'

'I'm available tomorrow from around lunchtime. We could—'

Glass cut across him. 'Too late, it has to be sooner.'

'If you're in a hurry I can give you my opinion of where your security's weak over the phone.'

'Not what I want.'

'Then, what?'

'Meet me at the club in sixty minutes.'

* * *

Nina stared at the screen, unable to take it in. Sometimes clients bought, sometimes they didn't – and sometimes they'd never intended to. Conrad had been a serious prospect – she'd met enough of the other kind to know the difference – very specific about what he was looking for and why. She'd Googled him: the banker was married with three kids and lived in Manhattan when he wasn't at their home in Sag Harbor on Long Island. On his wife's Twitter page he was craggy and tanned, playing with his children on the lawn with the sea in the background at the foot of their property; carving the turkey at Thanksgiving; or dressed to the nines at a Republican fundraiser in the Algonquin Hotel near Times Square, his arm round her, both of them smiling perfect white-teeth smiles that had cost more than most folk spent on a car.

The images told a story: the Conrads were people with a place in the world. Calling off so abruptly seemed out of character. And the tone of the email was different from the dozen that had passed between them.

Nina dialled the number. A well-modulated voice said, 'Claridge's, good morning. How can I help you?'

She took a deep breath and kept her anxiety under control. 'I'd like to speak to Mr Conrad, please.'

The receptionist had the information to hand. 'I'm so sorry, Mr Conrad decided to return to New York. He checked out an hour ago.'

* * *

Mark Douglas towelled his wet hair and studied his face in the mirror. Last night had been another late one – Tramp was almost closing when they left. Vicky had been a ball of touchy-feely energy, friendly, almost likeable, and he'd known she was on E. She'd insisted they drive around looking for somewhere that was open, throwing a strop when, eventually, he'd ordered them back to The Dorchester and handed responsibility over to her own men. Douglas heard she'd called Room Service for buttermilk pancakes with chocolate fudge sauce, a pint of freshly squeezed orange juice and four bottles of Tuborg Booster Strong, and realised he'd been wrong – she was on more than just ecstasy. As a vanilla dawn had broken over Hyde Park, he'd pulled his car into a deserted Park Lane and headed for home. Four hours later, Luke Glass caught up with him.

He was a man in a hurry and it was easy to understand why. Friday night had been a disaster for him and he needed somebody to pull his nuts out of the fire. The attack was brutal and would've been worse if Douglas hadn't come across it when he had: professionals did what they were paid to do and no more. The dead woman wasn't in anybody's plan. Slitting her throat was the hallmark of someone who enjoyed his work.

Mark Douglas was aware of the Glass family before he arrived in the capital. The brothers were well-known underworld figures, the kings of south London. Luke had taken over after Danny dropped out of sight; reports of him in Marbella had never been verified by the Spanish police – and if that was where he'd gone, he was still keeping his head down.

Tonight was the final night with Messina, the last time he'd have to put up with the arrogance, the mood swings, and the sulking when she didn't get her own way. He pulled on a fresh white shirt and buttoned it. The Sig Sauer .22 pistol – illegal as hell; owning one put you in line for a lengthy prison sentence – stayed in the drawer beside the bed. He'd need it. But not today. The meeting at LBC would be more than just a meeting. Glass would have questions. Douglas was sure he had the answers.

* * *

Vincent Finnegan was in pain. Sitting too long in one position stiffened his joints – he wasn't cut out for surveillance. In his darker moments, he wondered what the hell he *was* cut out for.

Three years earlier, when he'd bumped into Luke Glass in the Admiral Collingwood pub, Finnegan had been less than pleased to see Danny's younger brother. The Irishman, once a dandified enforcer known as much for his good looks as his ruthlessness, was eking out his disability allowance, barely taking care of himself. Luke had given him a job, more for old times' sake than anything else, and for the first time in a very long while he had a place in the world and money in his pocket. What a difference that made. He shaved every day and put on a clean shirt. There wasn't a woman in the picture. Probably never would be. Though if he got lucky, would he remember what to do with her?

For him to be even considering a relationship was a miracle. He'd been in the wilderness. Luke had led him back into the fold. Luke Glass was a gentleman.

The guy in the driver's seat hadn't had much to say for himself; they'd run out of conversation when the sky was still dark. All right with Vincent. Quiet was what he was used to, what he preferred to the mindless chatter everywhere.

Across the road, nothing stirred. Nina had spent the night at home – alone, as far as he knew. Around one o'clock, the light had gone out behind the heavy curtain. Finnegan checked his watch: 8.40 a.m. She'd be in bed asleep. Unusual for Nina, the original wild child and a gawky teenager when he'd worked for Danny. Well, she wasn't a gawky anything now. Just the opposite, in fact.

If he'd been twenty years younger... Better make that thirty.

The notion brought a rueful smile. Sometimes he forgot how broken Danny had left him, imagining himself the way he'd been, crippled and riddled with arthritis, rather than how he was now. George Ritchie had called three times during the night. The man must have vampire blood in his veins; he never seemed to sleep. Luke obviously trusted him but Finnegan hadn't made his mind up.

Ritchie was a man of few words on a good day. Their conversation had been notable for its brevity.

Ritchie: 'Anything?'

Him: 'No.'

It was going off all over the place. In another life he would've been in the thick of it but Luke wanted an eye kept on his sister, and that was good enough for Vinnie.

13

On the far side of LBC, a woman in a blue overall pushed a floor polisher across the black and white Italian marble tiles that had cost a small fortune, while two more busied themselves with the studded leather upholstery and mirrors. I didn't know their names and assumed they didn't know me. Though, how was that possible? In the last six months, I'd spent more time here than at my flat. The idea of running a club had come to me in the middle of a sleepless night and I'd launched into it without realising how much I was taking on. George Ritchie had tried to convince me we didn't need the hassle. I hadn't listened because the upsides seemed too great to turn down. Now I was discovering what he'd meant and why I was waiting on Mark Douglas to arrive.

Douglas wasn't how I remembered him: he was about my height, younger by a few years, and self-contained in a way I hadn't noticed in the wee hours of Saturday morning, when he'd broken up the assassins' party, killed one and sent the others back to the rock they'd crawled out from under.

Douglas was wearing a dark-blue suit, a white shirt open at the neck, and a pair of Tokyo Black Square sunglasses. Wisely, when he saw me, he pushed them up into his hair. Talking to people when I couldn't see their eyes was a thing with me – the windows of the soul and all that – I couldn't read them and that made me uncomfortable. Douglas was a good-looking guy, intelligent and alert even before he spoke. His Glaswegian accent had been finessed, the harsh rolling Rs softened, the consonants intentionally clipped, I guessed, to make himself understood. If something went down with one of his 'A' list clients, the last thing he needed was a failure in communication.

We shook hands and sat down. His grip was firm and dry; he didn't crush my fingers to prove he was tough: a good start. My offer of coffee was politely turned down as he sat, ready to hear what I had to say.

'First off, for what you did on Friday night, thanks.'

His reply was modest. 'You're welcome. They were up for it, all right. No knowing how far they'd have gone. It was lucky I came on them when I did.'

I'd had the same thought. It was impossible to tell what atrocity had been avoided and Douglas deserved more than a pat on the back. I said, 'Let's not waste each other's time. I'm asking myself why a smart guy throws paraffin on a promising career and puts a match to it.'

The question was intended to catch him off guard – the force of his reply surprised me.

'None of your fucking business, Mr Glass.'

'If you don't want to talk about yourself, then why are you here?'

His jawline stiffened; he raised his chin and his eyes locked on mine. 'I'm not prepared to discuss my life with you or anybody else. Your security's a mess. I assumed you'd want advice on how to sort it.'

'You think that's what I need?'

'Isn't it?'

'I told you that on the phone.'

He was a polished performer who handled himself well – now and two nights ago in the lane. My interest was in what lay under the surface. We stared at each other while he processed my silence and I could almost see the wheels turning in his brain.

After forty seconds, he said, 'You're... offering me a job?'

'That depends on your answer to the first question.'

His shoulders relaxed. He flashed a glance round the empty club and across at the cleaners, making certain he wouldn't be overheard before he responded.

'You've done your homework?'

'Would you expect anything less?'

'No. Okay. I'll tell you what I'm going to tell you. Whether it's enough is your decision, but it's all you're getting.'

'Fair play, let's hear it.'

'My parents were killed in a car crash when I was young. I was brought up by my father's elder brother, who'd been a policeman in Glasgow. No big star, just a copper on the beat. Joining the force was to repay him for what they'd done for me. They were my family. I owed them. Maybe you can't understand that?'

He thought he was telling his story. In fact, he was telling mine.

'My uncle said the day I put on the uniform was the proudest of his life.'

'Touching. What went wrong?'

Douglas made a face. 'Nothing went wrong. Police Scotland snapped me up. Because I had a degree, I was a candidate for the fast-track programme. People imagine it's a cushy number. It isn't. You have to be twice as good as everybody else and still aren't accepted by the other guys.' He played with his fingers and allowed himself a half-smile. 'Unfortunately for my critics I was good at the job.'

'Tommy Walsh.'

Mark Douglas looked at me with new respect. 'You *have* done your homework.'

'I always do.'

'Not long after that somebody presented me with an opportunity.'

'What about your uncle? If you got caught it would break his heart.'

'He'd died. So had my aunt.'

'Clearing the way for you to go over to the dark side.'

It was a joke; he didn't laugh, and I regretted saying it.

'I wasn't blind. I saw what was going on around me. If it wasn't me, it would've been somebody else.'

'And then you got found out.'

He sighed, though not with regret. 'And then I got found out, yes.'

My next question was obvious. 'They didn't prosecute. Why not?'

'And take the chance I'd blow the lid off the whole thing? No, we parted company on equal terms. I kept my mouth shut and my record stayed clean.'

The bitterness in his laugh might not be deserved; nevertheless, it was there.

'After that, what did you do?'

'Became a cliché: got drunk for a while, sobered up and came south. It's what people from that part of the world do. We're famous for it.'

It was time to give Mark Douglas a history lesson. 'When my brother was running things, we found out we had a mole, a sergeant in the Met. Danny lured him to Fulton Street – know where that is?'

'No.'

'Believe me, you don't want to find out. He tied the guy to a pillar and made holes in him with an electric drill. Lots of holes. It was like a slaughterhouse, blood everywhere. Except, that isn't how it finished. Turned out it was the wrong guy.'

'Am I supposed to be scared?'

He was good, I'd give him that. I said, 'You're plausible. Maybe too plausible, haven't made up my mind yet. Somebody who works for me believes even talking to you is a mistake. To his way of thinking, Friday night was too much of a coincidence and he's wary. I'm still not sure he's wrong. But here's the thing: if you're an undercover cop on a mission to infiltrate my organisation, then *this* is your moment of truth. You can walk out of here, go back to your masters and tell them you failed. No hard feelings. It takes a brave man or a very stupid one to try something like that. But step beyond this point and you won't be as lucky as you were in Glasgow. The river police will fish your body out of the Thames, minus the hands and the head. A friend of mine up in Walthamstow has a scrapyard; he'll toss them in the boot of an old Ford Taurus that's had a run-in with a brick wall and say no more about it. Next time I bump into him, I'll buy him a pint.'

I studied his face for a flicker of fear and found none.

'Does that mean I've passed the audition?'

'You're in until you're out is what it means.'

'And what exactly will I be doing?'

'George Ritchie handles everything on the streets south of the river. You'll be responsible for the top end – Glass Houses, Nina's real-estate company; the construction company – still small, but growing; and the club.'

'Sounds like a tall order.'

It certainly was and why we'd got our security wrong.

I chose my words carefully. 'You're not foolish enough to believe Friday was about lifting a night's takings. The businesses I mentioned are clearing houses for cash that can't be easily explained. Ours and our associates'.'

'Nice.'

'But the people I'm referring to are demanding. And dangerous.'

Douglas was getting the picture and realising he was in a position of strength. I expected him to haggle. Instead, he said, 'I trust your homework involved calculating what it would take to get me on board?'

That didn't deserve an answer. Of course, it had.

He laid down a condition. 'I'd want to bring in my own people.'

His handsome features tightened. I understood why Glasgow had brushed him under the carpet and made a mental note never to play poker with him. He said, 'Don't tell me horror stories about electric drills and expect me to work with what I've seen so far. I'll be bringing in my own men.'

George Ritchie had made the same point.

'How many?'

Douglas thought about it. 'Two. Three at the most. I'll vouch for them.'

Before I could speak, he cut me off.

'It's a deal breaker, Mr Glass. The stakes are too high – for you and for me.'

'Are they police?'

'Not any more.'

'When can they get here?'

'A couple of days. We'll do a security audit and I guarantee you're not going to like it.'

'I'll like it if it works.'

* * *

Outside on the street, Douglas pulled the sunglasses down and walked to his car, aware his life had just changed. No more playing nursemaid to over-indulged hopped-up stars who thought their talent allowed them to be terrible people. Luke Glass had a problem and reckoned he was the man to put it right. Flattering. Douglas didn't let it go to his head. The south London gangster had known about him before he even sat down and was studying his reactions rather than listening to his response to the questions. This morning was his second experience of Glass and he was everything he'd heard – tough, smart, cautious: not somebody you wanted as an enemy.

The job was his, a long travel from his last day as a police officer in Glasgow and the fight with DCI Symington – the final act in a sordid drama.

* * *

The voice, shrill and all too familiar, roared from the other side of Helen Street Police Office.

'It took a while but I've finally got what I need. Say goodbye to your career, Douglas. You're a disgrace to the uniform.'

The Manilla folder landed on Mark Douglas's desk with a slap, sending papers into the air like startled birds. Around the squad room conversation ended abruptly; wary eyes turned towards Detective Chief Inspector Symington.

DI Douglas put his pen down and slowly lifted his head. He wasn't surprised: this had been coming for months and he was ready to meet it. From day one, Symington had made it clear he was out to get him. Douglas was a new breed of policeman – in top shape physically and well educated. Donald Symington was neither and never had been.

The DCI pulled himself to his full six feet, dark eyes glittering malice, chin jutting provocatively, waiting for a response to his public accusation.

Knowing he wouldn't be getting one wound him tighter; his fists clenched and unclenched at his sides as anger rolled off him.

He leaned on the edge of the desk. 'I know you're dirty, you bastard, and now I can prove it.'

Douglas stretched to pick up the sheets from the floor and didn't reply. His silence was exactly the behaviour Symington abhorred – dumb insolence he wasn't prepared to tolerate. He opened the folder and took out the report.

'Your fancy qualifications won't impress too many people when you're behind bars. And that's exactly where you're going.'

The junior officer didn't react; he wouldn't give Symington the satisfaction.

The DCI turned to the room. 'Detective Inspector Douglas believes he's smarter than the rest of us. Thinks his degree from Strathclyde University entitles him to stick his snout in the trough. He doesn't get that's not on in this unit.' He glared at the DI but spoke to the audience, enjoying the drama he'd created.

'When you see him coming, stand aside or he'll knock you down. Our colleague's got places to go and he's in a hurry to get there.'

Symington took a page from the folder and began reading. Before he got to the end of the first line, Douglas came round the desk at a run and snatched it from him. The two men locked together, grappling over the paper. Douglas broke free, stepped back and lashed out, catching the senior man squarely on the jaw. Symington stumbled and fell, hitting his temple on the arm of a chair on his way down.

Instantly, policemen who'd been spectators were on their feet. One of them gripped Douglas in a bear hug and dragged him away.

Symington's eyes flickered and opened, glazed and unfocused, as though he didn't understand where he was. Until he saw Douglas and his thin lips parted in a sneer, satisfaction written all over his ashen face.

'You're finished in the force. Finished! Lucky if you don't do time.'

Crazy delight danced in his eyes.

Douglas took the warrant card from his wallet and tossed it on the floor beside Symington.

'Tell you what, Donald, stick the job and your report up your arse.'

He edged out of the Police Scotland car park into the afternoon traffic on Helen Street and turned onto Paisley Road West. A breeze had sprung from nowhere, rustling the branches of the trees, low cloud hung in the sky and it was humid; a storm was coming: a portent?

Donald Symington wasn't wrong – Mark Douglas was finished in the force. And in Glasgow. In reality, he was just getting started.

* * *

Douglas slid behind the steering wheel, checked his wing mirror and pulled into the traffic. Everything he'd heard about Luke Glass was true; he didn't suffer fools and he'd be good to work with, so long as Douglas did what he was told. Not something he was famous for.

He used one hand to steer and called on his mobile with the other. The person on the other end didn't speak. Douglas said, 'Get yourselves on the first train.'

14

DCI Carlisle's footsteps echoed in the dimly lit basement corridor of the Curtis Green Building on the Embankment, the current home of New Scotland Yard. The subterranean complex was a claustrophobic maze. No one came here; few even knew this place existed. The old Met had been tired and cramped; Carlisle hadn't liked it – its successor, with its flashy exterior, open-plan office space and hot desks, took a bit of getting used to. The detective heard a noise and stopped in his tracks. Over his shoulder, pipes from the abandoned heating system, lagged and heavy with cobwebs, ran in a line back the way he'd come. He felt his heartbeat quicken and cursed the secrecy surrounding the meeting he was going to. But only for a moment. What he had to report was vital, as important as anything he'd ever been part of. If word got out, a sting a long time in the making would come to nothing.

In his youth, John Carlisle had been handsome. Now, his hair was thinning, grey at the temples; he needed spectacles but was too vain to wear them. Almost his whole working life had been spent in the Metropolitan Police Service and, at forty-nine, he'd climbed as high as he was going climb. The DCI wasn't complaining. When he'd joined, if someone had told him he'd rise to detective chief inspector, he wouldn't have believed them. Carlisle was unmarried; he'd never found the time; the Met was his family. Anyone who betrayed it was his enemy. Before he handed in his badge, he had one final thing to accomplish – clearing out the bad apples that besmirched the hard-won reputation of the service he loved.

Operation Clean Sweep could make that happen.

Outside the door at the end of the whitewashed tunnel, a uniform stood to attention. He saluted and Carlisle went in. The room was no more than a glorified store cupboard, home to dusty boxes, paint tins and rusted iron radiators. In the centre, sitting at a folding table left by some forgotten tradesman, two officers – both Deputy Assistant Commissioners – waited for him.

Carlisle acknowledged the senior men and took a seat. They didn't speak to each other or him because, beyond their work, they had nothing in common and neither appreciated being dragged out on a Sunday. Carlisle checked his watch and drummed his fingers. One of them raised a disapproving eyebrow and was about to say something when the door opened and a fourth man came in. Assistant Commissioner of Specialist Operations William Telfer was a legend in the service. Known behind his back as Billy T, he was as revered in the ranks as any copper on the force because of his no-nonsense approach to policing the streets of the capital; Telfer was the reason they were in this godforsaken shithole yards from the Thames.

He nodded to the group and signalled the DCI to begin.

Carlisle cleared his throat and addressed his superiors. 'You're familiar with the history, so I'll keep it short. Operation Clean Sweep was brought into being to address the problem of police corruption in the Met. As the officer in charge, my first challenge in infiltrating a criminal organisation was to find the right people, people who can live every day with the unimaginable stress of knowing, once they were in, they'd be under constant scrutiny, and that the smallest slip would mean their death.' He looked at their faces. 'That takes very special individuals.'

The intolerant DAC hurried him along. 'But you found them?'

Carlisle allowed himself the ghost of a smile. 'One of them, yes. Eventually. Which brought another problem. We'd targeted the Glass family, the biggest criminal enterprise in London. Ruthless bastards. Finding our insider, building up their backstory, then getting them into the game was never going to be quick or easy.'

Telfer said, 'I hope you're going to tell us you've succeeded?'

Carlisle felt eyes bore into him; suddenly, the atmosphere in the room was electric.

'Not yet. What I can say is we've got the right person, and it looks as though an opportunity is about to open up. Any break in the chain of confidentiality, it could disappear and our officer with it.'

'Is Danny Glass in the picture?'

'The short answer is: we don't know. Three years ago, he mysteriously dropped out of sight. Rumour has him in Spain, Portugal, the South of France, even the Caribbean. Danny may still be pulling the strings. Even if he isn't, his brother Luke wouldn't hesitate to neutralise any threat. An undercover officer who infiltrates their organisation and gets caught can expect an agonising end.'

Carlisle scanned the faces. 'The insider's identity is the best-kept secret in Scotland Yard. Only a couple of people outside this room know who it is. And that's how it stays.'

Telfer said what the others were thinking. 'God help him, he's a brave man.'

Carlisle corrected him. 'With respect, sir, I never said it was a man.'

* * *

Kenny and Colin Bishop, known as the Awkward Squad behind their backs, were cousins who behaved like an old married couple, stumbling through a series of meaningless squabbles and ancient resentments that flared and were forgotten in their hurry to get to the next petty dispute: people who should never have been together but somehow were. Being in their company was an experience best avoided; the constant wrangling frayed your nerves. Chalk Farm boys born and bred, they couldn't agree on the day of the week and hated each other. But a lot of money passed through their firm and I'd managed to persuade them to let LBC clean it for them. The Bishops' shipment wasn't due to arrive until Wednesday; three days away. If they got spooked and pulled out, it could start a run I wouldn't be able to stop.

Kenny was keen for a powwow. Apparently, the cousins were sitting on a pile of cash and needed our arrangement to go ahead almost as much as I did.

He said, 'Where do you want to meet?'

The club would've been safer but they couldn't think I was hiding.

'Wherever suits.'

'Okay. Little Venice at two.'

His suggestion surprised me and I hesitated. 'Will Colin be up for that?'

'You're having a laugh, aren't you? Fat bastard wouldn't walk the length of himself. I'll blame you. Tell him it was your suggestion.'

Even on a sunny Sunday, their war of attrition never ended. He happily explained his logic. 'It's a two-mile hike to Camden Lock. With a bit of luck, he'll have a heart attack and drop down dead. Wouldn't that be nice?'

* * *

I left the car in the lane and took the Tube. Two faces I hadn't seen before travelled with me, thirty-somethings, one black, the other white. Spotting them wasn't hard: the T-shirts and baseball caps were fine, but it was too warm to be wearing jackets. Underneath, they'd be carrying.

At Warwick Avenue I got off and strolled towards town. I was early, the Bishops wouldn't be here yet, so I sat on a wooden bench in Rembrandt Gardens and tried to get my head round the last thirty-six hours: people had been executed in cold blood; money had been stolen; my reputation was on the line and I might have a sister I hadn't known about yesterday; a stranger had just informed me my security was shit and I was going for a walk with the Odd Couple.

Apart from that it was just another lazy Sunday.

Big cities have one thing in common: only the very rich or the very poor live in the centre. Little Venice was the exception. Secret London – the side most folk were unaware existed.

The Basin, close to where the Regent's Canal and an arm of the Grand Union Canal met, was like glass. When I was seventeen, I'd brought a girl here on a day very like this. We'd held hands and I still remembered her whispered 'I love you' and how it made me feel. Two weeks later she dumped me for another guy.

A boy of eleven or twelve fished for roach off the side, completely absorbed in threading bait on a hook. Out on the island, the reflection of an enormous willow tree darkened the water, the tips of its slender branches trailing. I was in the shade, but up on the road on the other side, the sun bleached a line of white Regency-style houses, where women in sunglasses, hats, and print dresses licked ice creams and hung on the tanned arms of the men with them.

Suddenly, I needed a holiday.

When Kenneth Bishop suggested meeting here, my instinct was

to say no. Staying out of sight until we knew what was going on made sense; in the circumstances, it wasn't feasible: places to go and people to see – after the Bishops it would be the turn of Bridie O'Shea in Kilburn.

If somebody wanted me, they could come and get me.

There were worse places to die.

* * *

The cousins arrived together, bickering their way towards me, Kenny Bishop, tall and beanpole thin, Colin, short and overweight, both talking at once, mouths going, nobody listening. Comical if you were in the right mood. Today, I wanted to bang their stupid heads together to make them stop. Then, I realised how it worked: Colin was a bad-tempered little clown but it was Kenny who kept it going, winding him up and complaining when he reacted.

Or maybe none of that was true. Maybe I was rationalising behaviour that had gone beyond explanation.

Dressed in suits, they looked more like old-fashioned insurance agents than millionaire scallywags. I didn't laugh too hard – the feuding cousins had put their differences aside well enough to button up most of north London and make a fortune in the process. Kenny was Mr Reasonable, Colin, Mr Touchy. How they'd spent their wealth said something about them: Colin had bought the properties on either side of the house he'd been born in and knocked them into one. Kenny lived in a six-bedroom town house in Chalcot Square, Primrose Hill, near the zoo. Not an entirely inappropriate location for his cousin. Rumour had Colin Bishop down as gay and addicted to cocaine; insecure about his appearance and prone to take offence – he'd stuck a broken bottle in a guy's face in Kentish Town because he thought he was taking the piss. Unfortunately, Colin Bishop thought everybody he met was taking the piss. Behind his back, most of them were.

I didn't like them. I liked their money. But it came at a price.

Listening to their fucking yammer was that price.

We started walking and for ten misguided minutes, I believed it might be all right. The cousins had gone quiet – a rare thing – taking it all in. Over my shoulder, I sensed the two new friends Ritchie had on me weren't far away. The Bishops appeared to be alone. They wouldn't be; they'd have people here, too.

Kenny watched a tour boat chug by, the skin at his eyes crinkling in the glare. The happy tourists prompted him to speak. 'You know,' he said wistfully, 'I could live here.'

Colin sniffed and sneered. 'Who're you kidding? You'd hate it. Too many people for a start.'

'No, I wouldn't. I like people.'

'Yeah, you would. Imagine it with the rain coming down in sheets.'

They were off. I filtered them out and soaked in as much of the scene as their vexatious presence would allow. Further along, someone I recognised leaned against the fence at the top of the embankment. Felix Corrigan nodded and I nodded back. George Ritchie really was taking no chances.

Four narrowboats painted black and orange, purple and green, red and brown, blue on blue were moored under a leafy part of the path. If I'd been alone, I would've taken the time to drink it all in and enjoy it. I wasn't. I was with these two.

The stalemate couldn't last and, though I missed the signal that passed between them, I knew one had. Kenny glanced at Colin and spoke for both of them. 'We're hearing things that give us pause, Luke. Word is you're in a bit of bother.' His face was flushed. He tugged a leaf off an overhead branch and threw it in the water. 'Sounds like you've upset somebody. To say we're concerned, well...'

Colin came at me like a terrier worrying my ankles, in my face, mixing accusations with questions he answered himself. 'You talked us into trusting you. Given what went down the other night, who would? Not the Bishops.'

'Colin—'

'All the main players are in, you said. No opposition, you said. Unless you've got a bloody handle on it, the deal's off.'

I looked at the sun beating down on the water. 'Colin—'

'We're not talking pennies here, Glass. We need assurances. A guarantee that—'

His cousin caught his arm. 'Shut it, Col. Let the man speak.'

Colin Bishop was sweating, breathing heavily through his nose. He wanted to go for me – part of me wished he would. It would've been fun to toss the outraged little bastard into the canal, but it wouldn't keep the deal on track. Even so, I was tempted. A jogger bought him a reprieve.

I reasoned with him. 'That's why I'm here, Colin. Except, I didn't talk you into anything. I presented you with a business proposition, which you agreed to.'

His eyes were ablaze with the conviction of someone who believed his own bullshit. His breath smelled of caramel and sour cherries and I realised he was drunk. They both were. I hadn't been early; they'd got here before me and squeezed in a session, most likely in The Bridge House just off the towpath. Colin threw caution to the wind and rubbed it in. 'Yeah, before you took a right pasting. Before you got turned over.'

The urge to hurt him was almost too much. I let him get it out; he was going to, anyway.

A husband and wife and their three kids were coming towards us. I faked a smile and waited till they'd passed before replying. I was angry – a lot was riding on this conversation and these fuckers had turned up pissed. I said, 'I'll level with you. It's common knowledge the club took a hit on Friday night. But it's sorted.'

'So you say.'

I repeated the words slowly for effect. 'That's right. *So I say*, Colin. You calling me a liar? Because there's nothing good down that road, trust me on this.'

Kenny listened to the exchange but didn't contribute. Colin teetered on the brink, weighing whether it was worth a beating, in the end deciding it wasn't and stepped away, anger draining from his bloated sweating jowls.

'We have to be sure. You'd do the same.'

No, I wouldn't.

'As for guarantees... in our dog-eat-dog business...' I allowed the sentence to peter out. 'Let me ask you this, both of you. Apart from Luke Glass, who's lost anything?'

They stared at me like the dimwits they were. Lucky dimwits, but dimwits nevertheless.

'I'll tell you, shall I? Nobody. Nobody's lost a coin. And nobody will. From here on in, I'll cover any shortfall. That's a licence to print money. I'd take it, if I were you. Just know this is a one-time offer. Pass on it and you're out. There's no way back.'

People strolled beside the glorious houseboats in fantastical colours anchored all along the towpath. In Little Venice, the willow tree would still be casting its shade in the Basin and I wondered if the boy had caught anything. But I'd had enough of Kenny and Colin Bishop to last me a while, or at least till their cash was delivered in three days. I left them with their mouths hanging open, speechless probably for the first time in their contentious lives, and walked to the next exit up to the road.

Felix would be there. Guaranteed.

15

The Bishops were a hard act to follow. Bridie O'Shea managed it without breaking sweat.

We hadn't arranged a time. There was no need. All day every day, Bridie was at the table in the back room of Kavanagh's, the pub she'd inherited from her husband, playing a never-ending game of patience, with a bottle of O'Hara's Irish Stout and a glass of ruby port and lemon sharing the limited space with a 50g tin of Amber Leaf, a packet of Rizla Blue, three mobile phones and a notebook. The door beyond the long bar would be permanently wedged open so she could glance up from the cards, stare through the haze of cigarette smoke hanging like a veil in the air around her and see what was occurring in her boozer.

But for all the public visibility, entering her presence was by invitation only. With fair hair greying at the roots, she looked like a dissolute grandmother, a casualty of mother's ruin and Capstan Full Strength. In reality, she could buy and sell the lot of us if the notion took her.

How much I knew about her surprised me: the young Bridie had had no interest in the issues scarring her homeland. That changed when she caught the eye of Wolf Kavanagh, a man two decades older than her and a bomb-maker for the Provisionals, and followed him to England on Christmas Eve, 1972. She was seventeen and an avid pupil. Three months later, the IRA launched its first terror campaign in London with four car bombs. Two were defused, the other two – outside the Old Bailey and the Ministry of Agriculture – went off, injuring two hundred people. Ten arrests were made, including Gerry Kelly, Dolours Price and Marian Price as they boarded a Dublin-bound plane at Heathrow.

At heart, Bridie was a good Catholic girl; she didn't sleep with Kavanagh until after they married in 1975. A faith that disallowed sexual intercourse out of wedlock with the man she loved nevertheless somehow found a place for the killing and maiming of women and children.

I didn't get it.

Wolf Kavanagh gradually lost interest in the Cause and filled the gap with protection, prostitution and robbery with violence; he died of cirrhosis of the liver in 1982, leaving his widow a criminal enterprise run from the back room of the pub on Kilburn High Road.

And so it began.

By the time Tony Blair felt the hand of history upon his shoulder and signed the Good Friday Agreement on behalf of the British government in 1998, Bridie had reverted to her maiden name and been out of politics the better part of twenty years. Her values hadn't altered; she'd never had any. Nowadays, her core objectives were simple: making money and making sure she didn't miss a black ten on a red jack.

* * *

The Bishops had taken time from me I was never getting back. I didn't have the energy for another confrontation. Felix didn't ask what was wrong. Instinctively, he just drove. We were in Highgate before I told him to turn around. The anxiety in his voice too obvious to miss. 'You all right, boss? You okay?'

The truth was complicated and uncomfortable so I lied. 'I'm fine, Felix. Putting it together, one piece at a time.'

He nodded like he understood. If he did, he was doing better than me.

'Where to?'

'Kavanagh's, Kilburn High Road.'

He knew who the pub belonged to and must've heard the 'by invitation' rule, because he said, 'Expecting you, is she?'

'Unfortunately, she is, Felix. Finnegan set it up.'

'Where is Vincent?'

'Ritchie's got him keeping an eye on Nina.'

Felix would be counting his blessings. My sister was a gig everybody was keen to avoid.

I pushed the door of Kavanagh's open. Heads turned in my direction and conversation stopped like a scene from a cowboy movie: strangers weren't welcome in these here parts. The barman stared at me, red veins criss-crossing his face as though somebody had drawn a map of the London underground from memory. He fingered a scar on his left cheek that ran from Mile End to Tottenham Court Road, the skin dirty white and pinched where the repair had been botched. It was an old wound; he'd have been a young man when he acquired it. In the moment the blade bit into him and did its evil work there would've been no pain, just a warm, wet sensation, a delayed tingling in the severed nerves, then the devastating realisation he was forever changed. And it hadn't ended there – three fingers were missing from his left hand.

In the far corner, a guy in a checked shirt and a bootlace tie was changing the strings on a guitar. I heard an 'Oh, Lonesome Me' coming and hoped to Christ I'd be gone before he started to sing.

I guessed Bridie's office had been a storeroom: there was enough space for a table, two chairs, and not much else. Her fingers were thick, the cards in her left hand old and bent at the edges; when I came in, her eyes didn't leave them.

'Sit down. What're you drinkin'? She paused and looked up. 'Might as well be friendly. As my Wolf used to say, "If you can't make a friend, don't make an enemy."'

'Very wise.'

Bridie was wearing a lilac blouse over a black skirt that fell to the floor, and sandals. She'd been slim and pretty, once. Now, she was neither. But the spark Wolf Kavanagh had been drawn to burned still behind grey eyes. Those eyes had seen more than I ever would.

She placed the seven of hearts on the eight of clubs and laughed a tobacco laugh. 'Maybe it is, and maybe it isn't. All I can tell you is I never met a more argumentative man than Wolf Kavanagh. Cause a row in an empty house so he would, and that's the God's truth.'

She ran the letters together to make one word: Godstruth.

'But he was smart enough to marry you.'

Her eyelashes fluttered; grey eyes met mine, wary and suspicious. 'So that how it's goin' to be, is it? Talkin' shite to an old woman. Flatterin' her to get your way. A typical man.'

I leaned closer. 'Will it work?'

Bridie laughed again. 'Well, it's worth a try.'

The hand was a bust. She recorded the failure in the notebook, swept the cards into the centre and shuffled like a Mississippi riverboat queen.

'When I was seven years old, my grandfather told me a lie. Thought I was too young and wouldn't notice. Men have been lyin' to me ever since.' She changed the subject. 'How did you get on with them Bishops? Enjoy your walk along the canal, did you?'

This lady was the best-informed woman in London without leaving her cubbyhole. And I recalled that in 1973, when they arrested Dolours and Marian Price getting on the plane, our Bridie hadn't been with them: a teenager fresh off the boat, yet even then she'd been smarter than everybody else.

'I shouldn't be askin'. It's none of my bloody business.'

I sensed the barman behind me in at the door and answered her original question.

'Lager by the neck.'

She raised an eyebrow. 'Not whiskey? With the weekend you're havin'?'

'The whisky I drink doesn't have an e in it.'

'Then more fool you.'

'As for Kenny and Colin, they're... an interesting pair.'

She snorted. 'Interestin' my arse. A couple of eejits is what they are. Blow on them hard enough, they'll fall over. Includin' them in anythin' is a mistake, as you've no doubt discovered.'

Ash fell from her cigarette onto the table; she flicked it to the floor.

'Your man said you wanted to talk.' She meant Vincent Finnegan. 'Did you imagine sendin' a broken-down rebel with the message would make a difference? Maybe we'd have a few jars and talk about the old days?'

Bridie leaned towards me and broke into 'Sean South of Garryowen'. Singing it like a secret. Mocking me. Telling me I'd misjudged her and not to do it again. Then, she stopped, her lips curled, her voice changed and she said, 'I was out of that bloody fiasco before he'd thrown his first rock at a soldier on the Falls Road and run away to boast about it to his wee pals.'

'Vincent Finnegan wasn't always a cripple. In his day—'

She cut into my history lesson. 'What do you want from me, Mr Glass?'

Her directness was a stark contrast with the cousins. 'We took a hit on Friday night. It was bad, Bridie.'

'Tell me somethin' new.'

I started to speak. She held up her hand, her accent thickening with annoyance. 'You're about to say it's under control, I see it on your face. Don't. Because that'll make you the same as every man I've ever met: a feckin' liar. And it would mean we'll never be friends. That would be a shame.'

She was offering me a chance to level with her. Before I could respond, a glass and a bottle of McGrath's clinked on the table. Up close, the barman's eyes were yellowed, the scar a white worm on his dark cheek. I handed the glass back to him. 'By the neck means I don't want this.'

When he'd gone, Bridie said, 'Niall's in a bad way.'

'I can see he is. What's wrong with him?'

She shrugged. 'Same as Wolf. The drink's done him in.'

'What happened to his face?'

'The same as happened to his hand.'

We were quiet until I said, 'I'm not here to lie. I'm here to ask you not to pull out of our arrangement.'

'If you valued my support so highly, why leave me to last?'

Moisture frosted the surface of the bottle, condensing into beads that raced each other to the bottom. I picked up the lager and drank half of it down. Her question was valid, but I'd anticipated it. 'First, the Bishops are easily rattled, you're not. Second, the stolen money belonged to Jonas Small. Will that do?'

Bridie was on a roll: a red seven went to a black eight; the three of clubs landed on the four of diamonds; she snapped the nine of hearts onto the ten of spades, smoke trailing from the forgotten cigarette in the ashtray at her elbow. She remembered and lifted it to her lips but didn't put it in her mouth till she'd said what she had to say.

'I gave up botherin' what other people did a long time since. Our deal stands. For now.'

'Appreciated. Thanks.'

She downed the port and shook her head. 'Don't thank me too soon. That's a yet, not a never. The problem you're facin' is bigger than you imagine.'

'What're you hearing?'

Bridie ignored me and redirected her attention to the cards. I'd had as much as she was prepared to give. The seat scraped the floor when I pushed it back. As I turned to leave, she grabbed my wrist in her meaty fingers. 'Are you a gambler, Mr Glass?'

'Are you?'

She smiled into the past and through the smoke I caught a glimpse of the Donegal girl who'd followed a man into the heart of a hostile country, rosary beads in one hand, an Armalite in the other.

'If I hadn't been, Wolf would've had no use for me. Fertiliser bombs are unpredictable bastards. Take the bloody hands off you, so they will.' Bridie lowered her voice, although there was only her and me in the room. 'I'm willin' to bet this pub and everythin' in it, Jonas Small had a proposition for you, would I be right?'

She didn't need me to tell her so I didn't.

'If it's a proposition you're after, I might have one myself.'

'LBC isn't for sale.'

'Pleased to hear it. But don't be too quick to turn me down. You might regret it.'

I didn't ask and she didn't explain, which was good because whatever she had in mind, the answer was still no. Cleaning their dirty money was the only bed-sharing I was interested in with these people.

She raised her glass of stout in a toast. 'If you can't make a friend, don't make an enemy.'

'A nice philosophy.'

She wrote a mobile number in the notebook, tore the page out and thrust it towards me. 'It is, it is. Except, sometimes... and this is the Godstruth... it just can't be avoided.'

Out on Kilburn High Road, Felix was behind the wheel. In two days, I'd been face to face with the biggest names in the London underworld.

Bridie O'Shea was the best of them.

But like everybody else, she had an angle.

16

Elise Stanford only had to admire something and Oliver made sure she got it. In the early years her wants had been modest: a birthday present of a brooch with diamonds so tiny you needed a magnifying glass to see them, a new washing machine and tumble dryer, delivered the same afternoon the old one packed in or, on one memorable occasion, a puppy she'd spotted in a pet-shop window; a cute little mongrel with a button nose. They'd had Suzie for a decade. When she died, Elise had cried herself to sleep. Nowadays, it was Botox in Harley Street, holidays in the Caribbean – last time they'd chartered a yacht with its own crew all to themselves – and a personal trainer to help keep the figure he loved so much trim and supple.

Not every woman was so lucky, and while other wives complained to each other about the men they'd married, Elise let them get on with it.

When they met, Oliver Stanford was at the start of his career in the Met, young and handsome, full of plans for their future together and how great it was going to be. Elise had believed him and he'd been right.

But her wonderful life came at a price: Oliver was gone when she woke up in the morning and often wasn't back until late. Sometimes, especially with the girls not at home, she was lonely. More than once, Elise had been sure he was having an affair. He'd laughed when she accused him of being unfaithful, scolded her for being so silly. It was the demands of the job, he'd said: first to arrive and last to leave, the only way to stay on top and the reason he'd risen so high in the ranks.

She was the wife of Superintendent Stanford, in case she'd forgotten, and he wasn't finished.

Far from it.

Saturday had been fun until that bastard Glass arrived and spoiled it. For the rest of the afternoon, Oliver had been withdrawn and when their guests had left she'd said, 'Darling, do you really have to speak to these people yourself? I don't like the idea of them coming to the house. Couldn't you delegate it to one of your detectives?'

'I could. Of course, I could. But talking to them face to face means I know when they're lying to me.'

Oliver's way of saying no.

On Monday morning, it was still dark outside when she heard him tiptoe across the bedroom floor as he always did so as not to disturb her. Elise's eyes fluttered; she sighed, rolled over and returned to the perfect world her husband had created.

Stanford showered and went downstairs. His life was ordered – how he liked it. He was too old for surprises. Every day began the same: two cups of decaffeinated coffee, two slices of lightly toasted bread thinly spread with butter, then a walk with the dogs before driving into the city, missing the worst of the traffic because he was so early.

He took a bite out of the toast and washed it down with coffee: almost forty hours later and he still wasn't right. Luke Glass hadn't wasted a sunny afternoon coming all the way to Hendon just to say hello – he'd needed a scapegoat and decided Stanford was *it*. The deal they'd had since his brother bowed out was working well. Danny had been a psychopath. Luke was less reactive, more measured. At least, he had been. Showing up unannounced was new. Something inside Stanford had snapped when he'd seen him standing by the side of the house – his house – watching Elise, watching their friends.

Who the hell did he think he was?

Glass was blaming him for what happened to his businesses. Wrong. There had been nothing about the attacks on the streets. Not so much as a whisper, otherwise he would've warned him and he would've been prepared. The gangster wasn't thinking straight. Shotguns with Liverpool accents, he'd said it himself: out-of-towners, down for a quick scoff and home.

Fuck all to do with the capital. Fuck all to do with him. Everything to do with Luke Glass.

And yes, the bastard had a point: he should've contacted him, even if there was nothing to tell, because, at the end of the day, he was a Glass – capable of almost any bloody thing.

The nightclub was the star of his criminal empire. Anything involving LBC had the potential to ruin Stanford; he intended keeping a close eye on how this – whatever it was – turned out. You never could tell what was in the future. If somebody was set on bringing the gangster down, changing horses was an option. Meantime, he'd do what Glass wanted. Not for him. Not for that bastard. For himself; he'd too much invested, involved too many of his contacts, for it to go belly up now.

Possibilities ran through his mind like ticker tape, so many wide boys more than capable of trying their luck. Except, nobody benefitted from a war. And it would be messy. So, why? The same question Luke Glass was asking himself. And when he couldn't come up with an answer, he'd come to Hendon to take it out on him.

He hadn't seemed scared, though maybe he was. His territory covered everything significant south of the river – worth millions. Perhaps that fact hadn't escaped a rival yet to reveal themselves.

Not good news for any of them. The city had been relatively quiet of late. The last thing Oliver Stanford needed was a turf war – they'd already had one with Danny and Rollie Anderson. Everyone knew how that had turned out. In a word: ugly.

He'd wanted to tell Glass on Saturday. If he were here right now, he'd say it to his face.

'Somebody other than me doesn't like you.'

* * *

The dogs crowded his legs, wagging their tails, excited paws scratching the flagstone kitchen floor. Scotties were cute, his daughters loved them, though they wouldn't deter an intruder, would they? Stanford wished he'd bought Dobermanns or Irish Wolfhounds. Yeah, a couple of Wolfhounds would've been better. Wolfhounds were huge – the largest dogs in the world – easy-going animals, calm, intelligent, helluva guard dogs. For a super in the Met to even have to consider protecting his family was a sign of the times. Glass hadn't barged in shouting, making a scene in front of his guests. No, he'd held back, kept his distance, stayed in the shadows unnoticed. But the fact he'd come to his house in person all the way from south London said it all.

If that wasn't a threat, what was?

Oliver opened the front door quietly and stepped into the early morning, with the Scotties pulling on their leads. Stanford tightened his grip, holding them back; he wouldn't be hurried. For him, those initial seconds when cool air washed over him were the best. London was a shithole – he'd read that breathing in the city was the equivalent of smoking a hundred and sixty cigarettes a day. This was fresh. Clean. It had been a long time since Oliver Stanford had felt clean.

He didn't notice the Audi at first. When he did he almost vomited – the beautiful machine was wrecked. A thug with a Stanley knife hadn't been satisfied with one or two cuts; a spider's web of scratches raked the sides from front to back, near the gate a wing mirror lay cracked and broken on the ground – no doubt the other one would be close by – the windscreen was shattered and SCUM was written in large yellow letters on the bonnet, the paint luminous in the breaking dawn and – to cap it all – the four tyres had been slashed.

Stanford didn't look inside – he could imagine what he'd find.

He dragged the disappointed dogs through the front door, shut it behind him and stood with his back pressed against it, sweating and shaking with anger. Saturday's conversation with Glass screamed in his head. Crossing the line with the gangster had been deliberate; he'd enjoyed doing it. A small victory. Payback for the cheeky bastard assuming he could waltz into his private life when-ever it suited him.

But knowing he had the power to destroy the whole fucking lot of them wasn't enough. He needed to be alive to do it. And Glass had given him a demonstration of how easy it was to get to an officer in the Met. Even a superintendent.

His immediate concern was for his wife: Elise couldn't see this. It would freak her out. She wasn't stupid. She'd put it together with Saturday's uninvited guest and correctly conclude something was seriously wrong. Trying to convince her it was an act of mindless vandalism wouldn't work. She'd never believe it.

Stanford dialled a number on his mobile with trembling fingers, the hatred he felt for Luke Glass fixed on his ashen face. The urge to tear the gangster's head off was overwhelming until he remembered just who he was up against. His psycho brother hadn't quit and gone to live in Spain. He was under the ground. Six feet under. Luke Glass had put him there.

The number rang out. He tried again, holding on. Eventually, a voice heavy with sleep coughed into the receiver, said, 'Fuck off,' and hung up.

Stanford dialled a third time. When it was answered, he hissed, 'Hang up, Victor, and in twenty minutes, you'll have two squad cars at your garage. Not the legit business in Willesden Green, the yard off Cricklewood Lane you don't talk much about.'

Victor Russo was a sallow forty-five-year-old second-generation Italian. While his brothers and sister sold ice cream and fish and chips, he'd become a mechanic. Early on he realised he was never going to get rich fixing people's engines and changed direction, establishing himself as the 'go-to' guy if a high-end value motor was what you fancied – any model, any series, any colour, stolen to order: Mercs, BMWs, Range Rovers. Even the odd Roller on occasion. And there was a waiting list for his services. Stanford could've busted him a dozen times over. Instead, he'd left him to operate.

Russo knew but asked anyway. 'Who is this?'

Stanford ignored him. 'Whatever you were planning, forget it and get your arse up to Hendon.'

'To your house?'

'To my house. Take away what's left of my Audi and start putting it back together. My wife's asleep. I want it gone before she gets up.'

'But... Mr Stanford—'

'And there's broken glass all over the drive. Sweep it up and call me later with how much it's going to cost.'

Stanford weighed the mobile in his hand, still rattled by the crude message. By itself, it meant nothing: in a week the Audi would be in the drive, good as new. But it wouldn't come cheap – the repairs would run to bloody thousands.

How much it would cost to fix the car made him think of money. *His* money. On instinct he connected to the offshore bank that would bring his career to a juddering halt if its existence was discovered. The juicy number hitting his account every month hadn't gone through.

Stanford swore under his breath. 'You bastard.'

His second call was to his office at Scotland Yard, high above the Embankment. 'Send a car for me, don't feel like driving this morning. Not to the house. Hendon Central. The driver can pick me up at the old cinema. No trouble, the walk will do me good. Need some fresh air. Busy week coming up. A lot to think about, you know how it is.'

* * *

The smart thing would've been to call in sick. Oliver Stanford didn't do sick; in all his years as a copper, he could count the times he'd missed work through illness on one hand. Today might've been the day to change that – he was agitated and unsettled, his mind not on the job. At nine forty-five, as he was heading for the door on his way to a strategy meeting on the top floor of the Curtis Green Building, his mobile rang. Stanford read the caller ID and almost let it go. Victor Russo would've done a quick assessment of the damaged Audi and be keen to get the go-ahead. Given a choice, he would've gone to his meeting and kept the mechanic in Willesden Green waiting. A reminder of how much this shit was going to cost wasn't what he needed right now.

The superintendent laid the papers he was carrying on his desk and sat on the edge. 'Is it done?'

Russo heard the anxiety in the policeman's voice. 'Relax, it's taken care of.'

'Elise didn't see you?'

'Not a chance. Your wife doesn't even know we were there.'

Stanford breathed a sigh of relief. 'So how much?'

'No idea. Not yet. That isn't why I'm calling.'

'Then what?'

There was no easy way to break it. Russo said, 'You didn't look inside the car, did you?'

The hairs on the back of Stanford's neck stood up; he sensed something bad coming.

'No. Why? What've they done?'

Russo hesitated. 'Whoever smashed up your Audi left a shoebox in the passenger seat.'

'A shoebox?'

'Yeah, that's what I thought. Till I opened it.'

Oliver Stanford felt his chest tighten. He gripped the desk, dreading to ask but needing to know. 'What... what was in it?'

The words fell from Russo's lips like stones from between his fingers. 'A bullet.'

PART III

17

Nina wasn't a 'morning person' and never had been, only arriving early if there was a viewing arranged. Turning up at her office in time for lunch was common. Who was going to tell her off about her punctuality? She was the boss. Since Luke had her working the graveyard shift at the club, she'd been lucky to crawl into bed before three.

Not today. Luke would read the Riot Act for her no-show on Saturday and Sunday.

Well, too bad, brother; she'd warned him. If it had just been the club, okay, she could've handled fawning over celebrities, stroking their egos. But 'special services' wasn't her thing. Nina wasn't easily offended. Matching up monied tossers so they could paw beautiful young idiots and pay for the privilege was absolutely not for her, no matter how often Luke explained the benefits. It wasn't her problem if he didn't listen.

The stolen weekend had done her good; she was relaxed and refreshed. Not, as was so often the case, suffering the combined effects of sleep deprivation and a hangover. Sex, albeit not award-winning sex, and eight hours straight. No wonder she felt good.

But the sudden ducking out by the New York client still rankled. In her head, Nina had already added the commission to the very respectable total in her bank account. It felt as if somebody had dipped their hand in her bag and stolen her purse: a loss and a lack of respect. It was still the middle of the night in the States. Later, she'd call and give the arrogant, ignorant bastard an earful. Fucking Americans. They thought the world and everybody in it belonged to them.

On the drive in she couldn't tell if she was being followed, guessed she probably was and wouldn't be getting her freedom back any time soon.

Her office was on the fifth floor. The view was the reason she'd taken it, although it was nowhere near as great as the one from Butler's Wharf. Impressive, nevertheless. Nina rolled the blinds up, opened the windows, and was sitting behind her desk with a cup of coffee as the first rays of the new morning lanced the skyline and bathed the city in golden light.

She opened her diary to check her schedule for the week ahead – two appointments, one on Wednesday, one the day after. Both confirmed. Plenty to be hopeful about.

On her computer, the usual slew of enquiries would be waiting for her response. People didn't understand how much went into setting up a viewing, especially if the property was occupied. In London, many were bought for their investment potential rather than a place to stay. The very first deal she'd done was for a mid-terrace house in Fulham. At 2.5 million, modest by the standards of the capital. Glass Houses' fees were 2.75 per cent. Nina had cleared sixty-eight thousand seven hundred and fifty pounds. Cool. Until she remembered it was her only sale in four months.

Glass Houses' fees were higher now and their enquiry-conversion rate bore comparison with just about any agent in London.

When Luke's development came on-stream, they'd clean up. And this was just the beginning.

She sipped the coffee and opened the PC to find dozens of emails, some of them from time-wasters, woolly about budget and what they expected it to buy. She recognised an address. Nina read the message and almost dropped the cup in her hand. No reason was given, no explanation and no suggestion of an alternative date.

The soulless 'Sorry' at the end felt like a careless afterthought.

Her Wednesday appointment was cancelling on her.

* * *

When I woke up on Monday morning, my eyes felt gritty and there was a hollowness in the pit of my stomach that wasn't down to Friday night: dead bodies piled in the back of a van; Jonas Small's stolen money; the Bishop cousins' pitiful attempt at coercion, and even Bridie O'Shea's insidious rendition of an IRA classic in Kilburn were part of the business I was in. Something else scratched like chalk on a blackboard inside my brain: a woman who said she was my sister had burst into my life. My reaction, once I'd stopped laughing, should've been to show her the door. After her involvement with the Lewisham and Lambeth hits, she could consider herself lucky to be getting off with her good looks intact. But I hadn't. And not because of a birth certificate that might or might not be real. Charley – if that was her name – had ignored George Ritchie's disbelieving taunts and looked straight at me, meeting my gaze without flinching. The fuck-you arrogance, the lack of fear, were all too familiar. I'd seen them often enough in Danny and Nina not to recognise them.

I'd no memory of my mother. If Charley *was* my sister, she could answer questions that had haunted me, things I'd wondered about since I was a kid. Today or tomorrow my phone would ring.

George Ritchie would be on the other end of the line confirming or rejecting her claim.

Maybe it was better not to know.

* * *

From his tone it was clear Oliver Stanford was still smarting from the reminder George Ritchie had delivered. Given a choice, he wouldn't have come. Unfortunately for Ollie, that wasn't how it worked. He hadn't liked his nice car getting done. I couldn't have cared less what Superintendent Stanford liked or disliked, so long as he did what I was paying him to do.

In sunny Hendon, he'd left off from barbequing sausages to bare his teeth at my uninvited appearance, marching me away from his well-heeled friends before I could embarrass him.

Big mistake.

He was waiting at Fulton Street, standing in the middle of the derelict factory's concrete floor, hands on his hips, clearly unhappy about being dragged south of the river, and went the surly, unhelpful route, answering only what he was asked, offering no details.

I said, 'Anything on the gang who turned my place over?'

'Nothing. Your picture drew a blank.'

'What's the word on the street?'

'There isn't one.'

'How hard have you tried?'

'I'm an officer with the Met, not a fucking magician. It isn't there.'

He was beginning to irritate me. His next statement told me some of what was really behind his attitude. 'You stopped my money.'

'So, it isn't the car that's upset you?'

'That was out of order. Elise could've found it.'

'What if she had?'

'I don't want her involved. She doesn't know what I do and she doesn't have to know.'

'How very considerate of you, Oliver. Can't have Elise in on how the bills get paid, delicate flower that she is. That would never do. She's pretty bloody good at spending it though, isn't she? No problems with that.'

Stanford was losing it. 'Your business is with me. Nobody else.'

'Then start doing what you're supposed to be doing, looking out for my interests.'

He was breathing hard, his hands shaking. I'd never seen him so angry. 'What about the money?'

I sighed. 'You really are a greedy bastard, Stanford. I'll pay you what you're worth to me. At the moment, that's fuck all. I asked you to check on Mark Douglas and you didn't.'

The policeman was defiant. 'Yes, I did. Of course, I did. He's clean.'

I could've hit him for insulting my intelligence.

'You aren't serious?'

'What do you mean?'

'Do you actually expect me to hire a fucking head of security for the whole bloody show... on that? And was I supposed to guess or were you ever going to tell me?'

He stammered, 'D-Douglas is clean... he's okay... he's—'

I could've let him off the hook; he hadn't earned it. 'Not good enough. Not even close. Put a report together and get it to me today. Any more half-arsed fucking about and you're out.'

Silence.

His voice changed; a sly smile played on his lips. 'Not a good idea, Luke. In fact, a terrible idea... for both of us.'

My turn to lose it: 'Are you threatening me, copper? Because if you are, you're making the biggest mistake of your sorry life. One of us will win and it won't be you.'

Stanford backed off. But not all the way. 'What happened to my car was too public. And it's costing a fortune in repairs. Naturally, I'm pissed. Are you surprised? Not contacting you after the hits was wrong, I've admitted that. But coming to my home in broad daylight isn't on. Let's call it a draw and put it behind us. We need each other.'

No, we didn't. He needed me. Or, more accurately, the cash landing in his offshore account every month.

'Start earning your corn, Superintendent, or—'

All the pent-up hostility, years in the making, poured out of him. 'Or what? You'll kill me? Is that what this morning was about? Because, if it was—'

I said, 'Go home, Stanford, you're not well. Time to take the pension and let somebody else have a go before you give yourself a breakdown. I've no idea what you're on about.'

He held out his trembling arm and opened his hand. 'You bastard,' he said. 'You fucking bottom-feeding bastard. What if Elise had found the car and discovered your little surprise?'

Stanford's sneer was as heartfelt as anything he'd done in his life. 'It's in the genes with you people, you can't help yourselves.'

Sunlight glinting off the bullet in his palm reminded me of the filling in Jonas Small's ugly mouth and I understood why the policeman was so upset.

Nice one, George.

* * *

Nina stood at her window, absently clicking the pen in her hand, nervously biting her lip. Across the river, the morning sun washed the gleaming white limestone of St Paul's on Ludgate Hill in warm light as the city shucked the weekend off and got back into harness.

She was anxious in ways that couldn't be explained. Selling property was a tough business, competition was fierce, cancellations were common. The capriciousness of buyers couldn't be overstated: in her experience, a deal wasn't done until the commission was in her account. Clients were more than opportunities to make a profit, they represented a ton of work and it was a bummer when one slipped away. Only, this wasn't one. It was two.

The call-offs didn't concern her so much as how they'd been done. In both cases, the emails were abrupt and impersonal; the tone of the American's last message bore no resemblance to what had gone before and might've been written by somebody else.

Algernon Drake came into her head. Usually Nina's lovers were hungry for more. She hadn't heard from Drake, perhaps because he felt humiliated. The barrister had powerful friends and a huge ego. This could be his way of hurting her. Nina pressed his number and heard it ring out.

He answered, sounding delighted. 'Nina! What a pleasant surprise. I was just thinking about you. How are you, my dear?'

'I'm fine, Algernon.'

'Algie.'

'Algie, of course.'

'Missing me already?'

What an arse he was. His performance hadn't affected his opinion of himself. Nina said, 'Thank you for a wonderful time. I'm sure you're going to love living in the flat.'

'The flat...' He seemed to have forgotten it. 'Oh, yes, I'm certain I will, though I won't hold onto it too long. I intend to punt it in a month or two. Glass Houses can handle the sale, how's that?'

'Great. I'll look forward to it.'

Drake was breathing like an asthmatic Labrador; she recalled at the height of her passion wondering if he was about to have a heart attack. Nina grimaced and held the mobile away from her ear. He said, 'Small talk is for small people, I always say. Let's dispense with it and get to the point, shall we? You want to meet me? That's usually why a woman calls a man at this time in the day. Am I right?'

He really was a disgusting letch.

She faked a giggle. 'Almost, Algie, we'll hook up very soon, I promise.'

The vagueness of her answer passed him by. 'Well, I'm here whenever you need me.'

Nina wanted to puke.

Drake said, 'Sorry, I can't chat – have a meeting in chambers with a Conservative lord who's a friend of the PM. Bloody idiot's been at it with a maid who worked for him in Eaton Place. At first, he claimed he was only helping her out. Unfortunately for His Lordship, her son's his image: blond hair, blue eyes, just like his daddy. A DNA test will end any hope he has of wheedling his way out of it. The fool had two families on the go at the same time. Can you believe it? No surprise his lady wife has kicked him out. He's staying at his club, getting drunk and making a nuisance of himself. Won't be able to afford that much longer. Divorce will ruin him, not to mention the scandal when the newspapers get wind of it. Better to admit it and salvage what can be salvaged, because that's just the tip of the iceberg. The horny bastard's been up to all sorts – prostitutes, threesomes, Soho massage parlours, you name it. If it moves, chances are he's had his Right Honourable dick in it.' He chuckled. 'Can't keep it in their trousers, these people. When will they learn, eh?'

Algernon didn't do irony.

After Drake rang off, Nina sat behind her desk and stared at the wall. She could cross off the idea the barrister had anything to do with the cancellations. Hearing his voice, remembering what she'd done with him, filled her with loathing; he could take his bloody resale somewhere else. She scrolled through her directory looking for a link between the contacts. If there was one, she didn't find it. One was local and fairly recent, the other – the New Yorker – went back to the beginning of the year.

And, now she thought about it, was there really a problem at all? In the grand scheme of things, a couple of rude no-shows meant little. She'd allowed George Ritchie – old woman that he was – to spook her. Who wouldn't be freaked with men in a car parked outside the front door, knowing that wherever you went, they were following?

She picked up the phone to call her brother. Luke would give her a roasting, there was no escape from that. Worth it if it meant Ritchie called off his dogs. Except, he wouldn't. Even raising the subject was a waste of time. Reluctantly, Nina closed her mobile down and went back to answering her emails.

* * *

The majority of enquiries were from people who'd spent Sunday trawling real-estate websites, scribbling figures, doing their best to convince themselves they could afford a house above their price range. The ones that most interested Nina had already sold and were deciding what their next postcode would be. Serious buyers. In London, it would be rare if they hadn't come out ahead and were pondering whether to continue their progress up the ladder, or settle for what they could comfortably afford and take the pressure off. Nina was in no doubt what they should do. Go for it!

Life was too short to do anything else. Her dream was a house in Holland Park and a cottage in the Cotswolds – Bourton-on-the-Water, Castle Combe, somewhere ridiculously pretty.

She was working on it.

Around ten, Nina joined the girls in the office to drink coffee and chat about what they'd all done at the weekend. Algernon Drake didn't get a mention. He'd served his purpose, just about; there would be no rematch.

She closed the door and concentrated on a couple from Crouch End looking to move nearer town, asking what 1.4 mil would get them in Islington. There was a short answer to that: not much.

A new email pinged in the inbox. She broke off thinking how to let the Crouch Enders down easily and opened it. Like the others it was terse, though it wasn't a cancellation – an offer on a two-bed terraced house in Camberwell that was all but done and dusted on Friday afternoon had been withdrawn without explanation.

Nina reached for her mobile. It was time to call Luke.

18

The good weather was still here. I drove with the window down, one hand on the wheel and Coldplay's 'Viva La Vida' blasting from the radio. On another day it would've lifted me. Mark Douglas's men were arriving later, Ritchie's reinforcements from Newcastle would already be here and Oliver Stanford would finally get off his arse and start doing what he was well paid to do.

I parked the car and went to a coffee shop near Little Portland Street, sat outside on a cane chair, sipping a macchiato espresso, and watched the world go by. For the first time, I came close to believing Ritchie and Nina had been right, that opening LBC had been recklessly ambitious.

The disappointment on Kelly's face flashed into my mind and suddenly I felt desperately sad. But that ship had sailed and today my head was out to get me.

I was at the club when my mobile rang – the first of many calls I'd be taking and making in the next few hours. Mark Douglas said, 'Just checking in. My guys are arriving at Euston station this afternoon. I'll pick them up.'

'What's their background?'

'Ex-police and special forces.'

'Before you do anything, Ritchie will check them out. You can vouch for them till the cows come home, if he doesn't clear them, they'll be on the next train back to wherever they came from. Okay?'

Douglas wasn't fazed. 'Not okay. I told you already. Either I'm in or I'm out. Your people fucked it up royally. Now the same failures are going to judge me and the guys I bring in? No chance. I'm not having that and neither will they.'

Pushing back wasn't what I'd expected from him, but if I'd been him my reaction would be the same. I let it go and moved on. 'The Bishops' money's due on Wednesday.'

'Yeah,' he said. 'Need to talk to you about that.'

'I'm listening.'

'I want to change the plan so the cash is delivered to us. That way, it won't be our responsibility until we have our hands on it in an environment we can control and defend. Anything that happens on the way isn't our problem.'

It made sense.

My sister sounded rattled. Eventually, she'd have to face me and was expecting a bollocking for her disappearing act: she wouldn't be disappointed. That wasn't what was bothering her. This was Nina. More like Danny than she'd ever admit: a vindictive hothead, never far from exploding if she imagined she was being disrespected. The last I'd heard from her was when she'd furiously ended the call on Saturday. Her attack on Ritchie was misplaced. She couldn't get over the fact George had been Rollie Anderson's right-hand man, and there was little he could do to change her mind, even if he tried, which he didn't. He hadn't come straight out and said it, but he wasn't a fan of hers, either. Ritchie had followed my orders; her complaint was actually with me. If Nina wanted to take it out on somebody, she was looking in the wrong place.

'Luke, it's me.'

I tried to keep sarcasm to a minimum and failed. 'Nice to hear from you, Nina. Where are you?'

'At the office.'

'How was your weekend? Everything okay?'

Normally, that would get me an earful. Instead, she said, 'No, everything's not okay. Three important clients have cancelled in the last twenty-four hours.'

'That's pretty common, isn't it?'

'Not like this. Not these people. I'll forward the emails and you can see for yourself.'

'All right. I'll take a look. And we need to sit down, you and me. You're a partner, you have to step up, otherwise...' I lowered my voice '... I'll cut you loose, Nina. I mean it. This is a game for big boys and girls.'

She'd already hung up.

* * *

The driver hauled himself up and unlocked the cabin, squeezed his stocky frame behind the wheel of the 'dozer, and checked the gear-stick was in neutral. Sweat beaded his forehead. Under the yellow hard hat his scalp itched but if he got caught not wearing it, he'd be in trouble. Two days of sun had compacted the criss-crossed clay ruts on what, because of the rain, was a quagmire most of the time. He pressed the rubber bulb of the ignition and waited for the powerful machine to cough into life. When it didn't, he tried again. After the third unsuccessful attempt, he climbed back down and went looking for the foreman.

* * *

No matter what time of the day or night I called him, George Ritchie answered right away.

He anticipated my question. 'Before you ask, she checks out. Congratulations, you've got another sister. It wasn't easy to track down her history on a weekend but my contacts came through.' He paused. 'How much do you want to hear?'

'How much have you got?'

'Enough to convince me she's who she says she is.'

'Then, tell me.'

'Okay.' I heard him take a deep breath. 'After she walked out on your father, your mother went to Scotland.'

'Scotland?'

Ritchie said, 'With very little money it's fair to assume her options would be limited. Presumably, she wanted to get as far away from him as possible.'

I wondered if she'd known she was pregnant.

'How soon after she did a runner was the baby born?'

'Seven and a half months in New York, like the birth certificate says.'

'New York? How the hell did she get to New York from Scotland with no funds?'

'Not such a stretch when you understand where she landed north of the border.'

Ritchie had uncovered a helluva lot. He was pleased with himself and was spinning out the information. I let him have his fun. 'Where, George?'

'Dunoon.'

'You've lost me.'

'The USA had sailors stationed at the Holy Loch. I'm guessing she met one of them just as he was about to be shipped back home.

They were living in New York when Charlene – the baby – was born. He knew he wasn't the father.'

'Because it wasn't his name on the birth certificate?'

'Yes. So, he must've been okay with it.'

I stopped him. I had even more questions than before he'd started speaking. This wasn't the time for them. 'No, no, you've convinced me.'

'What're you going to do with this?'

'Not sure.'

He said, 'The way I see it, you don't have to *do* anything. A sister you didn't know you had shows up out of the blue. So what?'

Ritchie was right, except it wasn't how I felt. 'She's family, George. That has to mean something – the importance of family is the one decent thing I got from Danny.'

His reply reminded me he'd lost family of his own along the way. 'Mmmm. Hope you know what you're letting yourself in for. Have to say, she came across as a bit of a handful.'

I hoped so, too, and changed the subject. Nina had forwarded the emails from her clients. I'd read them and agreed with her. The cancellations and how they were worded was strange. My sister understood the high-end real-estate market in this city, where the buyer had an almost endless choice. Fair play to her, she'd worked hard at it; her clients liked her. The final emails were brusque. Ritchie's take on it would be worth hearing.

I said, 'I've just had Nina on.'

'Still mad about the weekend, is she?'

'Probably, but that wasn't why she called. She's lost three clients in twenty-four hours and she's concerned because it's unusual. She's thinking something's going on and she might be right.'

Whenever he could, Ritchie ducked anything involving my sister. I heard his reluctance. 'Given what's happening, I wouldn't be surprised, though it's not much to go on. Let me have a look at them.'

An incoming call interrupted the conversation. I said, 'Hold on, George. Have to get this.'

Glass Gate was my first foray into construction. It needed a steady hand. The foreman I'd hired had been in the building game since he was sixteen and been bossing sites for ten years; he knew his stuff and pulled the trades together with the minimum of overlap. I liked that he took decisions rather than bothering me every five minutes. Thanks to him, work was on schedule. We had an on-site meeting once a week and a face-to-face in my office at the end of the month with a contract site manager. My accountants handled the paperwork. I kept an eye on the cashflow. For him to be calling was unusual and, in the light of recent events, didn't bode well.

He understood time was money and dived in. 'We've got a problem, Mr Glass. Somebody's been monkeying with the plant. Two of our machines are out. The watchman called in sick last night. It wasn't until the bulldozer wouldn't start, then one of the diggers packed in, that I took a closer look. Sure enough, a hole had been cut in the fence.'

'What's the damage?'

'Assuming it's a no-brainer, like sand in the filters, the best anybody can do is three days turnaround. It's the delay we want to avoid.'

'How much will that affect us?'

'Not as much as it would've a couple of weeks ago, though bad enough. I'll have the projections for you later.' I pictured him running a finger through his grizzled jaw. 'Funny thing is, on this job we haven't had any run-ins with the locals. That's why I wasn't worried about not having cover.'

'Do whatever you have to do. Just get it sorted, okay?'

He rang off and I went back to Ritchie. 'Some bastards fucking about with the plant at the Gate.'

'Thought you had a nightwatchman?'

'Phoned in sick. Lucky for him, or he might be lying in hospital. They cut a hole in the fence.'

'Serious?'

'Serious enough. Time really is money in that business. Which reminds me, I had a visit from a very unhappy policeman. Whining about how we're treating him. Thinks he's the injured party, can you believe it?'

'Maybe it'll encourage him to get his act together.'

'He'd bloody well better.' I laughed. 'The car was a bad start to his week. Then he checked his bank account and discovered I'd put a stop on his money. Stanford's lifestyle burns cash so that hurt. But he really didn't appreciate the bullet. You outdid yourself on that one, George.'

His silence should've warned me. It didn't. Eventually, he said, 'What bullet?'

'In the shoebox you left in Stanford's car.'

'Luke... I've no idea what you're talking about.'

The silence between us couldn't have been more ominous. With it, the pieces fell into place – the attack on LBC, the emails at Glass Houses, the machinery at the Gate and, waiting to be discovered, a bullet in a shoebox – fleshing out a picture clear enough to make sense.

We were being attacked on all fronts.

I said, 'LBC. One hour. I'll call Mark.'

19

Charley lay on the bed. It had only been two days but she was tired of waiting. Since her dramatic entrance on Saturday, George Ritchie would've been digging night and day into her background, hoping to prove she was an imposter and show her the door. Old George was wasting his time. Whether he liked it or not, she was Luke and Nina's sister – the blood in her veins identical to the blood in theirs. Conceived in south London during a drunken assault on her mother, she'd been raised in another country and called another man father, but she was Charlene Glass. Family. And she wanted her share.

* * *

I arrived first and went to my office in the basement. Usually, I didn't bring people to the windowless box in the bowels of the building, the room where the safe – the real safe, not the Mickey Mouse effort upstairs that the assassins had robbed – sat in a corner. The thieves had known the lay of the land on many fronts.

Not being aware of where the big amounts of cash were held was their only mistake. It made no difference. They'd got the briefcase with the two hundred thou inside.

Ritchie came in, pulled a chair out and sat down. We didn't speak. There was nothing to say until Mark Douglas joined us. I glanced across at George and noticed something was different about him. George Ritchie wasn't stylish and never had been; he wasn't that kind of guy. But since I was a gawky kid stealing cigarettes with my brother from corner shops and he was Albert Anderson's enforcer, he'd always paid attention to how he was dressed. Today, that wasn't true. His suit trousers were creased, the top button of the shirt underneath was undone and the tie drawn down. Unremarkable. Absolutely. Except, when I added it to the dark shadow on his jaw, it told a tale I hadn't heard before. Mr Unflappable had his mind on other things, issues more important than running a razor over his face. His eyes were red-rimmed and I remembered how quickly he'd answered my calls.

Because he hadn't slept.

* * *

Douglas pushed the door open and stood for a second, his eyes darting from me to Ritchie and back, curiosity mingling with annoyance. On the phone, Ritchie's name hadn't been mentioned and Douglas was wondering what he was doing here. He choked down whatever his feelings were, dropped his lean frame into the only other chair and waited for me to begin. In jeans and a black T-shirt, he seemed the opposite of his south side counterpart, rested and as fresh-faced as a shaving-foam model on his day off.

I brought him up to speed. 'Glass Houses has lost three clients Nina says were keen. Best guess: her computer's been hacked.'

Ritchie didn't appreciate the look Douglas shot at him. I stepped in and explained. 'Nine months ago, George hired a tech guy to install software protection. Given the nature of the business, it shouldn't have been an issue.'

'What happened?'

Ritchie answered. 'Nina takes her independence seriously. She wouldn't let him near her computers. Said she'd made her own arrangements.'

Douglas nodded. 'I'll get it checked out this afternoon and make sure it doesn't happen again. Independence is fine, unless it's a toss-up between it and your life.'

The right answer. My sister was about to meet her match.

'And plant's been vandalised on the building site.'

This time, he didn't rush to volunteer a solution. Neither did Ritchie. Douglas folded his arms across his chest and sat back, making the point that what he'd just been told had nothing to do with him. Irritation rose in me and I made a mental note to bang their heads together if they started any bloody nonsense. We needed all hands to the pumps, not some stupid power struggle while some unknown bastards dismantled what I'd built.

Douglas sensed I wasn't impressed and came in. 'Any chance it's a coincidence?'

'There's always a chance. Though it doesn't feel like it.'

Until I knew him better, Douglas didn't need to know about the copper I had in my pocket or the arrangements with my accountant.

Ritchie said, 'It could just be kids messing around. I'll put in a couple of the Newcastle guys and talk to the watchman. Find out if he really was sick when our machines were being crocked.'

This was the reaction I expected from these two.

The thought process of a Police Scotland fast-tracker revealed itself. Douglas said, 'What you've described is low-level nuisance-value stuff, intended to disrupt rather than cripple us. Nobody hurt, nothing stolen.'

Ritchie said, 'They're reminding us they're there and that it isn't over.'

George wasn't wrong. Douglas acknowledged it with a nod. 'It all goes back to Friday night. We agree the hit on the club was brutal, more violent than it needed to be. What we haven't got close to answering is why or who.'

Ritchie started to speak and changed his mind: Mark Douglas was on a roll, sifting the facts, searching for a breakthrough. He said, 'I was there. I saw them. They weren't kids. These guys were killers and I believe the damage was more important than the money. They already had that.'

'Are you saying they would've gone upstairs if you hadn't been there?'

'No, when their business is with the club, they'll go through the front door. So, let's do the first thing first. Other than you and Jonas Small, who knew about it?'

The next words out of my mouth were aimed at Douglas but sounded like an excuse. 'Paul Fallon, the head of security, insisted on bringing in his own men.'

'So, how many?'

'Me, six security people, two in the office, and Christ knows how many on Small's end.'

Douglas scratched his cheek – he'd got my jibe; his lips parted in a grim smile. 'You were wide open, and I'm going to take a wild guess you couldn't vouch for any of Fallon's guys. Were they on the payroll or was he handling them himself?'

'On the payroll.'

'Good. That gives us a chance to find out who they were connected to.'

Silence from me and George Ritchie.

Douglas said, 'The woman—'

'Rose.'

'Was she addicted to online gambling?'

He wasn't expecting an answer and didn't get one. But he'd made his point. There was too much we didn't know; we were wide open. His head bobbed thoughtfully. 'And that's before we get to Jonas Small. Who the fuck did he tell?'

Apart from his wife.

Douglas stood up and went walkabout. He stopped his tour of the office and turned towards me. 'In terms of protecting ourselves, between Glass Gate and Glass Houses, we're stretched. Add the club and the problem doubles. Throw in the cast of *Ben Hur*, large amounts of money arriving late at night, and we're not exactly difficult to hurt, especially with help from the inside.'

I guessed George Ritchie wasn't keen to hear any of this, neither was I, yet there was no denying it. I blamed myself for running before we could walk. Our businesses had grown; the security around them hadn't.

Mark Douglas shared a stare between us. He'd told the truth, uncomfortable as it was. Only a fool would bury their head in the sand. He said, 'I want your permission to make the necessary changes. As it stands, we're in the dark on just about everything. We could be hit anywhere. From today, that won't be the case.'

I said, 'What do you want?'

'The guys Paul Fallon brought are history. After tomorrow, they'll no longer work at the club. We need better. As I said, the next assault could just as easily come through the front door.' He caught the look on my face. 'Only until this threat's behind us. There are men in this city who understand what's required without having it spelled out for them.'

'What else?'

'To begin with, let's assume there was a leak and that it came from our end. My guys will have a look at who Fallon brought in and narrow it down. We can figure it out from there. Meantime, George is handling Glass Gate and I'll deal with Nina.'

Under my breath I wished him luck.

Mark Douglas was a fox. 'And we don't ferry the cash. Not any more. It's too dangerous. Nothing but downside in it for us. Your... associates... will deliver it.'

When he'd told me on the phone it had made sense. Unfortunately, it wasn't the deal I had with Small and the others; they wouldn't be best pleased. Douglas said, 'We – you – can't be expected to cover for them every time they put cash into the system. Again, at least until we're swimming in clear water, the arrangement has to change. Will that be a problem?'

'If it is, they can fuck off and find a better deal.'

The meeting had gone on longer than I'd imagined. Mark Douglas had taken charge and acquitted himself well. By comparison, Ritchie, taciturn on a good day, hadn't contributed very much. Now, he said, 'Can I remind you there's been nothing on the south side?'

The old stag was making his presence felt, pawing the ground, telling us he was still a force. But his memory was selective – no mention of Lewisham or Lambeth.

'And your point is, George?'

'We've had no problem south of the river and haven't had in the three years since Danny left.'

'How is that relevant? Every major player in London stands to benefit from the club. Thanks to LBC, they'll all do very nicely.'

Ritchie was working up to something. I wished he'd just come out with it. In the time I'd known him he'd been confident in his ability and his professionalism. Oblique references to his performance weren't how he normally behaved. He'd been against LBC from the beginning – that was no secret – about the only thing him and Nina agreed on. At the door, he turned and sowed doubt on an already uncertain situation.

'If it's just about money, I believe you. What if it isn't?'

20

I'd watched Danny deal with people and wondered why he was aggressive from the off, sometimes before they'd even opened their mouths. Now I got it. Holding onto what he'd built was as much about perception as anything. Now, I got that, too.

The man on the other end of the line could do surly for England; Colin Bishop had answered his cousin's phone. Talking to him – about anything – was a waste of breath and I was tempted to end the call. But this was Monday afternoon. In two days, the Bishops were expecting their money to be picked up. They weren't going to like what I had to tell them.

'What?'

I didn't introduce myself; the fewer words spent on this guy, the better.

'Put Kenny on.'

He recognised my voice. 'Am I not good enough for you, Glass?'

I resisted. 'Just put Kenny on.'

'Speak to me.'

It had taken less than twenty seconds to want to strangle the stroppy bastard with my bare hands. I said, 'Put your cousin on and stop fucking about.'

'He isn't here.'

Colin Bishop was an arsehole with everybody – I didn't take it to heart.

'Tell you what, Colin, forget it. When it happens, you can explain it to him.'

That got his attention.

'When what happens?'

'Never mind. Tell Kenny I called.'

'Hold it. He's around somewhere.'

The conversation was childish, typical of Colin Bishop, though more than enough to confirm what I already knew: somebody motivated could neutralise the cousins' power. North London looked like it belonged to them. In fact, it was ripe for a takeover; these clowns wouldn't get their act together to resist a serious assault. It wasn't in my plans. I had plenty to be getting on with. On another day, that might not be the case.

In the background, a bad-tempered exchange, like a couple of old queens in a 1960s Joe Orton play, ended with a door slamming. With these two, it never stopped.

Kenny Bishop was less of a wanker than his cousin. That said, he was still a knob. He came across, cheery and bright, as if we were pals who hadn't seen each other in a while. Maybe he'd forgotten the meeting the day before in Little Venice – I certainly hadn't: on the towpath, when his boozed-up partner had threatened me, he'd stood back and let him get on with it.

'Luke. Didn't expect to hear from you so soon.'

'We need a face-to-face.'

He laughed as if I'd said something funny. 'We must stop meeting like this, people will talk, eh?'

I'd no idea who his godawful chat appealed to. It definitely wasn't me.

'Fancy another stroll along the canal? Sink a few in The Bridge House, maybe?'

'No, you come to me. LBC at three.'

'My, my, you are in a hurry.'

'And before you get within a mile of the place, get your cousin to button it. He's gone after me twice, Kenny. Three will be once too many.'

* * *

Nina looked around at what she'd created. A lot of money had been spent here and it showed. The office on the fifth floor was impressive: burgundy sofas and outsized coffee tables casually strewn with copies of this month's *Tatler, Elite Traveler,* and *Bespoke* – a Middle Eastern magazine published in English aimed at high-net-worth individuals from the Arab world. Her eyes settled on the bank of screens, continuously showcasing houses and flats the company had brokered, and the reception desk – an eye-catching Perspex cuboid housing a scale model of Luke's new luxury property development, Glass Gate. He was building it; her company would sell it.

When he'd come out of Wandsworth, Luke had told her he intended to leave London and start fresh somewhere new. If he had, everything she was seeing here would never have been born and she'd be the oldest rebel south of the river, working for Danny and hating every minute of it.

None of that had happened. Instead of turning his back on the whole bloody lot, Luke had taken over from their lunatic brother and discovered he was a natural. But he wasn't the same man she'd visited twice a month for seven years – and maybe that was to be expected. Heading the family business demanded everything he had. There was a woman somewhere in the background, though he rarely spoke about her. Shelley... Kelly... something like that.

The thought hit home; her selfishness embarrassed her and she felt her face flush. Since Danny, she'd acted like a spoiled child, happy enough to spend the money, yet reluctant to take responsibility for anything beyond Glass Houses.

Ridiculous. Stupid. She was a partner, for Christ's sake. It was her name on the licence.

The attack on Friday night was a tipping point. Just when Luke needed her, she'd left the club to meet Algernon Drake of all fucking people. That kind of behaviour had to stop. Someone was coming after them. Her brother couldn't do it by himself.

Nina was at her desk when her mobile rang. Luke wasted no time on small talk and she realised he was still angry with her. She got in ahead of him. 'You're on to tell me our meeting's cancelled, right?'

He ignored her friendly jibe. 'Wrong. And don't be late. It's important.'

All her life Nina had baulked at admitting she was wrong; saying sorry didn't come easily to her, but an apology was overdue. 'Listen... about the weekend.'

Luke shied away from whatever she had to say; she heard the tiredness in his voice. 'I don't want to hear it, Nina. I really don't.'

'Please, listen. Let me get this out. You're my brother. If you can't depend on me, who can you depend on? And I haven't been there for you. For the family. I've been out of it. But I want you to know that from now on, I'm all in – 100 per cent.'

The silence seemed to go on forever. She began to regret allowing him to see her vulnerability. Inside her, the old Nina rose to rail at him.

Luke beat her to it, speaking quietly, almost tenderly. 'We've all been out of it, not just you. Even George Ritchie. We've had the south side to ourselves. It's been too easy. We've got lazy and slow. Ripe. Somebody's reminding us if we want to keep what's ours, we have to fight for it. I'm ready for that fight.'

'So am I.'

'Good to know.'

Nina smiled down the line and whispered the words Danny had used whenever it had looked like he was losing them. 'Team Glass?'

Luke laughed. 'A step too far, maybe. If I ever pull that crap you have my permission to give me a slap. I'm just glad to have my sister back. Let's quit while we're ahead. I called to tell you Mark Douglas is on his way to you.'

'Who?'

'Mark Douglas. The guy who saved our arses on Friday night. I've hired him.'

Nina felt a thrill of excitement run through her. 'Celebrity Security?'

'The very same. Paul Fallon's dead. Douglas proved he's got the stuff, so he's in. We're being attacked on all fronts. Your cancelled clients are the tip of the iceberg. We have to establish how much damage has been done. Work with him, Nina. And when Douglas arrives remember he's on our side and don't fuck him about.'

* * *

Traffic made travelling any distance in London a nightmare. Mark Douglas edged through the capital, stopping and starting every few minutes. He'd spent most of the afternoon lining up a new security team to replace the jokes that poor bastard Paul Fallon had brought in. Nina Glass would be expecting him. He hadn't forgotten her or their conversation, heavy with sensuality. In other circumstances his response would've been to take her up on her offer. Except Nina was Luke Glass's sister.

The guy in the passenger seat held onto the strap of the canvas bag he always carried, his unkempt beard and wispy moustache giving him the look of a left-wing activist or, more accurately, a geek with a degree in computer science and the only guy Mark Douglas would let within a mile of this stuff.

His question was an attempt at conversation rather than a genuine enquiry.

'We looking for anything in particular?'

Douglas kept his eyes on the road. 'Somebody is noising us up, accessing confidential information. So, like I told you on the phone, we need everything checked and swept – offices, the staff, Luke and Nina's flats.'

He almost added George Ritchie's lair above the King of Mesopotamia pub and changed his mind – the old guy knew the score.

'Paul Fallon was Head of Security. I want to find out how good a job he did.'

'Where is he?'

'He's dead.'

He nodded and went back to staring out of the window.

* * *

Nina was in her office at the far end of the room, on the phone, pacing the floor, her head bobbing as she spoke to whoever was on the other end of the line. When she saw them coming towards her, she cut the call short and waved.

Mark Douglas was struck by how little she resembled the lady in the club. The provocative vamp had been remodelled. Her hair was swept up. She wore a cream blouse, a navy-blue two-piece suit and modest heels. Nina smiled and held out her hand. Douglas took it but caught a trace of wariness in the corners of her eyes. Understandable. Her business was under siege.

He said, 'We met in LBC.'

'Luke told me you were coming. How's this going to work?'

It wasn't just the outfit that had changed. There was no sign of the smouldering seductress.

Douglas turned to the techie. 'You might as well get started.'

He closed the door and Nina asked, 'What's he going to do?'

'Check everything, including your people. It's early days and, so far, we haven't a clue who's behind the hits or whether they've burrowed inside the operation. But they're pros, no doubt about that.'

Nina might not have heard. She watched stone-faced as her staff handed over their mobiles and stepped back from the computers. The corner of her mouth turned down and Mark Douglas realised what was on her mind. 'You're thinking one of them might be working against you. You could be right. Everybody's the enemy, until we can prove they're a friend.'

Douglas reassured her. 'Chances are, they're not involved. But we only get this one opportunity to surprise them if the leak came from this office.' He pointed to the bearded techie. 'Introduce us as security experts, which means when your people hate somebody, it won't be you. Tell them hacking has been reported, and this is a necessary precaution. Then, send them home. You'll see them tomorrow. They can have their mobiles back as soon as they've been checked.'

'What, you think somebody's bugging their phones?'

'It's possible, though it's really who they've contacted we're after.' He held out his up-turned palm. 'And I'll take your phone, if you don't mind.'

'How long will your guy be?'

Mark Douglas shrugged. 'Two or three hours, hard to say. Why?'

'I'm meeting Luke at five. That gives us time for a drink.' She smiled. The vamp from the club was back. 'Of course, if you're too busy...'

* * *

I was in the bar drinking soda and lime when the Bishops arrived. Today was their first time in LBC and, by the looks on their faces, maybe the first time they'd been anywhere that didn't have linoleum on the floor, Formica on the tables and a spittoon within gobbing distance. Individually, they were rich; together the cousins were worth a fortune. But money could only buy so much; under the skin they were still a couple of thugs from Chalk Farm – unsophisticated, not very bright bully-boys, who'd cornered the market in hookers and drugs from Enfield to Barnet and everywhere in between.

The meet would be short: I'd do the talking. They'd do the listening. That wasn't negotiable. Neither was what I was about to tell them.

Colin picked up where he'd left off on the canal towpath, angry and belligerent. 'All right, Glass, we're impressed. Now, why the hell're we here?'

I spoke to his partner. 'Your cousin's been watching too many tough-guy movies, Kenny. Remind him he's in my drum. Tell him to show some respect before I break his fucking arm.'

Kenny Bishop laid a restraining hand on his cousin's shoulder. 'He doesn't get out much, Luke. He's easily excited; can't help himself. But he does have a point.'

'The plan for Wednesday has changed.'

Colin fell on it like a hungry rat. 'What do you mean *changed*?'

'It isn't happening, at least, not the way it's set up.'

Kenny pursed his lips – this wasn't what he wanted to hear. 'Because of Friday night? But that was a one-off, wasn't it?'

'Was it? Are you sure about that? Because I'm not. From now on the mountain comes to Muhammad.'

My mangled quote went over Colin's head. 'Muhammad? What're you on about, mate?'

Kenny explained it. 'He's saying they're not collecting the cash.'

'Then, who does?

I put him out of his misery. 'You do.'

It took a moment to register before the moron said, 'That's not what we agreed.'

'We're shaking it up, Colin.' I spread my arms. 'Mea culpa. It's got to be done. Suppose they go after it at your place, you ready for that?'

He wasn't happy. When was he ever? 'You can't go altering the terms.'

'I just have. Somebody's on to us. Should we carry on as we are and let them do us again?'

Colin turned to his cousin. 'I don't like this, Kenny. This guy's moving the goalposts. He thinks—'

I'd had enough. 'Tell you what, boys, forget it. My advice: if you find a better deal, take it. See yourselves out.'

Colin's bloated frame strained the buttons of his jacket. He'd pushed me over the edge and lost them their deal. He let his partner do the talking – a pity he hadn't thought about it earlier; he was about five minutes too late. Kenny saw the arrangement that would make them richer than they already were slipping away. 'It won't do any good to be hasty. Everybody, calm down, and Colin, shut the fuck up. How many times do I have to tell you?'

Inside, I smiled. On the Regent's Canal he'd been fine about his mad-dog relation having a go. Today, Kenny Bishop was sober and the greedy bastard in him didn't want to miss out. Suddenly, he was the peacemaker, gently gripping my arm to reassure me there was no problem, that everything was fine.

He waited until it was safe to continue. 'Luke, you aren't cool with what's agreed. Okay. I understand. But maybe you're overreacting. What're the odds on getting done again?'

I had an answer for him. 'The odds, Kenny? The odds are zero. Because we won't be coming. Wednesday's a bust. Don't expect us. On Thursday, I'll call with new instructions. Have the cash ready. And if that doesn't work for you...'

The Bishops were up against it, finally realising Luke Glass wasn't compromising.

Kenny said, 'We'll make it work.'

Colin wanted to speak – behind his idiot face, the cogs were grinding. I goaded him, praying that, no matter what was at stake, he wouldn't be able to put a sock in it and I'd have the excuse I was looking for to take him apart. The outward signs of an internal battle were visible – Bishop breathed hard through his nose, his teeth ground together and his thick neck flushed red.

I saw it and said, 'One word, just one, and I'll drag you back to Chalk Farm by your fucking balls, fat boy.'

21

I'd pushed the question of a second sister to the back of the queue of issues shouting for my attention. George Ritchie confirming the birth certificate was genuine had left me no way out. Charlene, or Charley as she preferred to be called, was a Glass.

The news brought no rush of emotion, no longing to hug her and welcome her into the family. But from the moment she'd breezed into the office above the King Pot, in my heart I'd known. Nina hadn't been told. Without proof, it was better for all concerned she wasn't in the loop. Nina's assurances she'd changed didn't convince me. She was still a headstrong teenager hiding behind the self-assured woman she'd become. Discovering she had a sister would be one helluva shock.

Heels clacked and echoed in the stairwell. At the door, she paused, lowered her head and smiled at me. She was wearing black skin-tight leggings, underneath a long red blouse.

Charley pulled her hair to one side and sat down. 'I'm here, so I'm guessing that means you realise I'm telling the truth.'

I cut the performance short. 'Don't read too much into it. What do you want?'

I was giving her a hard time. Deliberately. She was a Glass – she'd proved it – in my book that meant she was in. You only got one chance to set the boundaries and I already had a stroppy sister. I didn't need two.

The question surprised her. 'I should've thought that was obvious.'

Everything about her was obvious – but she had style, I'd give her that.

'Listen, we're talking. That's further than many people get. Top tip: don't blow it. I'll ask again: what're you doing here? What do you want? I mean, really want?'

'I want a job. Not to be too pushy, I want to be a part of whatever's going on.'

My turn to do the smiling: 'Take a ticket and wait your turn, is that how you think this works? All you need is the right name and the rest falls into your lap?'

Charley sighed and looked away.

I said, 'Sorry, am I boring you?'

She ignored me and pulled out cigarettes and a lighter. 'Mind if I smoke?'

'As a matter of fact, I do. You've got one minute to convince me why I shouldn't kick your fat arse into the street. Starting now.'

She had her response ready. 'Because you can use somebody like me.'

'Not if playing the long-lost-sister card is all you've got.'

'Even long-lost sisters have to pull their weight, and I will.'

I sat back, trying to get a handle on her. She wasn't overawed, confidence oozed out of her and, again, it was impossible not to catch the resemblance to Nina and Danny. She leaned forward, as if she had a secret to tell. I stayed where I was and let her do her thing – it had got her this far.

'Our mother died eighteen months ago. Big surprise. She left some money. I could've come to London then. You should be wondering why I've waited. And why I tried so hard to get your attention.'

'Let me guess – the cash is running out.'

'Wrong. I've known about the three of you for thirty years. I'm here because this is the time.'

'The time?'

'At the end of the day, family trumps everything and I'm ready to be part of mine.'

Nice speech. Tugging on the old heart strings, but not too much. I folded my arms and looked at her. 'You see, Charley, you've had the advantage. You knew about us. We didn't know about you. Maybe we're not ready.'

This woman had had a game plan from the beginning – now, she was rolling it out. 'I hear you need all the help you can get. Apparently, I'm not the only one who's found flaws in your set-up.'

Her first misstep. Just when I was starting to like her.

The amusement left her eyes. 'Face it, Luke, you need me. LBC has been open six months with Nina fronting it. With respect, she doesn't have what it takes, you must know that.'

'And you do?'

The red lips parted in a smile I was getting used to. 'If you have to ask, I've overestimated you. And that would be a shame because a sister likes to look up to her brother.' Charley leaned closer. 'You aren't going to disappoint me, are you?'

* * *

Nina didn't do sorry. If she'd had a Paul-on-the-road-to-Damascus revelation, I'd take it. Some people never really grew up. I'd resigned myself to the fact she was one of them and was happy to be proved wrong.

She kissed me on the cheek and sat down. She seemed happy and relaxed. Of course, she didn't know the bombshell I was about to lay on her, otherwise her mood would've been very different. Charley was upstairs in the bar, waiting for my call. Even in our dysfunctional family, being 'the little sister' counted for something and all her life Nina had traded on it shamelessly to wheedle what she wanted out of her brothers. Her new status would take some getting used to and I wasn't convinced she'd willingly relinquish her crown.

I began in neutral. 'How did your staff take to getting kicked out?'

She shrugged. 'Security comes first.'

'Douglas hasn't come across anything that shouldn't be there, so far.'

Nina frowned. 'No idea if that's good or bad. It's never simple, is it?'

She could say that again.

'Okay, why am I here?' She settled herself ready for the big reveal. 'You said it was important.'

'It is. Very.'

'Let me guess. You've found somebody to front the club.' Nina laughed. 'I spotted her in the bar. Not your type – you prefer skinny – so she can't be your girlfriend. Am I right? Got the stuff, has she?'

Once she'd met Charley, she'd never ask that question again. I stayed low-key. 'She'll do the job, if that's what you mean.'

'Are we going to interview her?'

'Not exactly.'

'What the hell does that mean? Either we are or we aren't.'

'We aren't. I've hired her.'

Nina glanced away and back again. 'Well, thanks for dragging me across London for nothing. Could've told me that on the phone.'

'I could've, except there's more.'

She shifted in her seat. 'Well, spit it out or do I have to guess?'

There was no easy way to tell her.

'Her name's Charley. She's our sister.'

The only sound in the room was the air-con droning in the background. I wanted to take her in my arms, but didn't – she had to come to terms with this herself. Her world, so much of what she'd thought she understood, was turning upside down and she was too stunned to speak. Instinct kicked in and I saw her silently rail against truth beyond her control. Her mouth worked; no words came. Her life had changed and there was nothing either of us could do about it.

Danny was gone. Three had become two – me and Nina. With Charley, we were back to three. It hadn't worked before. Why would this time be any better? I could see advantages – the reason I'd offered Charley a job – but Nina was a girl who went her own way in all things; she would be harder to convince, and, on the other side of the desk, she quietly ground her teeth.

I felt for her. She'd put whatever was going on with her clients aside and arrived determined to commit to the business for maybe the first time. Across the table, shock morphed into anger; tears weren't far away. Until now, the questions that came unbidden in the middle of the night had been pushed away and, like me, she'd got on with it. The existence of the woman upstairs in the bar made it impossible to run from that part of our lives any longer and we were being forced to confront the heartbreaking fact we'd avoided head-on.

Our mother had abandoned us.

No matter how many times I'd asked, Danny had refused to talk about it. Had carrying that around in his head turned him into the monster he became?

Then, what about me?

What about Nina?

She raised her chin defiantly, fighting down the emotions threatening to drown her – the reaction I'd expected. Days earlier, mine had been no different. Denial had taken Nina this far, why not further? Except, how we felt – unloved, rejected, judged and found wanting by a woman who should've cherished us and all the complex, complicated rest of it – was an open sore, a wound that had never healed. Until we faced it, it never would.

I said, 'Ritchie checked her out. She's Charlene Glass – Frances Glass was her mother. She has a birth certificate to prove it.'

'It could be a fake.'

'It could be, Nina, but it isn't. Wait till you see her – for Christ's sake, it's like looking at Danny. I'll get her to join us and you can judge for yourself.'

'Do what you like, I don't want to meet her. I don't believe we have a sister.'

We both understood she didn't mean it. This was the one chance to find out if our mother ever regretted leaving us behind. Neither of us would be walking away from that, though Charley had picked a helluva time to land this in our lap.

Nina turned her resentment on me. 'How long have you known?'

'Nina...'

'How fucking long?'

'Days. Just days.'

'She contacted you?'

'No. The hits on Lewisham and Lambeth were her.'

The latest in many surprises.

'What? I thought...'

'They were tied to the club. We all did. They weren't. She put it together.'

'Why?'

'To get our attention. Let us see she had the stuff. But she's made an enemy in George Ritchie. He hates her for showing how slack the operation's got in the last three years.' Remembering frustrated me. I ran a hand through my hair and carried on. 'Nobody's covered in glory here. We've been asleep. Charley's determined to wake us up.'

I reached out my hand. Nina didn't take it. 'She's a couple of decades too late. What the hell does she want?'

'Good question. Why don't you ask her?'

* * *

They say knowledge is power. That made Charley the strongest person in the room, because she could answer the questions we'd dragged around with us all our lives. It should've been liberating, exciting. It wasn't. Not knowing had allowed us to build fantasy excuses for why our mother had left three kids behind when she fled her husband. The truth might blow that away and I wasn't sure I was ready.

Charley sat silently watching us, her painted fingers clasped in her lap. I wondered what was going through her mind. When she was putting the plan together to make her grand entrance, was this how she'd pictured it ending? Beyond a job, I'd promised her nothing yet, in a room full of big personalities, her presence dominated. I gave us all time to adjust to the new reality, if that's what it was. Nina's lip curled at the corner, her features twisted like she was smelling something bad and there was a look in her eyes I recognised – I'd been on the receiving end of it plenty of times. Today, it was someone else's turn. She'd held back longer than I'd expected and wasn't interested in adjusting. She might never get there but the first words out of her mouth showed she wasn't messing around, either. 'If you're here, does that mean she's dead?'

Charley kept her answer short. 'Yes.'

'When?'

'Eighteen months back.'

'Where?'

'Upstate New York.'

'What happened to her?'

For the first time, hesitation. 'You don't want to know.'

The anger that wasn't far from the surface flashed. 'Don't tell me what I want to know. I'm asking what happened.'

'A fire. Frances smoked forty Marlboro every day of her life and finally succeeded in doing what she'd been threatening. She went to bed out of it, lit one last cigarette and closed her eyes.'

'Were you in the house?'

'No, I'd left.'

'Why?'

Charley chose her words: this was her show. 'We had issues. Frances wasn't the easiest woman to rub along with. Your daydreams of how it was are way off the mark. Whatever it says on the birth certificate, I didn't like her. You wouldn't have liked her, either.'

'Did she ever talk about us?'

Charley could've dipped her reply in sugar, fed it to Nina in small bites and she would've eaten it. She didn't. A low humourless sound saved for just this moment started deep inside her.

'When you can stand it, I'll tell you what she was really like. And, trust me, you won't feel so sorry for yourselves.'

Nina's need was greater than mine. She said, 'I've waited my whole life. Tell me now.'

Charley kept her eyes on her, assessing the impact of what she had to say, knowing it would be devastating. At the time, I was too caught in the moment to think about it. Later, I would realise she could've said anything, made up a lie, a string of lies if she'd wanted to minimise Nina's pain. That wasn't where Charley was at with this. She tilted her head and raised her chin the way I'd seen Danny do hundreds of times.

'Oh, she talked all right. Sometimes all she did was talk. Just not to me. Lying in bed in the room next door to me, drunk, raving for hours about the past. I'd never met my father but I knew all about him because she screamed his name and accused him of every sin under the sun. After her second marriage ended, she hauled me across one state after another. I had my sixth birthday in Tulsa, my tenth in a trailer on the Gulf Coast. By fifteen, we were back north living in a hovel on the outskirts of Chicago, the only white folks in an all-black neighbourhood and she was the busiest hooker in the 'hood.'

Charley paused. 'Getting the picture?'

We didn't answer and she got to the point. 'You're asking did she regret leaving her children. The answer is, no, not once, not ever.'

I saw hurt flood Nina's face. So did Charley. It didn't move her to soften her tale; her lips pressed in a crimson line and she delivered the killer blow. 'As far as Frances was concerned, she was better off without you – all of you. All of us. She only took me because I was in her belly.'

It was a harsh assessment, in its own way as shocking as anything we'd heard. Unlike Nina and me, Charley had had a lifetime to come to terms with it.

I spoke for the first time. 'When did you suss that out?'

'As soon as I could put two thoughts together.'

'How did you feel?'

She turned her dark-brown eyes on me. 'About the same as you do right now.'

'So how did you know about us?'

Charley shook her head. 'Still chasing an idea of the perfect mother, aren't you? You've carried this image of a woman you barely recall, whose claim to fame is that she gave birth to you. Didn't need anybody to tell you about your old man. You remembered him, all right, and had her pegged as trapped and helpless. You've spent your lives making up excuses to justify what she did to you.'

Charley grunted in lieu of a laugh and examined her manicured nails. 'And along I come and spoil the party with the uncomfortable truth. Our mother was a drunk and a whore and if she'd fucked off and left me, I would've thanked God for cutting me a break. As it was, I got out of there as fast as I could. Two days before my sixteenth birthday.'

She'd carried the pain of being our mother's daughter alone and needed to offload it.

Nina said, 'You said she died. If you weren't there, how did you know?'

'An old neighbour kept in touch and told me there was a fire. The liquored-up bitch had burned the boarding house she was staying in down. The landlord identified her body.'

Charley gave us a minute to take it in; there was no warmth in her eyes and I believed she'd been holding onto her little speech a long time. The chance to say it had finally come; she'd seized it with both hands. Maybe for her, it squared the account. It had done nothing for Nina – she seemed to have grown smaller, hugging herself like a child. She didn't cry but she would. When she was alone. What we'd just been told was worse, far worse, than Danny, me or Nina had imagined. Leaving us behind had cost our mother nothing because she didn't love us. It was going to take a while to process and I didn't have room for it right now.

Charley said, 'Hard to imagine you were better off without her, but you were. Look what you've become.'

I said, 'None of that explains how you found us.'

She brushed something off her clothes with a flick of her wrist. 'Over the years I pieced it together. Drunks say things they don't remember the next day. I was sober. I remembered everything. Don't mourn her, she wasn't worth it, though I can see from your faces you hate me for what I've told you. You should be thanking me. Daniel and Frances Glass were our parents. Two flawed people who produced four exceptional kids. The three of you and me. You got stuck with him. Believe me, you got the best of it. You had each other. I had no one but myself.'

I looked at them, sitting opposite me: sister No 1 and sister No 2. As alike and as dissimilar as it was possible to be. Charley, a super-confident rough diamond, and Nina, a damaged teenager hiding in a sophisticated woman's body. What they had in common was me and a shared future. There were interesting times ahead, that was for sure, as these women vied for pole position: one clinging to something she believed was her right, the other determined to have what had been denied her. Suddenly, I was relieved the secret sibling hadn't been a boy.

The final word was mine and I was determined to have it. They weren't so very different. Not at all: under the skin, they were children carrying a lifelong hurt, each believing the other had had it easier than them.

I knew. Because that was me, too.

I spoke to Charley. 'Trading horror stories – and be sure, we have ours – won't take us where we want to go. Danny did a lot of stuff, most of it you don't want to know, except he was right about one thing. He believed in family.'

Nina said, 'When it suited him.'

I ignored her and carried on. 'Danny's gone and isn't coming back. We – the three of us – are what's left. Who did this, who got that... none of it matters. What does is in this room: Luke and Nina and Charley.'

Nina cocked her head to one side; she was listening. Charley's expression didn't alter; she'd come expecting a fight and wasn't getting one. Blood alone wouldn't be enough – she'd earn her place or it would end – but for the moment, she was in.

I said, 'We can waste time chewing over old bones, resenting, even hating each other, and that's okay. But don't forget what we've achieved. We came from nowhere – fucking less than nowhere – now we own south London. And we aren't finished. Not by a long shot. We'll succeed because, at the end of the day, we're family. The Glass family. Nothing and nobody beats that.'

22

The last few days had been a bastard. I'd spread myself too thin and was feeling it. Unfortunately, the drama was far from over. Three years of peace had lulled me into a sense of security that had blown up in my face: somebody out there had gone out of their way to damage me. I was hurting. Down 200 K and the game hadn't long started. Losing the larger players would be bad news – avoiding that happening was crucial. Later, I'd call Bridie O'Shea and explain the change of plan; the old rebel was a pragmatist, a lady you could do business with, so I wasn't expecting a hard time. The Bishops made a noise – didn't they always? In the end, all they were being asked to do was deliver their own money, for Christ's sake. From then on, the risk was with me. But the real opposition would be the guy I was meeting next. My promise to cover the loss hadn't stopped him humming and hawing and scratching around the edges of Danny dropping out of sight, all the while treating me like his favourite nephew, almost a friend.

Except, I knew better: Jonas Small didn't have friends; he had interests.

I parked in Flat Iron Square and walked to Borough Market. From his voice on the phone, I'd guessed Jonas Small had been expecting to hear from me. He'd spoken quietly, deliberately, the gravel in his tone less harsh, and I wondered if he'd cut the smoking down from a hundred to just the sixty a day.

It was early, his 'Indian' restaurant wouldn't be open, so we arranged to meet in Southwark – a compromise between his part of London and mine.

I saw him before he saw me, leaning against a wall outside The Market Porter pub, his hands thrust into the trouser pockets of the same king of comedy suit he'd had on in Brick Lane. The cigarette dangling from his lips and the butts on the ground at his feet told me I'd been wrong about a change in his habits. When he finally noticed me, he took a last puff, crushed the smoke under the heel of his shoe and stood upright. We'd agreed to come alone. I hadn't stuck to it and I'd bet neither had Jonas. Trust had to be earned. With him, it never would be. He smiled – but then he always smiled – waited for me to reach him, fell in step beside me and asked a question I wasn't remotely interested in answering.

'Lukie boy! Did you know there's been a market here for nigh on a thousand years?'

Small could do both sides of a conversation and often did. Listening was optional, somebody else speaking just a pause to let him gather his thoughts.

'Yeah. A thousand years. Love a good market. A while back, some poor bugger got poked in the eye with an umbrella here. Died, he did.'

Jonas was at his chatty best, firing out obscure pieces of information to an audience who couldn't have cared less. With his scattergun chat and the loud clothes, it would be easy to write him off – I wouldn't make that mistake.

He admired the elegant glass and metal façade at the entrance, at odds with the industrial architecture of the rest of the place, and held out his arms. 'Bloody marvellous, ain't it? Makes you proud to be a Londoner. The Market Porter opens at six o'clock in the morning if you're ever choking. Strike that. Forgot who I was talking to.'

We strolled between the stalls. Two or three traders recognised him and waved; he waved back. Jonas stopped to examine a display of apples and bananas and said something I didn't hear to the woman behind the stand. She laughed and he lifted a peach, pressed the soft flesh and pulled a coin from his waistcoat. She shooed his money away and we walked on.

Small bit into the peach and for a moment he was quiet. Juice ran between his tobacco-stained fingers onto the ground from the fruit he'd never intended to pay for: a tiny deception but a massive clue to his character. He was a conman, and he was good at it.

He weighed the peach in his palm. 'My wife's clairvoyant, did I tell you that?'

'Don't think you did, Jonas, no.'

'Yeah. She can see the future. Fucking spooky sometimes. Knows what I'm going to say before I do.' He nodded at the wonder of it. 'This morning, I'm coming out the door and she says "He wants out of the deal. You mark my words, Jonas, Luke Glass wants out."'

His moustache was damp, a fragment of peach flesh lodged in his beard, but his eyes were clear. '"He wants out." Her very words, as God's my judge. You going to tell me she's right? That you got me here to call it off?'

'No, not at all.'

He exhaled, like something heavy had been taken off him, took out a packet of B & H and lit one.

Small laughed, a reminder of the wolf's head on Aldgate Pump. 'Not looking forward to telling Lily she was off the mark. Then again, there's a first time for everything, ain't there? I'm well pleased to hear it. *Very* pleased. Our arrangement got off to a shaky start, no denying it, but backing out... not how business is done. Couldn't see Danny backing out.'

The peach stone dropped to the ground; he kicked it away with his foot and looked back along the line of stalls. Our acquaintance had been mercifully short, though I knew him enough to realise something was coming. I wasn't wrong. He stroked his bearded chin, as if a blinding flash of insight had arrived and he was about to share it. He rested his hand on my shoulder like an uncle offering wise counsel. 'This money thing with the club. It's good. In fact, it's excellent. Except it won't work. Not in the long run.'

'Really?'

'Yeah, really.' He sounded sad. 'The risk's too high. Just been proved, hasn't it? Two hundred grand down the fucking Swanee. And, okay, you'll cover it this time.' He waved a questioning finger in my face. 'But it's a big nut to swallow. I wouldn't do it. No chance I'd bloody do it. Not twice.'

'What is it you're saying, Jonas?'

Small searched for the words in the air above me. 'We're vulnerable. Some bastard's already taken advantage. Others will see that and get... encouraged, understand what I mean?' He waited to let it sink in, his mitt massaging my shoulder. 'We could make a nice few bob or we could come a right cropper.'

'That's business, Jonas.'

'True, true, although it doesn't have to be that way. If we pooled our resources there isn't a firm in London who'd dare come within a mile of us without getting their balls shot off.' He hooked his fingers into his waistcoat pockets and puffed out his chest. 'Strength in numbers. Oldest defence in the world. 'Course, the percentages would need to change to accommodate the new arrangement. Fifty-fifty sounds about right. That said, to sweeten it and since you've done the donkey work getting the club up and running, I'm prepared to consider sixty-five-thirty-five. No, I tell a lie. Sixty-forty.'

He couldn't be serious. Except, he was.

In the restaurant in Brick Lane, I'd gone along with his stream of consciousness bullshit.

And I'd listened to enough of it.

I spoke slowly, choosing the words so there would be no misunderstanding. 'Jonas, let's you and me get one thing straight. I'm not Danny. He has no part in this. You're dealing with me. Understand? Me. Luke Glass. If you're not comfortable with that we'll go our own way and no hard feelings. But another fucking word about my brother and it's all in the bin. Danny's in Spain or Portugal or wherever he is, I couldn't give a monkey's. I'm here. LBC is mine. If you want to do business with him, get yourself a bottle of Ambre Solaire and fuck off out of it. Otherwise, enough with the 'Danny' shit.'

He stared at his shoes. Nobody spoke to him like this; he didn't appreciate it. Somebody had to and I was fine about it being me. 'Also, while we're here, forget the "we". There is no we. Though you're right on one thing. We were vulnerable. As an interested party you'll be relieved to know that's sorted. From here on in, the cash will be delivered to the back door of the club, where an army will be ready to welcome it or whoever else is along for the ride. Before was a lesson. And the lesson's been learned.'

I stepped back and looked at him. 'Is any of that unclear?'

He murmured something I couldn't make out.

'Come again, Jonas.'

'On his deathbed, Voltaire was asked to renounce the devil. Voltaire says, "This is no time to be making new enemies." Worth remembering.'

The wolf-grin spread across his face, the filling flashing in the light. He was full of crap. I ignored it and shook his unresisting hand. 'Glad we had a chance to sort that out. I'll be in touch. Tell Lily I said hello.'

23

A cool breeze rustled the branches at the bottom of the garden caressing Oliver Stanford's cheek as he stood in the shadow of his house, waiting for the moon to disappear behind the clouds before he made a move. Elise was in the conservatory, a glass of wine in one hand, a book in the other, blissfully unaware she was in danger. Stanford had had a wasted day. Distracted and unable to concentrate, his mind constantly wandered to the shoebox on the front seat of his wrecked car. Its symbolism freaked him. Thanks to the raid on LBC – the raid he'd known nothing about – his relationship with Luke Glass was at its lowest point in the three years since he'd taken over from his brother. Luke wasn't the animal Danny had been. But the bullet set off alarm bells in Oliver Stanford's head; it seemed he had a new enemy.

During his time with the Met, Stanford had had more than his share of villains spewing revenge when he'd collared them, angry threats thrown out as they were led in handcuffs from the dock to the cells below. No more than a final show of defiance from men who'd gambled and lost. Any copper who let that get to them was in the wrong job. The logic comforted Stanford but didn't negate the chilling significance of the warning.

Elise had been delighted to see him home so early. Arm in arm, they'd watched the sun drop over the horizon, then settled themselves in the latest addition to their house, until he'd spoiled the mood by announcing he'd brought work with him that needed his attention.

It was a lie. More accurately, *another lie* to go with the many he'd told her during their marriage.

Through the late-evening gloom, he'd noticed the barely perceptible pinprick glow of a lit cigarette, dancing like a firefly in the trees. His wife's lips moved as she read, her eyes staying on the page when he got up and went to his study. She'd thought, for once, she had him to herself and was annoyed with him.

When he was alone, Stanford acted quickly, taking a hollowed-out book from the shelf, removing the gun it concealed and thrusting it in the waistband of his trousers. He closed the side door behind him as quietly as he could and crept towards the garden. Once upon a time, a younger Oliver had prided himself on being a decent detective – he was about to find out if he still had those skills.

All the senior officer had to do was pick up the phone and two squad cars would arrive in minutes, sirens blaring. Except, there was no knowing where that would lead. Dealing with it himself made sense because whoever it was might have a tale best left untold, the price of decades of dishonesty.

Light from the conservatory spilled onto the patio. On the other side of the glass, Elise had her spectacles balanced on the end of her nose, engrossed in her story. That his actions might've threatened her safety was too painful for Oliver Stanford to consider. London was a jungle, yet there were rules – he couldn't be certain the figure hiding in the trees lived by them.

He kept to the bushes, bent low, every step slow and measured. A twig snapped like the crack of thunder when he shifted his weight from one foot to another and Stanford held his breath. In the stillness, he heard the metallic click of a lighter and saw a cloud of grey smoke rise between the branches and drift across the lawn as the stranger drew on a fresh cigarette. Suddenly, the policeman understood. This was a charade: whoever was hiding wanted him to know they were there.

A shaft of moonlight broke through the clouds. Stanford caught a face, a face he couldn't put a name to. Then the man melted into the night and was gone.

* * *

Stanford closed the study door and put the gun back in its hiding place in the book, beside the burner phone. He hadn't needed to use it. Another time, maybe that wouldn't be the case. He poured three fingers of Chivas, added a little water and drank a quarter of the amber liquid in one go. Slowly, gradually, his hands stopped shaking. He sat in front of the computer, undecided about whether to turn it on, staring at the blank screen, trying to separate thoughts from emotions.

First the bullet, now this.

If Luke Glass was telling the truth, the threats hadn't come from him: Luke had his own troubles. That wasn't to say the south London gangster wasn't connected. Stanford's association – he smiled grimly at his choice of words – with the family had begun with the older brother, who Stanford hoped was in a shallow grave covered in lime.

Wishful thinking.

What was happening had Danny Glass written all over it: the brutal and unnecessary violence in the attack on the club; the menacing figure in the garden – not the first time that little piece of coercion had been used – and the bullet in the shoebox, the kind of cruel joke he'd enjoyed. Classic Danny.

The more Stanford turned the details over in his head, the more obvious it became. Danny wasn't in Spain. Wasn't in the ground, either. No such luck. He was back. The crazy bastard was back.

Whatever had gone down between the Glass brothers, Danny had clearly come out on the losing end. It looked like he wasn't letting that result stand.

And suddenly, it made sense.

Slaughtering the men and slitting the woman's throat was vintage mad-dog Danny.

So why should Stanford care who ruled the roost? They were dragged-up gutter trash, always had been and always would be. Let them destroy each other. When the dust settled, he'd do business with whichever one of them was left. The difference was no difference.

Stanford took another sip of his drink; it didn't help and he knew why: his nice neat theory was bollocks. Luke Glass was at the beginning of what looked like a war. Whoever was provoking it had pegged Stanford as his ally. And if Luke Glass went down, Oliver Stanford was going down with him. Hanging back, allowing it to play out, wasn't an option.

He finished the whisky, poured another and dialled a number in Cornwall.

'Ted? It's Oliver. Sorry to be calling so late. We're fine but Elise is missing Sylvia terribly. Is it okay for her to come to yours for a week or two? Not me, no. Nose to the grindstone, I'm afraid. Criminals don't take holidays.' He faked laughter at the old joke. 'Tomorrow, yes. Great, I'll tell her. And thanks, Ted.'

* * *

Stanford was in the kitchen when Elise came downstairs the next morning. His side of the bed hadn't been slept in and he was still wearing the shirt he'd had on the day before. Usually, he'd have left hours ago to beat the traffic into Central London.

She remembered she was cross with him, the smile died on her face and she said, 'I waited. You didn't come up.'

Stanford said, 'I know. I wasn't tired. I lay on the couch. Sorry.'

'I heard you talking to someone.'

'Yes, Ted.'

'Is Sylvia okay?'

'Sylvia's fine. I called him.'

'Why? You don't even like him.'

'Ted's all right. You're too hard on him.'

'He's all right in small doses but he keeps asking us to join his bloody bowling club as guest members. Bowling! What makes him think I'd be interested? Bowling's for old folk. How long do you want us to go for?'

'Not us.'

'You are coming? Why would you want me to go there by myself?'

'I'll join you... later.'

Elise lost her temper. 'Don't lie. Don't lie to me, Oliver. There's something wrong, isn't there?'

Stanford inhaled. 'As a matter of fact, there is, Elise. Senior officers in the Met have been receiving threats.'

'Threats. What kind of threats?'

He waved further explanation away. 'The less informed you are, the better. Let's just say we're taking it seriously.'

'Has anyone been hurt?'

'No, not yet. Though that doesn't count for anything.'

'It isn't on the news or in the papers.'

'We've kept it quiet. Intentionally. We've a fair idea who's behind it, but until we can prove it, our hands are tied.'

'And you'd feel better knowing I'm hundreds of miles away, bored out of my head.'

'If the worst that happens is you're bored, I'd settle for it any day.'

Elise leaned forward and took her husband's hand. 'I love you, Oliver.'

'And I love you. Life without you would be unbearable. I wouldn't last long. That's why I want you well away from here. Will you do as I ask? They're expecting you. And tell Ted to sign you in at his bowling.' He smiled. 'He married the wrong sister and nobody knows it better than him.'

*　*　*

The moment Jazzer stepped onto the platform at Euston station he knew it was a mistake. London wasn't Liverpool; there was no place for him in this city. But she was here.

Yet another sleepless night had brought him to the point where he believed if he didn't do something, he'd go insane. Every time he closed his eyes, he saw her face, her body, the red lips sneering lust, laughing at him.

A taxi dropped him on Earl's Court Road outside The Blackbird pub. Going in for a quick one crossed his mind. In a rare flash of self-awareness, he rejected the idea. Jazzer had never had just one in his life, unless he was potless. Even then, he'd scrounge a second and a third from some daft bastard with more money than sense. Threaten them, if that was what it took. There would be plenty of time for drinking after he'd done what he'd come to do.

Finding the flat was no problem, exactly as he'd seen it in his nightmares. He stabbed the buzzer with his finger, expecting...

what? The woman to appear, throw her arms round him and whisper she hadn't been able to stop thinking about him? And if that fantasy came true, what would he do? What would James William Stevens' reaction be?

That had been decided long before he'd left Liverpool.

On the unmade bed in the room upstairs she'd taken something from him.

Jazzer wanted it back.

* * *

It took him a minute to realise somebody was talking. Jazzer slowly raised his head from the table. The barman lifted the almost empty pint glass and leaned on the chair opposite. 'No more for you, my friend. You've had enough. I can call you a minicab, if it's any help. Where do you live?'

His voice was soft – Irish, maybe, and kind. Jazzer was neither. He slurred an angry reply. 'Fuck off! Fuck off and bring me another drink!'

The barman shook his head. 'Sorry. You were well gone when you got here. Shouldn't have served you then.'

He put his arm round Jazzer's shoulder and walked him out. 'Watch yourself, okay? This is London. Get yourself home. Good lad. You'll be all right in the morning.'

The air was cool after the warmth of the pub. Jazzer flattened himself against the wall and tried to think. Earlier, he'd got no answer at the flat and gone for a drink to kill time. The last thing he recalled was ordering a pint and a double whisky from a smiling girl with big tits. After that, the barman was throwing him out. In between, nothing – the blackout had lasted most of the day.

Above his head, pinned to the bricks, a sign told him where he was. What he'd come to do flooded over him.

The Royal Borough of Kensington and Chelsea
EARLS COURT ROAD, S.W.5.

He forced himself to stand and lurched away, one unsteady step after another. People on the street saw the wild look on his face, the jacket half on, half off, and moved to let him pass. His eyes blurred, his head was a weight too heavy to hold up; he fought against an overwhelming urge to lie down on the pavement and sleep. Instead, he kept on, sweat filming his brow, his breath a storm in his lungs. When he got to the flat, he was exhausted. His shaking finger searched for the buzzer and pressed. Nothing happened. He pressed again. The darkened windows, the scene of his humiliation, mocked him, an animal growl starting in his throat. He hurled himself against the door, fists pummelling the panels, screaming impotent rage.

'No! No! No!'

Jazzer collapsed, sobbing like a child.

She wasn't there.

24

Superintendent Stanford spoke quietly into the phone. 'We have to meet. Today. Now.'

The policeman's blue eyes saw a different world from the one I lived in. We were on opposite sides of the track, always would be. And that was fine by me. It might've been his car the bullet had been planted in; its deeper significance touched both of us. He was right – we did have to meet.

I said, 'Where are you?'

'Paddington station.'

'Okay, Fulton Street in thirty minutes.'

'Too far. I don't have the time.'

'All right. Just this once. Soho Square. Make sure you're not followed.'

He laughed, short and harsh. 'Followed? Too late for that, I'm afraid.'

* * *

I expected him to be there when I arrived and he was, on a bench near the rustic black-and-white hut in the middle of the square, surrounded by young tourists lying on the grass, enjoying the sunshine. He was early – a warning I wasn't going to like what he had to say.

I sat down and waited for him to speak. Stanford didn't need to tell me storm clouds were gathering on the horizon; they were in his eyes. He leaned forward, balanced his elbows on his knees and stared at the paving stones.

'I had a visitor last night.'

'Somebody came to your house?'

'As good as. He was at the bottom of the garden, hiding in the trees. Except he wasn't hiding.'

'Did you recognise him?'

'Not clearly enough to pull him out of a line-up.'

'What did he do?'

'What he came to do. Make sure I saw him, and I did. First the bullet, now this, what the hell's going on?'

'That I don't know. But I've an idea why it's happening.'

Stanford waited for me to make sense of it for him. 'Everything north of the river is under attack – the club, Nina's real estate company, Glass Gate—'

He hadn't climbed the greasy pole at the Met by being stupid. He interrupted. 'And me.'

'Looks like it.'

'Who would know? Who would know about us? We've stayed underground ever since Danny.'

I shrugged. 'A good question. Clearly, somebody does.'

Stanford hesitated. 'It isn't him, is it? I mean, he hasn't come back, has he?'

As far as the world was concerned, my brother had quit the business he'd built from the ground up, leaving me and Nina to take over. Only four people knew the whole story and none of them were talking. Stanford was worried – he'd every right to be, though not for that reason. I gave him what I could to make him feel better.

'It isn't Danny.'

'How can you be so sure?'

'Because he wouldn't waste time on gestures. Outstanding scores would've been settled. You, me, anybody who'd crossed him – and he'd be holding court in the office above the King Pot with the jukebox playing The Who and the photograph of the Queen on the wall.'

'Just like the old days.'

'Just like the old days.'

He seemed to accept it. 'Okay, so it's not Danny. Who does that leave?'

I didn't speculate; there was no point. We'd had feelers out on the street since the raid on the club and come up empty. Apparently, nobody knew anything.

Stanford carried on. 'Maybe somebody doesn't like the direction you're going. Not just south of the river, now it's central, up west. There must be a few dissatisfied villains waiting on a chance to take you down.' A sly look washed across his face. 'Don't suppose George Ritchie would have anything to do with it, do you?'

'Forget it.'

'Sure, except he's played second fiddle to Albert Anderson—'

'I said, forget it, Oliver. George is solid as they come.'

Stanford scanned the kids on the grass – too young to be touched by the realities of the city they were living in – and floated a version of what he'd already said. 'Maybe, maybe. It could be you're moving too fast.'

The suggestion irritated me. 'Too fast? Too fast for who? Nobody's missing out. Toes aren't being stomped on. Everybody's happy and so they should be. We're making them money. We're cleaning their dirty cash. The big players – Jonas Small, Kenny and Colin Bishop, and Bridie O'Shea – are all involved.'

'Jonas Small's two hundred grand down.'

'Wrong, he isn't. That'll be covered by me.'

'Fine. So, what do you need?'

'Ears to the ground. Not only in London – in Manchester, Birmingham, everywhere.'

'What am I listening for?'

'Noises from out-of-towners who fancy a bit of vertical integration in the Big Smoke at my expense.'

Stanford nodded. 'Elise is on a train to Cornwall.'

The policeman had acted fast. Sending his wife to Cornwall was smart. I didn't remind him that if somebody was out to hurt him, it wasn't far enough.

It wouldn't have made his day.

* * *

I walked back to the club along a busy Oxford Street, turning over what Stanford had told me in my mind. The bent copper would kick his granny if the price was right. But he loved his wife and was spooked. Had Elise Stanford actually been in danger? I doubted it but, given what had happened to the woman in the office, I couldn't be sure. That said, sending her to Cornwall was one less distraction for her husband when I required his A game. Beyond was a bigger concern: somebody was aware of his connection to the Glass family. If they knew that, they knew everything. Which gave me one more call to make before I reached the club.

Barry French was a partner at Burton, French and Allan, the accountancy firm started by his grandfather. Their offices were in The Cut, not far from The Old Vic. Barry and Oliver Stanford had never met and never would – a pity, because they had plenty in common, up to their eyes in debt and greedy to take on more. Barry was thick-set and prematurely balding. If he kept his nose clean, eventually, he'd be the managing partner. Except he needed money now – not fifteen years down the line when his father retired. I liked Barry; there was no bullshit with him. He knew why he was doing what he was doing and played with figures with the same creativity Eddie Van Halen had played his axe. Nobody else got near our accounts. Three young kids and a fourth on the way guaranteed he'd be focused for the next couple of decades. We'd spoken recently when I'd told him about Charley, putting him on his guard in case somebody suddenly started taking an interest in Luke Glass.

Today's conversation was short and I did all the talking. Another reason I liked him.

When I got to the club, Mark Douglas was in the office above me, trawling through a stack of papers piled on the desk. In the room with him were two strangers parked behind PCs – late thirties, buzz-cuts, lean and spare – who didn't raise their eyes from what they were doing. My new head of security had been meeting his guys off the train at Euston. These two fitted the bill. And my initial impression was well wrong; they'd clocked everything about me in the first three seconds. Douglas broke away from his work and drew me into the corridor. Being in charge sat well with him; he was buzzing, confident and energised, relishing his role. George Ritchie's judgement was usually spot-on. Not this time. George was smarting from how easily Charley had exposed the security on the south side – the security he was responsible for – coupled with the fact I'd ignored his argument for consolidating what we had, in favour of opening the club.

Friday night had been a watershed – for LBC, for the whole organisation. Wherever I went, whoever I talked with, I got a sense of being closer to the beginning of what was happening than the end. People were scared. Clearly, Mark Douglas wasn't one of them.

He hooked a thumb towards the new guys, not bothering with names or introductions.

'They're down from Scotland for this gig and they'll be here as long as we need them.'

He got ahead of any objections. 'They'll report directly to me. You'll notice a few unfamiliar faces around the place from now on. Don't be alarmed. Your last head of security did a piss-poor job. The previous crew were useless. We'll do better – a lot better.'

I couldn't fault him; he'd moved fast. That said, he was putting himself on the line – any balls-up and the responsibility would lie squarely with him.

Douglas qualified his actions. 'Upstairs won't know what goes on here, but the club will be covered twenty-four-seven. If somebody decides they're coming through the front door they'll get more than they bargained for. Let's hope that doesn't happen. It wouldn't be pretty.'

He started to walk away and changed his mind. 'We're checking out everybody Paul Fallon brought with him, including the people who died in the attack.'

'Come across anything yet?'

'Yeah, as a matter of fact. The woman – Rose – didn't have an online gambling problem but she owed.'

'Think she was involved?'

'No, though she probably had a skim running on the takings.'

'Makes sense.'

'Where did you get her?'

'Paul Fallon brought her in.'

Douglas laughed. ''Course he did. She was his cousin.'

'Was Fallon dirty?'

'Honestly, it's too soon to know. Which brings me to Nina. I'll be seeing her later. Her system was hacked.' He shrugged. 'It won't come as a surprise; she's figured that out for herself.'

'Sounds like you're on top of it.'

'We are. There won't be a repeat of Friday.'

'I'll give you a time for when the Bishops' cash will be arriving on Thursday.'

'Thursday? What happened to Wednesday?'

'I prefer Thursday.'

* * *

Charley might be my sister but the truth was we were strangers. All I knew about her was what Ritchie had found out, what she'd told us about her mother – our mother – and an upbringing that sounded even crazier than our own. I'd given her the job of fronting the club and running the girls. If it turned out she was an idiot, blood wouldn't save her – she'd be on her way back to wherever she'd come from.

My gut told me that wouldn't happen.

When I went back to my office, she was behind the desk making notes on a sheet of paper. Her new status hadn't overawed her and, like Douglas's guys, she didn't look up when I came in. Charley's presence filled the room and I almost forgot it was my office and not hers. She was wearing a blue T-shirt, jeans cut off below the knees and sandals, and might have been in a Caribbean beach bar writing wish-you-were-here postcards, while she waited for a tall glass of fruit and alcohol to arrive; the shades pushed into her hair completed the effect. Silver, gold and platinum membership cards lay in front of her.

'You're in my chair.'

She didn't move, put the pen down and said, 'We're doing this wrong.'

'Are we? Five minutes in the door and that's your assessment?'

'I'm giving you my opinion. Take it or leave it.'

'I'm listening.'

'Before I washed up at your door, I did my homework. Everything I came across said you were smart. Nina's heart was never in the club, I get that. What's your excuse?' Her brown eyes stayed on me waiting for an answer that wouldn't be coming. Charley said, 'Then I understood: it was about focus. More accurately, the lack of it. LBC is big investment, a lot of money to put on the line. Why haven't the potentials been maximised?'

'I thought they had been.'

Her reaction was unexpectedly angry. 'No, you didn't. No, you fucking didn't. Don't treat me like a fool. We both understand what I'm talking about here. The club's an upmarket front. I'm guessing you're running a laundry service – 30 per cent of the membership don't exist but they eat and drink like there's no tomorrow.'

I let her speak.

'Glass Houses and Glass Construction will be the same. Phoney property sales and deliveries that never happened. Padded invoices for concrete, bricks, insulation, heating systems...' She paused for breath. 'Architect's fees that would choke a horse. The bigger the better. And at the end you sell Glass Gate units and make even more money. Have to give it to you – it's the perfect business model.' She clapped her hands, slowly. 'Very clever. Very, very clever. Only, with LBC you've missed a trick that can make what you've created the centrepiece of your empire. The place looks incredible – whoever designed the interiors did a great job. No surprise it's already one of the top half-dozen clubs in London.' Charley lifted a platinum card. 'And then it starts to falter because your attention has been on other ... things.

'People who've done well don't care who knows it. In fact, they insist on getting the word out. This is a private members' club but the last thing private members' clubs are about is their members spending their money privately. Most of them are showing off. A bargain, a "good deal", isn't what they're looking for. They want what they want and don't mind paying. So why are we giving it away?'

Charley was on a roll. Her brittle New York accent echoed in the room, frank and assured.

'LBC should be the most exclusive club in the world, not just London. And the most expensive. It's a goldmine. But the gold won't come out of the ground by itself.'

'Enlighten me.'

'Double the fees. Not quietly. Make a noise about it.' She anticipated my objections and held up her hand. 'Yeah, it'll be too rich for some people's blood and we'll lose them. Plenty more will take their place, believe me. Forget the silver card for stars when they're in town. Let them in for nothing. Worth it for the PR value, alone. The majority of members will not only accept the new charge, they'll welcome it.'

'You think?'

'I do think. Cost isn't the issue – unless it's too cheap. But the key is the platinum deal. We make it the most sought-after piece of plastic in London. Nobody *buys* an LBC platinum card. It can't be done because it isn't for sale – it's a non-transferable gift from the club to the biggest spenders. Platinum can make every fantasy you've ever had come true. Special services depend on having the right card and a charge is built into the bill the same as food and booze.'

Charley read from the notes she'd been making when I arrived. 'The girls are young and beautiful, but at the end of the day they're hookers no different from the ones I'm guessing George Ritchie controls on the south side. For the price of a membership, we're letting them use us, settling for selling a couple of bottles of champagne to horny tossers when we should be taking all of it. These girls think they need an agency. They don't. The club is where the connections are made. LBC is the key. We're outsourcing a big earner we should be keeping in-house. There's no loyalty. No incentive to be sure every penny goes to us. Whatever else happens, that needs to change. But it has to be subtle; it can't smell like a hustle. We put the pros on an exclusive retainer. A contract that guarantees both sides get what they want – money and security in their case. In return, they live clean, obey the rules and don't work anywhere but LBC. I'll vet them. Ten to start with.'

Charley had it all figured out. She waved the pen in the air, then pointed it at me. 'Where are the most expensive hookers in London?'

'Shepherd Market, always have been, why?'

'Wrong. From now on that particular honour will belong to LBC. To our girls.'

She was too sure of herself, her analysis too insightful. My sister had walked this road before.

I said, 'These women may look terrific. Some of them are pretty screwed up. We'd be taking on a mess of blues.'

Charley played with her sunglasses. 'Business comes with risk; we both know that. Rather than being put off, we do what we do everywhere else. Minimise it.'

'How?'

She sighed, looked away, and brought her attention back to me. 'Hooking's a tough life. Most girls finish with nothing. The trick is to hold onto what you make while you're hot and come out the other side in one piece. That's the dream. And that's our proposition. If you get sick, we'll look after you. If somebody's giving you a hard time, forget it, it'll be taken care of. You need time off to go home and see your family, no problem. Just don't be gone too long.' Charley sat up straight, rolling out her vision. 'We make it so a gig at LBC is as good as it gets. If you're with us, you've arrived. We can even make sure they get solid financial advice, same as happens with football players who'd blow it because they're young and think the big bucks will last forever.'

She smiled and her eyes were as warm as a bath. 'Admit it, it's a great idea. You like it, don't you?'

Nina had never wanted to be involved with the club. Property was her passion. I'd tried to fit a square peg into a round hole and failed. Bringing in an outsider had been an option, though an option I'd always been reluctant to take. Now, I understood why. The solution was on its way: Charley was that solution.

'Yeah,' I said, 'I like it. I like it a lot. Start putting it together.'

* * *

I rang the bell three times before Nina answered. At first, I thought she wasn't going to, then the door opened and I followed her into the flat. She was wearing a black robe with orange dragons and was barefoot. She looked tired, like she hadn't slept; her face wasn't made up and her hair hadn't seen a comb. I'd been around my sister's moods all my life and recognised the signs. Nina was depressed. It didn't take a genius to understand why.

She dropped into a chair and stared at me. 'I know what you're thinking and you're wrong. I couldn't give a shit. Got this far without her, haven't I?'

A lifetime of insecurities had been laid bare and Nina was scared. I was here to tell her it didn't matter. Our mother hadn't loved us. Which meant we were better off without her.

'Nina, listen, what we heard yesterday doesn't change a damned thing. Before then, it was you and me and it's still you and me.'

'Is it?'

''Course it is.'

Nina said, 'What about her?'

'What about her? You heard what she told us. Sounded to me like she got the worst of it.'

'How do you make that out?'

'Charley was dragged all over the country by a woman who didn't want her any more than she wanted us. She grew up with nobody. We had each other.'

'And Danny.'

'Yeah, and Danny. Don't forget he looked after us when we needed it. Now, when Charley finally raises enough bottle to hook up with her family, she's still on the outside. How must that feel?'

Nina folded her arms across her chest. 'Couldn't care less how it feels.'

'Not fair, Nina. You're holding a past beyond her control against her. Our mother left with a baby in her belly. We don't have to like it, but Charley's that child. As much a victim as you or me or Danny. She wants to be part of a family. Something she's never had. Give her a chance.'

Nina gazed at the wall. 'It isn't just her...'

It would've been easier to deal with this when the business wasn't on the line. Right now, I couldn't afford to fall apart because my mother hadn't loved me. Nina was struggling – she needed her brother to be there for her. I leaned closer and took her hand in mine.

'We can't pretend that circumstances forced Frances Glass to abandon her children, can't lie to ourselves that it broke her heart and she never forgot the kids she'd left behind. But it wasn't about us, Nina. She was in trouble before she packed a case and turned the key in the door. Even if she hadn't run away, she wouldn't have coped. And I don't believe it was because she'd married a man who was too fond of the booze, although who's to say that was all his fault?'

'He was an alcoholic.'

'Was he always like that or was it because his wife left and took their unborn child with her?'

Nina said, 'I don't know.'

'Neither do I. If she'd felt anything for us, she'd have found a way to get us back.'

The silence went on for a long time and I could see the conflict raging behind her eyes. If I'd helped, it didn't show. She needed somebody to blame, to lash out at. Charley fitted the bill.

Finally, she said, 'I don't like her. Keep her away from Glass Houses. I mean it, Luke. Away from anything I'm doing.'

'Agreed. She'll be working at the club. You won't be affected.'

'She's got plenty of show but is she up to it?'

'I think she is.'

'Sure?'

'Nina, right now I'm not sure of anything. Ask me in five years.'

'Five?'

'Okay, ten.'

25

I studied Mark Douglas for telltale tics of anxiety and found none. He seemed on it, relaxed and in control, his voice even and unhurried as he laid out the logic behind what he'd put in place. 'The last attack wasn't clever. A show meant to cause maximum damage. I'm expecting the next one to be more subtle.'

'That wouldn't be difficult.'

He nodded his agreement and went on. 'We've got people at Glass Houses in case whoever we're up against decides to diversify.'

'How did Nina take that?'

'Didn't ask. I'm trying to keep everybody alive. End of. Her and Charley have been warned to stay clear. The cleaners will be in this afternoon instead of this morning and every entrance is locked and manned. If they decide to blast their way in the front door, they'll be on the receiving end of a welcome they won't forget. I'll be at the back with my guys. We're as ready as we're ever going to be.'

He stopped speaking though I knew he hadn't finished. Douglas said, 'I'd prefer you weren't here when the money arrives. There's no knowing what—'

I interrupted. 'Forget it.'

On the surface, he was calm; fit and strong and a year or three younger than me. I'd bet on myself against him any day of the week and he knew it. He'd done his best to keep it from me: Mark Douglas was feeling the pressure. Good news. Over-confidence got you dead. Uptight and above ground was better.

'I hear you. Now, you hear me. LBC is mine – my club. Nobody's running me out of it. Not today. Not any day.'

'Okay, but stay in your office. I'll handle it – that's why you hired me.'

I smiled a hard, humourless smile, reached into the desk drawer and took out the gun. 'If somebody dies in the next thirty minutes, it won't be me. I bought security, not a babysitter. So, don't fucking insult me.'

* * *

In Chalk Farm, the rain drummed against the windows of the house in Prince of Wales Road. Down in the basement, Kenny and Colin Bishop's relationship was at a low, even for them. Since Luke Glass announced the arrangement had been changed, they'd argued bitterly about how to respond. Not the needling-each-other exchanges and squabbles blowing up and blowing over in minutes – real rows, screaming matches, almost coming to blows. Colin wanted to pull out. Glass could fuck himself. They'd clean the cash through somebody else. Kenny, the brains of the partnership, disagreed. This was an opportunity to be involved in something big, something with legs: a permanent solution to the difficulty making too much money brought.

The basement had been used by Colin Bishop's great-grandfather as a coal store when the family moved into the house two years before the start of the 1914–18 war. It was damp and smelled like something had died behind the skirting; black and green mould clung to the flaking plaster on the walls and the ceiling, and in places the decay was so extreme the original Victorian brickwork was visible.

Kenny Bishop sat in the only chair at a scuffed wooden table, filling an open attaché case with wads of notes bound together into five-thousand-pound bundles. He tallied the running total in his head and made one last stab at persuading his cousin not to go.

'You don't have to do this. The boys can handle it.'

Colin had already had a 'bump' off his fingernail before getting out of bed as he did every morning to help him shrug off the lethargy that was a symptom of his addiction. Today, the other half of the Bishop empire had made an effort: he'd shaved and was wearing a dark jacket over a white open-necked shirt and jeans.

He took a folded piece of paper from his pocket, carefully unwrapped it and arranged the powder inside in a line. Kenny said, 'Why you're wasting Charlie is beyond me. It'll have worn off.'

The reply was arrogant and unapologetic. 'Because I feel like it, okay? Stop telling me what to do. I don't like Glass. Thinks he's smarter than everybody else. Danny was the same. Superior fuckers. That family needs taking down a peg or two.' He fingered the gun in his pocket and repeated the lack-logic diatribe that had nothing to do with business. 'Getting involved with him was always a bad idea. Should've dug in my heels. Because I didn't, this is where we are. The bastard is leading us around by the nose.'

Kenny wanted to tell him that if anybody grabbed his nose, it would come off in their hand. Instead, he said, 'He's done what needed to be done. I don't have a problem with it.'

Colin sneered. 'And that tells every bugger in London everything they need to know about you, Kenny.'

'I go along to get along. You should try it instead of butting heads.'

'He's changed the fucking deal. We should've backed out, like I said.'

It was true: a lot had changed. Colin insisting on handing over the money himself, for one.

Two hundred grand was worth a roll around in the mud, but it wasn't worth dying for.

Kenny said, 'This is madness. What'll you achieve?'

His cousin didn't need to think. 'The satisfaction of seeing his face. Losing Jonas's cash has put the wind up big bad Luke Glass.' He laughed. 'Who'd have believed it, eh? He's scared and he's panicking. Well, he's about to realise the Bishops don't scare so easily.'

Kenny wasn't listening; he'd given up. There was no talking to Colin when he was coked up. And it wasn't a sometime thing; he was high every day. Glass had been hit and was minimising his risk – his reasoning was solid. The other way around, they'd do exactly the same. He put the last bundle of banknotes into the briefcase, closed the lid and set the combination lock. Colin held out his arm, half expecting him to take another shot at persuading him not to go through with it. He didn't; he was done.

Colin placed a reassuring hand on the gun in his pocket. 'Relax,' he said, 'I've got this.'

'Yeah, that's what the other guys thought.'

Upstairs, a driver and two bodyguards were waiting. Rough-looking geezers not big on small talk, whose jackets bulged on the left-hand side. Colin Bishop made it a four-man team – anybody who tried to hijack them this morning would be up against it.

It was ten thirty-six. The delivery was scheduled for eleven o'clock in the lane behind the club. Mid-morning traffic in the capital was unpredictable. Barring some serious delay, they'd be there in twenty-five minutes. Colin nodded to the other three and went out to the car; the engine was ticking over, quietly purring, ready for the road. The bodyguards climbed into the back. Colin got in the front, rolled down the window and looked up at the heavens, daring the rain to keep falling.

'Glass needs to know he isn't the only fish in the sea.'

Kenny stayed at the door. Typical Colin, everything was personal, always bent on settling scores, real or imagined, even if it meant getting him killed.

'You know your trouble, don't you, cuz?'

'No, but I'm betting you're going to tell me.'

Colin smiled and tapped the briefcase with a thick finger. 'You forget, we're the Bishops, you and me. And we own north London. Yeah?'

Kenny nodded. Colin's pupils were the size of saucers – the cocaine was doing the talking. But it wouldn't last. By the time they got to where they were going, the euphoria would've gone and he'd be ready to tear somebody's head off.

Felix Corrigan ignored the dull slap of the windscreen wiper and kept his attention on the black Peugeot edging through the gates out into the traffic. He counted four men in the car; three he didn't recognise and one he did: Colin Bishop's pumpkin face was unmistakeable. He said something to the driver and they joined the traffic heading for Camden Road. Bishop was in the front. As they passed, he looked directly at Corrigan without seeing him. Felix waited a minute, checking to see if anybody else was involved. When he was satisfied the Peugeot was all there was, he pulled into the flow and spoke quietly into the mobile in his hand.

'They're on their way.'

* * *

In the office above the King of Mesopotamia, George Ritchie imagined the scene in Central London: Felix and Vincent would be in the thick of it; he envied them. It had been his decision not to be involved with the club – the south side was his stomping ground. Luke respected it and had hired the younger Mark Douglas to head up security. Fine, except with what was going down right now it was impossible not to miss feeling his heart rate increase, the sweating palms and the adrenaline rush that told him he was alive.

His phone ringing brought him back into the moment. Ritchie pressed it to his ear.

'What've you got?'

The rustle of paper told him the man on the other end of the phone was reading off the information. 'His name's Stevens. James William Stevens. Jazzer to his friends.'

'And what do we know about him, apart from the fact he's a fucking idiot?'

'Currently unemployed. Spent eleven of his thirty-three years at Her Majesty's pleasure for two separate counts of robbery with violence.'

'You'd think he'd get the message and look for an alternative line of work.'

'He isn't smart enough to figure that out. It'll occur to him when he wakes up and discovers he's a fifty-eight-year-old man with arthritis in his knees and half his life behind bars.'

Ritchie said, 'Stand on me. He won't have to worry about arthritis. Where does he live?'

'The family started in Toxteth, near Sefton Park, and moved north to Bootle when he was in his teens. Our lad went wrong early. But prison didn't scare Jazzer; he didn't learn.'

'They rarely do. Anything on the other two?'

'Best guess, they're Ronnie Stoker and Thomas 'Tosh' Hughes.

Jazzer's known Hughes for a decade, shared a cell with him in Armley Gaol in Leeds.'

Ritchie pictured them lying in the dark on their beds at night, smoke from their ciggies drifting in the air heavy with the sweat of twelve hundred captive bodies, whispering about working together when they got out.

'And Stoker?'

'Stoker's his nephew. A natural-born mad-arse, apparently. By some miracle, apart from a two-stretch in HMP Altcourse for credit-card theft, he's managed to avoid doing the kind of time his uncle James and Tosh Hughes have under their belts.'

'A losers' convention.'

The man sighed and didn't disagree. 'The world's full of them, George. Anything else I can do you for?'

'No, we're good. And thanks, I'll take it from here.'

* * *

Oliver Stanford closed the PC and went to the window. His attempts at identifying the man in the trees behind his house had failed miserably and he'd lost hope. After a while, every face looked the same.

On a clear day from here he could see the Thames Estuary and, in the other direction, the chalk outline of the South Downs. Elise loved that part of the country. They'd often talked about moving when he left the service. He favoured Petersfield, the Downs' top town; she was drawn to Liphook. This morning, he could barely make out the other side of the river.

The grey skies above the capital matched his mood. Elise had only been gone a couple of days and already he was struggling to make sense of his life. He could've had one of his officers on the property – paid him privately and set him up in the bushes – and

Elise wouldn't have had to leave the beautiful home she'd created for them. That would've meant involving people so he hadn't considered it. Once you went down that road...

Without her, the house in Hendon was bricks and mortar, a place to live, not the totem of his upward rise it had symbolised not long ago. He'd tossed and turned, up and out of bed with every noise, peeking into the darkness from the cover of the curtains. A testament to his state of mind was the gun, no longer hidden in the book; now, it was under his pillow. And it was loaded. Fear was only part of it. Guilt as cold as the rain outside made sleep impossible and he cursed the ambition and the greed that had brought them here. Sending Elise away was like punishing her for some unspoken wrong. She was innocent; he was the one who'd brought danger to their door. She should never have married him. When she called, as she'd done both nights and would again this evening, hearing the unhappiness in her voice while he told the same litany of untruths left Stanford depressed. Her sister, Sylvia, was a stranger, her husband dull. Elise was hating every minute in Cornwall.

She'd asked when could she come back.

His response had devastated her. 'Soon. Very soon.'

Remembering how their last conversation had ended was painful. Elise had put her mouth close to the phone and said, 'I miss you, Oliver.'

He'd replied, feigning a cheerfulness he didn't feel. 'I miss you too, my darling.'

Then she'd whispered, so quietly Stanford almost couldn't hear her, 'I love you.'

And he'd realised she was crying.

Stanford sat down and reopened the computer. Whoever was giving the orders had it locked down tight. So far, his street sources had come up dry. Two possible resolutions remained. Luke Glass sorted it or he made the connection himself. He'd settle for either.

Elise deserved better than she was getting and her husband would make it his business to see she got it.

* * *

Bridie O'Shea stood at the counter rolling a thin cigarette between her fingers to go with the one hanging from her lip. The barman mopping the wooden floor sensed her eyes on him and glanced up. 'What? You're like the Hag of Beara, so you are.'

She didn't answer.

'For the love of Jesus – what?'

'Told you a thousand times – you're usin' too much water. It won't be dry before we open.'

Niall leaned on the shaft and she saw the hand and the missing fingers. 'If you're unhappy with my work you can always do it yourself, lady. Won't be easy, mind you, but I'll try and not to take offence.'

The banter, or something like it, passed between them every day. Nobody else spoke to Bridie O'Shea like that. Nobody dared. Niall could and did because he was the best friend she'd ever had. In the years after Wolf passed, he was the one who'd sat with her into the small hours, holding her hand while she told him her fears for the future, or about the latest faithless man to break her heart. If she got drunk and passed out – a frequent event back then – it was Niall who'd put her to bed.

There was nothing romantic between them and never had been. Niall was gay and celibate, though sometimes, when he'd had a few too many sips of Tullamore Dew, he'd reminisce about strolling the Cliffs of Moher with a boy he'd met in Dublin, his voice faltering as he described the sun setting over the Twelve Pins mountain range in far off County Galway, or the wild Atlantic waves pounding seven hundred feet below. And it would be Bridie's turn to hold his hand.

She poured tea into two mugs, stirred in three sugars and handed one to him. He took it from her. 'You're quiet on it this morning, lady.'

'I'm fine.'

He smiled. 'Fine but quiet.'

She sighed. 'I'm thinkin' about what's happenin' over-by. Everythin' tickin' along, until suddenly...'

'What've you heard?'

Bridie crushed out the cigarette and started on the new one, already reaching for the tin of tobacco and the papers. 'Nothin'. And that's the vexation of it.'

'Somebody knows.'

'And they're keepin' it to themselves.'

'There are only two reasons people keep secrets – money or they're shit scared. This Glass fella's in the middle. Are you worryin' he isn't up to it? Because, if you are...'

Bridie kept her eyes on the roll-up. 'He has to be, Niall – we're about to give him a helluva lot of our cash.'

* * *

The woman had the most perfect teeth Charley had ever seen. In fact, everything about her was perfect – the figure, the sallow skin; the pretence that whoever was speaking was the most interesting person in the world. Convincingly done and hard to resist, even when you knew it was a trick. She met Charley's gaze with frank green eyes, answering her questions in a cultured voice with a trace of an accent. She was beautiful and she knew it. This wasn't her first visit to Claridge's; a minor member of the Saudi royal family had invited her to his suite. Her name was Safiya; the Mayfair hotel was a long way from the fishing village she'd been born in south of Penang. By design, every trace of her former self had been eradicated. All except the fear of poverty and the greed it had spawned.

Safiya said, 'And you're offering how much?'

Charley told her and watched her reaction when she added, 'You'll also have private medical insurance and four weeks' paid holidays annually.'

'Pension?'

Charley smiled. 'Listen, honey, this is the best goddamned deal you'll ever get, don't kick the ass out of it.'

'Is that a no?'

'That's a have-a-nice-life. See you around. But not around LBC. That option's closed.'

* * *

'Turning off Euston Road into Great Portland Street. Be with you in five. Nobody with them.'

Mark Douglas nodded: so far so good. He brought his attention to Vincent Finnegan, high on the roof of the building opposite the lane.

'You seeing anything, Vinnie?'

Finnegan fingered the binoculars and scanned the traffic from one end of the street to the other. 'Nothing to concern us.'

'Okay, let's hope it stays that way.'

* * *

Barry French was surprised to hear it was Nina Glass on the other end of the phone. The accountant couldn't know she had a viewing scheduled in Holland Park for noon and was dressed to impress in a red Michael Kors sheath dress. Or that she'd spent an hour scribbling figures on the sheet of paper in front of her, then scoring them out. But he did realise she was on edge. It was in her voice and in her question. 'How much is my share of the business worth?'

'That isn't something I can answer off the top of my head.'

'Approximately.'

'It depends. You'd have to ask Luke.'

'Don't mess me about, Barry, how much? And why does it depend? I'm a partner. I'm entitled to a share.'

French replied cautiously. 'I'd imagine a lot needs to be considered.'

'Like what?'

French ran a finger under his collar, correctly guessing the family had had a dust-up and this was the result. 'Are we talking a half or a third?'

'A half. Has to be.'

'That's why you'd be better to ask your brother. He'll have it figured out. He usually does. Then it'll be down to how much he can lay his hands on and how soon you want it.'

'I want what's mine. What belongs to me.'

'Don't we all, Miss Glass, don't we all.'

He put the phone down and immediately called Luke.

* * *

The Peugeot stopped at the end of Hampstead Road and waited for the lights to change. Mid-morning traffic raced past, adding poison to one of the four most polluted thoroughfares in the city. Colin Bishop had stopped speaking. The men with him realised the high had peaked and he was starting to crash, a descent into a dark place only another snort could stave off. Anxiety washed through him; sweat broke on his brow. He quietly ground his teeth together, clutching the attaché case to him like a comfort blanket. His travelling companions saw the change and hoped they would be well clear when the comedown really got going. Colin was a nasty piece of work on a good day. Paranoid and aggressive, he was capable of almost anything.

Bishop sniffed, shifted in his seat and barked at the driver. 'Can't you go any fucking slower?'

The journey had taken twenty-eight minutes. The high had lasted seventeen.

* * *

The men Douglas had brought in crouched in position, guns drawn, unblinking, totally focused on the Peugeot's black nose edging into the lane. From reflex, I patted the gun in the waistband of my trousers and looked at my watch: three minutes past eleven. Six days since Friday – it seemed longer – but there would be no repeat of our mistakes: LBC was locked down tighter than a duck's arse. Beside me, Mark Douglas spoke into his two-way, checking with his spotters one more time.

The exchanges crackled in the air, tinny and distant.

'Vincent?'

'Nothing.'

'Don't move. Stay with it.'

'Felix?'

'One hundred yards out. They're alone.'

Douglas tried to sound relaxed. 'Okay. Follow the plan. Park across the entrance. Anything happens, they won't be able to get out.'

We'd had the Bishops' vehicle in our sights from the moment it left Chalk Farm. I wanted to avoid a fire-fight in the middle of the day and was ready to abort if we had to. So far, nothing suggested that was how it was going. The Peugeot crawled towards the door. I stepped into the lane in front of it. Colin Bishop's fat face glared at me through the windscreen, twisted with emotions I didn't understand.

He walked round the bonnet, holding the case to his body like a baby. I'd heard about his drug habit and thought little of it; he wasn't the first and he wouldn't be the last. What I hadn't factored in was the intensity: Colin Bishop hated me and nothing either of us could do would change that. Conversation wasn't necessary – we both knew why we were there. All he had to do was hand me the case and get back in the car. Simple stuff.

He threw it at me with both hands. 'Try not to lose it, eh?'

I caught it and felt the weight of its contents. 'I'll do my best, Colin.'

'That's what worries me.'

He grinned like a gold-medal winner in the idiot Olympics. Suddenly, the grin disappeared and he looked down at the red circle spreading on his white shirt just above the heart. Bishop staggered and fell to his knees.

Somebody in the Peugeot shouted, 'He's been shot. Colin's been shot.'

And for a moment, time stood still.

Colin stared at the scarlet stain and instinctively put a hand to his face. The stupid fucker had almost started the gunfight at the O.K. Corral with a fucking abuse-related nosebleed. A couple of the guys sniggered. Mark and I exchanged relieved glances, and he said, 'Show's over. Let's get this done.'

PART IV

26

THREE WEEKS LATER

Algernon Drake loosened his tie, took a sip from the glass of dry white wine in his hand and surveyed the scene from his balcony. It was after midnight. Across the river, Tower Bridge was an illuminated marvel against the dark night sky. Drake should've been happy – in court he'd given one of his finest performances, ruthlessly picking the prosecution's admittedly shaky case apart in his summation. The jury had taken less than an hour to find in his client's favour and he was in the mood to celebrate. For that, he needed a woman.

He closed his mobile, irritated and displeased. Nina wasn't answering her phone. Since their coupling there had been no contact. It had taken that whole weekend to get over the session. If he told himself the truth, he'd avoided a rematch. Nina was the female version of her gangster brothers: nobody fucked her, she fucked them – literally.

But after a day of winning, Drake was ready to be on the losing side, for a little while at least.

He tried her number again and heard a Martian voice tell him it was unavailable; she'd turned it off. The bitch was blanking him.

His fingers drummed the table. Suddenly, the extravagant praise about his sharp mind, his eloquence, the back-slapping and the handshakes in the corridor outside No 2 court seemed meaningless. In truth, he didn't give a damn about their opinions, good or bad: what did they know? He finished his drink, considered pouring another, and rejected the idea; alcohol wasn't the high he was looking for. Drake took out his wallet and rippled his thumb over the thin line of red fifties and purple twenties – probably around five or six hundred pounds. If he needed more, he could get it.

A naked Nina came into his head. Drake felt his throat go dry and wanted to call again. Then, he saw the card with LBC written on it and the decision was made for him: to hell with her; Nina Glass had had her chance.

* * *

Drake paid the taxi and stood on the pavement in Margaret Street pondering the wisdom of what he was doing. The club looked like many buildings in Central London, except it wasn't. The two dark suits at the door didn't give him a second glance. Inside, he swiped the card through the reader on the wall and waited. Behind the bar, the message that a platinum-card member had arrived was received and a hostess came to greet him. The girl was Asian, too tall to be Thai, with a trace of American in her accent – he guessed Hong Kong Chinese. Her dark hair, streaked with blonde, fell to the shoulders of her black dress. She smiled and shook his hand in a cool, firm grip.

'Good evening. Nice to see you. Follow me, please.'

At the table, she asked, 'What would you like to drink?'

Drake was enjoying being the centre of her world and forgot she was paid to make him believe it.

'Champagne.'

'Certainly. I'll bring our wine list over.'

'No, don't bother, you choose.'

She acknowledged his faith in her judgement with an imperceptible nod and said, 'Are you fine by yourself or would you like some company?'

Dropped so casually, so easily, into the conversation she could have been enquiring if he'd prefer Earl Grey or Lapsang Souchong. Drake pretended the notion hadn't occurred to him, hesitated, then said, 'What a good idea.'

The women arrived before the champagne – gorgeous and eager to please, making eye contact with him, each one chatting for a few minutes before excusing herself. Algernon Drake would've been satisfied with any of them but something about the fourth one intrigued him. She was different; they were young, she was younger still, with an energy he couldn't resist.

He lied for a living. Making conversation with a teenage prostitute would be easy.

'What was your name again?'

'Zelda.'

'Zelda? Unusual. I've never met a Zelda.'

She laughed and he noticed the perfect teeth. 'Then you've never lived.'

'Are there many Zeldas where you come from?'

'What, in Dublin? You're joking.'

'So why Zelda?'

She allowed her accent to thicken, the practised smoothness falling away, and Drake realised it was Sheriff Street Dublin rather than Castleknock talking.

'It appealed to me, will that do you?'

'Yes.'

'You're sure, now. Because I can make up a fairy story if you like.'

Drake refilled his glass and drank, suddenly overwhelmed by

her. She leaned closer, her scent filling his head, and whispered in his ear. 'You want me, don't you?'

The polished performer from the Old Bailey wasn't here. Drake felt his pulse quicken, his heart beat faster as he whispered in return, 'How does this work?'

Zelda wasn't more than seventeen years old. For all his experiences with women, the frankness from someone her age stunned Algernon Drake.

She said, 'Ask for the bill. I'll be on it. Then, we'll get out of here.'

* * *

Drake poured what was left of the wine he'd started on earlier and guided her out onto the balcony. Her reaction was predictable: she pulled in close, her breasts brushing against him, and under his breath he thanked Nina.

Zelda said, 'How can you afford this? How can anybody afford it? What the hell do you do?'

He gave his stock reply, an answer that amused him, one he'd been using for years. Tonight, it had a special irony. 'I provide a service to people prepared to pay for it. Same as you.'

She watched him over the rim, her lipstick smudging the glass. 'You're wondering why I do this, aren't you? A fine girl like me, eh? Don't deny it. I can see it in your eyes.'

'I'm wondering a lot of things – that isn't one of them.'

She slid her hand inside his shirt and stroked his chest. 'In some ways, men are more romantic than women, did you know that? A man will imagine a sad history behind me and see a victim.' She laughed. 'A woman would see a whore taking the easy option and that would be the end of it.'

Drake said, 'Sorry to disappoint you but I'm not even a little bit curious.'

She continued as if he hadn't spoken. 'And she'd be right. I do it because the money's great and I like sex.' Zelda changed the subject. 'Did you check your bill?'

'No, I never do. It would make me feel poor and I can't have that.'

'Then you don't know how much I just cost you.'

'I can guess.'

She peeled his jacket off. 'Close your eyes and think of a number.' Drake played along. 'Okay, now double it.'

'Really?'

She put her arms round his neck and stared up at him. 'It's my job to make sure you get your money's worth. What would you like me to do?'

'I'm... I'm... not sure.'

'Shall I call you Mr Drake?'

Drake unbuttoned her top and led her to the bedroom; he was nervous. 'Call me Algie. Will you tell me your real name?'

'My real name's Zelda. Do you need any help?'

'Like what?'

Zelda opened her bag so he could see inside. 'Like, whatever you fancy.'

'I don't do drugs.'

She gave a coarse dismissive grunt. 'Don't be stupid. 'Course you do, everybody does.'

* * *

They moved together with the familiarity of old lovers, easy and unhurried, savouring each other. His lips explored the youthful skin, taut and yielding at the same time. Zelda rolled on top, her naked thighs pinning him to the bed, nails gently scratching a path through the hair on his chest. He moaned and remembered her words.

it's my job to make sure you get your money's worth

The first pinprick of anxiety arrived as a sensation in his arm, no more telling than a bee sting. Algernon Drake ignored it. But the unease that followed was impossible to dismiss – a deepening sense of nameless dread. In seconds, he was sweating, drowning in fear; terrified and free falling, panic rising in his throat. Suddenly, he couldn't breathe – her flowery perfume was choking him.

'What's wrong? You're shaking.'

'I... I... don't...'

She held onto him. 'It's all right. Relax. You're having a reaction, that's all. It'll pass.'

Drake fought her. 'Let me up!'

'Stay calm. It isn't happening.'

He punched her. 'Get away from me, you bitch!'

'It isn't real, Algie.'

Drake manhandled her aside and ran from the room; she heard him crashing through the flat, arguing with people who weren't there. Seconds later, he was back, his face twisted and ugly with rage, the blade of a kitchen knife glinting in his hand. In the middle of the floor, the barrister made his stand, striking out at unseen enemies.

Zelda crawled to the end of the bed. Giving him the drug had been a mistake – he hadn't even wanted it. Drake jerked and danced like some possessed marionette, half-formed words tumbling from his mouth, while the blade cut the empty air in one deadly arc after another.

She tried again to reach him. 'Algie! Algernon! It's okay.'

His head came up like an animal testing the wind, turning towards her, no recognition of who she was or where they were.

Zelda saw his expression darken as his crazed eyes fixed on her and knew Algernon Drake was going to kill her.

The first thrust entered her breast an inch from the nipple, instantly turning the milky skin red; the second severed her windpipe releasing a crimson gusher that sprayed the bedclothes and up the walls. Then he was on her, thrusting and stabbing, again and again.

The effort drained him; he walked slowly, dazed and exhausted, to the lounge still clutching the knife, lay down on the couch and fell asleep.

27

I drove with the radio murmuring in the background, hardly audible, but as much noise as my aching head could stand. Champagne hangovers were the worst. I was in a strange space – no longer drunk but not yet sober. Through the window a young guy in denims and dreadlocks was making an early start, setting up a display of fruit and vegetables on the pavement outside a West Indian grocery store. I'd read Rastafarians had used their 'dreads' to instil fear in non-believers. I had my own methods, and they didn't include braiding my hair. It was three a.m. when I'd finally left LBC with a brunette who claimed she was a flight attendant with Finnair. Four hours later when the call came through, she was asleep and didn't stir. I'd stretched out a resentful hand to the bedside cabinet, dragged the mobile to my ear and listened. Her voice was shrill, the story garbled – fragments of apology jostling with barely contained rage as she described what she was seeing.

'Easy, Nina, easy. Take it slowly.'

In the background I heard a man crying. Her final words before she gave me the address and broke the connection had me on my feet.

'You need to get over here. This is really bad.'

* * *

Mark Douglas was standing on the cobbles in the middle of Shad Thames, waiting for me; he'd done well to get here so fast. Four and a half hours ago – it seemed like days – he'd walked me to the front door of the club, shaken my hand and wished me a good night.

Nina was leaning against the wharf's brick wall smoking a cigarette.

Douglas got into the car – he had something to say and wanted me to hear it before I spoke to my sister. 'Don't blame Nina. She isn't responsible for this.'

I felt a sudden surge of irritation. 'Don't blame her for what, Mark?'

He stared like it was a question he ought to have the answer to but didn't, then showed he hadn't forgotten his police training. 'Didn't know what route you'd want to go down so we've got their mobiles, the murder weapon's been bagged and I've taken a video. It... isn't nice.'

Nina saw me get out of the car, pulled deeply on the cigarette she was holding, exhaled slowly and watched me come towards her through the smoke. The cigarette dropped from her fingers. She studied it like the remains of a dead insect, her expression empty. My first thought was that whatever had happened had upset her. I was wrong – she was angry.

'Are you okay?'

Her reply was tart. Answering a question with a question. 'Why wouldn't I be okay?'

From behind me, Douglas said, 'Charley's on her way. Be here any minute.'

Mark Douglas, Nina, and now Charley. What the hell was going on?

He read my mind. 'Be warned, you're going to need a strong stomach.'

* * *

We climbed to the fourth floor, our footsteps echoing in the stairwell. Nina was a tough lady. Her reaction was enough to know what was ahead of me wouldn't be pretty. I'd only understood snatches of what she was telling me on the phone; I was about to find out the rest.

The front door was wide open. Douglas spoke quietly. 'The room on the right – she's in there.'

Heavy curtains covered the window; a lamp knocked onto the floor cast ghostly shadows over the naked body. Mark Douglas had told the truth about needing a strong stomach: a metallic smell stuck in the back of my throat and made me want to throw up and, in the half-light, blood stained the crumpled sheets and spattered the walls. In the centre of the room a mutilated woman lay across the bed, as dead as it was possible to be, her arms and legs splayed awkwardly, almost as if the torso and the limbs didn't belong together and had been forced into place like the wrong pieces of a jigsaw puzzle.

Her chest had taken the brunt of the attack, the wounds on the perfect breasts too many to count. Any one of them could've been fatal. But the slash at the neck had put the outcome beyond doubt, severing a major artery and probably the trachea, causing massive haemorrhaging.

After that, death, as violent as I'd ever seen, had come quickly.

There were all kinds of men in the world.

This girl had been unlucky – she'd met the worst kind.

I said, 'Do you know her?'

Mark Douglas didn't get a chance to reply – Charley picked that moment to arrive, dressed like she was on her way to dinner at Le Gavroche in Mayfair instead of the scene of a horrific crime in Bermondsey at half-past seven in the morning. She stood at my shoulder, the couple of stray hairs she'd missed when she was putting her act together falling across her cheek. Charley was seeing what I was seeing, yet didn't comment. It was hard to imagine an uglier end but the damage one human being had done to another left her unmoved. Her breathing was steady and even, unaffected by the atrocity in front of her and, again, I realised my suspicions about my sister and her past were on the money.

She answered without missing a beat. 'Yes. Called herself Zelda.'

'Zelda? Couldn't she have come up with better than that?'

'She liked it.'

'Who did this to her?'

Nina stood in the doorway at the end of the hall, framed by the light. We hadn't heard her come in. It was clear she hadn't shaken off her anger. She pointed an accusing finger at Charley, her shrill voice echoing in the hall. 'She did it! Everything was fine until she persuaded you that she knew our business better than we do.'

I said, 'You're blaming me?'

'Yeah, I'm blaming you.'

Charley took a step back, working to make sense of what was going on. Gradually, the pieces started to fit and she said, 'Wait a minute. Why're you here, Nina? This has nothing to do—'

'He called me.'

'Who called you?'

'Algernon Drake.'

'Algernon... you know him?'

'He's a client.'

'A fucking psycho is what he is.'

'No. He's a lot of things but this...' she hooked a thumb towards the body '... isn't him. Your girl gave him something. Have a look; he's wasted. What the hell are your skanks dishing out?'

I'd told myself confrontation wasn't inevitable, that we were family and could make it work. A lie. Too much water had run under too many bridges for both of them, the enmity was mutual, deeper than I would ever understand. They were siblings. But above that, above everything, they were rivals; the fight my sisters were squaring up to have had been on the cards from the minute I'd told Nina about Charley. The dead hooker in the bedroom and the man in the lounge who'd murdered her had no part in what was going on between them.

Douglas shouted, 'Get a grip, both of you! This isn't taking us anywhere.'

Like the bedroom, the lounge curtains were drawn and the room was uncomfortably warm. Every light was on. The furniture was stylish and modern and unmistakeably masculine: a glass and polished metal coffee table, twin maroon chesterfield couches and a beige carpet, its thick pile stained in a red trail from the bedroom. A naked man sat at the end of one of the couches, hugging himself, shivering though it was anything but cold. I guessed he was in his sixties, his grey body hair slicked and matted with his victim's blood. His lip was bleeding and there were bruises on his thighs. He rocked gently, backwards and forwards, in a world of his own and didn't look up when we came in. Finally, he raised his eyes, drug-glazed and red.

'She's dead, isn't she?'

It didn't deserve an answer. Mark Douglas gave one anyway. 'And you killed her, you sick fuck.' He dragged the man to his feet. 'Let's go for a wee walk down memory lane. Take a good look at your handiwork.'

Charley scrutinised the man's face, trying to remember him from LBC; his breath was foul. She'd been around drugs all her life – Nina was right, he was on something. She stood aside so he could see past her into the room. Zelda's nude body lay broken. Drake recoiled, his face twisted in horror and disbelief. 'Oh, God, no!'

'What did you take?'

'She... she gave me... something.'

Douglas shook him. 'Gave you what?'

He fell to his knees, moaning. Mark Douglas didn't let go; his fingers dug into the thin arm.

'I don't know. I don't know. I don't know.'

So far, I'd watched and listened and let Douglas handle it. Now, I stepped forward so he could see me. 'Algernon Drake?'

He looked up like a rabbit caught in the headlights. I turned the name over in my mind; it sounded familiar. 'Take him back to the lounge.'

Douglas started to object. 'But he's—'

I wasn't in the mood. Only weeks into Charley's grand vision and already it was off the rails. Somebody was to blame and I was trying to decide who. If this got out, the consequences could be ruinous. A dead hooker wouldn't make the front page of the newspapers, but any hint she was connected to the club could finish LBC for good.

'Just do it.'

Drake ran an agitated hand over his smooth pate; he was terrified and he should be. I gave him a minute to pull himself together. Sixty seconds wouldn't be enough – it was the only break he was getting. I hunkered down so he could see my face and understand the gravity of his situation and mine.

'Do you know who I am?'

'Yes.'

'Then you'll know the girl you murdered worked for me and realise the only hope you have left is to tell the truth.'

Paranoid eyes darted from me to Mark Douglas and back again as he processed what he was hearing. Behind Drake, Charley anxiously bit her lip – the dead prostitute was a potential disaster for both of us.

Algernon Drake pleaded with Nina. 'You know me. Tell them I wouldn't do this, Nina. Please.'

I put my hand on his shoulder and felt him tremble. 'Forget Nina, she can't help you. Start at the beginning. Take your time. And don't lie.'

He nodded, and for a moment I thought he was going to do the sensible thing.

'She came on to me. I was having a drink at the bar in the club.'

The blow struck his temple and knocked him to the carpet. I dragged him to his feet and slapped him twice, hard. He'd stabbed a woman too many times to count, yet this guy wasn't getting it.

'The girls don't "come on" to people. That isn't how it works. You asked for her. One more lie and you're going out the window head-fucking-first, Algernon. Try again.'

'I used the card.'

'What card?'

'The card I gave him.' Nina was standing at the door. She said, 'He's a client. He bought this flat through Glass Houses.'

'And you added a bit of value by tossing in membership to the club.'

This was good news for Charley, a twist she hadn't seen coming. She seized on it and spat her judgement across the room. 'You stupid bitch. Why? You'd got your commission.'

The question was irrelevant. Charley was off the hook and saw a chance to nail Nina to the cross. 'You couldn't get out of the club fast enough. Vetting who gets a card is a big part of protecting the girls. They have to believe there isn't some nut job running around with access to them in his wallet.'

'You weren't here.'

It sounded pathetic because it was. Charley swept it away. 'Nobody, repeat, nobody but me decides on that level of membership. Not even Luke. I'm responsible for the girls' safety. They trust me and I'm not letting a bimbo destroy that trust. Being the boss's sister doesn't cut it. For obvious reasons.' She sneered. 'Maybe I should stick my nose in your gig? See how you like it.'

Nina was smart enough not to reply. This one had gone to Charley.

But she was wrong. I decided who'd be getting a card.

Over on the couch, Drake was holding his head in his hands, making a noise in his throat like he was going to be sick. I ignored it and rewound. 'You said she gave you something. What? What did she give you?'

'What?'

'"She gave me something." What did you mean?'

Drake said, 'Can I have my clothes?'

'No, you can't. What did she give you? Answer me.'

'How would I know?'

'Did you ask her?'

'No, no, she offered.'

Righteousness drained from Charley's face. She saw where this was headed – she was back in the frame. Drake said, 'I... I... couldn't do it.'

'And Zelda suggested she give you something to help. Is that right?'

'Maybe. I think so. We were drunk. I can't remember. Where are my clothes?'

'A joint, or was it a pill?'

'She lit a joint and told me to smoke it. She called it another name.'

Charley's fingers gripped the back of the couch. 'What other name?'

Drake rubbed his eyes like a tired child. Charley was wide awake. A psycho losing it and butchering one of the girls was bad enough, but this...

She shook Algernon Drake. 'What did she call it? Remember! It's important!'

I barked an order. 'Get her bag. See what she was holding. Whatever she was into, I want it.'

Mark Douglas was already on his way. Nina hadn't moved; she was still at the door. When she'd given Drake the platinum membership card she couldn't have imagined he'd end up murdering somebody.

Douglas brought Zelda's bag into the lounge, knelt on the floor, and tipped the contents onto the coffee table. 'Christ, she's got everything under the bloody sun in here: uppers, downers, Prozac, LSD.' He read the label on a brown bottle. 'Ketamine – that's a horse tranquilliser. Who did she do business with?'

He sifted through the pharmacopoeia and picked up a plastic bag of shredded material and a small container of clear liquid, three-quarters full. 'Fucking hell! Mamba! She gave him black mamba.'

I'd been in the skin trade a long time. It was a hard game, especially on the streets; the women were vulnerable, all too aware their next customer might be Peter Sutcliffe or somebody with the same hang-ups. Danger was a given. For many, it was the daily indignities they couldn't stand. Staying clean was impossible; they needed to be able to take themselves out of the life they'd landed into. Soft drugs weren't a problem. There was no great harm in a little sideline and I wasn't against them selling to the marks. Except, none of that was true at this level. And some substances like synthetic cannabis – spice, fake weed, mojo or black mamba – were too risky and unpredictable to dabble with. Drake was lucky he hadn't suffered a heart attack. Instead, he'd killed Zelda in a psychotic episode.

Charley wasn't convinced; she shook her head in disbelief. 'Something isn't right here. Not this girl, no way.'

She could be shifting the spotlight off herself but I didn't think so. I turned to Mark Douglas. 'Call George Ritchie. He'll handle the clean-up.'

'Already on it. We'll check the girl's place. What'll we do with Drake?'

'He stays here until he straightens out. Keep somebody with him. When he sleeps it off, we'll make a decision.'

Nina reacted like the spoiled brat she was. 'Why am I involved? If he hadn't called me, I wouldn't even be here.'

She didn't realise how often in her thirty-odd years being my sister had saved her. Nina's ability to look at a problem and only register how it affected her was remarkable. This was one of those: I wanted to slap some sense into her.

'How about because you gave him the card? If that doesn't happen, none of this happens. But you did and that makes it your mess, so stop whinging.'

Charley smirked at the put-down and I bit back anger. Images of the mutilated female next door were fresh in my mind. She seemed to have forgotten them already. I didn't expect her to be broken up about Zelda – prostitution at any level was hazardous – but nobody had covered themselves in glory. The murdered hooker was a complication we didn't need, a fact that should've been self-evident.

I said, 'And before you get too smart, maybe you'd like to explain why one of your girls was carrying her very own pharmacy in her bag.'

The reminder of her shortcomings wiped the smirk from her face. In the last couple of weeks cash had shipped from Jonas Small, the Bishops and Bridie O'Shea without incident. Glass Houses hadn't lost any other clients and everything was cool on the housing development. All good.

Almost good enough to make it seem like the attacks had stopped. A dead hooker and one of London's leading barristers out of his head on black mamba told a different tale.

'If Charley's right, we're still under attack. I want everybody at the club in three hours and, Mark, we need to ID those drugs. Find out where they came from.'

'That's a long shot.'

'Long or not, it's the only shot we've got.'

For Charley, Zelda's death was very bad news. Luke hadn't singled her out, at least, not yet. She'd hired the young hooker – if it turned out the Irish prostitute was playing for another team... Charley left the thought unfinished. She hadn't met Danny. By all accounts, he'd been a madman. Luke wasn't like him. Then again, genetics didn't lie: Danny, Luke, her and Nina were the spawn of Daniel and Frances Glass. Fucked-up people who'd produced fucked-up children. Under the skin, those kids were all the same and Charley had no doubt how she would deal with any fool who'd invited a cuckoo into the nest. Brother or sister. It wouldn't save them.

The calls took less than twenty minutes. In every case the message was get dressed and get here. No excuses, no exceptions. The girls wouldn't appreciate being woken up. Tough titty. They could catch up on their beauty sleep later. Right now, everything was on the line. Sooner rather than later, the inquest would begin in earnest; unless she brought Luke information he could use, the spotlight would be on her.

The females arrived in ones and twos and gathered in a corner of the bar, most still wearing the previous night's make-up, talking quietly amongst themselves, wondering why they'd been ordered to the club. Charley let her eyes run slowly over them, nodding as if she was realising something.

'Does anybody know where Zelda is? She isn't answering her phone.'

She made a show of calling the number again, swearing when she got no response.

'Fuck! The silly bitch has turned it off. How many times does it need to be said? Always keep your mobile on.'

Her eyes ran over the tired faces. 'Open your bags. Everybody.'

A girl from Sydney objected. 'Why do you want us to open our bags? What's going on?'

The Australian had long legs and even longer eyelashes; tanned and slim and popular with the punters. Charley made a mental note to fire her. As soon as this was over, she'd be on her way back to Tumbarumba or wherever hellhole she was from.

'I'm curious to see what's inside.'

'If you're looking for hard drugs, you won't find any. I don't use. Don't take anything stronger than alcohol unless the client's into it. Even then, I'm careful. Most of us are the same. This is a great gig. Nobody's stupid enough to jeopardise it for a line or two of coke.'

Charley smiled a thin smile. 'Then you've nothing to worry about, have you? Fucking open it.'

She emptied the bags onto the carpet and sifted the contents – apart from a dark-brown lump of marijuana wrapped in silver paper and a couple of Es, the women were clean.

'What's all this about?'

Charley paused, pretending she was unwilling to comment. A blonde from Finland, sitting at the end, pressed her. 'Surely, we've a right to be told?'

'Okay. There's a ten-month wait for membership to the club. LBC is the in-place in London. Everybody who's anybody comes here. This morning we had a tip-off some of you are selling H to the punters.' Charlie went down the line, studying the faces. 'Do you have any idea the damage that would do? The press would lap it up. Overnight, our reputation would be in the gutter. My job is to make sure that doesn't happen. You're here because of me. That makes you my responsibility. If any of you overstep the mark, it's my ass on the line.'

She tried Zelda's number again. 'This is fucking unbelievable. Do you understand how stupid it is to switch it off? Your lives might depend on it.' She sighed and shook her head. 'All right. Enough stupidity for one day. What's Zelda on? One of you knows – the sooner you tell me, the better.'

The girls stared blankly at her.

'Is our anonymous caller right? Is she dealing? Did she know we were tipped off, that we were on to her? Is that why she's broken contact? I'll find out, I promise you, and anyone who kept silent will be out the door with her.'

The faces in front of her held none of the answers she was looking for. Charley pointed to the handbags. 'Pick them up. You can go. And if Zelda contacts you, tell her she's in big trouble.'

She spoke to the Australian. 'Not you.'

When the rest had left, Charley softened. 'Look, you seem like a nice kid. But you have to appreciate this is a big operation. Luke won't let anybody compromise it. What you've got isn't just the best deal in London, it's the best on the planet. That brings responsibility.' She put a hand on the Aussie's arm. 'If Luke can't find who it is, he'll let all of you go.' She snapped her fingers. 'Twenty-four hours later, ten new girls will be strutting their stuff. And understand this: once you're out, there's no way back.'

'What do you want me to say? I can't tell you what I don't know. I want to help, believe me.'

Charley looked away. 'I do believe you. My problem is I believed Zelda, too. You girls have a lot in common. Sister-close in five minutes, I've seen it. Who was supplying her?'

'If I knew—'

'But she was dealing?'

'I can't be sure.'

'Okay, let's try an easy one. Was she seeing somebody away from here? A boyfriend?'

The girl laughed. 'A guy? When would she have the time? I'm here five nights a week. The rest, all I do is sleep. Same story with most of us.'

'And last night. Tell me about that.'

She shrugged. 'Honestly, I was busy with my own thing. I hardly saw her except when she asked me for a cigarette.'

'I didn't realise she smoked.'

'She didn't. She just fancied one. I let her have a couple.'

'What then?'

'Nothing. She went outside to smoke it. When I left with my client, she was on the pavement talking to somebody.'

'Somebody from the club?'

'No idea.'

'Had you seen him before?'

'Maybe.'

'What did he look like? Think.'

Her brow furrowed, instantly ageing her, and Charley caught a glimpse of the girl in ten years. By then, she'd be back in Australia, married and respectable – a doctor's receptionist or some such – the perfect daughter-in-law, loved by her kids, adored by her husband. All blissfully unaware of who she'd been and what she'd done. After a while, spreading her legs for money would feel as if it had never happened. Now and then, on summer nights, with a warm wind blowing off the ocean, she'd have a few drinks too many and allow herself to be coaxed into talking about London and what a great city it was.

LBC, hooking, and this conversation wouldn't be part of it.

She said, 'What can I tell you? He was a guy. I mean, after a while they all look the same, don't they?'

28

George Ritchie arrived first and took a seat across the desk from me. He'd had his hair cut; it made him look younger. He seemed well, bright-eyed and alert, and waited patiently to be told why he was here. George was a great man to have in the boat. But he'd disappointed me. Charley's hits in Lewisham and Lambeth had shown he'd taken his eye off the ball. Everybody had a sell-by date. Maybe old George had gone past his. I hoped not because, right at this minute, I needed him as much as I'd ever needed him. I poured two whiskies from the bottle in the drawer and handed him one. He held it with both hands like a chalice, gazing into the glass, swirling the liquid in the bottom, and I was reminded of a prospector, sifting flecks of precious metal from sediment.

Ritchie said, 'The body's taken care of. We've no worries on that score. Setting the flat to rights will take longer. Felix says there's blood everywhere.'

'Thanks for that, George.'

He set the tumbler down, untouched. 'Drinking during the day doesn't agree with me. Learned that the hard way in Newcastle. Only ever do it when I'm with you!'

'One won't do any harm.'

A half-smile tugged at the corner of his mouth. 'Sure about that, Luke?'

'Right now, I'm not sure about anything, George. These women are on the best deal in London.'

I described the horror in the flat in Butler's Wharf and watched his eyes narrow as he took it in. When I finished, he said, 'And you're struggling to get your head round what it would take to buy one of them.'

'Yeah, something like that.'

'Two things shouldn't be overlooked: even if a High Court judge is drinking Moët out of her stiletto, a hooker's still a hooker.'

'Meaning?'

'Mayfair or Margate, they can't be trusted. Most of them are screwed up to begin with. They'll find a way to fuck up. Trust me.'

'You said two things.'

He lifted the whisky, changed his mind, and put it back on the desk. 'You mentioned her handbag was full of junk.'

'She'd every fucking thing in there. You name it, she had it.'

'Yet, she chose to give the guy black mamba. Not to be messed with even on a good day. She had to know that.'

'Then, somebody put her up to it. Used her to get to us.'

'Or made her a better offer. In which case, it isn't over, we're still under attack.'

'I don't get it – what would they achieve? It's not as if you can guarantee a result.'

Ritchie said, 'I'm betting everything she was holding had been tampered with. Boosted in some way. Maybe had LSD added to it.' He stared at me as the possibilities deepened. 'They're having you at it, Luke. Standing back and enjoying the show. At the very least, it's a reminder they're still out there and have their eye on you. The prossie dying – that's a bonus, an unplanned extra. But intended or not, it's enough to put the club out of business.'

I still didn't get it. 'If they're intent on coming after me, why not just come and get it over with?'

'Like I said, they're toying with you. And when your nerves start to fray, they'll show themselves.' Ritchie picked up the whisky, emptied the glass in one go and wiped his mouth on his sleeve. 'Of course, I might be well wrong.'

'Except, you don't think so.'

He shrugged. 'Who was the hooker and where did she come from?'

'Zelda.'

'Zelda? Jesus.'

'Charley hired her.'

It was the moment he'd waited for since the hit on the taxi firm and the betting shop – the chance to kick the woman who'd shown him up, not once but twice, when she was down. I studied his face for a trace of satisfaction and found none. Like the whisky, he'd turned it away until he was ready to deal with it on his terms: it said something about the kind of man George Ritchie was, a reminder of how dangerous he could be and why I'd brought him on board in the first place.

He quietly considered the information, then asked the question he'd asked a hundred times before. 'What do you want me to do, Luke?'

* * *

They were like mourners at the funeral of a friend who'd died unexpectedly, their faces blank. Solemn. Not quite believing any of it was real. But it was.

The chair next to Ritchie was free. Douglas could've taken it and didn't, which summed up their relationship. Until recently, I'd been a fan of George Ritchie and in some ways I still was. Except, he wanted it both ways – take no part in anything to do with LBC and criticise from the sidelines. Not on, George. Expecting anything from the old king and the young pretender was asking too much. I'd settle for them doing what they were paid to do. Nina moved beside Douglas. When she thought no one was looking, her finger traced the back of his hand. Charley was standing in the corner, as far from her sister as space allowed, pulling on a strand of hair, twisting it into a curl. She saw Nina's touch, displeasure darkening her eyes, and I realised Mark Douglas had unwittingly stumbled into a contest with him as the prize: his life was about to get complicated.

He could join the club.

I counted four sharp, intelligent people with plenty to contribute – the future of everything I'd built depended on them, yet there were chasms of distrust and worse between them: Nina and Charley, sisters and rivals who would never be friends; George Ritchie, still licking his wounds over being made to look a fool by Charley's stunts in Lewisham and Lambeth. He was a patient man; he'd bide his time but, one way or another, the score would get settled – it was who he was. From the beginning, there had been tension between him and Nina. I blamed her, not that it changed anything. How often had I had to tell myself Nina was Nina?

Except, my tolerance was zero – somebody was out to destroy me and, so far, was making a bloody good job of it.

I nodded for Mark Douglas to kick off. He said, 'George's guys have removed the body and are working on the clean-up. The flat's being swept, though I'm not expecting to find anything that helps with this. Drake's in his spare bedroom sleeping it off, with a guy outside his door. He won't be going anywhere till he understands we own him now.' Douglas shot a glance at Ritchie. 'George and I have already put feelers out to turn up Zelda's supplier. Doubt it mattered what was in her magic handbag. I'm guessing it had all been doctored. We've been to the hooker's place. Nothing there, either.'

'Nothing? That can't be right.'

He made a face. 'Yeah. Given what was on her, it's a surprise. But it's empty. Which suggests last night was the exception rather than the rule.'

He answered my next question before I had the chance to ask it. 'So, if it didn't belong to her, where did the pharmacy she was packing come from? One helluva selection of recreational fun to not be seriously into it.'

'I agree.'

'Which means somebody gave it to her, probably last night. When we finish here, we'll look at the security cameras upstairs. See who she talked to. What about her phone?'

'We checked both her and Drake's mobiles. As you'd expect, she had a lot of numbers in her directory. I'm having them traced but it won't be quick.'

'Okay, what about Drake?'

'Missed calls earlier on.'

'Who to?'

Douglas hesitated, being gallant – he needn't have bothered. I pressed him. 'Who did he call, Mark?'

Nina shuffled uncomfortably. I still didn't understand the full extent of her involvement but, unlikely as it seemed given the age difference, guessed she'd sold the barrister the Butler's Wharf flat and had a thing with him to seal the deal.

'Mark, look at me. Who did he call?'

'Nina.'

'How many times?'

'Three or four.'

Nina said, 'Yeah, he called me. I didn't answer.'

'Why not?'

She stuck out a defiant chin. 'He's a letch.'

That hadn't stopped her before.

'I wasn't in the mood. Okay?'

'Then it's possible he came to LBC looking for you, and when you weren't there, decided to try out his new card.'

Douglas shifted the focus of the conversation. He set a plastic bag on the desk in front of me, the blade of the knife inside, even the handle, stained dark.

'His paws are all over it.'

'You'd expect them to be, it's his flat.'

'But not in her blood.' He laid a memory stick on the desk and pushed it towards me. 'The video. Fucking gruesome. Freddy Krueger eat your heart out. Some nice shots of Drake and Zelda side by side on the bed. Added to his fingerprints on the murder weapon, a jury would be hard pushed to reach any verdict other than that Algernon Drake brutally murdered a teenage prostitute in his flat. Like to see the silver-tongued barrister talk himself out of that one.'

Seeing the knife, knowing the awful damage it had done, banished any lingering sense of doubt in the group, replacing it with a recognition of exactly what we were up against. I picked up the bag, intending to put it in the safe, and changed my mind when I saw the reaction round the room. Maybe it would be enough to put their differences on hold.

Charley's East Coast drawl dragged us back to the now. 'Drake wasn't the target. The gods were angry with him and put him in the wrong place at the wrong time. But anybody would've done.'

'And you know this, how?'

She killed the smirk starting on her face. 'Haven't you been listening? Nina just told us. If she'd been horny for Algernon he wouldn't've been near LBC. She would've supplied everything he wanted. Done it before.'

Nina took the bait just as she was meant to. 'You fucking bitch!'

I shut her down with a wave of my hand. If we didn't stand together, there would be nothing left to defend.

Charley laughed; her work was done.

I said, 'Cut it out, both of you – you're starting to piss me off.'

Douglas carried on. 'She bummed a cigarette off another girl and went outside to smoke it. A guy talked to her. We'll check the cameras inside and out. See if there was contact before the pavement.'

This was a breakthrough – the first since the nightmare started.

Charley said, 'I've told the girls we got an anonymous tip one of them was doing some serious dealing. Zelda's dropping out of sight makes it easy for them to draw their own conclusions.'

Five minutes in and already my sister was behaving like she'd been doing this all her life. Perhaps she had. You didn't lick it off the rocks; street smarts were learned.

Charley had been around.

We watched the security tape confirm the sequence, knowing how tragically it was destined to end. Algernon Drake ordered champagne in black-and-white, relaxed, sitting back as if he belonged. A girl joined him and they talked for a couple of minutes. When she left, another took her place. Algernon was choosy, obviously not willing to be rushed, until Zelda approached his table and the decision was made. They sat, heads close together, like the lovers they were never going to be: two hours later, he'd be in a psychotic episode and she'd be dead.

Douglas fast-forwarded to her tapping the cigarettes off the Australian and leaving, his finger poised to run it on. I stopped him. 'Let it play. See what happens.'

At the top of the screen, a man we hadn't been tracking slid off his seat at the bar and followed her. Douglas froze the frame and zoomed in: he looked to be in his mid-thirties, heavily built, with dark hair and thick eyebrows. If he'd paid his bill by credit card, we'd have a name. I wouldn't hold my breath – these people were too professional to give themselves away so easily. What we were watching wasn't some spontaneous interaction, it had been planned.

I said, 'Okay. Switch the tape.'

Nina stated the obvious. 'She's meeting him.'

Zelda walked up and down, her bag over her arm, glancing anxiously towards the front door, the cigarette in her hand unlit and forgotten. The stranger came through the door and they faced each other, him doing the talking, her doing the listening. The conversation was short. After less than a minute, he handed her something. She put it in her bag and went back inside.

'Anybody recognise him?'

Nobody did and we were back where we started.

29

George Ritchie hung back until the others had left and we were alone. I poured a whisky for myself and felt its fire burn my throat. It was time for some straight talking. 'Mend your fences with Douglas, George. He isn't the problem. The guy's in a job you didn't want, remember? Right now, he's checking everybody on the books trying to find a connection. Believe me, you're better off south of the river in the King Pot.'

Ritchie's expression gave nothing away, which told me I was on the money.

He lied effortlessly. 'No fences to mend. I'll work with anybody, you know that. If he needs me, I won't be hard to find.'

He wasn't being straight with me. Not the George Ritchie I'd known. Pushing it wouldn't get me anywhere.

'The drugs are likely a blind alley. Could've come from anywhere. But every thread has to be teased out.' He nodded as if he agreed and I said, 'Keep an eye on my sisters. Try to not let them see you. Interference doesn't go down well, with Nina, especially.'

Ritchie knew that already. At the door he turned. 'Feels like it used to be simpler than it is now – or am I telling myself a load of horseshit?'

'You're getting old, George, that's all.'

'Am I?'

'Yeah. And I'm pleased to see it, thought it was just me.'

* * *

The mobile rang out nine times – I counted – before she answered. I pictured her in her 'office' scanning the horizontal lines of red and black icons, making certain she hadn't missed anything.

'It's Luke Glass.'

Her voice was soft and smoky. 'Not on with bad news, I hope.'

'I'll be straight with you, Bridie. We've had no problems since the hit on the club but there's still stuff going down.'

'Stuff like what?'

She was fishing.

'As far as this goes, we're partners. You deserve to be told that whoever's behind it hasn't gone away. They're still out there.'

'And you're warnin' me.'

I corrected her. 'Warning, no. Let's just say I'm apprising you of the situation. Whether you go ahead with our arrangement or pull out is your decision.'

'It always was.'

'I appreciate that.'

'Except, that's not how I do business. If I agree to do a thing, I do it. Are you ready to listen to my proposition?'

'I'm not looking for a partner. I thought I'd made that clear.'

'Oh, you did. But...'

'But what, Bridie?'

'That was then and this is now.' She cut the call short. 'You have a good day, Mr Glass.'

* * *

I went upstairs, needing to clear my head and get a handle on the last ten hours; the cleaners had finished and the place was empty. I sat at the bar, close to where the stranger who'd followed Zelda outside had been, and surveyed the scene. Opening a club in the heart of London had always been risky, a huge financial commitment Nina had been against and still was. Ritchie hadn't been a fan, either. I'd believed the opportunity was too big to turn down and gone with my instincts.

Today, I wasn't so sure.

Bridie O'Shea was a tough old bird who wasn't afraid of a fight – even one she could avoid. For the moment, she was onside. How long that would last was anybody's guess. I liked her but her colleen-from-the-old-country routine was tired. Jonas Small and the Bishops wanted a piece of LBC. So did she and she made no bones about it.

Her cash was due to arrive at seven. Meantime, Mark Douglas and George Ritchie were working to tag the guy Zelda had spoken to on the pavement, while Stanford would try to identify the source of her pharmacopoeia as soon as I could get it to him. I'd sent him the image of the guy and heard fear in his voice when he confirmed it was the same man he'd seen in the trees at the bottom of his garden.

My mobile rang, startling me. And suddenly, the garrulous avuncular Jonas Small had become a different animal, direct, economical with the English language. He didn't bother to introduce himself.

'Any sign of my money?'

Offering to stand Small his 200 K was a one-time thing. He'd picked the wrong moment to get heavy about it.

'You know that's not how it works, Jonas. It's a process. I've got your money.'

'*You've* got it. Why doesn't that make me feel better?'

George Ritchie's stinging assessment of him flashed into my mind. 'It's here if you want to come for it.'

He thought about the suggestion, though only for a second. 'No. No, I won't. We'll meet.'

'Fine, but it won't be today. I'm busy.'

He brushed my objection aside, almost as if I hadn't spoken. 'Aren't we all, Lukie boy? Blackfriars Bridge in an hour.'

The line died in my hand.

* * *

Whatever Small had imagined the dynamic between us was, clearly, for him, it had altered. He dropped the elder-statesman-of-the-London-underworld pose, along with the pretence we had anything in common other than an ambition to make a shitload of money. I hadn't forgotten how aggressive he'd been, implying doubt over the security of the cash I'd pledged to cover. There had to be a reason. His money wasn't at risk and we both knew it. So why was he putting the grip on me all of a sudden?

Mark Douglas found me in the office, on my knees in front of the safe, filling a green Harrods carrier bag with cash. He put a hand on my shoulder. 'Luke, what're you doing?'

With all the shit that had been going on, my reply sounded crazy, even to me.

'Delivering something.'

'Deliv... You're not serious. Our guys can do whatever needs doing.'

'No, this one's mine.'

His fingers dug into me. 'Don't you trust me?'

I turned my head and looked up at him. 'It isn't about trust.

You've got enough on your plate, and besides... I want to handle this myself.'

Concern and disappointment mixed on his face – he felt slighted and couldn't hide it. 'Where are you going? Let me drive you, at least.'

'Blackfriars Bridge.'

He swore softly to himself and paced the room. 'Tell me what's happened.'

I stopped what I was doing long enough to put him in his place. 'None of your concern. When we get there, drop me and keep going.'

Douglas wasn't happy. 'You're the boss, which means you shouldn't be anywhere near this kind of stuff.'

'On another day, you'd get no argument. This is different.'

'Famous last words.'

'Sometimes it can't be avoided.' I lifted the carrier bag and checked my watch. 'Let's go.'

In the car, he didn't speak until we reached Russell Square, then he said, 'When this thing, whatever the hell it is, is over, you can have my resignation.'

'Mark, listen.'

He had nothing to lose and let me have both barrels. 'No, you listen. I was bored out of my skull babysitting Vicki Messina and the rest of them. It was a cushy number. Nobody would describe what we do as that. So, there has to be...'

He didn't finish the sentence. I tried to reach him. 'You're taking this personally when it isn't.'

Douglas's mouth closed and he breathed slowly through his nose. We made a right turn near Smithfield Market into Farringdon Street and overtook a blue Mondeo with a 'Baby on Board' sign in the rear window. His face was white with anger, the strength of his reaction surprising.

I'd offended him. And not just professionally.

At the bottom of the road, he pulled up at the Underground. As I was getting out, he saw Felix Corrigan and Vincent Finnegan waiting at the end of the bridge shaped like a pulpit, a reference to the Black Friars. His hands closing round the steering wheel, knuckles threatening to break the skin. I said, 'I know these guys. Your team have enough to do. Don't read more into this than there is.'

Douglas didn't acknowledge I'd spoken; he edged the car into the flow and didn't look back.

I crossed the road, dodging in and out of the traffic, keeping a tight grip on the bag. Felix and Finnegan were known quantities, guys who'd proved themselves in the past. George Ritchie hadn't hesitated when I told him why I needed them. Mark Douglas was understandably pissed – I got that. Where I was going, I had to have complete faith in the men at my back. Small had been too confident. Too pushy. Too fucking sure of himself. Somehow, he'd got wind of the dead hooker and saw an opportunity. And he was just daft enough to try it on. The 200 K wasn't a problem. At the end of the day, it was my life on the line, not anybody else's.

Felix asked what they were anxious to know. 'What's occurring?'

I raised an eyebrow. 'That's what we're here to find out.'

It was an uncomfortably warm afternoon, the air muggy. In an angry sky, dark clouds, heavy with rain, melded together: a storm was coming – it fitted my mood to a tee.

Traffic poured across Blackfriars in a never-ending stop-start procession. On the far side, the distinctive figure of Jonas Small and two of his men watched us, alert, tooled-up and ready to react. Felix and Vincent returned their hard stares but stayed where they were. I walked towards the middle of the bridge, Small did the same from his end, like Cold War spies being exchanged in some remote Polish forest in the pages of a John le Carré book.

When we'd met in Borough Market, I hadn't noticed his arms and legs – thin and too long for his body. Today, the king of comedy three-piece suit he'd worn the last two times had been abandoned in favour of a brown corduroy jacket with leather patches on the elbows, a lime-green shirt, and a maroon waistcoat. With his gangly stride, from this distance he looked like a well-dressed stick insect on his way to the Ugly Bug Ball.

People hurried past in both directions unaware the bag bouncing off my thigh contained more money than some of them made in a decade. But Small knew. And as he got nearer, his mouth spread in his trademark wolf-grin, laughing at me.

I'd told him I was too busy, yet here I was.

He saw that as a win. By his reckoning, the first of many.

Wrong, Jonas.

Before he could speak, I yanked his lapels and threw him against the pink-and-white wall that made the bridge one of the prettiest in the city. Surprise darted in his eyes – whatever he'd expected, it wasn't this.

'Woah! Woah! Take it easy, Lukie boy.'

I tightened my hold, forcing him over the low-lying parapet, until the only things stopping him from falling were my fingers and his tailor. Up close, his breath smelled of stale cigarette smoke and there were broken red veins in the whites of his eyes. His fob watch had slipped out of the waistcoat pocket and dangled on the end of its chain. The timepiece had sentimental value: it reminded him how much he hated the man who'd sired him. Losing it would be a shame.

Over his shoulder, the Old Father made sluggish muddy

progress to the sea. I'd read the Thames was one of the cleanest rivers in Europe. It didn't look like it to me.

'Can you swim?'

'No. No.'

'Well, now's as good a time as any to learn, eh?'

'I... I...'

'A word of advice: don't drink the water. Christ knows what's in it.'

He was near to tears. 'Luke, please—'

This was fun. Reluctantly, I cut it short. Across the bridge, Small's heavies were running to their boss, guns drawn. Felix and Vincent would get here before them but a shoot-out in broad daylight on the streets of London wouldn't serve anybody's interests. I hauled him up, gasping for breath. 'Signal your goons to go back.'

He did as he was told, panting like a fifteen-year-old dog, his sixty-a-day habit telling on him. I slapped his face because I felt like it, then slapped it again for the same reason.

'Enough of the "Lukie boy". The name's Luke.'

'Luke, okay, Luke.'

The Harrods bag thudded against his chest; a bundle of notes slipped out. He reached for it, lost his balance, and almost went over the edge in what would've been the most expensive dip in history. I caught him – a mistake. Because Small realised he wasn't going to die today. A light came into his eyes and, with it, some of his old cunning. He assumed we were cut from the same cloth and clumsily tried to flatter me, his mouth curling in an approving sneer as what passed for a compliment escaped his thick lips.

'Thought Danny was the mad-arse.'

As an attempt to ingratiate himself it was pathetic.

'You really need to work on your conversational skills, Jonas. No more of the Danny shit, understand? And stop acting like you're worried about your money.'

He glanced quickly at his thugs and chose his words carefully. 'Told you before, I like to stay ahead of the game. You said the 200 K was covered. All I did was ask for it.'

'Not true, you were turning the screw because you want in. Listen hard – I won't say it again. You're in as far as you're getting in. If that doesn't suit, fuck off out of it. Another thing, when you count the cash, remember it's 180 thou, not 200.'

His face twisted – given half a chance he'd kill me and be digging into his chicken madras an hour later or boring people with his wife's homely pearls of wisdom.

'There's 10 per cent commission as per our arrangement. Like I said already – you get a better offer, my advice would be to take it. But don't mention LBC again or I'll break your fucking legs.'

Small took out his watch and studied it as if he expected to learn more than the time.

'All right, I won't. The subject's closed.' He leaned on the wall and stared down at the river, the bag of money forgotten at his feet. 'Does the name Roberto Calvi mean anything to you?'

I caught a glimpse of his filling when he smiled. 'You'd be too young. A baby.'

'Is there a point to this, Jonas?'

'Isn't there always... Luke? Calvi – "God's Banker" – that was his nickname, bit off more than he could swallow.'

'You've lost me.'

Except, he hadn't. I understood exactly where he was going.

'They hanged him from this bridge we're on.'

'Who did? Who's "they"?'

Small picked up the bag and peeked inside, pleased with what he saw: he was leaving with what he'd come for. 'Dissatisfied customers. Sometimes they take it hard.'

30

Niall Monahan watched the man rock gently on the balls of his feet, occasionally lifting his glass to study the dregs in the bottom and putting it down again, untouched. His pockmarked sallow face was unfamiliar. Definitely not a regular. Years on the run on both sides of the border had taught the barman to be suspicious; he never moved more than a few feet from the revolver behind the counter – washing pint mugs in the sink, while out of sight his fingers traced the loaded Webley. In all probability, the stranger was just that – a guy in for a dram. Monahan preferred people he knew.

When the stranger finally left, he slipped the bolt on the front door, quietly so Bridie wouldn't hear. She was where she always was, in the back room, sipping her stout, scribbling her scores in the notebook at her elbow. They hadn't said much to each other today – old friends didn't need words.

She sensed him before she saw him. 'Christ Almighty, Niall. Don't creep up on folk like that.'

'We have to talk.'

'Sure, talk away. But make it quick.'

He blurted out. 'You're not goin'.'

She lowered the cards and looked at him. 'Say again.'

'The money. You're havin' no part of it.'

Bridie scratched her ear. 'Givin' out orders now, are you? Must think you're Wolf. He was fond of doin' that. Confused bein' my husband with bein' my gaffer, poor man.' She laughed softly and smiled. 'So, I'll tell you what I told him, shall I? Away and behave.'

The rebuke echoed in the room. 'Clear enough for you, is it? Fuck off and let me get back to my game.'

They'd been together too long for the bluster to work. He ignored her and spoke quietly. 'Get used to it. You're stayin'.'

'I'm not... Jesus, man...'

'I'm serious, Bridie, it's not happenin'.'

'Glass called me. He has it sorted.'

'He doesn't and you know it.'

She sat back in her chair and faced him. 'What's brought this on?'

'In a couple of hours, we're deliverin' a bloody ton of cash to Luke Glass.'

'Yeah, like we've already done, Niall. What's changed?'

'My fingers are itchy. Been that way all week.'

He meant the fingers he didn't have.

'I saw how you acted round him – like a feckin' schoolgirl. Never liked his brother but you took to him, don't deny it.'

Bridie drew deeply on her cigarette and sighed. 'You're as queer as a bottle of bloody chips. Surely, you're not jealous?'

Niall said, 'I love you. I always have.'

'And I love you. What's that got to do with anything?'

He took her hands in his. 'Then help me keep you safe.'

'I am safe. I will be safe.'

'How can you be sure? There's no plan.'

She slapped his head playfully. 'Of course, there's a plan. Do you think I'm a complete feckin' eejit like yourself?'

* * *

Felix and Vincent had wanted to come to the club. Not on. Ritchie had loaned them to me as backup for an hour. That was it; they were his men now. I'd reckoned without Mark Douglas's reaction. He'd forgotten I was the boss and that I made the decisions – something he needed to accept if we were going to be able to carry on working together. If he resigned like he'd threatened to do, I'd be sorry, but I wouldn't stop him.

After the adrenaline rush, the office was eerily quiet and I had time to think. Liking who I did business with wasn't a priority – just as well in Jonas Small's case. The meeting place had been his suggestion and it was no random choice plucked out of the air. Small thought he was the smartest guy in the room – a mistake – and proved it, to himself at least, at every opportunity. I was always going to hear the story because he was always going to tell it. Today's history lesson had been about the ill-starred Roberto Calvi, Chairman of Banco Ambrosiano, which collapsed in one of Italy's biggest political scandals. The Vatican and the Mafia were involved – not people you want to be falling out with. Calvi had fled Italy and come to London. Which of his sins caught up with him on Blackfriars Bridge wasn't known and was a moot point because they killed him anyway.

And dead was dead.

In his unsubtle way, Small was pushing, still trying to deal himself in. Not clever. Danny had been a mad-arse, that much was true; he wasn't the only one. Our family had more than its fair share and he'd do well to remember it.

There was a knock on the door and Mark Douglas came in holding a sheet of paper. There was nothing stiff about him; he didn't avoid eye contact with me and launched into an update on this morning's meeting that felt like it had happened weeks ago.

Despite everything, I didn't want to lose this guy. 'Mark, I—'

Douglas said, 'Forget it. These bastards making clowns out of us isn't sitting well with me and I overreacted. Anyway, maybe the tide's turning. The guy at the bar had two drinks. A pro. The barman remembered him because he paid cash and didn't tip. In a place like this, nobody uses cash – the till records membership numbers for every transaction and spits out a receipt. Thank Christ or we would've had to check everybody who was in. And just as we thought, the membership's phoney: the name and address belong to an eighty-two-year-old man in Acton, a widower in the early stages of dementia. No relatives; just him. His carer comes in three times a day. Gives him his tea at half-past six.'

He grinned, building up to the big reveal. 'The carer checks out okay but she's got a boyfriend, a real loser with a record for credit-card fraud and resetting. We've got men outside the house. Tonight, once the old boy's sorted, we'll lift her and make her tell us which rock the lowlife's hiding under. What's going on is obvious, although I'd be surprised if it's just the old bloke they're ripping off.' He raised his head. 'Imagine stealing from an eighty-two-year-old. Soulless cunts. Be getting a slap, whatever they say.'

Douglas paused. 'I take it you've spoken to Bridie O'Shea?'

'Yeah, and it's on. She looks like your granny but I wouldn't mess with her.'

When he'd gone, I called George Ritchie. As ever, he answered right away. Choosing not to be involved wouldn't stop him following the unfolding story north of the river and he'd know about my meeting with Small.

'I need the guys again, George.'

'Any time, Luke. As many as you like.'

He paused and I sensed he was going to ask about Blackfriars Bridge.

'What's Small saying to it?'

'The usual guff. Wasting my time trying to put pressure on me about the club. He's a strange man.'

Ritchie agreed. 'He's that all right.'

'I'm looking for an excuse to break his jaw. If he doesn't stop quoting his wife at me, that'll do it.'

George laughed into the phone. 'Got an awful lot to say for a dead woman, hasn't she?'

'Dead? His wife's dead?'

'The rumour is Jonas caught her in bed with another man and offed the two of them.'

'When was this?'

'Way back. Nobody's seen Lily Small since 1987.'

* * *

Oliver Stanford pulled into the drive outside his house and turned off the ignition. Victor Russo had made an excellent job of the repairs to the Audi – good as new – though Stanford didn't feel the same about the car. When he looked across at the passenger seat, he pictured the shoebox and its intimidating contents and remembered why Elise was still with her sister in Cornwall.

He pinched tired eyes; it had been one bastard of a week, and it wasn't over. The drugs in the hooker's handbag had been laced with methamphetamine, commonly referred to as 'speed'. Smoked, snorted, injected or taken orally, the effect on an unsuspecting user could be devastating. Added to the inherently unstable synthetic cannabis – black mamba – no surprise the guy had gone off the deep end.

On the phone, Glass had been brusque. No appreciation for the favours he'd called in to get the test result so quickly. Stanford wasn't a fool; the relationship with the gangster or his brother had never been great. Sooner or later, it would end. What that meant for him wasn't something the copper let himself think about.

Normally, Stanford shunned police functions, leaving parties especially – listening to half-pissed boring bobbies tell each other lies wasn't his idea of a great night out. But there were times it couldn't be avoided. Tonight was one of those.

John Jacob Shaw – Jocky to his many pals – was the living proof it was better to be lucky than smart. The lazy incompetent bastard was retiring after three decades of fooling some of the people all of the time. Shaw was popular with the powers on high so showing his face made political sense.

Stanford was sick of playing the game; he didn't have it in him any more. This was the last. And if his bosses questioned why he didn't show up, fuck it, he'd tell them the truth.

The key slipped into the lock and he stepped inside. Immediately, Stanford sensed he wasn't alone and reached for the hammer he'd hidden in the umbrella stand after the stranger in the garden's nocturnal visit, his fingers closing round its wooden stock, the weight of the head heavy in his hand. He gritted his teeth and slowly pushed the kitchen door open.

Elise was sitting at the table they'd bought on a rainy Saturday morning from Habitat in Tottenham Court Road; she looked wonderful. When she saw her husband, she jumped up and ran to him.

'Don't be angry, Oliver. Please, don't be angry with me. I couldn't stand being away from you another day.'

She fell against his chest and he held her, gently stroking her hair.

'I'm not angry, darling. I'm not angry at all. I need you here.'

* * *

The light from the window hurt Jazzer's eyes. His temple throbbed; he groaned and curled himself into a ball. He was on a bed – his bed – fully clothed, his head aching, his lips cracked and dry, no clue how he'd got there. Jazzer had been fourteen years old when he'd had his first blackout after downing three litres of Strongbow with his mates in Stanley Park. Since then, loss of memory had become an accepted part of his life. Everybody he knew joked about it, wore it like a badge. So, what was there to be concerned about? His last clear recollection from today was the faces of his friends, at the bar laughing with a stranger who thought it was safe to wind him up about the woman in London.

The only people who knew were Ronnie and Tosh – they must've told him – and egged the mug on to give him the juicy details. The bottle appeared in Jazzer's hand as if some unseen force had passed it to him and pressed his fingers to the neck. Then the man was on the floor screaming, blood pouring from his head, and Jazzer had felt rough hands hauling him outside.

Tosh was shouting: 'Fuck's sake, Jazzer, he was joking. What's wrong with you?'

Somebody called him an animal. After that, there was nothing except an emptiness where the afternoon was supposed to be. He rolled off the bed and stood, dizzy, blinking stupidly at the wall. Still drunk, though sober enough to realise he couldn't go back to that pub. There were bloodstains down the front of his shirt.

Jazzer stuck his hand into his trouser pocket and came out with a wad of fivers and tens and twenties – what was left of the money she'd paid him. If he could turn the clock back to the meeting in the Holiday Inn in Lime Street, he'd tell her what she could do with her job. And she'd have to find another idiot, some other guy to humiliate instead of him. An image of the unmade bed in Earls Court

Road rushed to meet him; he turned away, almost like warding off a blow, wishing a blackout would swallow him.

* * *

Bridie leaned on the open car door and spoke to Niall, alone in the back, his good hand firmly gripping the holdall on the seat beside him. In the evening light, his eyes shone; he'd washed his hair and put on a fresh shirt – at long last the forgotten soldier had a purpose. He was happy and she realised how much her need to protect him had cost Niall Monahan. The bomb he'd been putting together had taken half of his hand; unintentionally, she'd taken his pride, as well.

After the accident, Bridie had given him the room upstairs on condition he left the IRA. That way, she could keep him safe. He'd been crushed, too weak to argue, when she'd announced there was no role for him in her businesses. His nerves were shot. He was lucky to be alive. But the blast had cut a hole inside him he'd been filling with alcohol ever since.

Not today. Today he needed his wits about him and he was sober.

Bridie fussed like a mother on her only child's first day at school. 'Now, no hero nonsense.' She pointed to the guy in the passenger seat. 'We're in radio contact with Luke Glass.'

'I heard you.'

She tapped his forehead. 'Aye, but is any of it goin' in?'

Niall faked irritation. 'You're startin' to annoy me, girl. Do you imagine sayin' the same thing over and over to a fella will make any feckin' difference?'

She saw the livid scar, the marks on his face, and remembered the night after the pub closed: they'd been talking about the past, the old days. He'd gone to his room and returned with a faded photograph of a shy young man taken on a summer day, the green Wicklow hills in the distance behind him. Niall had been proud and so he should: the teenager had long eyelashes and clear skin; a fine boy. The local girls would've fancied him and been disappointed if they'd known he couldn't love a woman – he barely knew it himself. With one exception: he loved her. Always had. And she loved him.

She spoke quietly, the words catching in her throat. 'It makes a difference to me.'

'Then you're a bloody fool, Bridie O'Shea.'

'It's true, I am. Only... I'm fond of you. Can't help myself.'

He pretended to mock her. 'Now she bloody tells me.'

Bridie replied with her familiar bluster. 'All right, have it your own way. Just don't forget—'

'Sweet Jesus!'

'Do what I'm askin', Monahan, or you'll answer to me.'

31

Oliver Stanford threw his hands down and swore at the mirror. 'For Christ's sake, Elise. Fix this thing, will you? Whoever invented the bow tie should've been put up against a wall and shot.'

Elise stood in front of him, measuring the ends, making sure one was longer than the other.

'It isn't difficult. It takes patience, darling, and you've never had a lot of that, have you?'

'Not when the car will be here in five minutes. Thank God you're back.'

'You don't want to go and it's making you irritable.'

Her husband didn't disagree. 'I object to sitting through boring speeches praising a man I despise along with a bunch of people pissed out of their minds.'

Elise teased the tie into place and stepped back to critique her work. 'Very handsome, though I'll never understand why you insist on wearing a real one. The clip-on kind look just as good.'

'No, they don't. Besides, a senior officer in the Met can't be caught with a clip-on.'

'If they're all drunk, what does it matter?'

'It matters to me. It says something about the man.'

She stood on tiptoe and kissed his cheek. 'That he's superficial?'

'Worse, he's trying to impress and is prepared to cut corners.'

She laughed. 'Is that why you dislike Jocky Shaw so much?

'One of many reasons.'

'He's always nice to me.'

'That's because he'd like to get into your knickers. And before you get all girly and flattered, he's the same with every woman.'

'I haven't been a girl in a long time, and I don't feel flattered, thank you very much. I just doubt he's as bad as you make out.'

'You're right. Bad isn't a fair description. Fucking awful is nearer the mark.'

'I know you complain about him, I've heard you often enough, but, honestly, is he any worse than the others?'

Stanford didn't need to think about his answer. 'In a word, yes. The job's too much for him. Been a disaster since his first day. Started badly and fell away. I can't remember a single initiative he's been responsible for. He couldn't spell strategic. A follower not a leader. The men don't respect him. Is that enough reasons?'

'Quite enough, thank you. At the Christmas party he brought me a sherry and told me to call him Jocky.'

Stanford smiled grimly at his reflection. 'Wonder what would happen if I tried that.' He turned to his wife. 'And for the record, Jocky's a nickname he invented to make him seem approachable. Like everything about him, it's a con. He's a liability. The service is well rid of him.'

'Who'll take over?'

Her husband understood. Elise was even more ambitious than him. In her artless way, asking if he was in the running. As she helped him on with his jacket, he lowered her expectations. 'Any idea how many supers there are in the service?'

'How many?'

'A hundred and ninety-seven.'

'Then it's a shoo-in.'

* * *

The city was quiet, gearing up for the night. Through the window, Niall caught glimpses of streets and places he hadn't seen in years. His world had shrunk since he'd stepped off the Liverpool train at Euston and taken a taxi to a bedsit in Camden, where a friend of his brother had offered him the floor until he sorted himself out. The cab driver had heard the broad accent and seen an easy mark, taking him on York Way as far as Tufnell Park Tube station, before doubling back. Niall watched the meter clock the money up and smiled at the casualness of the racist stereotyping. He'd never forgotten the look on the driver's face when the two one-pound coins had dropped into his upturned palm and he'd said, 'Thanks for the tour, mate.'

The cockiness of youth – for sure, he'd been given more than his fair share. Added to a quick mind and a handsome face, only a fool would've bet against him achieving great things.

The bomb had changed all that. He'd ended up depending on the generosity of Wolf Kavanagh's widow, asking nothing of him because he had nothing to offer except friendship.

Until now.

The men in the front seats kept their eyes on the road; Niall knew them, of course, from the pub – always at the end of the bar, keeping themselves to themselves, drinking Bell's neat – the universe he'd return to after this was done. He touched his cheek, feeling its rough landscape, the unimaginable ugliness of it.

His fingers itched – the fingers that weren't there – and he tightened his hold on the bag.

Like the instant the spark met the ammonium nitrate, too fast to avoid, a blue Mondeo overtook them and slewed sideways, blocking the road. Four men jumped out, guns drawn, shattering the windscreen in a hail of bullets before a word had been spoken. The driver and the guy in the passenger seat died instantly without getting off a shot or warning the club.

Niall readied himself for the inevitable and didn't hide. The leader walked to the car, taking his time, toying with his weapon as if he hadn't decided whether he needed it. Niall's missing digits were on fire, more painful than the awful moment, frozen in time, when they'd been separated from the rest of his hand in a flash of orange light. Then, there had been nothing – no searing hurt, no nanosecond of knowing. All that came later when he regained consciousness in the hospital.

The hijacker opened the back door and pointed the black barrel at his head, nodding as if he understood. 'The Irishwoman sent you. Smart.'

'Nobody sent me.'

'Give me the bag.'

Niall thought about Bridie: when they told her, she'd cry and retreat to the sanctuary of the room at the back of the pub, to the cards and those damned cigarettes. But she was strong, she'd got over Wolf and she'd get over him.

Deep inside Niall Monahan felt something lost return.

If it wasn't him here, it would be her.

He'd saved her.

The man with the gun spoke again, his piercing eyes boring into him, his voice tight with impatience. 'Give me the fucking bag!'

Niall slowly lifted the holdall off the floor, unzipped the top and turned it upside down, shaking its emptiness in a final show of defiance. His ruined face spread in a grin.

'And don't you be spendin' it all at once, now, you hear?'

* * *

It was seven-thirty. The money should've been here at seven. I stood at the back door of the club with Mark Douglas and his two guys, expecting a car from Bridie O'Shea to turn into the lane. The men Douglas had brought on board were similar enough to be brothers: slim bodies and broad shoulders, lantern jaws and eyes that never left the Margaret Street entrance. They didn't acknowledge me and held their weapons out in front of them, poised and ready, like the mercenaries they so clearly were.

Douglas understood the significance of the delay, glanced anxiously across at me and stated the obvious. 'This isn't good. What do you want me to do?'

'Nothing, yet.'

Five minutes passed with no sign of the vehicle. Douglas couldn't hide his concern.

He knew. So did I. It was happening again.

I was too preoccupied to notice the security guard from upstairs until he touched my arm to get my attention and almost had his hand broken for his trouble.

'Sorry, boss, there's somebody asking to see you.'

'Not now.'

'Says to tell you her name's Bridie.'

She sat inside the door like someone waiting to be interviewed for a job they needed but didn't want. Bridie O'Shea wore a tan raincoat and a blue scarf; a faded carpet bag lay at her feet. Seeing her away from her usual habitat without the endless round of cards or swirling cloud of cigarette smoke was odd. I'd no idea why she was here, unless it was to tell me face to face she'd changed her mind and was dropping out of our arrangement, which would explain the non-appearance of the cash.

She smiled when she saw me and nudged the bag with her foot.

'Is this what you're lookin' for? Two hundred thousand pounds, as arranged.'

My confusion showed. 'I don't understand.'

She said, 'I see you're not a man who's big on surprises. Even the nice ones. I'll bet you got a fright when you opened the bag Niall gave you?'

'Niall? Bridie... Niall hasn't been here.'

It took a moment for what I was telling her to register. When it did, she took out her mobile and made three calls, visibly ageing in front of me when none of them answered and reality hit her.

'Bridie, let me get you a brandy.'

I thought she hadn't heard but she had.

'No, I have to get back. We'll talk tomorrow.'

* * *

Bridie O'Shea was no stranger to tragedy. In her Republican days, the indiscriminate violence she'd crossed the water to be part of had brought sorrow to scores of innocent bystanders caught up in a struggle she'd aligned herself with to impress the man she wanted. Today, it was her turn. Her men were dead, their journey cut short in broad daylight on those same London streets. We didn't have the details. Along with the rest of the country, we'd hear them soon enough. By the time the next news cycle came around, the names of the dead would be forgotten – the images of bloodstains and splintered glass would linger.

I was tired of fighting an enemy who refused to show themselves. Furious at always being a step behind. Never sure where or when an attack was coming. Taking my frustration out on somebody would be easy, except opening the club had been down to me and I hadn't been alone – somebody had been watching. Waiting for the right moment to make their move. The vultures would be hovering, biding their time to strip the carcass clean: LBC, Glass Houses, Glass Construction – all on the line; all up for grabs.

The rules of the game never changed: if you couldn't defend yourself, you wouldn't survive and didn't deserve to.

We'd survive or we'd die trying.

George Ritchie was having my sisters picked up; they'd be here shortly. Mark Douglas had every entrance other than the front door locked down. At ten o'clock, as far as the world was concerned, it would be business as usual on Margaret Street. Behind the scenes was another story. Ritchie had called to reassure me everything on his side of the river was sound and that half-a-dozen guys were armed and ready to join me if I needed them.

Good to know. So far, I didn't. Although that could change in a heartbeat.

Charley arrived first, dressed like a movie star, ready for another night as the club's hostess. I told her what I understood about how it had gone with Bridie O'Shea. She let me speak and didn't interrupt. When I finished, she said, 'The girls have to be put in the picture.'

She was right. If we'd learned anything from the Algernon Drake experience it was that no one and nowhere was safe. Her concern was appreciated but it had to be handled carefully. The hookers were in the dark about Zelda. As far as they knew, she'd received word from Ireland about her mother and gone home.

'Just remind them to be careful who they pull.'

Charley agreed and left to go upstairs. It was still early days though it was working out with her – behind the Christina Hendricks persona was a sharp mind. Unfortunately, the same couldn't be said of Nina. She arrived, looking tired and sullen, and slumped into the seat opposite me. My sister had never had a filter, a sense of how the wind was blowing, and didn't have one now, her opening statement enough to tell me where her head was. In my face from minute one.

'Maybe I should move in with George Ritchie – every time I turn around one of his guys is ordering me to get my bag and follow him.'

'Nina, listen—'

'The old letch would like that, he's—'

'Nina—'

'How much longer are you going to allow this fiasco to go on? Somebody's laughing at us. Fuck! The whole town's laughing at us.' She ploughed on. 'We're acting like a bunch of wankers, for Christ's sake. Danny would've found out who's behind it and crushed them after they stole Jonas Small's money.'

The Danny reference was a jibe too far. I put my hand over her selfish mouth. She realised she'd pushed too far. The words hissed from between my gritted teeth. 'Ritchie's crime is he's trying to save your worthless life, and so am I. The family's being attacked. Systematically picked apart. Chose a side, Nina.' I took my hand away. 'As for Danny – compare me to him again and you're out on your arse with nothing.'

'You can't do that.'

'Yeah? Try me.'

Mark Douglas knocked on the door and came in before she could dig a deeper hole for herself. He shot a glance at Nina and then at me. 'The hit on Bridie's guys is all over the Internet. Nothing from the police.'

'What about the club?'

'Short of barricading the front door, we're as ready as we'll ever be. Got Fraser and Hume up there, though they're not exactly LBC types. I'm keeping them in the kitchen, out of sight. Chefs are scared shitless. If our enemy comes at us, we'll give a decent account of ourselves.'

Douglas seemed confident – unfortunately, some situations were beyond even him. Minutes after Charley came back down to the office, it all kicked off, and there were no prizes for guessing who started it.

Charley closed the door and leaned against it. 'Only a couple of girls in. I've told them what they need to know. Made it sound like a standard warning – nothing special to be concerned about. They'll pass it on.'

'Thanks, Charley.'

Nina butted in. 'Are we expected to stay here all night?'

'Depends, Nina.'

'On what?'

'What happens next. My guess is nothing will. But I'm not betting your life, let alone mine, on it. When the members start arriving, go upstairs, have a couple of drinks and mingle. Only a couple, don't overdo it – we need our wits about us.'

'What wits?'

If Charley had kept her mouth shut it would've ended differently. She didn't. 'Don't you think you should cut Luke a break?'

Nina didn't hold back. 'What I think is that you should keep your Yank nose out of our business.'

Charley pushed off the wall. 'Isn't it about time you dropped the spoiled little bitch act and be your age? Or maybe it isn't an act. Maybe it's who you really are. Either way, I'm tired of it.'

'And I'm tired of seeing your fat arse squeezed into an Una Burke, so where does that leave us?'

'The real problem is you're pissed because she left you and took me. Admit it.'

Mark Douglas was standing between them – he might as well not have existed. Nina screamed and flew at her sister, grabbed a handful of hair and dragged her into the centre of the room. Charley stumbled, regained her balance and held Nina to her in a bearhug, thrashing and panting until they both crashed to the floor, scratching and kicking each other.

Nina straddled her, punching her, shouting, 'Bitch! Bitch! Bitch!'

Charley covered her face with her arms and chose her moment to throw Nina off. I was tempted to close the door and let them get on with it. Douglas looked at me for guidance. I nodded and he pulled them apart, still spitting and cursing, though not before a painted talon raked his cheek.

I said, 'Charley, upstairs now and get ready to do what I pay you for.'

I rounded on Nina. 'Get out of here and don't let me see you again until you grow up! Mark, take her home. I'll get George Ritchie to send over a couple of babysitters, make sure she does what she's told.'

* * *

When I'd calmed down, I went upstairs into the world I'd created, where all that mattered was how many strangers knew your name and how many zeros were at the bottom of your secret account in the Caymans. As I strolled across the imported black and white marble floor, under the chandelier that had been freed from a chateau in the Loire Valley at a cost too painful to dwell on, a waiter balancing a bottle of Krug Private Cuvée champagne and four Waterford hot pink flutes on a silver tray glided soundlessly past. A woman with the biggest Afro I'd ever seen gave me a come-on stare and said something to her companion. Both were stunners and I was flattered, until I realised they were two of Charley's girls. From the mirrored booths around the walls, faces I didn't know smiled at me: the men were tanned and rich, the women young and good-looking, no doubt dressed in the current 'must have' designer labels, wearing their partners' wealth on their fingers and round their necks. They were happy, and no wonder. The plush decor, the Amex Black Cards in their calf-skin wallets and Bottega Veneta handbags lulled them into believing they were the chosen ones and disguised their true identities: lucky bastards, casually knocking back some of the most expensive booze in London in a club named after them.

Me, I kept it simple – I was a whisky and Hugo Boss kind of guy.

There was no envy on my part and, of course, I could and would greet them like old friends. They were fools, clueless about the dramas going on behind the scenes, unaware they were being used to clean dirty money, earned from other people's addiction and back-alley sex. Or that any moment my enemy might come through the front door. If that happened, the temple would crumble round their ears and all the diamonds in Hatton Garden wouldn't be enough to save them.

Outside, rain fell silently on the city from a dark sky; my mind turned to Kelly. Since she'd dumped me, I hadn't thought about her. Standing at the door of LBC, I pictured being crushed between her smooth thighs as she moaned, threw her head back and climaxed long and hard. I'd phone her, except the timing was wrong, and, quite rightly, she'd tell me to do one.

Mark Douglas wasn't back yet; he was taking his time. I stood in the elegant entrance under the domed roof beside the huge statue of Fortuna, the Roman goddess of luck, alabaster coins cascading from the horn of plenty nestled in the crook of her arm.

The capricious whore had done fuck all for me so far except cost me money and take up space.

She wasn't alone.

32

Mark Douglas kept his eyes on the road and the red tail lights of the cars in front, following the sweep of Regent Street, slicked with rain, to the neon madness of Piccadilly Circus, crowded with teenagers and tourists enjoying the big-city vibe. Nina stared out but said nothing; he knew she was hurting. Behind the crass behaviour was a fragile woman, damaged in ways Douglas couldn't begin to understand.

On Haymarket, he broke the silence. 'Are you okay?'

She replied without looking at him. 'Not really.'

'Want to talk about it?'

'Not really.'

Douglas hesitated, wanting to reach her but wary of her reaction. The jibe about her mother had set her off. He spoke quietly. 'I'm sorry you had to go through that, Nina. Charley shouldn't have said what she did. She pretends she's super-confident. Didn't sound like it to me. More like somebody struggling to find a place for themselves and screwing it up. Families are tough. Give it time.'

She faced him, her eyes dark and angry. 'And that's your advice, is it? That's the best you've got. "Give it time."'

'You got a better idea?'

'Yeah, tear her stupid head off her shoulders.'

He smiled. 'Well, when you put it like that...'

At the bottom of Parliament Street, he turned left and crossed Westminster Bridge as the quarter bells of Big Ben chimed on the half-hour, then continued on towards the Albert Embankment. The exchange had mellowed her. Nina said, 'Sometimes I hate him.'

She meant Luke.

'Every sister in the world has felt like that. It's natural.'

'Except, I'm serious. Do your sisters hate you?'

'Only got one – she's in South Africa. No idea what she thinks of me. Haven't seen her in twenty years.'

'Do you keep in touch?'

'We did, for a while. Not now. We're strangers. Whatever we had died with our parents. That's what I'm saying about families being hard. You're from the same gene pool, you're blood, that should bind you together, except all too often it doesn't.'

They skirted The Oval cricket ground and pulled up at traffic lights. Nina crossed her legs, slowly and deliberately. Douglas caught a flash of thigh she'd intended him to see. He swallowed, gripped the steering wheel and forced himself to focus on the threat to LBC – still live, still real.

In Denmark Hill, she directed him to a quiet street and a white Georgian house with a square of well-tended garden at the front. Douglas said, 'Didn't have you pegged as the gardening type.'

'I'm not. A man takes care of it for me.'

The implication was unmistakeable. Douglas ignored it, turned off the ignition and started to get out. Nina said, 'Where're you going?'

'Have to see you safely—'

'For God's sake. I'm not a child, despite what my brother thinks.'

Douglas leaned into the car. 'You're not taking this seriously,

Nina. Your family's in danger. People have already died. Now, let me do my job, eh?'

Nina scowled, fished her keys out of her bag and marched to the door. In the lounge, she switched on a table lamp and flooded the room in warm light. Douglas paused; the interior was elegant: one wall featured a five-panel Rio Silver mural in a modern banana leaf pattern, behind a white leather couch resting on the polished hard-wood floor and a deep-red oblong Indian rug. A set of African tribal figures, males and females, carved in ebony, claimed the far corner, while charcoal line-drawings and black-and-white photographs of Victorian London framed the original fireplace.

Under his breath, Douglas whistled: Nina Glass had eclectic taste – and style.

'Nice place.'

'The perks of being in the business. When something comes on the market, I get first shout, and I know what the owners are prepared to accept.'

'You've done well.'

She went to the kitchen and called to him; it seemed her annoy-ance at her brother was forgotten. 'Drink?'

'No, thanks.'

'Go on, just one.'

'Okay, one it is.'

Nina came back with two glasses. 'I owe you an apology. What's going on is scary. Maybe I'm in denial. As for Charley...'

'Forget about her.'

She handed him a cut-glass tumbler. 'You're from Scotland so I guessed whisky, am I right?'

'I never say no.'

She waited till he'd checked each room in turn, making sure no one was there. They clinked glasses and watched each other over the rim. Nina moved in closer, gently touched the cut on his cheek and ran a manicured fingernail down his chest. 'What else do you never say no to?'

Douglas felt himself go hard. He stepped away and put a hand on her shoulder. 'Nina... this isn't the time, really it isn't. Luke's expecting me back.'

Her eyes were bright, her lips parted defiantly. 'To hell with him.'

'I'll tell him you said that.'

'Tell him anything you like.'

He put down the glass. 'You're really not taking this seriously enough, Nina. I told you, people have died. Don't you get that? Doesn't it mean anything to you? Luke believes he could lose everything, and so do I.'

Her arms circled his neck, she lowered her head and looked up at him like a naughty little girl. Douglas couldn't decide whether to kiss her or slap some sense into her.

'And I might be next – is that what you were going to say? Don't be so predictable, Mark. Predictable is dull. I don't do dull.'

He took hold of her hands, irritated by her performance. 'Please, Nina. Your brother has enough on without worrying about you. I'd stay. I want to stay. But it's the wrong time.'

She turned her back to him and walked away. 'A man only gets one chance with me. If he's stupid enough to pass it up...'

Nina left the rest unsaid.

Douglas closed the lounge door and stood in the hall, torn between lust and anger, every atom in his body aching to take her in his arms. Desire crippled him; he felt weak, tried to leave and couldn't; his legs refused to take him. He'd had his share of women – more than his share – but his need for this one was greater than anything he'd known. The face of the woman who'd had her throat slit rose in front of him, her lifeless eyes urging him back to the club and his duty. He shook his head, fighting against it, willing the memory to leave him alone so he could be with Nina Glass.

In the lounge, Nina sighed and kicked off her shoes – having a man reject her was an experience she wasn't used to. She sipped the alcohol, the taste strangely harsh and unpleasant, and lay back.

Suddenly, Douglas kicked the door open and stood in the frame, breathing heavily through his mouth. He dived at her, pulling at her blouse with enough force to pop the buttons and reveal the firm breasts underneath. The bra was ripped away as though made of paper; he threw it into the corner with the African carvings, his lips searching for her nipples. In seconds, the skirt and everything underneath were gone and he had her naked. While Douglas devoured her, Nina undressed him, until they were skin on skin. He towered above her, surveying the toned body, savouring the feast laid out for his pleasure. Painted nails raked his flat stomach, her slim legs parted and he buried himself in her to the hilt. Nina gasped under his thrusts, arched her spine and climaxed. Then, they went at each other like animals. When it was over, he lay on the Indian rug, closed his eyes and waited for his heartbeat to return to normal.

Douglas couldn't be sure if he'd fallen asleep – it was like a dream; she was calling his name. He followed the sound to the end of the unlit hall. A street lamp washed the darkened room. In the pale light, Nina was in silhouette, kneeling on the edge of the bed, facing away, her head low, thighs spread wide.

She sensed he'd joined her and spoke, her voice hoarse with lust. 'Again. Take me again.'

* * *

After Bridie O'Shea and my sisters, the rest of the night seemed positively dull. Nothing out of the ordinary happened. When

Douglas got back, we shot the breeze, watching and waiting, happy to be wasting our time. Around 2 a.m., I called Bridie and eventually managed to get an answer. She sounded drunk, slurring her speech and losing track of who was phoning. The little I'd had to do with her had me convinced she was indestructible – a west London fixture, untouched by pain.

But under the skin, everybody was the same.

33

Stanford had been right about the speeches – tedious and unfunny; a parade of sycophantic anecdotes about what a great guy Jocky Shaw was. It was enough to make you puke.

But he'd been around. He knew the rules and played his part, laughing when everybody else laughed, at pains not to reveal how much the after-dinner cigar smoke bothered him. At a break, he went to the toilet and found himself next to Commander Iain Bremner. Senior officers used these occasions to bond with the men under their command, knocking back whiskies with the best of them, getting a round in when it was their shout, and generally pretending to be one of the lads. Racist comments and off-colour jokes were met with guffaws that would mean trouble if repeated in daylight.

The two men nodded to each other. Beyond the door, the murmur of the raffle being drawn drifted into the Gents. Bremner took a bundle of tickets from his jacket with his free hand, stared at them as if he hadn't seen them before and stuffed them back in his pocket.

'Never won a thing in my life – have you? The old football pools, the lottery, even the tombola at the church bazaar. A waste of bloody time and money.'

There was a slur in Bremner's voice, his eyes were heavy, and Stanford realised the commander had had a few too many. More than a few: he was drunk. He said, 'Another good man gone. Soon be our turn.'

Stanford humoured him. 'The end of an era.'

'Indeed. Indeed. We'll miss Jocky.'

Suddenly, the hypocrisy was too much to take. 'Will we, sir? You sure about that?'

Bremner considered the question, then put a clammy hand on the other man's shoulder to steady himself. 'Well said, Superintendent. We spout such terrible bollocks at these jollies. Easy to fall into the trap. A couple of brandies, a glass or three of wine, and we'll swear black is white.' He stared at his shoes, slowly shaking his head. 'I worked with him for a year – 2008, I think it was – a useless lazy bastard of the first order. Pissed me off so much I requested a transfer to get away from him. Can't complain. Indirectly, I owe him my career. But I've never met a copper who liked him.'

'Neither have I.'

'Not a bloody one.'

'Hard to believe from what's being said out there.'

'Sheep, the fucking lot of them. Christ knows how Shaw's got away with it, but he has.'

'Friends in high places and a talent for fooling some of the people all of the time. A gift not many have.'

'Spot on. Wish I had it.'

'We all do.'

Bremner drew himself straight. 'Miss him? Will we fuck.'

'Between ourselves, sir.'

'Between ourselves, of course.' He started to leave and stopped. 'What's your name?'

'Stanford. Oliver Stanford.'

Bremner nodded. 'Of course. Thought I recognised you. A rising star, from what I hear.'

'I do my best. Nice to know my efforts haven't gone unnoticed, sir.'

'Far from it. Say this for you, Stanford, you're not afraid to speak your mind. There's a place for that in the Met. Or there should be. These days the service is full of arse-lickers. Give me a call when we've sobered up. I'd like your opinion on a few things. Could do with a breath of fresh air. My people tell me what they think I want to hear. Save themselves a bollocking at the time, but it's no damned good in the long run.'

'Absolutely, sir. Anything in particular?'

Bremner continued as if Stanford hadn't spoken. 'The PM isn't happy with the rising crime figures. Not the look he's after. Election's still a long way off but unless they improve, his law and order platform's screwed and he knows it. Needs a big win if he's to have any hope of getting back into Number 10.'

'Anything I can do?'

Bremner leaned against the door. 'As a matter of fact... Operation Clean Sweep mean anything to you?'

'No.'

'Glad to hear it.' He tapped the side of his nose. 'Top bloody secret. Shouldn't be talking about it, really. Pretend you didn't hear that, will you?'

'Not easy, sir, now you've whetted my curiosity. I won't sleep tonight thinking about it.'

Bremner clapped his shoulder. 'Sorry about that, sorry about that, Superintendent. Fucking unfair to give you a sniff and leave you hanging. Big mouth. Can't hold my water – or so my wife says.'

The commander was three sheets to the wind; Stanford chanced it. 'You can trust me, sir.'

Bremner's muddy eyes studied his face. 'Can I? I believe I can at that.' He gathered his confused thoughts, jaw slack, mouth forming unspoken words. 'Law enforcement in the twenty-first century is fucked. Absolutely shafted. Reduced to a bunch of soundbites to keep the masses from panicking. Don't have to tell a man like you. The war on this, the sodding war on that.' He laughed, grimly. 'Whatever we do we're humped and that's the truth of it. Nobody says it out loud – defeatist talk. Not politically correct. Who wants to hear we're beaten before we even get started?'

Stanford nudged him back to the topic.

'Where does Operation Clean Sweep come in?'

'Simple. Drugs, money laundering. London's become the filthy-money capital of the fucking world. It's out of control and getting worse. We need points on the board. Make it look like the PM's a tough guy. And for the first time in Christ knows how long, it looks like we've got a break.'

'With Clean Sweep.'

'You're catching on.' He put his hands to his head. 'Christ, I'm going to be bad in the morning. *And* I'm bloody working.'

The lie came out of nowhere. 'So am I, sir.'

'Yes, but you're younger. In better shape than me.'

Stanford took the conversation back to where it had been. 'What's it about?'

'What's what about?'

'Clean Sweep.'

'Oh, corruption in the force. Rooting out the bad apples.' He rubbed his nose. 'I know, I know. We're knee-deep in bent bobbies, always have been. These stings can take years. Not soon enough for the prime minister's agenda. This is different. We've got somebody on the inside. Right at the centre.'

Stanford felt the hairs on his neck rise; he blinked but didn't speak. His heart jumped in his chest. For a moment, he thought his legs would give way. If Bremner had been sober he'd have heard the quiver in his voice. 'A mole?'

Bremner nodded. 'Word is, a ghost squad and they're the best.'

Stanford faked delight. 'Great stuff, sir. The bastards have been getting it their own way for too long. Which outfit's been infiltrated?'

The senior man put a drunken finger to his lips and smiled a sly smile. 'Let's just say it might be better to avoid a certain nightclub until the dust settles.'

Thank God the old bugger was too far gone to see the line of sweat on Stanford's top lip.

'Luke Glass? Christ Almighty!'

'We'll get whoever he's in cahoots with. And we'll get him as well. I'd bet my pension on it. He's taken on a Scottish copper – a headstrong fucker who blotted his copybook and left Glasgow in a hurry.'

'And he's the insider?'

'With his record? When the lid blows off, the Scotch bastard will fall with his pals.'

'So, who've we got in there?'

'That, my friend, is the best-kept secret in London. Even the PM doesn't know the details. The commissioner, the deputy, and maybe two or three people in the whole of the Met have that information and I'm not one of them. Ridiculous, considering I'm part of it.' He studied the palms of his hands. 'It's locked down tighter than a badger's arse.'

Stanford swallowed hard. The commander didn't notice and carried on. 'But if it goes the way it should, it'll be the biggest police corruption scandal since Operation Countryman in the seventies.'

'Before my time, sir.'

'And mine.' He closed one eye and squinted. 'How fucking old do you think I am?'

'That's not what I meant, sir.'

'The media will lap it up.' Bremner drew the headline in the air with an intoxicated finger.

'BENT!'

Stanford's tongue felt thick in his mouth; he struggled to get out the words. 'Any officer who drags the good name of the service in the gutter deserves to go down.'

'My feelings, exactly. We'll get Glass and his associates. Two for the price of one. Spent thousands trying to nail his brother so, when it happens, it'll be sweet. Danny came out of nowhere. No bugger rises as fast as he did without help from our side. Can I assume you'd be interested in being involved?'

Stanford was stunned. 'Absolutely. Is that possible? I mean, can that be arranged?'

Bremner winked. 'A whisper in the right ear won't hurt. As you said, friends in high places and all that, eh?'

The door creaked shut behind him. Oliver Stanford waited a few minutes before following; he was trembling. Everything he had, everything he'd achieved was threatened by what he'd heard. Luke Glass was building a reputation as a successful businessman. It wasn't the truth – the gangster was what he'd always been and always would be: a career criminal. Sooner or later, no question, he'd go down. In the end, his kind always did. Stanford had no intentions of going with him. How he'd manage to avoid it wasn't clear. But he would. By God, he would.

When Jocky Shaw finished his retirement speech and accepted the inscribed crystal decanter and glasses, the room rose to applaud one of their own. Through the crowd Stanford saw Commander Bremner up on his feet with the rest.

* * *

Jazzer pushed the door open and staggered out into the night. A thin sheet of rain fell silently – he didn't have a coat and couldn't have cared less. Jazzer was drunk and he'd been drunk every day since London. He was at the befuddled stage, slurring his words, losing his line of thought, struggling to keep his balance. The pub he'd been in wasn't his usual haunt. He couldn't go there any more – they'd barred him after he'd given that loser what he deserved.

It was no loss. Liverpool was full of fucking pubs. Ronnie and Tosh were no loss either, if it came to it. All they did was remind him. Remind him of her.

A taxi with its 'For Hire' light on turned the corner at the end of the road. Jazzer stopped unsteadily at the kerb, leaned against a lamp post, and held his arm out. The driver slowed, saw the state he was in and drove on – his shift was finishing in an hour; he could do without somebody being sick in the back of his cab. Jazzer gave him the finger, mumbling.

The world was full of bastards.

He didn't realise he wasn't alone until the baseball bat cracked against his shin, breaking it in two. The pain was instant and unbearable – Jazzer dropped to his knees; a second well-aimed blow snapped his collarbone like a dried-out twig at the end of a long hot summer. Powerful hands dragged him to his feet and laid into him. No words were spoken. When he was on the ground, bloodied and beaten, boots replaced fists.

Jazzer's eyelids flickered and closed – the pain meant nothing to him.

Everybody had to die some time.

* * *

Oliver Stanford loosened his black bow tie and poured himself a very large whisky; he needed it. Elise was expecting him to make love to her when he came home. Not tonight – he'd too much on his mind for sex. The chance meeting with the commander, barely able to stand, had rocked his world. Tomorrow, assuming Bremner remembered the conversation, he'd regret it. Was offering him a role in Operation Clean Sweep just the booze talking? Or a clumsy attempt to cover the slip of a drunken tongue? Either way, it didn't matter – Stanford was in the shit. Big time.

His relationship with the Glass crime family, first with Danny and now with Luke, had been going on for years. And Bremner was correct. Danny couldn't have travelled as fast and as far without someone in the know. That someone had been him.

He'd taken care to keep contact minimal – not always possible with the hot-headed older Glass brother demanding to see him at a moment's notice. That said, there was no paper or digital trail from the gangster to Stanford's door. The few times he'd been in the club he'd made sure it seemed like an innocent night on the town, and when he'd called, he'd used the burner phone he kept hidden in a book in his study.

But with an insider recording times, dates, meetings and conversations, none of it would save him. All it needed was for his name to slip out and it would be over. His colleagues were hardest on their own; they wouldn't rest until they'd nailed him. In prison, criminals he'd sent down would have him exactly where they wanted him. He'd be tortured, raped and beaten. Until one morning, the guards who'd been paid to look the other way found him hanging in his cell.

Just another bent copper who'd got what he deserved.

Stanford was sweating, close to losing it, barely holding on. His thoughts raced to the past and the brown envelope from Danny Glass – the first of many. How heavy it had felt in his palm. It was an opportunity – that was the lie he'd told himself – only a fool would turn down. His girls were growing up; he'd wanted the best for them. What father wouldn't? And Elise had hated where they lived. For doing almost nothing, they could move. Then, it had been a bigger place in a better neighbourhood, private schools for his daughters – the holidays, the cars, the house in Hendon. Right or wrong hadn't come into it. A man provided for his family any way he could. There was nothing more to be said. Until the conversation tonight in the lavatory with the drunk officer, Oliver had been in denial, refusing to consider how the end game, when it came, would play out.

Then Glass had moved the goalposts and come to his home in broad daylight. Dangerous and reckless – the action of a man under pressure. Stanford recalled the heat of the grill and the sun on his face, then peering through a cloud of blue smoke to see the south London gangster standing at the side of the house. Fucking Christ Almighty! His eyes had run frantically over his guests, patiently waiting for their lunch, paper plates and plastic cutlery in one hand, glasses of wine in the other, chatting, enjoying the day.

Getting Glass out of the garden before anybody recognised him had been the priority. Luke hadn't appreciated being ushered away. Too bloody bad. He'd forgotten the rules, rules that had kept both of them out of jail.

When he'd left, Stanford had plastered on a smile and rejoined the party, studying every expression, suspicious of the slightest look, analysing each exchange.

Did that mean he'd got away with it? Or had somebody at the barbeque recognised the south London thug, put the pieces together, and made the phone call that would end life as Oliver Stanford had known it? If the answer was yes, he'd lose it all – the job, his freedom; his girls would disown him. Divorce wouldn't be far behind.

Paranoia got the better of him and he imagined himself as Clean Sweep's first major scalp, his picture on the front page of every newspaper in the country.

They'd make an example of him. Throw away the key.

The clock on the wall ticked away the minutes, the hours. Stanford willed it faster so he could call Luke Glass, forcing himself to take deep breaths, calm down and think it through: the only thing that could screw him was Glass. If he'd dropped his name, someone would've reacted. Above all else, coppers hated bent coppers who got caught; one of them would've had to let him know they were onto him. His brain searched for an off note, a snide remark, a sneer that said, 'You're dirty.'

If there had been one, he'd missed it.

He'd call Bremner in the morning, get himself on the investigation, get the name of the insider and hope to Christ it was closed down soon.

Whatever else, the relationship with Glass was doomed. If by some miracle Stanford avoided exposure, he'd look out for himself from now on, because nobody else would.

A noise behind him startled his already frayed nerves. The study door opened. Elise wore the scarlet bra and pants he'd bought as a Christmas present. She'd dressed for him and Stanford felt a pang of guilt.

'Oliver, why haven't you come to bed? I'm waiting for you.'

Stanford snapped at her. 'For Christ's sake, Elise, don't sneak up on me like that.'

'I wasn't. I spoke. You mustn't have heard.'

'I'm sorry, darling, my nerves are a bit on edge.'

She repeated her question. 'Aren't you coming to bed?'

He thought on his feet and tried to appear calm. 'I can't. I have to go out again.'

'But you're off duty.'

He took her in his arms, praying she wouldn't hear his pounding heart. 'They need me.'

She looked up at him. 'I need you. Doesn't that count for anything?'

'Of course, it does.'

'The job. Always the bloody job.'

He kissed her forehead. 'I'll make it up to you, I promise.'

'You'd better. I hate this underwear. I only put it on for you. Women never buy red. It doesn't go with anything and shows through your clothes. If I'd had the receipt, I'd have exchanged it.'

Stanford smiled. 'Next time, I'll get white. You go back to bed and I'll see you in the morning.'

At the door she turned and for a moment the girl he'd married two decades earlier was in the room: trusting and kind and too bloody good for him.

With Elise gone, the house was quiet. Stanford toyed with his whisky, considered having another and changed his mind. He crossed the study, removed the hollowed-out book from the shelf and opened it. The mobile inside had only ever been used to call one number – the number he called now.

Luke Glass answered on the fourth ring. Stanford heard the familiar voice on the other end of the line and hated himself for what he'd become. He'd sold his soul and the debt was coming due.

He kept it short. 'Fulton Street in one hour. Be there.'

34

As I bumped the car onto the broken pavement overgrown with weeds the memories that came were jarring and painful: a tin door hanging at an angle on a crumbling brick wall; a rusty padlock welded by time to the metal; the sour smell of disuse and decay; the beating of wings in the rafters above a cold concrete floor and opening my eyes to find Danny grinning at me like the madman he'd been.

Inside, shafts of dawn pierced what little remained of the roof. In the half-light, Oliver Stanford waited, hands thrust into the pockets of a dark-green wax jacket. The dinner suit and bow tie hanging loose at his neck said he'd spent the previous evening on the tiles, probably pissing it up with his police cronies. I'd seen him drink to excess in LBC, when the booze – my booze – was free, and wouldn't have been surprised if he was drunk. His terse call in the middle of the night, ordering rather than asking me to meet him, could only have been made by somebody who'd had a tincture or three too many in the pub with his mates to give him courage.

But Stanford was sober.

I walked towards him, my steps echoing in the silence, conscious of the revolver's weight at my side. He stayed where he was, nervously balancing on the balls of his feet. As the distance between us closed I saw his eyes were strained and tired, the skin around them tight and lined. He was a good-looking bastard, if smug and condescending was your thing. But overnight, the copper had aged.

I looked at my watch. 'Five o'fucking clock in the morning! This better be good, Stanford!'

His mouth opened and closed like a guy who'd had a stroke trying to speak. Driving through the deserted streets, I'd struggled to keep my thoughts in check. But fear was contagious and Stanford's had infected me. Seeing him wrestle with what he had to say, knowing it had to be bad, I felt it slither in my belly like a serpent.

I said, 'Why're we here?'

He whispered, 'I need out.'

'Say again.'

'Out. I need out. They know.'

I lost it and slapped his face, hard. 'What the hell are you talking about?'

'Operation Clean Sweep.'

'What?'

'They've got an insider.'

'An...'

The serpent's forked tongue caressed my insides. I shuddered. Stanford caught my arm. 'You've seen what they do to police in prison. I'd die in there. And Elise would be—'

I dragged him across the floor by his lapels, crawling on his hands and knees, hauled him to his feet and pinned him to the wall. He clutched his chest, head lolling from side to side.

'I can't breathe. For God's sake, I can't breathe.'

I slapped him again. He slid down the wall. I hauled him back up.

'Talk, copper, or I'll kill you, right here right now.' Stanford moaned. 'I need you to calm the fuck down and start at the beginning. Word for word.'

His eyes were wild; pleading. 'I'll lose everything. I can't go to prison.'

'I heard you the first time. Spit it out.'

It didn't take long to tell his tale. When he'd finished, I made him go back to the start and tell it again. The story was the same, the important details unaltered, and it didn't sound any better the second time.

The attack on Bridie O'Shea's men meant we were still under the cosh. Stolen money, even gun battles in broad daylight, were events we could respond to. The bombshell Oliver Stanford had dropped blew all that out of the water. He was terrified of losing his freedom and the nice life he'd built as a bent bobby, apparently unaware that not six feet away was a bigger threat. Me. The lily-livered copper was the weakest link in an already weak chain. There would be no happy ending for him.

Stanford rested his hands on his knees, his breathing almost back to normal. From somewhere he found a spine, looked up and said, 'Don't contact me again, Glass. I'm out.'

I blinked – surely this fool couldn't really believe it worked like that?

Apparently, he did.

'The only ones who know about me are the family. Danny isn't around. That just leaves you and Nina.'

'And George Ritchie. Don't forget George.'

He hadn't included Felix Corrigan. Or Vincent Finnegan and two or three dozen foot soldiers who'd make persuasive witnesses for the prosecution. I let him run with his fantasy, until he saw the pity in my eyes and reacted.

'What? What? You can't seriously think we can carry on. We're fucked. It's over.'

He opened his palm and I saw the dull glint of a bullet – the one from the shoebox on the front seat of his car, turning it over in his fingers, his face shining with sweat.

He had a speech rehearsed and was determined to make it. 'They're coming after you, Glass. Just like somebody came after me and my family.'

A thin smile played on his lips; there was no pleasure in it. 'Doesn't feel nice, does it?'

'Apples and oranges. That wasn't the police.'

'Of course, you're right, it wasn't.' He held the cartridge up. 'I'll take my chances with whoever left this. At least, that's a war I might win. This isn't. My side won't give up. Not ever. Even if you beat them this time, they'll come back. With lawyers and warrants and judges. Resources you can only dream about. Until they nail you. If you're smart, you'll shut everything down. Why not? You've made enough.'

Stanford's face shone. He couldn't know I'd had the same conversation with myself during the long nights in Wandsworth. And, lying on my bunk in the darkness, come to a decision: when they let me out, I wasn't going back.

Except Rollie Anderson had been waiting to kill me for what I'd done to his father.

Now I was here. And when I did quit, it would be on my terms.

Stanford wiped his forehead on the sleeve of his jacket. The next words out of his mouth sealed his fate. 'If I go down, every one of your low-life family is going down with me. All the way to the fucking bottom.'

A bent copper who had lost his bottle was a sickening sight, and threatening me was a huge mistake – I wanted to strangle him with my bare hands. But he was correct about the arrangement coming to an end – just not how he imagined it. I'd inherited this creature from Danny; the man was a reptile who should've been put out of his misery when I had the chance.

Too late to cry about that. I needed him to get it together. Danny had insulted and humiliated Stanford constantly and publicly. At the time, I'd just come out of prison and thought it was Danny being Danny, putting the boot in because he could. Now I got it.

Seeing the gun in my hand concentrated his mind. It did with most people. I said, 'This is how it's going to be. The commander's bound to be rough as a badger's. Let him have time to come round, then give him a call.'

'But if they already know...'

'Obviously, they don't or Bremner wouldn't have spoken to you.'

'He was pissed out of his head. He didn't realise what he was saying.'

I pressed the barrel of the gun under his jaw and saw it etch a perfect circle on his skin.

'A name, Oliver. Bring me a name. Nothing is more important than the insider's identity. Got it?'

'Yes... yes.'

'Then we understand each other. Any questions?'

'No, no questions.'

'Oh, one more thing. This idea of yours about quitting. Sorry, but it's a non-starter. Forget it. Once you're in, there's no way out. Ever. Didn't Danny explain that? Remiss of him. My brother was a big-picture guy – details bored him.'

I pointed the gun at the roof and pulled the trigger. The sound was deafening, reverberating in the empty space; birds flew noisily into the air above us as the bitter taste of cordite caught the back of my throat.

'Deliver a name and we can talk about renegotiating your deal. Now fuck off out of it before I change my mind, shoot you and make it look like suicide. Come to think of it, that's not a bad idea. It's you they're after, Ollie.'

* * *

I stood at the tin door half off its hinges and watched him race up Fulton Street, trailing a thin line of blue smoke behind him. It never rains but it pours, so they say – Stanford's nice car was burning oil. His life and everything in it was in serious danger of going down the Swanee and he was terrified. His tall frame hunched over the steering wheel, wild eyes fixed on the road; at that moment hating me more than anyone on the planet. I hoped so. It would mean I wasn't like him.

Oliver Stanford was a pathetic coward, a hollow man with no redeeming vices. And he was right: prison wasn't an option for him. Suicide would be the easy way out.

I knew it and so did he.

But the news he'd brought was bad. The worst. Infiltrating an organisation like mine, insidiously burrowing to the heart, was every undercover detective's dream. Corruption would only be the start of what an insider would find. I slid behind the wheel and switched on the ignition, sweating under my collar although it wasn't warm, and listened to the engine purr. A helluva lot of people on both sides of the river worked for me. Those close enough to do real harm I could count on my hand.

One of them was a traitor.

Stanford would do what he'd been told. Later this morning, he'd call his drinking buddy and take him up on his offer of joining Operation Clean Sweep.

And the games would begin.

Security around the identity of the mole would be difficult – maybe impossible – to break and Stanford would be starting at the bottom. I'd made a big deal about him getting a name. In truth, it was unnecessary – something to get the policeman back on track. You could never be sure; he might get lucky and get intel we could use going forward. I wouldn't hold my breath.

The insider hadn't got what they wanted otherwise we'd have coppers all over us, though it didn't take a giant brain to narrow down the likely suspects and I only had myself to blame: Mark Douglas or my new sister. Douglas had been ruled out by Commander Bremner. But with Charley, the signs had been there from the very beginning – she'd been too practised, too assured, too in control. And now, I understood why.

I hammered the steering wheel with my fist, burning up with rage.

'Fuck you, Charley! Just as I was starting to like you!'

The clock on the dashboard read 6.25 a.m. Mark Douglas would be in bed asleep. Time to wake him up.

* * *

When I opened the door, two security guards stepped out of the shadows with their weapons raised and pointed at me. Good to know they were doing their job. In the wee hours, walking through the lounge with music drifting up from the club, surrounded by the great and the good toasting their golden lives with my booze and paying through the nose for the privilege, it had been possible to believe, even with the godawful shit going on, that I was still untouchable. Now I understood how the captain of the *Titanic* felt as the deck tilted and creaked beneath his feet and his ship began its relentless slide into the cold Atlantic water.

LBC – the Lucky Bastards Club – was a mirage, an illusion dissolving before my eyes. The forces marshalled against me – from without and within – kept coming.

For sure, there were regrets – a lot of regrets. Further down the line I'd think about them.

Oliver Stanford was a useless tosser, a weasel of the first order. Once, he might've been worth having around. Those days were well gone; the copper had stopped earning his corn a while ago and was a liability with no future. When this thing was over, his card would be quietly cancelled.

But he wasn't wrong about one thing. Shutting down made sense. South of the river would keep operating under George Ritchie and Nina would have Glass Houses – she'd be happy with that. I'd be left with the construction company, LBC, and a lifestyle beyond my wildest dreams.

All things considered, not the worst deal.

And, oh, yeah, I wouldn't be in prison.

It was tempting, no doubt about it, except it wasn't my style.

When the time came, I'd walk away. I wouldn't run.

If they had the evidence I'd already be in the cells. That I wasn't meant they hadn't put the pieces together, probably because my Judas sister had only just arrived.

At the bar, I raised an empty glass to an optic, changed my mind and took the bottle. I wasn't short of bad habits – drinking whisky at ten past seven in the morning wasn't usually one of them. But the old checks and balances were in the bin. Danny had bored the arse off me with his 'Team Glass' obsession. Behind his back, me and Nina had laughed. Not any more.

Today, loyalty was more precious than gold, the difference between freedom and twenty years at Her Majesty's pleasure.

The whisky went over in one go and I poured another. Getting drunk had a lot of appeal, though it wouldn't help. Anger made me want to lash out at the world and everyone in it, but the person I was most annoyed with was myself. Nina had railed against accepting a sister we'd never heard of turning up and joining the family. I'd overruled her, believed Charley's story and invited the enemy in. What a bloody fool. The people she reported to would've cracked the champagne open and congratulated each other at how easy it had been. Dead easy.

* * *

Douglas must've been a cat burglar in a previous life – I hadn't realised he was there. He glanced at the whisky and back at me. Wisely, he didn't comment. I pushed the bottle across to him. He shook his head and left it where it was. His eyes were heavy, like he hadn't slept much. I guessed sister No 1 might have had something to do with that.

He waited for me to begin, understanding something had gone very badly wrong for us to be meeting this early. If I hadn't been on edge, I wouldn't have said what I did. It was late in the day to start fighting for Nina's virtue – she hadn't put up much of a struggle.

The directness of my question took both of us by surprise. 'I hope you know what you're getting yourself into.'

Douglas stared but didn't respond. He said, 'Want to tell me why I'm here?'

I said, 'If I told you we had a mole in the organisation, what would you say?'

'A what?'

'An insider. An undercover copper.'

Douglas tilted his head, some of the tiredness left his face, the edges of his mouth curled in the beginnings of a smile. Then, he realised I was serious and it died on his lips. 'I'd say you were having me at it.'

'You'd be wrong.'

My tone got to him. He tensed. 'And you think it's me?'

'What makes you say that?'

'For one thing, I'm the obvious candidate. Ex-copper, last in, well placed in the set-up. I wouldn't blame you for jumping to the wrong conclusion.'

'George checked you out, remember?'

Douglas's response was unexpected; he laughed. 'So what? Creating a fake background isn't hard. Anybody could do it. So convincing you'd believe it yourself.' He shook his head. 'If I was you, my face would be in the frame.'

'A couple of hours ago, it was.'

He got up and paced the floor. 'How sure are you?'

'I'm sure.'

'Yeah? This might be the next stage in the game – the info might be bad?'

I might have taken this possibility more seriously if the source hadn't been a senior officer in the Metropolitan Police force who couldn't hold his ale.

'Believe me, I'd prefer it wasn't. It's solid. With you ruled out it can only be one other person.'

His eyes narrowed, unconvinced. 'Who's feeding you this?'

'A little bird.'

He walked to the bar, came back with a glass and poured himself a whisky. 'You're seriously telling me your sister's an under-cover copper?'

'Yes, I am.' I drained my drink and splashed myself some more.

'I don't get it. Why would your own flesh and blood come after you?'

'We're a pretty fucked-up family. Or hadn't you noticed?'

'Not what I see.'

'I wish I had your vision.'

He rolled his glass between his palms, not wanting to look at me.

'What's our next move?'

'You mean *my* move. Finish it. Today. Before she can do more damage than she's already done.'

Douglas didn't like what he was hearing. 'Isn't there a way to use this to our advantage? Use her?'

'No, the solution is to weed her out as fast as we can.'

He came back at me. 'Fair enough, except you handling it is a bad idea. When it happens, you should be miles away with a dozen witnesses, preferably coppers and High Court judges.'

On another day, I would've agreed with him. But this was personal. I couldn't shake the anger bubbling inside me or the disappointment at allowing myself to be duped.

I'd wanted her to be my sister and that was the truth. Wanted it too much.

Douglas was willing me to be cautious. I wasn't having any.

'I clean up my own mess. Before she dies, she'll tell me who she's working for and exactly what they know.'

He went up against me. 'I understand why you feel the way you do, but you're making a mistake. They'll have her under twenty-four-hour surveillance. Chances are she's wearing a wire, which means any conversation will be on tape. I'm your head of security and I'm giving you advice. It can't be you. That's a no-brainer. But we need somebody inside the Met, our own man, so we can stay ahead of this kind of shit. I could put out feelers, if you think it's an idea.'

It was, a great idea in fact. Unfortunately, like everything with my family, it was years too late.

His eyes fixed on me – no tiredness in them now. Before I could answer, his mobile rang. He turned away to take the call. Everything he'd said was right. I could think of a dozen men who would do what had to be done without me being involved. All it needed was a word and my sister would discover what Fulton Street was really all about. Being a woman wouldn't save her. Nothing would save her.

Her dead body would join the others in the New Forest. A hundred years, maybe even two hundred, they'd find what was left of her and speculate why a female ended up in the ground with a bullet hole in her skull.

Douglas was nodding, serious and animated. When he rejoined me, he was on fire.

'We've got the carer's boyfriend, the scum who stole the old guy's credit card?'

I remembered.

'Is he talking?'

'Not yet. Once we start cutting bits off him, that'll change.'

35

If Bremner could hold his liquor Stanford wouldn't even be aware of Operation Clean Sweep and the jeopardy he was in. His relationship with Luke Glass was already on thin ice and wouldn't survive much longer. The commander's drunken invitation to join the undercover op was a gift from the gods. Yet, he hesitated. Bremner had been pissed. If he didn't remember the conversation it could be awkward. Very awkward.

But it had to be done.

Stanford called the switchboard and got connected with Bremner's office. A clipped female voice answered and he introduced himself, feigning a breezy self-confidence he didn't feel.

'Good morning. Can I have a word with the commander?'

'Who shall I say is calling?'

'Superintendent Stanford. He's expecting me.'

'Just a moment.'

He held the phone away from his mouth, exhaled deeply and waited. Half a minute later, the woman was back. 'I'm sorry, Commander Bremner's in a meeting.'

Stanford recognised the lie as soon as she spoke but carried on, willing himself to be wrong.

'When will he be free?'

'I don't have that information.'

Back in his office he slumped in his seat, shaken by the obviousness of the rebuff. He'd been a bloody fool to read so much into the previous night's encounter. At the end of the day, it had been a smoky room full of bladdered coppers letting their hair down. Bremner was boozed-up and garrulous. Stanford's assessment of Jocky Shaw as a lazy, useless bastard had forged a moment of common ground. No more. Expecting it to be there in the morning was asking too much: The commander had forgotten. Forgotten his gaffe. Forgotten him. Simple as that.

Stanford picked at the rejection like a scab until it started to bleed. Maybe the opposite was true. Maybe Bremner recalled it all too well, was embarrassed by his lack of professionalism and preferred to let it die – the reason he hadn't told his secretary to ask him to call back.

He drew a hand across his forehead, relieved at the ordinariness of the explanation; it comforted him. Until a third possibility reared its head, sending his pulse racing. He was compromised. The whole thing had been a set-up. A test to see how he'd react.

He hadn't disappointed them.

The bastards knew about him and Luke Glass.

They knew and were getting ready to drop the hammer.

* * *

Charley didn't disguise her annoyance when I told her to meet me in LBC. She was a Glass – taking orders wasn't what she did. I tried to keep anger out of my voice but almost failed when she pushed back. 'Can't it keep? I mean, it's Saturday. I'm still in bed. It was almost four when I got home. Any later and I'd be having a fling with the milkman.'

'No. It has to be now.'

My abruptness instantly altered her tone. Her defences went up, suspicion rising as she processed the conversation and what was behind it.

'Don't I get to know what this is about?'

'You will soon enough.'

Somebody capable of doing what she was doing had spent years training for every eventuality, including the moment her cover was revealed, and wasn't likely to break down and confess as soon she was under pressure. For her and her kind, danger was a constant, the consequences of discovery a risk they somehow learned to live with. It took a special person to do what Charley was doing. On another day, I would've credited her courage in facing me down, knowing the game was over. Not today. Today she was the enemy.

'I'm asking you to come to the club so we can talk. Which part don't you understand?'

Her reply dripped insolence. It might've been Nina talking.

'The part where you want me to drop my plans but won't say why.'

I let a couple of beats pass, hearing her breathe at the other end of the line. She was a cool bastard, I'd give her that. There was no fear in her voice, not so much as a flicker.

'It's important, Charley.'

'To you or to me? You see, brother, when people say something's important, usually they mean it's important to them. Have you noticed that? Want to try again?'

'Trust me.'

She held the phone away and laughed. 'Trust. Don't get me started. If only I had a dollar—'

'Cut the crap! Get here, or I'll come and drag you by the fucking hair.'

* * *

Zac Fraser had been here before: on a cold night in Helmand Province the captured Taliban fighter was sallow-skinned and silent; a warrior wearing a green turban, a heavy coat, and a black-and-white checked scarf over his shoulders. A lifetime in the sun had left the skin on his face as worn as saddle leather, the flesh weathered and wrinkled. When Fraser had taken the thick cartridge-belt slung across his chest and stripped him, grey eyes had observed them, unafraid. And Fraser had known that whatever they did they wouldn't break this guy because he was a believer, willing to die with his secrets intact. For him, death was part of the deal – his reward was waiting on the other side of the veil.

The interrogation had ended with a bullet to the man's temple.

Two days later in a village fifteen klicks to the north, thirty-five civilians, mostly women and children, had been wounded in an explosion. He'd failed in southern Afghanistan. He wouldn't in south London.

A naked man sat on a wooden chair in the centre of the room, hands bound behind his back, bony ankles fastened to the chair's front legs by plastic ties. He was in his thirties, though looked older, his face gaunt, concave cheeks a match for the ribcage showing through his emaciated body. Food had ceased to be important to him: he was an addict, prepared to do anything for the next high and the one after that. Stealing an old man's identity hadn't bothered him; it wasn't the first time he'd conned a pensioner and it wouldn't be the last. Selling the information financed his habit.

The unanswered question was who'd paid for it.

He'd been beaten. Not badly. Just enough to soften him up.

Blood from his nose had dried in a dark line on his upper lip and his left eye was closed. He heard Douglas come into the room and tensed. Fraser brought out a Smith & Wesson bayonet knife and ran the tip of his finger along the black, razor-sharp edge, grinning like a maniac for the prisoner's benefit – a routine they'd used before.

Douglas missed his cue to join in. He sounded edgy. 'Where's Hume?'

'Outside.'

'What the fuck's he doing outside?'

He didn't expect an answer and didn't get one – Fraser wouldn't rat out a mate. Douglas crossed to the window and looked down. In the scrubby courtyard, two floors below, Hume paced the cobbles, speaking into the mobile pressed to his ear.

'Get him up here.'

When the two men returned, Douglas glared at Hume and turned his attention to the naked prisoner, hunkering down as though they were just two friends having a chat at the end of a long working week. He said, 'In the movies they always come away with shit like "I'm going to count to five" or "You've got thirty seconds to make up your mind".' He laughed. 'You and me know that's bollocks. If you're going to do something, just do it, am I right?'

The terrified man struggled against his shackles, chaffing his wrists and ankles raw against the plastic holding him, eyes crazy with fear.

'Listen, mate. This is what's happening. I'm going to ask you who you passed the old guy's identity to and – no ifs, no buts, no one, two, three nonsense – you're going to tell me. Without the fucking about. Otherwise...' Douglas pointed to Fraser playing with the knife '... he's going to yank your scrotum and slice your dick and your balls off. Do we understand each other?'

* * *

Felix and another guy were standing inside the office door when Charley arrived. On the phone, she'd told me she was in bed – the latest lie to fall from her luscious lips. I didn't believe her: nobody could put together what she was toting in a hurry. She glanced at Felix and his friend, smiled a half-smile and raised a carefully plucked eyebrow.

'Are these goons for you or for me?'

I said, 'Okay, Felix, you can go.'

The office wasn't large. It wouldn't have mattered – Charley dominated it the way she dominated every room she walked into. She was wearing a navy-blue blouse out over jeans, her hair under a turban of green and navy silk. The bag at her side matched the scarf, the scarf matched the shoes, every stylish stitch thoughtfully considered. This woman was royally fucking us, yet still had time to look like she'd stepped off the front pages of *Vogue*. In spite of how I felt about her, I was impressed.

She sat down and crossed her legs. 'I don't see it.'

'What don't you see?'

'The fire. The emergency, the no-it-has-to-be-now shit. Where is it?'

She was the real deal, no doubt about it, holding the act in place until the end. But I'd had enough. I steepled my fingers, studying her. 'Who the fuck are you? Tell me, I want to know.'

'Back to that?'

'Yeah, back to that.'

'I'm your sister.'

'Strange as it may seem, that's the only bit of your story I'm buying. Maybe I'm asking the wrong question. Maybe it should be, "What are you?"'

For a second the mask slipped and unease flickered behind her eyes. I saw it and realised the truth wasn't far. 'George Ritchie checked you out. You are who you say you are. I accepted that weeks ago or you wouldn't have got within a mile of this place. I'll try again.'

She interrupted before I could speak. 'Wherever this is headed, whatever's on your mind, Luke, you're wrong.'

'Am I? I don't think so. I really don't, Charley. We've got an insider.'

'An—'

'An undercover copper. A mole. Somebody trying to destroy us.'

Charley's head went back and she laughed, long and loud. Under the navy shirt her tits bobbed like plastic ducks at bath-time. She stopped, looked at me, and started again, tears streaming from her eyes; she wiped them with the palm of her hand. 'And you think it's me? You think I came all the way across the pond to take you down? Why would I do that, brother?'

Whoever had coached her could be proud of themselves; they'd done a fine job. She was more convincing than anybody I'd ever come up against, denying, even when the signs pointed to her, brassing it out like a true professional.

'That's the part I can't figure out.'

'Maybe because there's nothing *to* figure out. I've never been on the inside of anything. That's why I'm here.'

This woman was good. Really good.

'What fucked-up resentment did our bitch of a mother put in your head, eh?'

Her expression softened, the mocking amusement disappeared and there was hurt in her eyes. Her head moved slowly from side to side. 'You still don't believe me?'

'I believe you're who you say you are. What I don't understand is why.'

She was making me doubt myself – that was her gift. I wondered how many men had been persuaded against their better judgement and how it turned out for them.

I'd never know. It was time to end the charade. My fingers closed round the gun in my jacket. She saw it and her jaw fell slack, her tongue pink against white teeth.

'Really? Really, brother?'

'Don't call me that.'

The stubby barrel drew level with her chest. Doing her here was madness. I didn't care. I needed it to be over. Felix and Vincent would clean up the mess – that's what I paid them for. Lately, they'd had plenty of practice.

The tension was broken by my mobile. For a second, I considered letting it ring, then changed my mind. Mark Douglas's words rushed like a flash flood down the line. Suddenly, I felt like a sleeper waking from a bad dream, disturbed and disoriented, stupidly staring at the weapon in my hand, unsure how it had got there.

He sounded breathless, as if he'd been running. 'Tell me you haven't... tell me she's all right.'

'She's here, Mark.'

'Thank God. It isn't her, Luke. It isn't Charley.'

Her eyes moved from the gun in my hand and back to me. I hadn't realised it was still pointed at her. Across the room, Charley's expression morphed from surprise into something I didn't want to name. Her features crumpled; she was close to tears. And I finally got it. Charley might be tough as old boots on the outside, but she'd trusted me, her brother, her family. As understanding of what had just happened dawned, she knew her status hadn't changed after all – her whole life she'd been on the outside and she still was.

I had been wrong but so was she. If it had been Nina, I'd have shot her, too.

Sister or no sister.

'Charley, I—'

She cut me off, her voice heavy with sadness and disbelief. 'You were going to do it. You were really going to shoot me.'

I lowered the weapon. 'You don't... I'm...'

I'd crushed her and it was too late to make it better. Charley wagged a disappointed finger, warning me to leave it where it was.

'Don't. Don't say it, Luke. Not if it isn't real.'

* * *

Douglas heard the exchange in the room at the other end of the line. When Luke came on, he sounded weary. Mark said, 'We've got a name.'

'Who?'

'Colin Bishop.'

'Colin? Not Kenny?'

'Just Colin. The piece of crap in front of me sold him the old man's details. That's all he knows. Between him and his girlfriend they've had a nice sideline going on. Been at it for a couple of years. What do you want me to do with him?'

'Ritchie's guys should be there soon. They'll take him. Great work, by the way.'

Douglas ran his tongue over his dry lips and glanced across at Hume. 'As for the other thing, no worries, it's sorted. Or, at least, it will be tonight.'

36

At twenty minutes to midnight an orange moon hung above London town. Two miles away, the river would be an amber thread silently snaking through the city. Inside the door of LBC, Fortuna towered over me, impassive and aloof. People arriving at the club recognised who I was and nodded, probably imagining Luke Glass had it all going on. Tonight, nothing could be less true but the goddess had come through – we had the name of the bastard who'd been yanking our chain.

My plan to leave after I came out of Wandsworth seemed a lifetime ago. I'd listened to Danny's 'Team Glass' shit and let him persuade me to stay.

That was my first mistake. It hadn't been my last.

Colin Bishop was a drug addict who couldn't organise his way out of a paper bag. Acting without his cousin, Kenny, was a red flag. Somebody was working the fat bastard from behind. When I knew who, I'd know everything and retribution would follow.

Charley hadn't showed for work. No surprise. Tomorrow I'd call her and try to put what I'd broken back together. I didn't fancy my chances.

Mark Douglas's girlfriend was propping up the bar, asking every five minutes if anybody had seen him. At some point I'd put Nina in a cab and send her home before it got ugly. Douglas was busy clearing up his own mess. His arrogance had compromised us – one of the guys he'd brought in was an undercover cop. Until this morning, hiring the Glaswegian ex-copper had been one of my better decisions. When this was over, we'd be having a chat.

* * *

The detached house in Hendon had been Elise Stanford's dream, something she'd believed they could never afford. Because of Oliver's hard work, they had. But the service got everything and occasionally she wished they spent more time together. Elise switched the TV off and glanced across to the armchair by the fire. Oliver had hardly said two words all night; he was worrying. Lately, he'd been a different person, shunting her to Cornwall and avoiding sex. Men were different from women: women were more open, talking about their troubles. Oliver had old-fashioned ideas about husbands and wives. He wasn't a sharer, bottling things up, dealing with them on his own.

Elise said, 'I'm going to bed. Are you coming?'

She knew what he was going to say before he opened his mouth.

'You go ahead, I'll be up soon.'

'It's Saturday night. Surely you don't have work to do?'

He faked a weak smile that didn't come close to fooling her. 'Bits and pieces. Bits and pieces.'

She sighed. 'Well, try not to be too long, eh?'

'I won't be.'

At the living-room door she stopped and looked at the handsome man she'd married two decades earlier. The suntan had faded, there were bags under his eyes and his hair was thinning at the temples; he'd aged and she hadn't noticed.

Elise said, 'I love you, Oliver.'

'I love you, too, my darling.'

'But...'

'But what?'

'I'm lonely.'

'Are you? I'm sorry, I didn't realise.' He spread his arms in a gesture of powerlessness. 'This damned job...'

She screwed up her courage and blurted it out. 'Maybe you should think about retiring? Let somebody else carry the weight for a change.'

Stanford felt as though he'd been punched in the stomach.

'Retiring?'

'And we could drive around Europe for a couple of months, stopping at all these lovely vineyards before we're past it.'

The policeman felt emotion well up inside him. His wife was unhappy. In the early days, living in the shoebox basement flat in Bayswater, dreaming about the French trip had kept them going on the last rainy Tuesday of the month before his salary as a PC hit the bank, when they were down to beans on toast and dreading the electricity bill. That pipe dream had got lost, hadn't been mentioned in years. Stanford found being reminded of it strangely comforting.

Elise said, 'We'd get by on the pension. I mean, we'd just have to, wouldn't we?'

He laughed. 'We'd have a bloody good shot at it.'

'The Met have had their money's worth out of you. Make the decision before somebody makes it for you. Perhaps it's time.'

He was sincere. But he knew the moment she closed the door behind her his fevered mind would take him back to the damning conversation in the toilet, with Bremner slurring his words, telling him about the insider in Luke Glass's organisation as his world soundlessly collapsed around him.

He spoke quietly. 'Perhaps it is. Perhaps it is, Elise. Hold on, I'm coming upstairs with you.'

* * *

The older George Ritchie got, the less sleep he needed. His lifelong habit of going home every evening by a different route had been all but abandoned. It wasn't necessary; there was nobody left to go up against them. Running the operation had been a breeze. Until the double hit in Lewisham and Lambeth had exposed flaws and weakness in the system, born of complacency. Without a rival to keep them on it, they'd lost their edge. Luke had his own problems, otherwise he'd have had plenty to say. With the threats he was facing on the other side of the water, Eamon Durham and River Cars had been forgotten.

But George Ritchie hadn't forgotten. For him, it was a personal affront that couldn't go unanswered. The hardman from the north east had a way of dealing with it that was all his own.

Upstairs above the King of Mesopotamia, Felix Corrigan and Vincent Finnegan waited to be given the green light. Ritchie leaned back in his chair. 'We all set?'

Felix said, 'All set, George.'

Ritchie's brow furrowed. 'Good. Good. You know exactly what I want?'

'Yes.'

'Any questions?'

Vincent said, 'No questions, but Luke won't like it.'

Ritchie was pragmatic. 'That can't be helped.'

'I'm saying, he *really* won't like it. She's his sister.'

'Heard you the first time, Vinnie. Is this your way of telling me you're out?'

'I'm in. We're both in. And we get why you're doing it but...'

George Ritchie was a career criminal, known for his patience. While talentless hotheads overreacted with violence to every turn in the road, he stayed calm. What they were about to do flew in the face of that reputation. Then again, maybe it didn't. The Geordie was making a point. Who liked it or didn't like it played no part in his thinking.

He said, 'Where is it?'

'Not far.'

Ritchie smiled a thin smile and looked at his watch. 'Plenty of time for a drink if you need one.'

Felix replied for both of them. 'Take you up on that later, George. Right now, alcohol would only get in the way. We need clear heads.'

Ritchie nodded his approval; it was the right answer. 'That you do, lads.'

* * *

A security guard touched my arm and whispered the message he'd been sent to pass on. I kept my expression neutral. Not easy. With the shit going down around me, the last thing I needed was Nina causing a problem. My sister thought all she had to do to get what she wanted was stamp her foot.

This time, she'd called it wrong.

She was missing her boyfriend. If she forced my arm up my back, I'd tell her where he was, though, guaranteed, it wouldn't enrich her life. Douglas was off sorting the problem he'd caused before it destroyed us. Nina liked him. For what it was worth, so did I. Right now, his tart was making an arse of herself.

She was at the bar, dressed for battle, the silver dress so tight it might've been sprayed on. Her black bra strap was showing. Nina was too gone to notice. She turned towards me, her face flushed with alcohol, telltale traces of white powder on her nose: high as well as drunk.

I put my hand on her arm. 'You're going home.'

She swayed on the stool and shrugged me away, slurring, 'Fuck off. I'm a big girl.'

'Yeah, well, start acting like it.'

'I own 50 per cent of this place, in case you've forgotten.'

Arguing with her was never a good idea and like this, it was impossible. But I wasn't in the mood for her nonsense. 'Maths never was your strong suit. Your interest is 30 per cent.'

'Thirty!' She giggled. 'What've you been smoking, brother?'

I took her wrist and squeezed. 'Not tonight. I'm warning you, not tonight. Another word and I'll throw you out in the street where you belong.'

Her face twisted in contempt. 'Who do you think you are?'

'Twenty per cent.'

Through the booze and the coke, she somehow realised she was on dangerous ground.

'Where's Mark? Why isn't he here?'

'He's busy. Get your bag.'

I dragged her off the barstool; she tripped and I caught her. Close up the smell of whisky was overpowering. All over the club, people broke off from their conversations to check out the commotion. Nina saw the look in my eyes and shrank from it as I pulled her to me.

'I'm done carrying you. Done making excuses for you. Get it together or get lost. As for your boyfriend, he works for me – you'll see him when you see him. Conversation over.'

'And I'm done with your don't-make-me-angry shit. It was 50 per cent before she stuck her face in the frame, and I don't recall being asked if I wanted to hand a perfect stranger nearly half of my stake. You do what you like with yours, brother, I'm keeping mine. Didn't take her long to worm her way in, did it? Well, not with me. Never with me. Do you hear me? Never!'

I could've broken her bloody neck, there and then. 'I'm sick of you, Nina. Fuck off out of my sight.' I pushed her towards the security guard. 'Pour her into a taxi and send her home.'

* * *

The car rolled to a stop under a tree and they sat listening to the engine cool. They'd driven slowly, careful to stay below the speed limit in case some zealous coppers pulled them over. Across the river, the city was a neon blur. Fraser drew a hand through the stubble on his chin and looked at the reflection of the moon on the river. 'Why here? It's too public.'

Douglas answered. 'You know why.'

'Yeah, but central London's asking to get caught. We could dump it down river.'

'That won't do the job.'

'All it'll take is an insomniac walking his dog—'

'Listen, we're doing it my way. Live with it.'

Fraser heard the anger in Mark Douglas's voice and backed-off. 'If you say so.'

'I do say so.'

He exhaled deeply. 'Okay. I didn't expect it, that's all.'

Douglas's reply was terse. 'Neither did I.'

The exchange was a symptom of the pressure they were under. Fraser wasn't wrong – it was too public. Given a choice, Mark Douglas wouldn't have picked this place or this time. He'd had no choice. In a few hours, some Sunday-morning mudlark foraging the foreshore would discover more than broken roof tiles and the long stems of Victorian clay-pipes. Douglas didn't envy them.

His partner's concern was understandable; he took the edge out of his voice. 'We do what we have to, you know that.'

Fraser glanced over his shoulder and finished his thought. 'Yeah, except I didn't see it coming. Did you?'

They opened the boot and stared at the reason they were here: the dead man was unrecognisable, half his face blown away by the bullet, moonlight washing what little was left, fragments of bone and brain sticking to his clothes like dead flies.

Fraser said, 'Christ, what a mess.'

'We're sending a message.'

'Yeah, loud and clear. Nobody's going to miss it.' He turned away from the mutilated man and whispered to himself, 'Poor bastard.'

Douglas took the arms, Fraser the legs, and between them they carried him down the embankment's granite steps. Yards away, the Thames rolled silently past. At low tide, the rotted wooden stumps of an old mooring rose out of the wet ground. It was stony, their shoes sank in the slimy shingle and they stumbled, almost falling.

Fraser cursed. 'This is fucking madness.'

Douglas ignored him and waded into the cold water, hauling the body behind him. When it was waist-high, he let go and watched it float into the night. So far, they'd been lucky. Fraser scanned the road behind them, checking for the passer-by, the witness who would send them to prison for a very long time.

There was no one.

Back in the car, Douglas started the engine and pulled away, conscious of his sodden trousers against his skin; if that was his biggest problem, he had no problems. He drove through the empty south London streets feeling himself relax for the first time since the call from Luke, telling him they had an insider.

A lifetime ago Fraser had asked a question. Douglas answered him. 'You asked if I saw it coming.'

'Did you?'

'No. And that makes me wonder what else I'm missing.'

* * *

Charley crawled across the floor and emptied what was left of the bottle into her glass, missing the lip, spilling most of it. In her dragged-up life there had been many bad days with a mother barely able to take care of herself, let alone a daughter. But not like today. Her own brother had been seconds away from killing her. When she closed her eyes, she saw the gun's ugly barrel pointed at her and knew he was going to shoot. The call from Douglas saved her. Twenty seconds later, it would've come too late.

She would've been dead.

Charley staggered to the room and threw herself on the bed, sobbing into the pillow for herself and the family she'd never had and never would have.

She was on her own. Like always. Nothing had changed.

37

I tossed and turned, before finally admitting defeat and getting up. Above London, the moon had moved on, leaving a dark, starless sky that perfectly fitted my mood. Washing my face made sense, until I caught the haggard reflection in the bathroom mirror and wondered where the boy who'd stolen fags from the corner shop had gone. The difference was more than the ravages of time: that kid was having fun.

The last twenty-four hours had been a wild ride, starting with Oliver Stanford's phone call and the bombshell he'd dropped in Fulton Street. I'd considered cutting the copper adrift. What an error that would've been. Stanford was insurance: you paid the premiums for the day you really needed him.

That day had come.

From then on, nobody had covered themselves in glory, me especially. Next to what I'd almost done, even Mark Douglas's royal fuck-up was forgivable, a mistake he'd corrected in an attempt to save his own arse.

Both my sisters hated me. This morning, only one of them deserved a call, and it wasn't Nina.

When it couldn't be put off any longer, I tapped the number, nervously drumming my fingers on the coffee table as it rang out at the other end. After the fiasco yesterday, I half expected her to hang up as soon as she heard my voice. I didn't expect the scream that went on forever, or my heart beating wildly in my chest as I ran to the door with the sound of her terror in my ears.

And in that instant, I knew I'd outdone myself in the fuck-up stakes: I should've acted as soon as Douglas got the name instead of holding back.

Charley was paying the price.

Colin Bishop had come after my family.

I'd managed to get a frantic call off to Mark Douglas, one hand on the wheel, as I raced through the quiet streets. He was waiting for me at the door of Charley's flat and saw me take in the splintered frame and the broken lock.

He held his hands up to reassure me. 'She's okay, Luke, she's fine.'

'What happened?'

Douglas shook his head and went inside. I followed, dreading what was coming. Charley was in an armchair, bent forward cradling a glass of brandy, or maybe it was whisky, unrecognisable from the woman who'd faced me down with a gun pointed at her. That lady was confident and unafraid, absolutely convinced her own flesh and blood wouldn't pull the trigger. From the moment she'd realised she'd called it wrong, her trust in me and in her own judgement had started to slip away.

This was where it had ended.

Black lines of mascara ran down her ashen face from tired eyes. A cream silk dressing-gown draped her shoulders, the belt untied. I guessed Douglas had put it there and appreciated the gesture. The empty bottles on the floor told part of the story, though not all of it. Charley had fallen fast and hard. Knowing the role I'd played made me feel sick. But I hadn't been responsible for this. Something more, something awful, had occurred.

I hunkered down and took her hands in mine, feeling the softness of her skin.

'Hey, sis.'

She didn't look at me. Mark Douglas answered the question he'd avoided seconds ago. 'It's in the bedroom.'

The curtains were closed, the light dim; the single bed was crumpled but hadn't been slept in. What Douglas wanted me to see was in the darkest corner. It took a moment for the metallic smell to register then, as my vision adjusted to the gloom, I gasped and stepped away, suddenly understanding what had made my sister scream: his head rested on the back of the chair, sightlessly staring at the ceiling, the face so battered and beaten his mother wouldn't have recognised him. His throat had been severed, the wound red and ugly. Wire binding his hands cut criss-crossed lines into his wrists where he'd struggled against the inevitable and the gag plugging his mouth had stopped his cries.

Colin Bishop's men had known their business; slicing the trachea below the larynx prevented him making a sound. Thirty seconds to a minute later, lack of oxygen alone would've brought death. Mercifully for the victim, unconsciousness had happened much sooner. Listening to the gurgling coming from his throat while his heart pumped until there was nothing left would've been gruesome.

It was crude and cruel: a horror show.

Charley had screamed. I couldn't imagine any other reaction. Yet, the most disturbing thing was the blood: it was everywhere – scarlet on white, soaking his shirt, on the carpet at his feet, even staining the edge of the bedspread. Understanding the significance wasn't difficult. He'd died here. They'd killed him in this room.

From the evidence next door my sister had been out of it.

What if she hadn't been?

In the lounge, I tried again to reach her, quietly coaxing her to speak to me.

'Who is he, Charley?'

Her eyes flickered, like a sleeper waking from a dream.

'Who is he?'

She turned her ravaged face towards me and whispered, 'Jazzer. His name's Jazzer.'

'Jazzer?'

She nodded, slowly.

'You know him?'

'I know him.'

* * *

I called Nina and said I was on my way over without telling her why. She'd assumed she was in for part two of the bollocking I'd given her in LBC and sounded subdued. Understandable, given the state she'd been in last night. The list of people who didn't want to speak to me grew by the day – her name was never far from the top. Tough titty. It was time for sister No 1 to step up.

Gradually, the colour returned to Charley's cheeks. She was fragile, the shock of the mutilated man in the chair still with her. Pushing for an explanation wasn't an option so, instead, I squeezed her hand and said, 'I'm sorry.'

Some of the old fire flashed in her. 'That you didn't shoot me when you had the chance?'

'No, really I am. You—'

'If you're going to give me your life story, for Christ's sake, make it interesting.'

'When you screamed, I thought Bishop had sent somebody to kill you.'

'Bishop?'

'Yeah, Colin Bishop – he's the snake behind what's been going on.'

Her expression hardened and she looked at me. 'You think what's in the bedroom is Bishop?'

'Yeah, it's the bastard's next move and his last. He'll pay for this, Charley, trust me. What I don't get is how he's connected to you.'

I realised I was on the wrong track before the words were out of her mouth. Her free hand covered mine. 'Luke, Jazzer's the guy who hit Lewisham and Lambeth. I paid him. Jazzer worked for me.'

* * *

Nina was still wasted: the party hadn't ended at LBC. At this rate, she wouldn't see fifty. She peered round the edge of the door and got her retaliation in first. 'Before you start, you better accept you can't control me. Not you. Not anybody. Don't even fucking try. And for the record, you can shove your club. I won't be back.'

'That not why I'm here.'

'Then what?'

'Something's happened.'

'To Mark?'

She opened the door, fumbling for her cigarettes, her hands shaking so badly it took her three goes to light one up.

'Mark's okay but Charley isn't.'

I gave her the short version, minus Lewisham and Lambeth, and laid it out. Her reaction was pure Nina. She shucked off the hangover and laughed a brittle, mirthless laugh drawn from a well of anger and misplaced resentment deep inside her.

'You want me to bloody babysit? You can't be serious.'

'She's family and she needs us.'

'I couldn't give a flying—'

'She needs us.'

Nina threw her head back and blew smoke into the air. 'Stop before I start crying.'

I wanted to slap her stupid face.

'Believe me, this isn't her idea.'

'Why me? Did you toss a coin and I lost?'

'There isn't anybody else.'

She pointed the cigarette at me. 'There's you. Since you're so fond of her, you do the dirty work.'

I felt anger hot on my cheeks. 'I do, Nina. Every day. Or are you too out of it to notice? I'm making sure we're still in business next week.'

She stood in the middle of the room, feet apart, one arm folded across her chest, playing the rebel – the part she was born to play – to the end. But it wasn't real; the hangover was back and she was feeling it.

'The answer's no. Absolutely not. Next question.'

'Then you're out. You won't starve – far from it – but it won't last, not the way you're going. I don't ask you for much. This is important. If you can't deliver, won't deliver, it's over for you.'

'That's blackmail.' Her lip curled in a sneer. 'You're no better than Danny.'

She realised she'd crossed the line and took a step back, paranoia from last night's drugs rolling in her eyes.

'Refuse me on this and there's no future for you and me, Nina. Everything I said last night will come true, only worse. Your call.'

* * *

The second confrontation in hours with Nina had drained me. She'd picked a bad time. Didn't she always? I pulled into the side of the road and waited until my brain caught up and my emotions calmed down. In her bid to get my attention, Charley had made a mistake. She hadn't been aware who George Ritchie was, otherwise she'd have had second thoughts about crossing him. It took a lot, but if anybody was unwise enough to provoke him, they'd quickly learn why people had been happy to see him leave his native Newcastle. The hits on the bookies and the taxi firm were assaults on the reputation of a proud man, a dangerous man. The result was lying in Charley's bedroom with his throat cut. She was too shocked to join the dots, though she would.

Ritchie had better take good care of me because he had not one but two of my sisters against him. And Glass women made bad enemies.

He answered his phone so fast I knew he was expecting the call. What I had to say wouldn't take long. 'Charley got your message. This is where it ends.'

His steady breathing came down the line. None of this was a surprise to him.

'And, George, get that fucking mess cleared up.'

* * *

Bridie O'Shea, 'The Irishwoman' as Kenny Bishop called her, and Ritchie had a lot in common; mellowed by age, deceptively ordinary, until some clown crossed them. A visitor to Kavanagh's wouldn't suspect the grey-haired lady playing patience in the tiny back room was one of the biggest villains in London, and had been for more than two decades.

Mark Douglas had given me a name. Bridie deserved to be told before I blew the fucker away.

Unlike Ritchie, she kept me waiting. Hearing it was me neither pleased nor displeased her; she was beyond caring and it showed. Two days ago, Niall Monahan had been alive, bickering with her like always. Now, she was on her own again, except this time she wasn't young, the loss was greater, the energy to rebuild her world not there.

Her voice was hoarse, edged with grief. 'Luke.'

'Bridie.'

She assumed I'd called to ask about Niall. 'The police released his body late last night. I'm on my way to see him.'

I didn't offer to go with her. For sure, she would've turned me down. In her shoes, so would I. Sharing enemies didn't make us friends.

'Are you okay?'

'I don't know.'

The honesty of the answer touched me. I said, 'I know who did it.'

'Who?'

'Colin Bishop.'

'Man, you're haverin'. Bishop's an eejit.'

'The eejit who killed Niall.'

She sighed and changed the subject back to Monahan. 'You should've seen him in his prime. God, he was a fine boy. If I'd met him before Wolf...'

Bridie needed to talk it out; she'd forgotten I was there.

I said, 'We'll speak when you come back from the morgue.'

'Yes, we'll speak then.'

'And, Bridie, I need you to do something for me.'

* * *

With the exception of George Ritchie, everybody I'd spoken to was having a bad day. Oliver Stanford was no exception. His tone was surly. He was alone and he'd been drinking.

'Before you say anything, you ought to know I'm in my study trying to work up the courage to put a bullet in my brain.'

I didn't give a damn. 'I'll believe it when I see it, Oliver, though I won't hold my breath. My guess is that when Elise comes back from church you'll still be in the land of the living. Larger than life and twice as ugly.'

He sneered down the line and I imagined the hate on his face. 'You really are a soulless bastard, aren't you, Glass? At least with your brother—'

I'd had enough Danny comparisons to last me till next Christmas.

'Shut up and listen, copper.'

Fear made him brave. 'No, you shut up, you piece of trash. You're probably right about the bullet. I'm a coward. I've always been a coward. But there's something you should know. Elise and I have talked it over and, first thing tomorrow morning, I intend to resign from the Met.'

I laughed, although it wasn't funny. 'Forget it, Ollie, it isn't happening.'

'You don't understand. I've promised Elise.'

'Well, unpromise her. You're staying exactly where you are until I tell you different. And you can stop peeing your pants, the insider's sorted. Unless they've already sussed you, you're in the clear.'

It took a moment to register. 'Sorted? Does that mean what I think it means?'

My turn to sneer. 'Oh, for fuck's sake, grow up, Stanford. When you told me about the mole, how else did you imagine it could end, eh? Think taking him aside and having a quiet word would do it?'

'All the more reason for me to go. Elise says they've had their money's worth out of me. So have you. Getting out makes sense.'

Cheeky.

'Listen. There's noise coming – a lot of noise. I'm expecting you to put yourself in the middle of it. Steer any investigation in the other direction, away from the family. Operation Clean Sweep isn't one man – when they lose contact with the mole, they'll send somebody else. That's how it works. You've had an invitation to join the team.'

'I tried. Bremner wouldn't take my call.'

'Then, that's your new challenge, isn't it? Get on it or you and I are going to have a problem.'

'What'll I tell Elise?'

'Try the truth for a change. Might be surprised at her reaction.' I put my mouth closer to the phone and drove the message home. 'Don't mug me off, Ollie. It isn't over until I say it's over.'

38

The mortuary attendant had dirty fingernails and dead eyes; empathy wasn't a word he understood. Mortality left him unmoved. For him, grief was a profitable sideline, and in his years on the job he reckoned he'd seen them all: adults who drew away like frightened children when the sheet was removed and had to be coaxed to come closer; the disbelievers, sleepwalking through their pain too stunned to speak, unable to comprehend the sudden void in their existence or the hurt that would never heal; and the few like the old lady in front of him, stoic and calm, there to say a quiet, private goodbye.

Admirable, though it didn't change the price.

He pegged her as late sixties/early seventies, greying at the roots, the complexion smooth and fresh as a girl's, until the smoker's dip at the corners of the mouth. She pressed notes into his outstretched palm, telling him what she wanted in a soft Irish accent. He gave the money a cursory glance, stuffed it in the pocket of his white overall and led the way.

The cadaver was second from the end in a row of metal cabinets. The attendant rolled it out and drew down the sheet. Niall

Monahan's face might've been carved in soapstone, his skin the colour of putty, the marks from the blast like hairline cracks in unfired porcelain. Even in death his long eyelashes were beautiful. A strand of hair had fallen across his forehead. Bridie tenderly smoothed it in place. From behind her, the attendant's harsh voice shattered the silence and stole the intimacy from the moment.

'No touching.'

She pulled her coat tighter and glanced over her shoulder. 'I need a minute.'

'Okay. One minute. But no touching. Then you're gone before anybody gets here.'

When the door shut, she leaned closer, whispering like a lover. 'I would've told you years since and maybe I should have, except you would've been unhappy and you'd had your share of that. This is the truth, the truth nobody knows but you and me: Wolf Kavanagh was a bastard. He used me. Like a fool, I let it happen. Marryin' him was a mistake I lived with for nigh on twenty years. After the funeral, when his cronies had drunk their fill and slurred how sorry they were for the umpteenth time, I threw the lot of them out and did a wee jig on the bar. It was the happiest day of my life, that's the God's truth.'

She traced the dull line of the scar from underneath the eye to his jaw with her finger. 'Then you came along, brave and kind and gentle. Everythin' I'd dreamed of. But you were gay and I...'

The words fell away, not needed – he'd known.

She toyed with the edge of the sheet, tempted to see for herself the bullet wounds that had ended her friend's life and changed her mind. Memories were forever. She already had the best of them.

'We had some good craic, though, didn't we?'

Bridie smiled. 'Oh, I can hear you, Monahan. I know fine what you'd say. "Now she tells me." And you'd be right.'

She kissed the cold lips. 'Rest easy, lovely boy. Whoever did this to you will regret—'

The sound of the door opening broke the spell. 'Time's up.'

She replied without taking her eyes from Monahan. 'Keep your voice down. Show some respect, man.'

* * *

Kilburn High Road was quiet, a far cry from how it would be twenty-four hours later choked with Monday morning traffic pouring into the city centre. The distant sound of a church bell ringing mocked the thoughts in Bridie O'Shea's head – bad thoughts, thoughts a good catholic girl should never have. That girl had died the moment she saw Wolf Kavanagh's manly frame and lust quickened her pulse.

Light from the window streaked the counter Bridie had danced on after Wolf was in the ground and she was finally free of him. Wherever she looked, she saw Niall: at the bar polishing glasses, blethering with the regulars, mopping the floor before opening time like he'd done a thousand times or more and missing the half of it. Kavanagh's was closed and would stay closed. More important issues needed her attention. If that meant losing customers or even the licence, she couldn't give a tuppenny damn.

Bridie felt old and alone and close to tears. It wasn't a day for port or stout. Today it had to be whiskey. She poured Bushmills into a tumbler and carried it through to the back room he'd called her 'lair' when they were on bad terms with each other. Shuffling the cards was a reflex, laying out a hand second nature. Old habits were the hardest to break. The Irishwoman had set hers aside decades ago, trading them for more lucrative ones in west London.

They weren't lost, they were hidden, waiting to be rediscovered.

The Bushmills burned the back of her throat. She lifted a mobile from the table and pressed it to her ear. Luke Glass answered on the second ring. Bridie said, 'Your request – I need five days but I can deliver. Colin Bishop would be wise to put his affairs in order. And just so you and me understand each other, Mr Glass, if you're thinkin' different, forget it. I'm havin' him; he's mine.'

* * *

In Little Venice it was too early for the boy with the fishing rod and not warm enough for ice cream and sunglasses. Like before, the branches of the weeping willow on the island traced lines in the water. Last time I'd been here I'd come to talk and was on my own. The cousins had had other ideas, drunk, gagging for a confrontation they thought they'd win. There would be none of that today.

Kenny Bishop hurried towards me along the towpath, his tall frame bent as though he was leaning into a gale-force wind. The Bridge House wasn't open yet. Even from a distance I could tell he was sober. And worried. With good reason. What I'd given him on the phone was enough to get him to meet me. His reaction when I let him have the rest would decide whether I strangled him and dumped his body in the canal or let him go home for Sunday lunch with his wife and kids.

Kenny's weedy face was flushed – not from booze, from fear. He'd reached the same conclusion and, without his cousin to back him up, didn't fancy the odds. He slowed the final steps to walking pace, reluctant to come closer. The Bishops should have gold-star membership of LBC. They'd made it; they were rich. Fair play to them, being thick as shit hadn't held them back. There was a moral somewhere in there but I didn't have the energy to look for it.

Money changed people. Not Kenny and Colin. They'd started out inner-city boys and still were; the bar was set low at the club but not low enough for them to clear it.

Bishop swallowed and wiped his mouth with his hand. What I

was about to hear had been rehearsed all the way from Primrose Hill. Now the moment had arrived, the script in his head went in the canal and he was going with ignorance as his defence.

His voice shook. 'I didn't know, you have to believe me.'

He was wrong, I didn't.

'Convince me.'

'Colin was fine with your brother bossing south of the river. Nobody in their right mind would go up against Danny Glass.'

'Rollie Anderson did.'

'Yeah, and look how that turned out for him.'

I remembered.

'Then you took over.'

'And?'

'Started...'

'Started what, Kenny? Spit it out.'

'Fucking about. Moving up west. Opening a club in the heart of the city. Col thought you were taking a liberty.'

'What did you think?'

'I told him it didn't affect us one way or the other. Doing business with you made sense.' He made a pathetic stab at reaching me. 'Nothing gets in front of making money, right?'

Further along, a boat chugged towards us. In the stern, a middle-aged guy relaxed in a striped deck chair, smoking a pipe, reading a broadsheet; he didn't look up. Kenny Bishop waited for it to pass by before he continued. 'I thought he was cool with it – as cool as Colin is about anything. Until you called, I'd assumed he'd let it go.'

I kicked a grey stone into the water and watched the ripples disturb the surface. Kenny Bishop loosened a button of his shirt, preparing himself for the judgement that might signal the end of his time on earth. He scanned the steep bank beyond the trees, weighing whether he could reach the top before I dragged him down and finished him. It was a tough call. If I'd been a betting man...

I said, 'Your version is it's all Colin.'

He nodded.

'Don't much like him, do you?'

Bishop produced a rare flash of humour, brave in the circumstances. 'Not true, he's family. 'Course I like him. Just don't like him around.'

I stopped myself from giving him a round of applause. 'Why should I take your word for it?'

His eyes danced in his head. 'Because I'm telling the truth. Whatever's going on, I'm not part of it... not part of any of it.'

'Then you're asking me to believe a muppet like Colin set the whole thing up. Without your help. Without you even suspecting. I was born at night, Kenny, but it wasn't last night, you get what I'm saying?'

Panic flared in his eyes. 'Somebody else must be in on it with him. Has to be.'

'Sounds like you're grasping at straws.'

A light came on and he saw a way out. 'Luke, ask yourself who was keen to do business with you, to keep doing business. As far as I'm concerned, you're an opportunity, not a threat. Why would I upset the apple cart?'

'Then, who?'

He cast around for a name to fit his theory. 'A new firm. Somebody under the radar.'

'There aren't any new firms. There's you, Bridie O'Shea or Jonas Small.'

Kenny wasn't so different from his cousin. When his back was to the wall, he lashed out.

'My money's on the Irishwoman. Don't trust that old rebel bastard as far as I could throw her.'

39

The five days Bridie O'Shea said she needed were the quietest in a long time. Nina kept her distance; Charley moved back to her own flat and carried on running the girls at LBC as if nothing had happened: peace seemed to have broken out between my sisters. A temporary situation? Given their fiery personalities, maybe, but I'd take it.

George Ritchie was smart enough to quit while he was behind. He'd made his point. The dead man in the bedroom disappeared and didn't get a mention.

No word from Stanford, though, for sure, he'd have breathed a sigh of relief when he heard a body had washed up near Battersea Park. Sixty people a year were fished from the Thames. Suicides or poor bastards out of their head on pills and cheap wine who got stuck in the mud at low tide and drowned when the water rose. This wasn't one of those but I wasn't worried – the policeman had a vested interest; he'd bury it in the stats.

Now it was ten to ten on Friday night. Light rain spattered the windscreen and, for the first time in months, it was cold. Summer was over. I was in Prince of Wales Road with Felix and Vincent across from Colin Bishop's childhood home, the three houses he'd knocked into one, about to bring the whole sorry saga to an end.

Danny had been the gangster in the family; that was his trip. I'd do what had to be done and get back to being a businessman.

Further down the street a car pulled in and flashed its lights: Bridie had arrived. She rolled the window down to speak to me and I caught the hard Irish faces she'd brought with her.

I said, 'Are you okay?'

'Okay as I'll ever be.'

'Good.'

'The funeral's next week, once that's behind me...'

'I'll be there.'

'Don't bother. You didn't know him.'

A subtle reminder of my status. Tonight, we were on the same side. Tomorrow, that might change.

I said, 'Leave it in the boot. It's open.'

She pulled off a glove and took my hand. 'It's been a while, be careful. I'm out of practice.'

'I will.'

'Don't forget our deal. I'd hate us to be fallin' out.'

'In the boot, Bridie.'

When Kenny Bishop left Colin's place in a grey Mercedes, three men were with him. Taking the heavies guarding his cousin out of the picture was a smart move on his part: it meant he'd be alive in the morning. We climbed the wall at the back of the property, our footsteps cracking like thunder on the gravel. A security light burst into life and we stopped, holding our breath, expecting a guard loyal to Colin to come at us from the darkness with a couple of Dobermanns. It didn't happen. After sixty seconds, the light went out and we moved on.

In the King Pot, we'd discussed where in the house Colin would be. Kenny, in his new role as Judas, had told us he spent the week-ends in his den, watching blue movies, drinking vodka and getting wrecked on coke. It sounded too good to be true – Fortuna was starting to pull her weight.

Not before time.

The original plan had been to burst in, all guns blazing. A phone call from George Ritchie to Kenny meant that wasn't going to be necessary – the basement door was open, another present to us from Cousin Kenny. He really didn't like Colin, did he?

I took out my weapon – the one I'd almost shot Charley with – and climbed the stairs to the ground floor. The bastard was in an armchair facing away from me, the back of his bald head shining. On a large-screen TV in the corner, a group of naked men were enjoying themselves. Two lines of white powder waited beside a three-quarters-full litre of Absolut that would be dead come Monday morning. So would Colin. He didn't know I was there until my shadow fell across the floor between him and the orgy, way too late to react.

When he looked up, I understood why – he was going for gold in the Out-Of-It Olympics.

His addiction was biting hard, the deterioration in him shocking to witness: his eyes were bloodshot, the dilated pupils like small planets in a very different face from the one I'd wanted to punch. Cocaine was an appetite suppressant; loose skin hung under his chin reminiscent of a pelican's bill, his shirt so big at the collar it might've belonged to somebody else.

I wondered when he'd last eaten. Not that I gave a damn. At this rate, Bridie wouldn't have to kill him. He was doing a great job of it on his own.

He left off from cutting another pile of powder. 'Well, well, well. Look what the cat dragged in.'

I caught the front of his shirt with both hands and pulled him up out of the chair. When my forehead met his nose, they probably heard the crack in Canning Town. His features imploded. Red rain fell on the table, stippling the lines of crack, and Colin Bishop screamed.

He fell back already beaten, his face a bloody mess. I said, 'Hello, Colin. Sorry to be a party pooper but you know how it is.'

'You've broken my fucking nose, you bastard!'

I kicked the table over; vodka crashed against the fireplace and a white cloud rose into the air. 'Since when are you bothered about your nose? I've done you a favour, mate.'

His eyes watered. He moaned and gingerly felt his face. 'How did you get in here?'

'Long story, Colin. Tell you some other time.'

Felix and Vincent pinned him against the wall. He stank of BO – his drug of choice really was the gift that kept on giving. I took what was left of his fleshy jowls in my hand and squeezed. 'Give me what I'm here for and I'll leave.'

'Go fuck yourself, Glass. You must think I'm thick.'

He'd got that right.

Felix kicked his legs wider and gave him two to the kidneys. He cried out and slumped to the floor. I hunkered down beside him. 'You are, Colin. 'Course you are. Thick as they come, now that you mention it, but I won't hold it against you.'

He saw the gun, realising through the coke haze that his weekend wasn't going to go quite how he'd planned it, and weighed my promise against what he knew about me.

'I don't have a fucking clue what you're talking about.'

I stood. 'See. Now you're insulting my intelligence and that's not nice. We can both admit that on your own you couldn't find your arse with a torch. It's nothing to be ashamed of. It is what it is. Last chance.'

'And then you put a bullet in me?'

'Don't be so negative. Then you can get on with your miserable life. Look, I'll make it easy for you. I already know. All you'll be doing is confirming it.'

Behind his red eyes the wheels were grinding. His options weren't great. Finally, he said, 'If I tell you—'

'I won't touch a hair on your head. That's a promise. And it's the best deal you're ever going to get. I'd take it, if I were you. Trust me, I won't lay another finger on you. You have my word on it.'

He mumbled something.

'Speak up, Colin, can't make out a fucking word.'

'It was Small. He hates you even more than I do.'

I patted his fat cheek. 'Thanks, Colin. Nice doing business with you.'

When I came out of the room, Bridie and her men were waiting. She said, 'Remind me to never play poker with you. I'd lose.'

'You don't believe that.'

'Let's hope we never have to find out.'

As I walked down the hall, realisation arrived for Colin Bishop and he shouted after me.

'Glass! You promised! You fucking promised!'

He was right, I had. And I hadn't broken that promise. I wouldn't lay a finger on him. At the door I stopped until I heard him scream. Colin would be doing plenty of that before his night was over. It couldn't happen to a better guy.

* * *

But this is what I know: people are greedy; they can't help it – it's how they're made. Sooner or later avarice gets the better of them and they fuck up. Jonas Small should've seized the chance I'd given him with both hands and held on. Instead, he'd turned against me. I'd tolerated his mad-arse chat, his patronising 'Lukie boy' crap, and his wife's latest gems from beyond the grave.

No more. I was done.

* * *

It had stopped raining; the air tasted fresh and the sky over Brick Lane was clear. The nightmare was ending and it felt good. One more thing remained and I was up for it.

I left Felix and Vincent in the car and walked to the alley beside the Bangladeshi restaurant Small thought was Indian. A moggy foraging the bins heard me and scurried into the darkness. Jonas would've been wise to do the same. I'd come for him.

Light from the kitchen threw a vanilla rectangle on the ground. Inside, two men in chef's whites spoke to each other in Bengali. They saw me and the talking stopped, glanced nervously at each other and raised the knives they'd been using to slice chicken breasts. My quarrel wasn't with them. I pressed a finger to my lips – a language we all understood – laid a bundle of notes on the stainless-steel worksurface.

'Put those down before somebody gets hurt.'

Uncertainty clouded their chubby illegal faces but they did as they were told. I pushed the money towards them. 'Find another gig, guys. This place is closing down.'

The knives were professional steels, solid and heavy and razor sharp. I relished the damage they were about to do.

'When the police ask, you never saw me. London might look big. It isn't. My men would find you in five minutes. Trust me, you wouldn't be happy with how that turned out.'

They thought for about three seconds, scooped up the cash and ran.

Tomorrow they'd be unemployed. Better than being dead.

Small was sitting where he'd been the last time I was here, at the back, cleaning the fob his father had given him with a hanky. If it was possible, the grey and yellow king of comedy suit looked even more ridiculous than before, the salmon pink shirt underneath spectacularly at odds with the rest. I wondered if he was colour-blind and nobody had told him. When I came through the kitchen door, he saw the knives and his expression froze midmouthful. Behind the eyes, his brain processed the world of shit he was in and went with what he'd done all his days: he brassed it out.

Bad decision, Jonas.

Small pretended he was pleased to see me, though in his heart he had to know his time was up. But old habits died hard; he couldn't help himself.

'Lukie, boy! I mean, Luke. Belter curry tonight. Chef deserves a pay rise.' He winked. 'Won't be getting one, mind you, but still.'

I grabbed his hand and flattened it on the table. He got what was going to happen, tried to pull away and failed. The blade passed through his palm, splitting the flesh as easily as it had cut the chicken breasts, and embedded itself in the wood underneath, the hilt trembling like a tuning fork.

Jonas roared against the pain. 'You bastard! You fucking bastard!' and was still shouting when I spread him low across the table like a medieval heretic and sank the second blade into his left hand. He screamed as blood from both wounds soaked into the tablecloth, the slightest movement bringing fresh torture. Small glared hate at me and started to say something that was drowned out when I twisted the knives.

'No more, Jonas. All I want to know is why. What the fuck was more important than making money?'

'Go fuck yourself, Glass!'

I took hold of his hair and smashed his face on the table; the gold filling came loose and fell to the floor as though his body was breaking up, one piece at a time.

'Now, answer me. What the fuck was more important than everyone getting rich?'

Behind me, the door opened. His eyes darted over my shoulder to Felix and Vincent.

And that was the moment he realised nobody was coming to save him.

Blood trickled into his beard. He growled his tobacco laugh. 'Why? An upstart like you wouldn't understand.'

'Let me be the judge of that.'

His breath was shallow and laboured, an old man who'd run his race and lost. He bared his teeth in a final act of defiance. 'Okay, I'll tell you. I'll fucking tell you. Your brother understood the rules, the unwritten rules.'

Not remotely true. Danny had trampled over everyone and everything.

'He kept to his side of the river. But you, Lukie boy, you had to push it, didn't you? Had to take what wasn't yours.'

'You're mental. All I did was offer you a business opportunity.'

'And I offered you a partnership. A partnership with Jonas Small. Should've bitten my arm off. Especially once I'd shown how vulnerable you were. Screwing with you was easy. A piece of piss. Hitmen, hackers and hookers have one thing in common. Pay them enough and they'll do anything you want. London's full of them. I said to myself, Luke's a clever boy. He'll see sense.'

One thing had bothered me more than anything else, a twist I hadn't been able to get straight in my mind: why a hooker would risk everything and go over to the other side. And now I knew. The deal of the century hadn't been enough. She'd seen more and she'd wanted it. Greed had cost Zelda her life.

Felix set Bridie O'Shea's bag on the table. The East End gangster forgot the pain paralysing his arms and struggled, the veins in his neck stretched like cords under the skin. 'I've been the king of

London since you were in short trousers! The king! You took my crown, you bastard! You won't have it long. Somebody'll knock it off your head, you see if they don't.'

Small sucked air through his mouth like a landed fish, exhausted by the hatred that had driven him to go up against me. Felix hung the bag strap round his neck.

Jonas liked to be ahead of the game: when the bomb exploded, he'd be the first to know.

He hacked in his throat and spat a red bubble on the carpet. 'That Irish whore in Kilburn gone back to her roots, has she? Should've rotted in prison for what she did.' He grinned and I was reminded again of the wild animal on Aldgate Pump. 'Fucking terrorist bitch.'

Vinnie passed me the black box, no different from the device I used to open my garage door. But when I pressed the red button on the top, Small would cease to exist. Pinned by knives and outnumbered, he stopped struggling and accepted his fate: an old wolf knows when it's time to leave the pack. Jonas Small was an old wolf.

'One more question, Lukie boy. Call it a last request. What happened to Danny?'

Telling him would've cost me nothing, except he didn't deserve to know.

'You'll be seeing him before me, Jonas. Ask him yourself. And say hello to Lily while you're at it, you weird fuck.'

* * *

Our footsteps echoed in a deserted Brick Lane until we reached the car parked seventy yards further up. Felix looked across from behind the wheel and I was aware of Vincent's eyes boring into the back of my head, willing me to end this thing, once and for all.

I pressed the red button and turned away from the blast.

Nothing happened.

I pressed again. Still nothing.

Bridie O'Shea had been a twenty-three-year-old virgin the last time she made a bomb; she'd warned me she was out of practice.

Fortuna was still fucking with me.

I opened the door to get out. Vinnie grabbed my arm and stopped me.

'Not yet.'

An eerie silence settled over the Lane, the air, charged with expectation and uncertainty.

Vincent's fingers dug into my shoulder. 'Not yet, Luke.'

Suddenly, the front of the restaurant exploded in a roar of fire and smoke. Glass and stones fell from the sky as the Chittagong closed for good – Jonas Small had been its final customer.

Finnegan loosened his grip, Felix started the engine, and we pulled away from the kerb. In the rear-view mirror, the curry house burned. I waited until we were on Commercial Street before I asked. 'How did you know?'

Vincent pursed his lips and started to whistle. I recognised the tune Bridie had sung to me in Kavanagh's: 'Sean South of Garryowen'.

Once a rebel...

Colin Bishop had got what he deserved. So had Jonas Small. Bishop's motivation was easy to understand: he was a greedy bastard. Small's was the product of ego and a lust for power.

Kings and crowns?

What a load of bollocks.

EPILOGUE
LBC

The club closed on Mondays. Usually, the only people in the bar would be me and the cleaners. Not today. Brick Lane and all that had gone with it was the past; my focus was on the future. And that future was sitting in front of me.

I'd let the dust settle, literally, before asking them to meet me at eleven o'clock. Nina hadn't said she'd come, but she was there on the button, wearing a green V-neck jumper and faded jeans, her blonde hair tucked behind her ears, more relaxed than she'd been in a long time. I guessed I had Mark Douglas to thank. Nina needed a guy she could depend on. Maybe he was the one.

She saw me and smiled. I smiled back.

Charley arrived a minute later, dressed to the nines, stunning as usual. Black was back. Shirt and cords, offset by half a hundred-weight of Aztec costume jewellery with a gold sun pendant in the centre.

My last attempt to pull us together had failed. I sat down on a stool facing them and went into my pitch. 'For the last couple of months, this family has been under threat. The strain has been tremendous. But that's behind us. On Friday, it all changed. We changed it.'

Nina interrupted. 'You changed it, Luke.'

I acknowledged the compliment and went on. 'Our rivals, the people behind the attacks on us, have been sorted – the details aren't important. If you've seen the news or read a paper, you'll be aware a body was dragged from the Thames. What you don't know, what nobody knows, is it was an undercover cop who'd found a way inside our organisation.'

I had their attention. Charley leaned closer.

Nina broke the silence. 'Who was it?'

I held up my hand. I'd answer their questions but not now.

'That just leaves us. The three of us: the children of Daniel and Frances. Because that's what we are. The world isn't the same as it was a few days ago. When I explain, you'll understand. For the moment, it's enough to say we rule this fucking city. We rule London. It's ours. The only people who can hurt us are in this room.'

It was decision time – an end to nonsense and petty squabbles – and they realised it.

'I have to know, once and for all, if you're in or out.'

There was a light in their eyes I hadn't seen before. I walked to the bar and came back with a bottle and three glasses: three glasses – the irony didn't escape me.

'Now, do I crack this baby open or what?'

* * *

New Scotland Yard, Curtis Green Building, the Embankment

It was still dark when Oliver Stanford slipped quietly out of bed, careful not to wake Elise, and went downstairs to the kitchen. He stood at the kitchen window, watching the first shafts of dawn's early light break through the trees where a stranger had stalked them from the bottom of the garden. The memory made Stanford shudder: life had become a bad dream. But, at least, the weekend hadn't added to his problems. The murder of Colin Bishop – kneecapped and shot execution-style in the back of the head – had the fingerprints of the IRA all over it, which meant that, fortunately, the mess had landed on Counter Terrorism's pile instead of his. Maybe Glass had involved the Irish bitch in Kilburn.

Stanford was physically and emotionally drained; his head ached and his eyes were puffy. No matter how tired he felt, he couldn't sleep. Jocky Shaw's leaving do might've been months ago instead of the previous weekend, the meeting in the derelict factory in Fulton Street with Luke Glass even longer.

The gangster wanted him as close to the beating heart of Clean Sweep as he could get. Easier said. After all his talk – booze talk, admittedly – Bremner hadn't taken Stanford's call and he was worn out trying to convince himself the senior man had been hungover. No surprise, given the state he'd been in. Except...

* * *

The middle-aged receptionist outside the commander's office barely raised her head when he approached her desk. He straightened his spine and pulled himself to his full height. 'Superintendent Stanford. Commander Bremner asked me to come and see him.'

The woman got up, knocked on the door, went in and closed it behind her. Thirty seconds later, she was back. The smile couldn't have been less sincere. 'I'm sorry, Superintendent, the commander's diary is full today.'

'What about tomorrow?'

'And tomorrow. If you'd like to make an appointment, I could fit you in, though it would be next month, I'm afraid.'

The policeman's fear took him to the stairs rather than the lift; he couldn't be with people. He'd been a bloody fool to believe the loose-lipped bastard in the first place. There was no place for him on Clean Sweep, never had been, and the thoughts he'd fought against resurfaced.

Was Bremner embarrassed and covering his drunken arse?

Or was he sending a message? Telling him they knew he was dirty.

If they did, it was over. Luke Glass would have no use for him.

* * *

The King of Mesopotamia

George Ritchie never looked back: what was done was done. He'd been left no choice with the guy from Liverpool. The old gangster had known Luke would understand his sister had gone over the line, and he had. The same couldn't be said for Charley – if her and Nina put their differences aside and teamed up, he'd be in trouble.

Jonas Small's demise had created a vacuum in the East End. Luke had wasted no time in taking over. Felix had been promoted. Fair enough; he'd earned it, though he'd have to watch his back, because right now, in Limehouse or Whitechapel, Dalston or Waltham Forest, for sure, somebody would be planning a move of their own.

Not today. Maybe not tomorrow.

But soon.

Luke had offered him the territory. A younger George would've jumped at the chance to run both. But then a younger Ritchie might've gone up against Luke Glass. And London could've added one more turf war to the list.

* * *

Kavanagh's, Kilburn High Road

Bridie O'Shea poured herself a large whiskey. Her reflection stared back from the mirror behind the optics – nothing like how she saw herself in her head. Time was a bastard. Living was a bastard too, but it was better than the alternative.

The service had been short. No priest, no Bible quotes, none of that. Niall wouldn't have tolerated it. The cronies who'd hugged the end of the counter every day of the week, egging him on to tell them stories, had been there. And that was it.

Her and half a dozen tired old tossers: not much to show for sixty-odd years on earth.

She went through to the back room and peeled off her coat. The cards lay on the table, just as they'd been left on Friday night before the car had picked her up and driven her to Chalk Farm. When he was in his cups, which towards the end was often, Wolf had talked philosophically about the manner of death. Bridie hadn't understood then. Now, she did.

Colin Bishop hadn't died well. Or quickly. The Provisionals had their own ways: torture and executions were formal affairs, like the judgment of the courts. And just as final.

The first bullets had taken Bishop's ankles, after that both of his knees from behind. Dark blood and fragments of bone had stuck to his trousers. If he'd survived, he would've been a cripple. Seeing Bishop on the floor, hearing him beg for mercy, had given Bridie O'Shea no pleasure. Nothing would bring Niall Monahan back. When they'd pulled Colin Bishop upright onto his destroyed legs, screaming in agony, she'd put the hood over his head herself, pressed the gun to the back of his skull and fired.

In the aftermath and every minute since, Bridie was reminded of how right she'd been.

Niall was still gone. She was still alone.

A newspaper she'd been too sad to read lay on the chair. Images of a bombed-out restaurant in the East End told her she hadn't lost her touch; the old skills were still there, had always been there. Waiting for the day. The lighter clicked; a cloud of smoke rose above her. She threw the whiskey over in one go and pushed the glass away, hesitated for a moment, then placed the red eight on the black nine.

The Flask, Flask Walk, Hampstead

Nobody recognised the guy sitting outside the pub reading the Monday edition of *The Times*; there was no reason why they should. Hampstead had more than its share of famous people. DCI John Carlisle wasn't one of them. Although it was sunny, he kept his tan raincoat on. When he saw who he was meeting turn in from the high street, he didn't wave. The man sat down and Carlisle said, 'Quite a weekend your boy had to himself. A murdered gangster with all the hallmarks of an IRA execution thrown from a moving car in the centre of the nation's capital is exactly the kind of optics the PM's desperate to avoid.'

'Fuck the PM. He's a dick.'

'My feelings exactly, though add an explosion into the mix and it isn't hard to see where he's coming from. If it looks like the Provisionals are making a comeback, all bets are off. The Good Friday Agreement's dead in the water, and so is his career.'

Mark Douglas couldn't have cared less. 'He can take his pick – terrorism or his crime figures. One of them's fucked. Get used to it.' He drummed his fingers on the table. 'The immediate problem is Glass knew he had an insider. How the fuck did that get out? Who told him?'

Carlisle made a face and shook his head. 'Honestly, we've no idea. The operation's airtight. You could count on one hand the people in on it.'

'Not good enough... sir. One of those people almost got me killed. It's my life on the line. If I think they're starting to suspect me, I'm coming in.'

'Understood. We agreed at the start that call has to be yours. But it would be a shame, Mark. You've done better than we could've hoped in our wildest dreams. Setting you up with Celebrity Security so you could get closer and maybe get noticed was a long shot. But it was the only shot we had of breaking into the family. Head of Security for Luke Glass is a big win for our side. Who'd have thought that was even possible?'

'Plain old luck. And, right place right time. But getting a result won't be quick. Luke's smart and very careful. He keeps me at arm's length from what's really going on. Not a whisper about a contact in the force. We are sure there is one, aren't we?'

Carlisle didn't reply and Douglas had his answer.

The DCI said, 'Why weren't you at Brick Lane?'

'Luke took the people he trusts completely and that isn't me. Not yet.'

'You call him Luke. You like Glass, don't you?'

Douglas dismissed the question. 'Wouldn't matter, one way or the other. As far as who he's working with, I'm out of the loop.'

'What about the sister, Nina? Anything with her?'

Mark Douglas hesitated before answering. 'Too soon. I'm just in the door. If I start dropping questions into the conversation, she'll suss me.' He looked up and down the Walk, keen to get the conversation on something else. 'Where's Simon Hume? Because I don't need anybody bumping into him in Marylebone High Street.'

'Sunning himself in Gran Canaria or somewhere. Lucky sod.'

'Whose face did I blow away?'

Carlisle shrugged. 'A John Doe nobody will notice is missing.'

Douglas returned to the fear gnawing the pit of his stomach. 'Whoever told Glass his organisation was compromised is Old Bill.'

'Almost certainly. But they think it's sorted, think you got rid of the problem. That puts you in the clear.'

'Only for the moment. As it stands, I'm on borrowed time. A false move and it'll be me you're hooking out the river. Glass was ready to shoot his sister, what would he do to me? Luke only trusts me up to a point. Beyond that... expecting me to deal with more than one enemy at a time is too much. Find out who told Glass or it's over. I'm pulling the plug.'

'Mark—'

'I'm serious. Do a better job or this is over.'

POSTSCRIPT

Luke Glass has consolidated his hold on the London underworld. LBC is fast becoming the most exclusive club in the city and his high-profile luxury property development, Glass Gate, is in the final stages of completion. All ten units have already been sold.

Nina Glass manages Glass Houses, her real estate business. She is rarely seen at LBC.

Charley Glass is the uncrowned queen of the gossip columns, often photographed with film stars and celebrities. A fragile truce exists between her and her sister.

Mark Douglas remains head of security for the Glass organisation north of the Thames. He is still in a relationship with Nina Glass.

George Ritchie has tightened security south of the river; there have been no fresh attacks.

Superintendent Oliver Stanford is still an active duty officer with the Met. He has not been seconded to other duties.

Jonas Small is believed to have died in the explosion in Brick Lane that destroyed the Chittagong restaurant. The bombing had the stamp of the IRA, though no one has claimed responsibility.

Bridie O'Shea controls a significant part of north London; she talks about the old days and moving back to Ireland.

Six weeks after his cousin's body was dumped from a moving car, Kenny Bishop handed the reins over to his nephew, Calum, and retired.

Felix Corrigan runs the territory that formally belonged to Jonas Small, east of the Aldgate Pump. Vincent Finnegan is his right-hand man.

James William Stevens [Jazzer] is listed on the NCA's central national database of missing persons. Mr Stevens has not been seen since leaving a public house, alone, in Liverpool.

Shortly after brokering an out-of-court divorce settlement for a prominent Conservative lord, Algernon Drake died of a heart attack at his flat in Butler's Wharf.

Operation Clean Sweep is ongoing.

Read on for a sneak peek at the next Glass family novel, Hustle, from Owen Mullen...

1

POLAND STREET, SOHO, LONDON

Day 1: Friday – 2 weeks before Christmas

It had been a cold day in the capital, the coldest of the year, and with the temperature dropping snowflakes fluttered and fell on the crowds hurrying about their business on Shaftesbury Avenue. A guy in a Santa beard and jeans torn at the knees knocked seven bells out of the Wizzard classic, 'I Wish It Could Be Christmas Everyday', loud and raw, his breath condensing in the chilly air. He wore a red-and-white woolly hat and gloves with the fingers cut off so he could play. On the ground in front of him a collection of coins, mostly silver, lay in his open guitar case. The woman in a cashmere coat rushing by had gone for a walk to kill time before her appointment. Now, she was late and didn't give the busker a second glance. In Wardour Street, she passed St Anne's churchyard and kept going. Across from The Ship public house, once a watering hole of John Lennon and Jimi Hendrix, she made a left, then a right into Poland Street where her car was parked, walking purposefully, in no doubt where she was going.

The entrance to the building was lit by a single bulb hanging from the ceiling inside the doorway. She hesitated, drew her expensive coat around her and climbed the stairs. Behind her, a car pulled to a stop near the green-and-gold façade of the Star and Garter. Like the busker with the guitar, she didn't notice the three people in black reefer jackets who got out, or the good-looking guy with the stylish blonde hair leading them.

In his office on the second landing, Jan Stuka was waiting. With more than sixty years in the trade, the old jeweller had no need to advertise his talents. He'd owned the room in Poland Street for decades, though only came here when he had a client to meet. Stuka was a craftsman, an artist, a stout little man with a goatee and spectacles, who could've set up shop in Hatton Garden like so many others and guaranteed himself a comfortable living. Instead, he'd gone a different route, fashioning bespoke pieces using only top-quality gems, singular creations for those interested in getting exactly what they wanted – the best.

When she'd explained she wanted a bracelet for a man with the inscription From N to M – all my love – he'd stared balefully over his wire-rimmed spectacles; romantic messages on an item she could've bought from any high-street shop left him unmoved, and for a second, the woman was convinced coming to him had been a mistake. The necklace brought a different reaction. As she'd described what she imagined, he'd mellowed, making notes in a small dog-eared book, asking questions in a guttural accent, even finding the enthusiasm to suggest the male jewellery might be a classic design, 18 carat gold cuff – simple and stylish.

Perfect; she was delighted: someone was going to be very pleased.

During her second visit he'd shown detailed charcoal sketches based on their previous conversation, including the otherwise plain bracelet and its inscription. Stuka was an old-school artisan craftsman; he didn't understand high tech computer modelling software and made everything by hand. The third time he'd proudly unveiled wax replicas of what he intended to produce, subject to her approval. This evening, they'd select the stones to make the necklace a reality – FL diamonds, flawless and clear, and pure blue sapphires, AAA quality. Finally, he'd tell her how much it was going to cost.

Not that she gave a damn about that.

On the landing, a bodyguard stood to attention, steroid-induced man-breasts pressing against the fabric of his shirt, thick arms folded. He didn't turn his expressionless face towards her until she reached him. When he did, there was no recognition in his dull eyes and she realised the guy was on more than hormones. Swollen fingers tapped the door, the electronic lock buzzed and released. Before he could react, the three figures she hadn't seen on her way in rushed from the shadows wearing balaclavas and pushed her through the door; the butt of a revolver crashed against the side of the guard's head and they dragged him into the room, screaming threats at the old man.

'Open the safe! Don't fuck me about or I'll blow you away!'

Max's well-modulated voice was at odds with the jargon. The jeweller didn't blink. 'Do this the easy way, granddad, and nobody gets hurt. Don't be afraid.'

'I'm not afraid.'

'Good for you. Just don't be a hero.'

Stuka was telling the truth: by the time the Soviet army arrived, Jan was six kilos underweight, suffering from tuberculosis and barely able to stand, yet he'd survived in a place where more than a million had perished, his parents and grandparents among them. After that, what was there to fear?

He pulled up his sleeve to reveal the tattoo – 6613145 – faded into the mottled skin.

Defiance burned in the old Jew's eyes. Anger thickened his accent. 'What would trash like you know about heroes?'

The slight didn't faze the robber. He said, 'On another day, I'd buy you a drink and you could tell me what it was like. We'd have an interesting conversation. Except, that isn't where we are, is it? And respecting what you've been through won't stop me putting a bullet in you. Whatever you believe, believe that. Now, open the fucking safe.'

Stuka spat on the bare floorboards at his feet. 'Nie.'

Behind his mask the thief smiled. 'I'm guessing that's Polish for no.'

He grabbed the woman by the arm, pulled her towards him and held the gun to her temple. She stiffened but didn't cry out. Max spoke to the jeweller. 'You should've died a long time ago. Somehow, you got lucky and didn't. Eighty years down the line you're fine about it. I understand.' He dug the muzzle into the female's smooth skin. 'Take a look at her. She's what? Thirty-five, thirty-six, maybe? How does she feel about it being all over? Ask her?' His finger closed round the gentle sweep of the trigger. 'In thirty seconds, we'll be leaving empty-handed and you'll both be dead. What I'd call a lose-lose situation. Imagine making it out of a Nazi camp for it to finish in a grubby little cubbyhole in Soho because of a few stones. What would the poor bastards in Auschwitz, Buchenwald and the rest of those hellholes say?' He shook his head at the irony. 'Do what I'm telling you or she gets it. Right here. Right now.'

On the floor the bodyguard groaned, regaining consciousness.

'The old fucker thinks we're bluffing. Let's show him we're not.'

Under the reefer jacket and the balaclava, the speaker was indistinguishable from the other two. The words were hard despite the soft tone. Coco went to the helpless man on the ground and straddled him, arms straight, pointing down, both hands on the revolver. staring into his terrified face, savouring his fear. The bodyguard realised what was coming and held his palms up impotently against it. 'No! No! Don't! It was me who told you.'

'And we're grateful.'

The silenced shots popped like balloons. Nobody would hear them outside the room. She stepped over the limp body and took up position at the only window as though nothing had happened.

Through the frosted glass, snow was falling on Soho. Stuka said, 'I've met your kind all my life. You're animals.'

The hostage hadn't spoken; the gun barrel carved a perfect circle on her neck. Tomorrow – if there was a tomorrow – there would be a bruise.

Max said, 'We're serious people – you saw what we did to the guard. Tell this old fool you don't want to die. Tell prisoner 6613145 to open the bloody safe before I blow your pretty head off.'

The jeweller's resistance was admirable but it was fading – he was afraid, though not for himself. For her. She took a deep breath. 'Don't open it. They're going to kill us, anyway.'

Stuka had seen unbearable inhumanity, yet he couldn't allow himself to believe what she was saying. He shook his grey head. 'No, no they won't. Not if I give them what they came for.'

'We've just watched them murder an unarmed man. They can't leave us alive. We're witnesses.'

He ignored her, turned to the safe embedded in the wall behind him and knelt in front of it. In the silence, the tumblers falling was the only sound. With the last click, the door swung open. Stuka lifted out a grey-metal box, set it on the desk and raised the lid. The robbers edged closer: this was why they were here. Inside were four small purple velvet purses with draw-strings tops. The jeweller spilled the contents of each one onto the desk in neat piles. Even in the poorly-lit office, the gems sparkled and shimmered.

'Why four? Why four pouches?'

'Diamonds and sapphires. Two pouches each: the very good and the very best. I only work with quality.'

'How much are they worth?'

Stuka eyed his captor with contempt. 'Anyone who looks at these and thinks only of money is a cretin. Sapphires take millions of years to form. A blink of an eye compared with diamonds.' He rolled a perfectly clear stone away from the others with his finger. 'The process that created this beautiful thing began more than a billion years ago. Perhaps even as much as three billion.'

He gave them a second to take in the enormity of what he'd told them, then tilted the desk; a fortune in stones cascaded in a drum-roll on the wooden floor and scattered – after the old man's history lesson, the last thing the thieves expected. The jeweller seized his opportunity, reached for the mask nearest him and clawed it away.

Coco screamed, 'Shoot him! Shoot him!'

Max hesitated, blinking rapidly, as though he couldn't take in what had happened and fired. Mr Stuka fell over the desk, his white shirt instantly turning red: shot through the heart, the man who'd survived the horror of a concentration camp died instantly.

Max shouted, 'Get the stones! Move, we need out of here!'

The third robber twisted Nina's arm up her back. 'What'll we do with this bitch?'

Coco had no doubts. 'She's seen Max's face. Put her down.'

'But not here. We'll take her with us in case there's a problem.'

'Don't be fucking stupid, Max. She knows who we are.'

The leader stood his ground. 'No more argument, she's coming.'

* * *

Out on the street, the car was waiting with the engine turning over. Behind the wheel, Henry couldn't hide his nervousness; he was still in his teens, younger than the others, and only here because he was Max's brother.

'Did something go wrong?' He saw the stranger and realised his question had been answered. 'Who's she?'

'Drive! Just drive!'

The wheels spun on the icy road. In the back seat, the woman sitting between Coco and Julian hadn't spoken since telling Mr Stuka not to open the safe. Jan Stuka hadn't listened and it had gone badly for him. The thieves, murderers now, took off their balaclavas: the guy in the front was handsome: perfect white teeth, piercing blue eyes set in smooth boyish skin, and blond hair expensively styled so it fell to one side of his face at the front. Beneath his jacket he wore a midnight-blue silk scarf casually tied at the neck. The girl was slim, twenty-two or three, with crimson streaks in her black bob matching her painted nails. Two minutes earlier she'd ended a life: no one would guess. Her breathing was steady and calm, detached from the callous crime that had left two dead in the upstairs office.

The third man pulled off the mask and let it drop to the floor from his slender fingers. His face was white, unnaturally pale, the lean jaw covered in designer stubble. Above it, a receding hairline made him look older than his years. Intensity surrounded him like an aura. At its core, an anger that curled the bloodless line of his lips at the edges. He spoke quietly, his tone sharp and crisp, each word heavy with foreboding.

'This is a mistake, Max. A huge fucking mistake. We ought to have finished her when we had the chance. She's dangerous.'

Max airily dismissed his objection. 'Be a good chap and put a sock in it, Julian. She's fine.' He turned in his seat and smiled at the woman. 'You're not going to be a problem, are you, darling?'

Julian lowered his grey eyes and resisted the urge to argue. The exchange revealed the pecking order in the group and the tensions between them. The driver didn't count – an immature boy out of his depth on a good day. The other three very different people with one thing in common – the absolute certainty they were superior.

It wasn't just the plummy accents or the assured way they held their heads: it was everything; and it rolled off them. Killing the jeweller and the guard had cost them nothing because they believed them to be nothing.

Outside the world went about its pre-Christmas business, unaware of the drama. On Wardour Street, heading north, Coco had never felt more alive. She snatched the woman's bag, emptied it onto her lap and sifted the contents. The soft-leather Hermes purse inside held cash and credit cards, lipstick, a comb and a compact. Nothing unusual. Until she read the cardholder's name.

'Well, well, well.'

Max saw the excitement on her face. 'What is it?'

'Guess who we've got here. Guess who this bitch is.'

'Stop fucking about, who?'

'Nina Glass. We've only kidnapped Luke Glass' sister. Christ Almighty.'

ACKNOWLEDGMENTS

It amuses me to see a name – in this case mine – on the cover of a novel, suggesting to the reader that what they hold in their hands is the work of a lone individual. Nothing could be further from the truth. To take a spark of an idea and work with it until it becomes a one hundred thousand word book, written and re-written, edited and re-edited, proofed, typeset, designed and finally sent out with a carefully considered marketing plan behind it, requires the gifts, talents and commitment of many people. I am fortunate to be one of them.

I am indebted to the outstanding team at Boldwood Books. As my publisher they promised a relationship, a genuine partnership, and have certainly delivered, so thank you Amanda, Nia, Claire and Megan. But Sarah Ritherdon deserves a special mention. Her unflagging energy, endless enthusiasm (who else would email me on a Sunday morning on her way out the door to go sledging with her children?) and innate understanding of storytelling, are the reasons this brief acknowledgement is necessary in the first place.

Most of those involved in the publishing process are unknown to me. Nevertheless, they have my gratitude. Among those I do know are my editors, Sue Smith and David Boxell; patiently smoothing the manuscript's rough edges, bringing clarity and correctness to the language. I imagine them shaking their wise heads when, like a headstrong teenager, I occasionally go my own way only to regret it a few pages later, backtrack, and bow to their superior knowledge.

DS Alasdair McMorrin of Police Scotland CID, and Kay Etherington of the Metropolitan Police Service. Both generous with their insights and their time. Invaluable sources of how things work in the real world of policing. All appreciated.

Decades ago, I fell in love with the city of London whose famous streets and landmarks are the ever-changing and constantly inspiring backdrop to the story of the Glass family. I couldn't ask for a better canvas to paint on.

And lastly, my wife Christine who believed when it was easier to doubt. I've praised her flair and ability in every book without coming close to describing the depth and breadth of her involvement. How about immense? Awesome, maybe? Or just plain old, thanks, baby?

Owen Mullen

Crete, April 2021

MORE FROM OWEN MULLEN

We hope you enjoyed reading *Insider*. If you did, please leave a review.

If you'd like to gift a copy, this book is also available as an ebook, digital audio download and audiobook CD.

Sign up to Owen Mullen's mailing list for news, competitions, updates and receive an exclusive free short story from Owen Mullen.

https://bit.ly/OwenMullenNewsletter

ALSO BY OWEN MULLEN

ABOUT THE AUTHOR

Owen Mullen is a highly regarded crime author who splits his time between Scotland and the island of Crete. In his earlier life he lived in London and worked as a musician and session singer. He has now written seven books and *Family* was his first gangland thriller for Boldwood.

Follow Owen on social media:

 twitter.com/OwenMullen6

instagram.com/heathercrimeauthor

bookbub.com/authors/owen-mullen

facebook.com/OwenMullenAuthor

ABOUT BOLDWOOD BOOKS

Boldwood Books is a fiction publishing company seeking out the best stories from around the world.

Find out more at www.boldwoodbooks.com

Sign up to the Book and Tonic newsletter for news, offers and competitions from Boldwood Books!

http://www.bit.ly/bookandtonic

We'd love to hear from you, follow us on social media:

facebook.com/BookandTonic
twitter.com/BoldwoodBooks
instagram.com/BookandTonic

Printed in Great Britain
by Amazon